The Doorway

An unanticipated journey into the
"Wild West" of the Philippines

BY MICHAEL W. SIMKO

authorHOUSE®

AuthorHouse™
1663 Liberty Drive
Bloomington, IN 47403
www.authorhouse.com
Phone: 1 (800) 839-8640

Published by AuthorHouse   03/17/2017

ISBN: 978-1-5246-5294-4 (sc)
ISBN: 978-1-5246-5295-1 (hc)
ISBN: 978-1-5246-5293-7 (e)

Library of Congress Control Number: 2016920955

Print information available on the last page.

THE DOORWAY
FOREWORD

Again I want to thank all my supporters, friends, consultants and colleagues as we went through the laborious process of getting THE DOORWAY published and in print. I greatly enjoyed writing the story and did my level best to create pictures in the minds of all my readers as we progressed from one stage of the story to the next. THE DOORWAY is a work of fiction and not a "tech" novel. I attempted to be as accurate as possible regarding the description of the equipment used, having a little experience with some of the equipment described. Of course this being a work of fiction there were parts where a little bit of dramatic license was employed to created to make the story more interesting. My primary intent was to take the reader on a journey. Not any journey, but a journey that most if not all would ever be given the opportunity to take. A journey to *another* "wild west", where just about anything goes including modern day pirates. The story is a combination of day to day reality, with office politics, disappointment, anger, fantasy, science fiction and romance- and yes I am a romantic. Also, all my stories, but one exception, will contain my trademark – a special dog in every story playing an important role in the story – no question, I am a big animal lover!

It is truly my hope that this will be a "I can't put the book down until I finish the story" type of novel for you the reader. I sincerely hope you all enjoy the story, as much as I did writing it.

Michael W. Simko, Author

THE DOORWAY
ACKNOWLEDGEMENTS

My very special thanks for all the wonderful help and guidance by my mentor and editor, Barbara P. Conklin who kept me accurate and the story moving along at a fast pace. Also not to be forgotten my many supporters, friends and fans, including, Jae Muhammad a special friend who helped me tremendously; also Danny Parkin, Mr. Designer Media who did a fantastic job creating the graphic images. Thanks to Steve and Amy Felix who did a great job of creating the additional images needed to further illustrate the story. Not to be forgotten, Jodi Koudelka and Asa Nelson among my biggest fans and supporters. There are many others too numerous to mention including Mae Genson and Joan Conners of AuthorHouse. Thanks to you all for you wornderful support.

This novel is dedicated to the loving memory of my wife, Pamela L. and my mother, Alma C

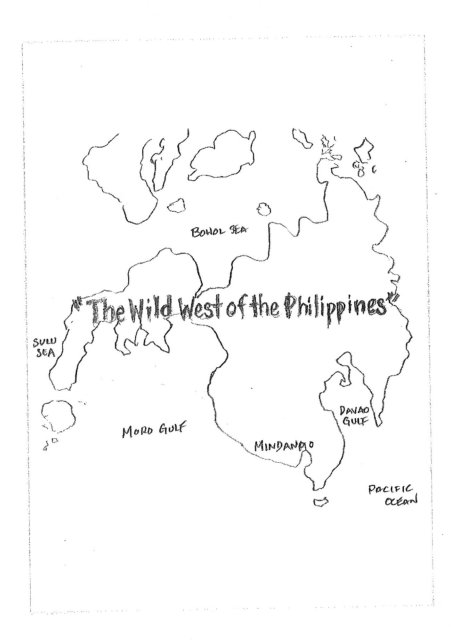

"The Wild West of the Philippines"

Chapter 1

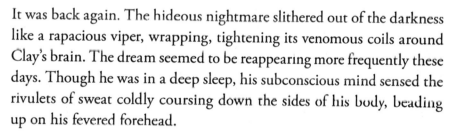

It was back again. The hideous nightmare slithered out of the darkness like a rapacious viper, wrapping, tightening its venomous coils around Clay's brain. The dream seemed to be reappearing more frequently these days. Though he was in a deep sleep, his subconscious mind sensed the rivulets of sweat coldly coursing down the sides of his body, beading up on his fevered forehead.

In the dream, Clay found he had just struggled out of a fetid, rotting, steaming jungle that lay behind him. The whole ordeal was the latest mental purgatory he had been forced to endure. The sweat really started coming as recognition came that he was back on that malodorous Philippine island. Yet, he knew in his heart he had left it behind so many years before.

Out of the humid mist to his front, the hideous apparition of the three men appeared, slowly moving toward him. He once again felt shock that he knew those battered faces as they had at one time been his best friends. Now as they seemed to glide over the ground, their bloodied hands reached out as if inviting him into their macabre group.

He could see their mouths silently beseeching the words to come and join them in death. He struggled in vain to back away from them in a terror approaching outright panic. He tried to flee, but as they slowly moved closer to him, it was as though he were tied securely in place with ropes and chains. As hard as he struggled to escape, he could not move. Cemented in place as they closed in on him, he felt complete terror by the apparition. He just wanted to scream.

In immobilizing fear, he looked in every direction for any escape from this advancing horror. Glancing to his rear, he saw the dense, brooding, man-eating depths of the green jungle hell behind him. A solid, impenetrable wall. There would be no escape. The memory of the oppressive, cloying, moist heat cloaked him like a warm, wet blanket. He could actually smell those rotting jungle scents of decay all over again.

Why was this happening to him? The images were so real in his mind, he believed he was back there, yet he did not recognize this particular location. He instinctively knew that if he *had* ever been there, he would have recalled it immediately.

The three images of what passed for the remains of men, pressed closer. He was appalled in his dream world by the appearances of his friends. He could easily remember where once they had all been youthful, handsome with smiling faces. Now they were hideous apparitions, bullet riddled, and covered in blood. He could see the open, festering wounds from bayonets and machetes. Horrified beyond words at the images, he recoiled backward in abject fear.

In the next instant, they were all around him, reaching out, grabbing hold of him, pulling him into their cadaverous group. He opened his mouth in a voiceless, terror filled scream, shouting over and over again, "No! No! No! Please! Please! I'm sorry! Sorry! Sorry! I couldn't help it!"

His voice trailed off as they circled him in a dance of death. His heart pounded harder as he shrank back in horror when they roughly grabbed hold of him, pulling and tugging. He tried vainly to jerk himself away from the horrid images, a silent scream on his lips. Guilt and overwhelming self-loathing washed over him like a dam bursting.

He should have been with them; he should have been there to share their fate. He kept repeating this to himself over and over again.

Their bloodied hands were on him now, pulling him and jerking him into their horrid visages. Trying to tear away from their grip, he felt himself being roughly shaken and pulled forward into a strangely lit, mist- filled, tunnel to their rear. They had a good, solid hold on him now and were forcibly dragging him forward toward their hell. He gave one last terrifying scream and then the shouted words penetrated his consciousness.

"Clay! Wake up! Wake up! Damn it! Stop it! Stop! You're having that damn dream again! Stop it!"

Clay Dixon opened his eyes and squinted at the glare from the lamp on the nightstand. He was shocked to see that he was still in his bedroom and not in the steaming, green hell of the Philippine jungle island. Sitting up on the sweat soaked bed sheets, it became fully vivid in his mind all over again - that final night at the end of his tour of duty. He had been a short-timer with only a few days left and then back to the world, as they all liked to say. Remembering the wild party, they had all promised to stay in touch after returning to the states. He'd been with his favorite bar girl and as the night wore on, he became very drunk. She had taken him upstairs to her apartment and after making love, he had fallen into a deep sleep.

He awoke at dawn the next morning to find that his buddies were long gone and he was alone. In a panic, he threw on his clothes and virtually ran all the way back to his base. He had originally been assigned to go on one last scouting mission with his buddies before being reassigned stateside.

When he got to the flight line, he found that the chopper had left him behind. He felt stupid and disgusted with himself that he had been so drunk. He knew they would razz him unmercifully when they returned. Clay waited on the flight line until late that night, but they never came back. Several search missions came up empty handed; they had just literally disappeared into thin air, never to be seen or heard from again. No traces were ever found. He never forgave himself. In his heart he knew he should have been with them. Clay carried this anchor around his neck every waking day of his life.

His wife looked down at the pathetic, sweat-drenched figure of her husband. He looked up at her with guilt-ridden eyes. All pity she might have felt in the past was gone. Clarice felt herself cross an invisible line of her own making. There was no turning back. No one should have to constantly put up with this, she thought angrily. I should have done something about it a few years ago when those crazy nightmares began. Doctors didn't seem to be much help, she now acknowledged. Where could she go from here? She knew the answer in her heart, but didn't voice it, even to herself.

He was about to say something in useless apology, as usual, she knew. She quickly cut him off, raising her arm and facing her palm outward at him to stop.

"I don't want to hear it!" she said tersely. "I've heard it one hundred times before. It won't wash with me anymore!"

"I can't help it!" he said in anguish. "It just comes and goes. I have no control. It won't go away."

"How much do you expect me to endure? I just can't take it anymore. I've had it! Either you find some way of making it stop or we need to go our separate ways. That's final! Even the doctors have totally given up on you!"

Clay recalled his own doctor, a family practitioner, an old friend, had tried desperately to relieve him of the nightmares, but could not help. He had referred him to another physician he knew who had experience in dealing with these kind of matters, what he considered to be post-traumatic syndrome.

Sitting there on the bed, Clay remembered the sessions when the kindly, older physician had tried to help pry the demons out of him. After a number of visits, the doctor had strongly suggested that he suspected Clay was experiencing an unconscious and deep-seated guilt feeling, and that if he kept these feelings inside of him, they would eventually tear him apart emotionally and ruin his life. The physician inferred that Clay was not opening up and telling him the whole story. Incapable of bearing his guilty soul to anyone, Clay could not dare reveal the secret he kept locked in the deepest, darkest part of his heart. He found it impossible to talk about it to anyone. Although he had tried on a few occasions, but only ended up breaking down in emotion-wracked sobs before he got the first few words out of his mouth. He had forced the memories down over all of these years. By totally throwing himself into his job, it had worked to some degree. Now he was under tremendous pressure at work and the memories and dreams had started to surface again on an intermittent basis and only in his dreams. He wondered how could he possibly relate his deepest secret to anyone? Thinking about it again, he would rather be dead than tell it to anyone close to him.

"Look, I'll go back to Doctor Obermayer and really work on it this time," he offered pleadingly to his cold, stone-faced wife.

"At this point, I think we're beyond that," she said frigidly. "I will have to give this some thought."

"The children..." He felt trapped.

"You always throw that at me, don't you?" She was screaming now. "Well, let me tell you something, I don't think they care one way or another\ because you've been more married to your job than to the children and me. You haven't been around long enough to get to know them. So, don't try that on me. It just won't fly!" Turning, she went into the bathroom and shut the door, closing the issue and leaving him alone to his thoughts.

Well, at least I've succeeded beyond anyone's expectations in my job, he thought, and have that to fall back on. Clay could still vividly remember how he had started on the bottom rung of the ladder right after he'd gotten out of the military, happy to even get a job. They'd thrown every shitty job that no one else wanted at him, but he was proud that he had endured and succeeded.

Clay could recall the many unpaid for, extra hours he had gladly put in, frequently acknowledging to himself with a twinge of guilt, at the expense of his family life. But he knew there were other reasons also. He had immersed himself in his work to push down that deep feeling of guilt he had carried around on his overburdened shoulders all these years. His wife's very expensive taste in style didn't help matters.

It was still very early, but he decided to get up anyway. He knew her mind was closed to discussion, so his only recourse was to get ready for the day and head for the office. He had a pretty good feeling that something momentous was about to happen soon, maybe even today. He had certainly worked hard enough for it.

That afternoon of the same day, the call came in. It was expected. Clayton Dixon had been anticipating it for a long time, but when he took the call, he still felt a tremendous surge of excitement and pride. He had given several years of his life and a lot more for that call, he inwardly acknowledged.

"Mister Dixon?"

He knew immediately from the flat, dry tone of the voice on the other end of the line when he said, "Yes, this is he."

"This is Lorraine, Mr. Campbell's secretary."

As if he didn't know who she was. A mental picture of the gray haired, rail thin, austere private secretary to Jordan Campbell, the president of the company, appeared in his mind. He could almost see the dry, lined face that was all business and rarely showed any emotion. You could never tell what she was thinking.

This humorous thought briefly crossed his mind that when she finally retired she had a whole new, lucrative career waiting for her as a poker player in Vegas. He chuckled briefly about that thought. No one ever knew what was going on behind those old style granny glasses, nor what secrets lay behind those cold, gray eyes of hers.

"Yes, Lorraine, what can I do for you?"

"Mr. Campbell asked me to call you. There will be a meeting at the home office. It will be in three weeks on Friday, the 31st. Can you be there?"

"Certainly," he replied, his heart skipping a beat. With bells on, he thought to himself. Finally he would be receiving his reward of the Vice Presidency that he knew he so richly deserved. The years had flown by very fast. He recognized, even though he was in his early thirties, he was still very young to hold such a lofty position in this company. He knew too that there would be some resentment.

"What time would you like me to be there?"

"At four-thirty sharp."

"Thank you, I'll be there." *The timing will be perfect*, he thought, *just before quitting time and just in time for a big celebration.*

"Thank you, Mr. Dixon" she said, "We'll see you then."

He hung up and sat quietly for a few minutes, letting his mind drift. "No Frills Lorraine," they called her, was living up to her reputation and certainly wasn't letting anything out, he thought. The very least she could have done was hint about him taking over the Vice President slot, but of course, with that dispassionate personality of hers, saying nothing was expected.

He felt confident that old Herb Sanderson, the Vice president and his mentor, was finally going to hang up his spurs this year. The old duffer had gone way beyond normal retirement, but they had let him do so because he had been one of the first employees with the company. Clay recalled hearing stories that the company was so poor and struggling to stay alive in the early days, they had paid old Herb part of his salary in stock certificates. Over the years during the booming economy, the stock had grown so much in value that he really didn't have to work. Even now, during these sluggish economic times, the stock still performed well. But Herb was finally bailing out, and when Clay thought about it, he wondered because it was so sudden. He'd thought the lovable, old coot was going to stay for at least another two years. Clay truly liked Herb and had learned a lot from him.

Of course, the ever-present rumor mill within the company was saying that old Herb was now spending a lot more time on the golf course than in the office here lately. The thought occasionally crossed his mind as to who was covering Herb's desk when he was absent. He often wondered if it was that opportunistic son-in-law of Campbell's that he instinctively mistrusted.

Six years ago he had recalled spending two weeks at the home office, filling in, while some of the upper echelon in management were ostensibly at a management seminar in the Bahamas. However, he had overheard later, during a coffee break, that they had spent more time on the golf links than in the seminar.

During his temporary assignment to the home office, he'd had a chance to closely observe Herb Sanderson, who was known as the workhorse. He recalled surreptitiously watching the older man at work at his desk. Herb had a squat, almost pear shape, accentuated by his baggy trousers that were held up by old-fashioned suspenders. He had once had blond hair, but it was now white and rapidly receding up his forehead. Clay remembered the old wire-rimmed glasses that perched almost on the end of his nose as he waded through the mountain of files and other work stacked haphazardly around his desk.

He remembered too the older man was always the first one in the office in the morning and was still there, hard at work at the end of the day when everyone prepared to leave. He claimed he did this to beat the heavy freeway traffic inbound during the morning rush and outbound in the evening, but Clay was now not so sure about that.

Looking back now in retrospect, a tiny bit of doubt crept its way into his mind. With the huge mound of work the older man had to deal with in his position, he almost had to spend those extra hours just to keep his head above water. Herb claimed that he could get more work done when no one was around, and that was probably true to a great extent, because his phone seemed to be constantly ringing and people were continuously interrupting him with their own problems. Regardless, he still seemed to spend an inordinate amount of time at his desk. Clay also remembered that old Herb had appeared to be a lot healthier looking in the earlier years, shortly after Clay had started with the company. That was not the case the last time Clay was in the home office. Herb looked very tired.

Clay paused in his thought train again for a moment as that little shred of doubt crept back into his mind. With a smile and no argument, he had already given *his* all to the company, taking on every crappy little job that no one else wanted. He didn't want to end up another "Herb Sanderson".

The cost had been high and there were moments when he sometimes wondered if it had all been worth it. The first victims were his adopted family. He had met his wife shortly after he had been released from the military. She had lost her husband to an auto accident and was a single mother with two young babies. He had volunteered to take on the responsibility and then married into instant family.

He loved his two adopted children. Clay had spent a lot of time with them in the beginning, but as he had to devote more and more hours to his job, they slowly grew away from him. Their mother had to take on the dual role of father and mother because he was either at the office or out of town on some company business. He seemed to be always at work, trying to meet some deadline. She never let him forget it. He felt his adopted children had grown up, coming to view him as just the guy who was rarely home and never seemed to have time for them.

Sometimes when he was alone, he wished deep in his troubled heart that he could have the opportunity to live those critical moments of his life over again. There were so many things he would do differently. Now, he thought with regret, the children had just entered those special prep schools his wife insisted on and he saw even less of them. In essence, he was a stranger to them, however, he argued that someone had to pay for the private schools his wife had chosen. He had many regrets, but there was no turning back now. His future life appeared to be carved in marble. He had chosen this path, though littered with thorns, and now he was compelled to follow through with his commitment. He desperately wished it could be different, but he knew in his heart that wasn't his destiny.

There had been an unending, running quarrel over the years about both the time he spent on the job and the proposed special schooling for the children. It reached the point where he welcomed being at the office and almost dreaded going home to the probability of another argument.

His wife had never been able or refused to grasp the fact that for her to have all the nice things she liked and insisted on, there was a price. Someone had to pay it, he knew, but she was unwilling to really help. Of course, he was making a nice salary now, but he was required to give much of himself to the job to justify that salary.

In one of their final spats he had told his wife that the children could get just as good an education from a local public or parochial high school, as the private, over-priced, prep schools she insisted on. That argument ended in a stalemate, neither one giving in. As a parting shot at her, he told her to get a job so that she could better support the lifestyle she insisted on living. The atmosphere in the house became more frigid than usual and they only spoke to each other now when absolutely necessary. He noticed she seemed to become more distant as each week passed and he had the feeling that something was going on, but he couldn't quite put his finger on it.

Chapter 2

In the following weeks Clay noticed that his wife spent considerably more time at lunch with her girlfriends, often arriving home long after the lunch hour. He knew from her previous actions that this was somewhat uncharacteristic of her normal behavior, but disregarded it as he was too busy with his own problems at work. A recent intense interest in women's groups and charitable organizations was puzzling to him. Clay recalled she had never shown this kind of concern for these types of affiliations in the past. He didn't begrudge her involvement, in fact he approved as it kept her busy. He just assumed she wanted to spend as little time around him, continuing to blame him for their family problems. He had phoned home several times over the weeks to try and patch things up, or to let her know he was bringing a client home for dinner, but she had not been there.

Clay had unconsciously overlooked and forgotten these apparent insignificant irregularities, his job totally overwhelming his mind, until the day he'd received an anonymous telephone call from a stranger, calling herself a *concerned friend*. The informant directed him to immediately go to a certain address in town. The unidentified person suggested, without elaborating, that he would discover something of great interest. He was originally not going to do anything about the mystery call, but idle curiosity, based on his wife's recent absences, got the better of him.

He followed the caller's directions and recognized a light industrial, warehousing complex. Arriving at the address, he found it to be a small distribution center for inspirational and motivational books and tapes. He recalled attending a charitable function there with Clarice the year before.

The front door opened at his touch, revealing an unoccupied front office. It looked like someone had been there recently from the light fragrance of a woman's perfume, which was vaguely familiar and the lingering smoke from the recently stubbed out cigarette in the ashtray.

With inordinate curiosity, he quietly slipped over to the heavy metal fire door to the warehouse, his heart already starting to beat faster. He felt like an imposter. Slowly turning the handle, he leaned against it and pushed it silently open a tiny crack to see inside. His heart pounded like a jackhammer, not liking the way he was acting and fearful of finding something he didn't want to know. His knees trembled a little as he carefully pushed the door open a little further.

In the ultimate betrayal, his wife stood, wrapped in a hot, passionate embrace, greedily kissing a man he vaguely recognized. Unaccountably the first thought that leaped into his numbed mind was black humor. With a cynicism totally uncharacteristic of him, Clay thought *that the pair must have really been inspired by all the inspirational books stacked around the room.* Then other black and murderous thoughts clouded his shocked mind.

They continued at it, hot and heavy for a few seconds more, until his wife suddenly gasped, realizing someone was watching. When she broke the kiss, she looked over toward Clay for the first time. There was a perceptible sharp intake of breath on her part and the fear of being caught blossomed in her eyes.

"Oh God!" was all she could voice, but the momentary guilt was quickly overshadowed by a flare of anger in her eyes.

Her sharp intake of breath caused her partner to look at Clay. To Clay, the guy looked comically like some dumb ass who'd dropped his pants to take a pee just as a covey of nuns strolled past him. The man's startled look turned into one of deep, pure fear as he came eye to eye with Clay. The sight of him must have caused the other man to wilt away from his adulterous act. He quickly disengaged from the embrace and started to edge away. Clay, a big man, even though he was out of shape, knew the short, soft looking guy had to be close to crapping in his pants! Clay felt an overwhelming temptation to grab him by the throat and throw him against the wall. He could feel the anger boiling up in him and could see the abject fear on the man's face.

Giving the door a hard push, slamming it against the wall, he watched the two adulterers jump like rabbits. Clay stepped into the room and slowly moved with murderous determination toward his wife's lover. His eyes, locked on the other man, burned with a fury he did not know he possessed. His wife stood to the side, speechless, frozen in terror, seeing a part of Clay she had never witnessed before - rage.

"This is going to cost you more than you think, you little sonavabitching weasel!" Clay exploded with rage. "This is one lesson you'll never forget!"

Slowly advancing like a giant jungle cat approaching its prey, Clay moved forward till he had backed the other man up against a nearby wall. His eyes drilled into the other man's eyes like red-hot pokers; the rage was palpable. He raised his hard, clenched fist above and slightly to his rear, ready to strike like an angered rattler. At the precise moment he started to swing it down onto the side of the man's head, he stopped. He lowered his hand and backed up a foot and stared at his adversary. Then he spontaneously broke out into harsh laughter, for a large, dark wet stain had appeared in the crotch area of the man's pants. *My God! Clay thought, not only did the bastard not try to defend himself, the little wimp pissed in his pants and I didn't even touch him!*

Forcibly pushing down the destructive, gut wrenching anger that had momentarily overwhelmed him, he turned to his wife and said with biting sarcasm, "You got yourself a real winner there, sweetie-pie! He's not even housebroken yet! Good luck! And don't forget to keep a good supply of diapers on hand!"

Getting control of the wild emotional ride he had just been on, his rational thinking slowly returned. *That little piece of toad-shit wouldn't be worth getting my stupid ass thrown in jail and jeopardizing my imminent promotion*, he thought.

Now, he'd had enough. The continued sight of the two of them boomeranged back on him and gave him a helpless, dead feeling inside, along with the utter disgust he felt for both of them. No matter what he said or did, he felt he had lost. Again he had let down someone else important to him. It was all he could think about, the guilt hanging like an ax over his head.

While the betrayal was an enormous let-down for him, he still found it hard to fathom after all they had been through together. He had put up with her extravagant spending habits and the children's special schooling, but he had always figured that he could work it all out. But after this, he found himself to be incapable to even think straight at the moment; he didn't know what to do or which way to turn. He gazed at them with great loathing for a moment longer, then quickly stepped back toward the office.

After her first surprised outburst, Clarice had kept her mouth shut, too surprised at being caught to say anything further. Now as he went through the door she furiously yelled after him, "You're going to pay for this you sonofabitching bastard!"

Glancing back one last time at her, in a parting shot he shouted, "Why Clarice, I didn't know you were so capable of such sweet sentiments! Temper, temper!" Before she could utter another word, he violently slammed the door closed behind him as if he had slammed shut a chapter of his life. He was disgusted beyond belief with all of them, including the woman who had phoned him. He assumed she was somehow connected with the guy that his wife had been screwing. The caller probably hoped I'd kick the stuffing out of the little toad to teach him a lesson, he reasoned. Clay had decided not to do so because neither one of them was worth it. He realized that if he had wiped up the floor with that little backstabbing bastard, the police would have immediately been called by his bitch wife and he had no one to bail him out of jail. It just wasn't worth it to complicate any further his already totally, fouled up life. In a way, he really wished he hadn't been told and he really didn't want to know about the affair. A feeling of failing himself and his family washed depressingly over him.

Leaving the building, he got in his car and drove aimlessly for a long time, feeling like he'd been punched, the wind knocked out of him. Finally, he forced himself to go home, made a strong double scotch and water in the family room and stared blankly at the television screen. Actually his eyes saw nothing on it; his mind dwelled years away and in a different land.

His wife came home late that evening, ignoring him and not saying a word about their encounter. She went straight upstairs to her separate bedroom and slammed the door. He got up and went up to her bedroom and opened the door. He could see Clarice was preparing to retire. Looking at her in silence, he struggled to find an answer to the main question on his mind. Why? After all this time! After all he had done for them. Why had she given up on him?

She showed no remorse and instead floored him with a statement he didn't dream she would ever make. "It's been dead for a long time, Clay, only you refused to see it.

"What?"

"You damn well know we've just been going through the motions until the children left home, even though you have refused to accept that fact! Now that they're at school, it's no longer necessary to keep up the pretext of a happy family."

"I never saw it that way. You know I had to put in the time so you could have all the things you insisted you *had* to have!"

She sighed. "Sorry, but there's no going back. It would never be the same again between us."

With a defeated slump to his shoulders he left the room and went downstairs to make himself another drink. Later that night, after falling asleep in a drunken stupor, he finally came awake and made his way unsteadily back upstairs. He staggered into his bedroom and collapsed on the bed with his clothes still on.

The following morning, he got up very early, made coffee, had a quick breakfast and left before Clarice got up. He figured she would wait till he was gone to avoid another confrontation. He arrived at the office before anyone else, glad to be away from the house. He slumped forward at his desk, with his face in his hands, thinking that it was in times like these that he dearly wished he could live a certain part of his life over again. He had a huge empty feeling within him as if he had nothing left.

Caught up with his workload, he purposely stayed late at work that day. He hurt too much inside to face his wife again. Arriving home that night, he noticed her car was gone. She had taken all her personal belongings and a sizable portion of the furniture and wall hangings and other possessions. Her terse note, lying on the kitchen table, informed him that she had taken only those items that she had originally picked out and liked. He was welcome to keep the rest. "Thanks for leaving my half of the towels, bitch! Thanks for the big favor, you conniving whore!" he screamed at his leather chair. He was crazy mad now! The note went on to say that she'd have her attorney get in touch with him and that she expected the house to be sold and when it was, she was to get half the proceeds. He angrily crumpled up the note and tossed it across the kitchen, thinking, you are one cold fucking bitch! Why did she have to go and do this when he almost had the whole thing wrapped up and in the bag! Promotion, more money, maybe even a bigger house! As these thoughts flashed through his exhausted mind, he felt crushed. She had it all tied up in a neat bundle, he figured, but he was in no rush to sell the house. Clay intended on staying there as long as he damn well pleased and she could kiss his bare ass! Even if the stupid place was almost devoid of furniture, he didn't care.

But that turned out to be a mistake. Coming home to an empty house every night, he had to live with all the good and bad memories haunting him, and they managed to take their toll. It tore him up as much as the break-up of the marriage. With his face in his hands and tears flowing freely, he came to the realization how important they all had been to him.

Now all that was about to change because of the promotion. At least, I still have my job and it should get a lot better, he thought. Maybe he might even get her back, even though a little voice in the back of his mind kept saying, "There's no going back." Could they ever be the same again as they were in the very beginning, he wondered. A new beginning? He now seriously doubted it.

Snapping out of his daydreaming, he asked his secretary to book him a room for Friday, the 31st at the hotel he usually patronized when he was at the home office for a meeting or other business. He assumed they'd make the announcement after his meeting with Campbell and then there would be a celebration party. He reasoned he didn't want to drive after the party as he knew he'd have more than a few drinks in him and with his luck, he'd be stopped on the interstate by the highway patrol.

As he thought back about the house again, he came to the conclusion that maybe this change would be a blessing in disguise. After training the new manager at his branch, he'd be required to move up to the home office. This freed him to sell the house and put all those haunting memories behind him. He'd be starting out with a clean slate. He would find a small apartment until the house was sold, then later he'd shop around for a nice, smaller-sized condo. With everything else behind him, he felt he was beginning to see the light at the end of the tunnel. Things had finally started going his way.

Sorting through the interoffice mail sent from the home office by courier, he came across a long white business envelope with his name typed on the front in caps and below that the word *personal* underlined in red. This puzzled him a bit because in any sealed interoffice memos, the sender was always identified on the front of the envelope. His curiosity piqued as he slit it open with his opener and pulled out the one sheet of folded stationary. Unfolding the crisp, white sheet, bearing the letterhead of the home office, he was mystified by the cryptic, one line message contained within. Typed in large, bold capitol letters, it said, "*WATCH YOUR BACK*!" There was no signature or any other identification on the sheet of paper.

Clay sat staring at the warning for several minutes, sorting through the compartments of his mind, trying to figure out who might have sent the mysterious warning and the real puzzler, why was he being warned? Now alerted, who did he have to watch out for? He didn't want to be blindsided, but he really couldn't think of who would be a threat to him considering his experience and seniority with the company.

Long ago, Clay had conceded to the fact that in any office there would always be an undercurrent of friction between some employees, no matter how minor. Also, he had recognized that in any company there would be office politics, especially in a large one like the home office.

Though he knew he could never stay clear of it totally, he learned to keep his mouth shut and not say anything about anyone at the home office even if they were a problem. He just worked through channels to clear the problem. He'd miss the casualness of his old office, but he couldn't complain, he was moving up in the world.

So with the enigmatic message, he really couldn't pin down any one person to watch out for or who might be a threat. The young son-in-law of the owner came across arrogant and overly aggressive, but Clay was of the opinion that the man was too green and inexperienced to be a serious threat to him. He didn't particularly like Jacky Prenotsky and dealt with him only when he had to and then in a strictly businesslike manner. He'd heard rumblings from others that Prenotsky was disliked and would step on anyone to advance his career.

As for his eminent promotion, he felt confident that he was the most qualified by experience, success and sacrifice. He couldn't think of anyone else that might even be a possible threat in that department. He was deep in thought about the message when Evelyn, his secretary, knocked and entered, as was the custom with the two of them in his office.

"Excuse me, Mr. Dixon."

"No problem. How can I help you?"

"It's after five-thirty and I'm getting ready to go home. Is there anything else I can do for you?" He looked at the gray haired woman that he'd inherited when he became the manager. He hoped that she would be able to go with him to the new office. What a fine person she was. This would be a nice reward for her unstinting loyalty to him. A substantial pay raise and a new office would be perfect to get her to come with him. She had no one to keep her here, he reasoned. All her relatives were upstate. This could actually bring them closer to her.

"I'm sorry Evelyn I just lost track of time. No, there's nothing else. Oh, by the way, when I get back from my meeting at the home office we're going to have to get together and talk. There possibly might be some good things brewing." As he said this, he smiled warmly at her, hoping she'd get the meaning.

"Certainly, Mr. Dixon, that will be fine." She was silent for a few moments and he could see that something was on her mind. Finally she said, "I truly hope things work out for you, Clayton. You're a good person." She smiled when she said this and he knew that she meant it.

He was a little surprised that she had addressed him formally by his first name. This was a rarity as she always had insisted on addressing him by his surname, out of respect, she always said. Something was on her mind, but he didn't have a clue as to what it could be.

"There was a concerned look on your face when I came in - is something the matter? Is there anything you might want to talk to me about?" She smiled her sweet and sincere smile.

"No, no, everything is okay. Just a little tired."

Clay always tried to avoid reading between the lines in what people said, but for some odd reason *what* she said made him wonder for a couple of seconds. For the briefest moment, he could almost swear he saw a sadness reflected in her eyes. Leaning back in his chair for a few moments, he thought about it. He knew she had a lot of friends locally and to get anything done at the home office she had to have some reliable contacts to accomplish anything there. Perhaps she'd heard a hint from one of her local girlfriends about Clarice's affair. Then again, she might have some kind of an idea of the maneuvering that could be going on at the home office.

Oh, well, he thought, don't worry about something that's probably not there. He quickly put the thoughts out of his mind.

"Evelyn, you are a very fine person. I know I don't say it often enough, but thank you for everything you do to keep this office running smoothly. I couldn't do it without you."

"Thank you, that's a very nice compliment and it's appreciated." Turning in the doorway to leave, she said, "Good night." She hesitated for a moment, looked at him and said, "And do take care."

For a moment he thought she was going to say, "watch your back".

After she left, he pushed all thoughts and apprehensions out of his mind. He got busy with his next task as he reminded himself he had a lot to accomplish before he left for the home office. He pondered for a few moments over her cautioning words and charged it off to her motherly concern for him.

Chapter 3

Clay was up very early on Friday morning. He felt exhilarated about his forth-coming trip, anxious to get on the road. He held himself in check and took his time getting ready, making sure he dressed carefully, putting on his best suit and tie. He didn't want to arrive at the home office too early, but did want to say hello to a few people prior to the meeting and get-together. It was almost like a holiday for him and he hadn't felt this good in a long time. He had managed to put his family problems to the back of his mind for the moment.

In a better frame of mind then he had been, he decided to indulge himself and drive up to the office in his pride and joy, a fully restored 1968 Mustang. He had seen the auto at an auction, checked it out and found the engine and body to be in sound condition; it mainly needed a professional restoration of the exterior and interior, due to its age. He had fixed all the exterior dings by himself and had the car professionally painted to its original maroon metallic. He had a new black vinyl top installed and had the complete interior redone. The little 289 cubic inch engine was in good shape and purred along the freeway like a contented tabby. It lifted his spirits where they needed to be for the coming meeting and promotion party.

Deciding against stopping by his office, he departed, feeling positive that if he did take out the extra time to stop he'd get bogged down with telephone calls or other pressing matters. He realized he was a worry wart, but felt for at least today any business could wait until he returned. He felt totally confident that Evelyn could handle just about anything and if there were any real pressing emergencies, he knew she could reach him easily on his cell phone or forward it to the home office.

He took his time driving, had a leisurely lunch on the way and arrived in the early afternoon. Before he went to the office he checked into his hotel. On the way up to his room, he decided to freshen up after the long drive before going to the office. He put on a fresh shirt and stood in front of the bathroom mirror adjusting his tie when he noticed his face for the first time. He had never really looked closely at it in the morning when he shaved, but now he took a critical look at himself in the mirror. The face that stared back at him had changed dramatically from the fresh faced, gung-ho trooper he had once been in the years that had rapidly and quietly slipped by him.

Is this what the years and the job have done to me, he thought? I'm not really that old, but I look it. The reflection staring back at him in the mirror had a puffy, slightly flabby look. There were lines across his forehead he'd never noticed before and deep crow's feet around his eyes where once there had been none. For the first time, he noticed the dark circles under his eyes. Have I really grown this old? His hair, once a nice chestnut brown was rapidly going gray with a drab look to it. His brown eyes, once fired with so much enthusiasm, now looked dull and tired. He stared at a body that had once been over six feet of muscular slimness. He could clearly see he had lost the angular good looks he had when he had been overseas and a lot younger. He was thirty pounds overweight and now had a body that looked something akin to a lumpy potato sack. *There's nothing here that three months of healthy exercise and a proper diet wouldn't change,* he mused, *if only I had the time.*

Where *had* the time gone, he wondered? What am I rushing to in this lifestyle I'm leading and what's going to be there when I arrive - an oxygen tent? Is it going to be worth all of this? He remembered from photos how he'd looked when he'd been in the Army on that special mission in the Philippines. For the briefest moment, he thought back to that time and felt the same sharp pang of regret every time he thought about it. In moments when he awoke in the night, he wanted to sob and sometimes did, much to Clarice's exasperation. His wife never could or wanted to understand and now he would never get the chance to explain it to her.

Thinking about the turns his life had taken and where he was now, there were often times when he dearly wished he could live a certain portion of his life over again. Would I do anything differently, he would always ask himself, or would I have a choice in the matter? *Get a hold of yourself, man*, he thought. It wouldn't be very positive to go to the office with these kind of thoughts on your face dragging down your mind.

Continuing to stare at his image in the mirror, his mind again drifted back to that time when he had been a lot slimmer and a whole lot younger. It brought back the memory of the photo one of his buddies had taken of him outside that ramshackle, corrugated tin-roofed, rat infested barracks they had slept in on the southern island of Mindanao. The Philippines, that other miserable, sweltering world, had been unbearably humid and dusty on that particular day so long ago. But he managed to look sharp in his freshly starched jungle fatigues with the special shoulder holster holding his 9 mm Beretta automatic, heroically perched on his left chest. What a time that had been, he recalled.

Life was very good then and they were all on their great adventure. He recalled how they all felt back then, that they'd live forever. Everyone of them had a feeling of their own immortality and of being impregnable. That was then, and now because of what he had experienced, he knew things were different.

He continued to stare at his face. The memories flooded in and it saddened him. The old familiar pang of guilt washed over him suddenly. Thinking about that time in the past, a self-loathing replaced the guilt feeling. In those moments, when he suddenly came wide awake in the night, he had an overwhelming urge to sob for them, and often he did, as quietly as he could so not to awaken his sleeping wife.

If only I had been there...he berated himself once again, and then let the thought drop away from him before he descended into that dark hole of depression. He had carried it all in his head all these years, as if it were yesterday, and would continue to do so as long as he lived. If only I had been there...his subconscious reminded him again.

Get a grip on yourself, man! He angrily forced himself back to reality. It would not be very good to go into the office with these kind of thoughts clouding his mind and showing all over his face, now would it? Forcing the negative thoughts from his mind he quickly finished adjusting his tie, put on his suit jacket and left the room. It was three o'clock in the afternoon.

The drive from the hotel to his home office took him only a few minutes on the freeway. Shortly thereafter, he pulled into the large parking lot of the building that where his and a couple of other companies were based. The clock on the dash of his car read three fifteen; he had arrived early, but he figured he could spend the extra time visiting with some of the people he knew at the office.

His company occupied the entire top floor of the four story, commercial building. Getting off the elevator, he strode toward the big double oak doors. The impressive main entrance even had a gold embossed company logo on each door. In anticipation of things to come, a spring to his step moved him down the corridor. Inside, a waist-high barrier about ten by twenty feet long surrounded the waiting area. This barrier, carpeted in a soft beige, had a walnut railing along the top. A few chairs occupied the space with a table and lamp. He looked around the open, spacious office and then glanced at the attractive young woman behind the desk. *This looks like I'm going to enjoy working here*, he thought.

"May I help you, sir?" the receptionist asked with a businesslike, practiced smile.

He hadn't been to the office in a while and obviously the girl who'd been here when he had visited last had been either promoted or had left for greener pastures.

"Thanks for the offer, but Mr. Campbell is expecting me," he said with an engaging smile. "My name is Clay Dixon."

A slightly strained look crossed her face at the sound of his name. Her voice came out a little more crisp and impersonal. "Let me call his secretary for you, and please take a seat."

Relax, girl. I don't bite, he thought. *I'm not going to threaten your minor, gate-keeping authority. But, you will not keep me out here cooling my heels when I've been with this company this long!* He reminded himself to have a brief talk with this little twit when he left today. She should have recognized him from pictures of the branch managers. The previous receptionist had always wisely directed him into the inner office immediately. *This one must be one of Lorraine's new, loyal hireling's, he thought.*

With a smile, now a little tight at the edges, he said in a firm voice, "That's not necessary. I know my way around. I've been here more than a few times before." The last sentence came out slightly snappishly and he regretted it the moment he said it. He turned around and stepped toward the swinging, waist-high door, the entrance to the office proper.

"But, sir...!" A noticeable strain appeared in her voice as he stepped through the barrier.

"That's okay, you won't get in trouble," he assured her. "I'll square it when I check in with Mr. Campbell's secretary, before I see anyone else."

With that, he was through the little swinging door and moving toward the main corridor of the area. This walkway ran around the perimeter of the floor. As he walked away, he saw her pick up the phone and rapidly punch in an extension.

Facing the reception area, a ceiling high, fabric-covered wall again announced the company's logo. On the other side, the large, waist high cubicle area held the typing pool. The head high cubicles in the central area made up the offices of the various midlevel managers, assistants and accountants. Other departments were beyond that.

Clay stepped to the left, heading toward the perimeter corridor and passed offices placed on both window sides of the floor. These spacious enclosed areas with windows facing out with a view, were the most coveted and occupied by the various higher officers. They were situated on either side of the central area in a subtle pecking order. The closer he or she was stationed to the corner chambers of Jordan Campbell, CEO, the more important they were in the unofficial hierarchy. This wasn't as rigid as it appeared, as Mr. Campbell had some relatives and in-laws working for him and *their* offices were cleverly interspaced between the others in the pecking order, even though their importance in the company might not have been as great. Although it was proclaimed that everyone was equal, it was common knowledge, but unspoken, that some were more equal than others, and this applied to the relatives. All of these workstations were enclosed in waist high to ceiling glass with blinds for privacy and solid doors with imposing titles on each. All the spaces on the perimeter of the floor had nice views of the city and Jordan Campbell had the best view of all. His spacious mini-kingdom, situated in the left hand corner of the floor, was considerably larger than the rest and had floor to ceiling, tinted, plate glass windows looking out on a spectacular view of the skyscrapers in the city center.

Clay made a right at the corner of the floor, and headed up the corridor. He knew this route would take him past Herb's office. He intended to stop in and wish him well and congratulate him on his retirement. He was a little puzzled by a strange undercurrent he started to feel as he headed up the corridor. Everyone he passed seemed to be overly intent on their work - not one of them greeted him.

Am I becoming paranoid? What are these vibes I'm picking up, he thought briefly. On previous trips everyone had been very cheerful, friendly and open to him. *Was something going on? Does it have to do with me?* The thoughts were coming quicker now, as a tiny knot of apprehension curled like a small worm around his spine. He knew something was in the air.

Passing some of the entrances to the larger cubicles, he had elicited similar responses as if they were somehow distancing themselves from him personally. What the hell was going on? Puzzling. He tried to look at it positively, recalling that things had always been fairly informal in the past. He rationalized that perhaps things might have gotten *overly* informal and maybe someone had "cracked the whip", to straighten things out.

He headed up the aisle toward Herb's and Campbell's offices, intending to stop in and see Herb. He genuinely liked the old guy. Moving past the long conference room on his left, something caught his eye. The room was glassed in on the aisle side with blinds on the inside that were normally kept open in case a secretary had to interrupt someone in a meeting for an important phone call or other urgent business. Normally they were closed when managers were discussing new business strategies of a confidential nature.

Someone had partially closed the blinds today, but Clay could still see who was in the group. He was surprised to see the conference going on with all the managers in attendance. He had not received any email about a gathering at this time. Perhaps someone had neglected to inform him, which he found unusual and they had started without him. He scanned his memory again but didn't recall anything about any kind of assembly. He had a sudden cold feeling in the pit of his stomach. Was someone doing an end run around him? This chilling thought suddenly hit him in the face like a hard snowball. Who?

When he looked through the partially open blinds, he saw several people he contacted regularly, including the managers from the other branch offices. This surprised him even more that he had not been notified about any planned strategy session, whether he was invited or not. He had always been advised of any conference. He had a gut feeling that what he observed wasn't a normal meeting.

He was surprised to see who sat at the head of the large polished oak conference table, conducting what looked like a proverbial dog and pony show. Jacky Prenotsky, Campbell's son-in-law, held court, as he liked to do, always in the spotlight. Egotistical, little bastard, Clay thought. Prenotsky, slick and brash, an experienced political animal and infighter, who always strived to shine in front of the boss and often did so at the expense of someone else. He had a self-important demeanor that often rubbed many people the wrong way, including Clay. He loved making people look stupid in front of the chief executive officer and when he pulled off one of the coups, he had a sarcastic snicker that made some people want to pop him one in the nose. In so many words, he put them on notice that they couldn't touch him and they'd better not even try to get even. He had good reason to have this attitude as he had come into the company at the urging of Campbell's wife and operated under the protective wing of Campbell himself. Prenotsky had married Campbell's only daughter, the spoiled apple of Campbell's eye. No matter what, the little weasel could do no wrong because of familial connections.

Clay figured that all the behind the scenes maneuvering and machinations Prenotsky constantly instigated, ensured he'd step into Campbell's job when the old coot croaked. From all the training Herb and he had given the little snot, Clay felt positive the schemer would inherit his old branch office. He wondered how the smart-ass little prick would go over in his relaxed, friendly office, probably about the same as a dog, rolling in fresh cow dung, with tail wagging, wanting to share his fresh perfume. Most likely a lot of the people in his office wouldn't put up with his crap and would quit, leaving him high and dry, with no experienced help. He wouldn't lose sleep over that one, he thought.

Clay remembered that he had always tried to live with Prenotsky's personality, on the premise that you can't change a leopard's spots. He dealt with him when he had to or was ordered to and worked with him or around him to get the job done. He often bit his tongue and kept his mouth shut, without letting Prenotsky know what was on his mind, even when he wanted to grab him by the throat. However, he was constantly on the lookout for the little wise guy's "bear traps" and "ambushes".

As he peered in at the meeting, he wondered if he'd been seriously ambushed this time, but just didn't know it yet. Prenotsky glanced and took notice of him, saying a few words to a secretary seated with her back to Clay. After he said it, some of the managers and others he knew from the home office turned to look. Clay felt embarrassed, like he was eavesdropping, but when the others saw him standing there, guilt crossed their faces. He recalled watching his sixth grade classmates caught stealing fish out of the classroom tank. Same thing!

It was run for cover and save thy ass time! When the secretary, who he knew, stood up and moved to the window, she gave him a weak smile and shrugged her shoulders, as if to say she had nothing to do with whatever had happened. She then closed the mini-blinds, giving him a clear gesture that the meeting behind those blinds did not include Clay Dixon. He felt like storming into the room and throwing the little hypocrite through the window.

With deep and growing concern, he quickly moved up the aisle. His hands were sweaty and he absentmindedly wiped them on his pants. He wondered what important job Campbell had given the little weasel. Hell, the little conniver couldn't even run a pushcart stand properly, much less an important position in this office. Most everyone knew that the petty tyrant was a master of Machiavellian moves and did their best to avoid him. Others, as was frequently the case in a large office, figured to gain favor with the boss and sided with him.

When Clay reached Herb's office, the first thing he noticed was that his mentor and old friend wasn't there, although there was a secretary he knew slightly, working in the office. The woman's back was turned toward him and she had her head buried in a file. Herb's longtime secretary was nowhere to be seen. Hmm, that was also very strange, he pondered. Again the question popped into his mind. *I wonder what the hell is going on?*

Standing there outside the open door to Herb's office, he felt that there was something rather odd about the interior, but he couldn't quite put his finger on it. Then it hit him! The whole place looked remarkably neater, as if someone had been working at organizing all the files and other things in the room. The haphazard clutter, Herb's hallmark, had disappeared. The random stacks of files, papers and reference books had been removed from chairs, couch and bookshelves. The reference books were neatly ensconced in the dusted and polished bookshelves. It was very odd as there had always been a fine patina of dust all over the bookshelves and his desk. The irregular piles on and around the desk were now stacked neatly on the credenza behind the desk or had apparently been filed away. He felt a moment of sadness. While Herb had the appearance of being disorganized, he always, without exception, knew where every single file or bit of information could be located, in the stacks of clutter around him. Quite a feat, Clay conceded, and it was also his trademark. Now, very strangely, his mentor was gone. He had to be, Clay thought, because nobody could have or would have dared to do this to him.

Stepping into the office he spoke to the clerk. "Excuse me, Alma."

On hearing his voice, she glanced up from the filing cabinet, a look of consternation crossed her face, He could tell from the sheepish look that she'd known he was in the room the whole time.

"Mr. Dixon, you startled me! I didn't know you were there," she said a little lamely.

He ignored it, but knew better. From past experience he knew she never missed a thing. "That's okay. Didn't mean to surprise you. Let me ask you a quick question, Alma."

"Certainly sir, if I know the answer," she hedged.

"What happened to Herb? When did he leave? Nobody said anything to me and I didn't even know that he was gone."

"Mr. Dixon, I'm sorry, but I honestly don't know. They just told me to come in here and straighten up this office."

From the look on her face, he knew she was telling him the truth. "Well, surely you must know something. Like when he left and is he coming back?"

"I recall they had a big meeting in Mr. Campbell's office on Monday afternoon. It was still in session when I left at the end of the day."

"You specifically used the word they. Can you at least tell me who was in the meeting?"

Alma's eyes darted furtively to the doorway, like a small animal looking for a dangerous predator. Lowering her voice to almost a whisper she said, "I'm sorry, Mr. Dixon, but we've been ordered not to talk about it. But…I do know that Mr. Campbell, Mr. Sanders and the two Vice Presidents were in the meeting."

"Oh?"

"Yes, and oh, by the way - Mr. Prenotsky was also in the meeting."

"Prenotsky was there? That's very unusual. I wouldn't think he'd rate being in a meeting like that." *Has a palace coup taken place, he thought with a great deal of growing concern.*

Alma lowered her voice to a whisper and said, "And that's not all!"

"Oh? What else went on?"

"All I can say is, I heard shouting coming from the office a couple of times. You couldn't help hearing it, even through the closed door of the office."

"That's very interesting. What else?"

"Lorraine acted as if nothing was going on."

"She would!"

"Then later on, she came by our desks and told us we'd better keep it to ourselves, if you know what I mean."

"Yes, I unfortunately do." He recalled the implied threat she often used so freely with the people working under her. He'd experienced her stiletto-sharp tongue a long time ago and never forgot it. He detected the stealthy sound of footsteps approaching outside the office. Raising his index finger to his lips for silence, he went on innocently in a normal tone of voice, "Well, I'd just thought I'd drop by and say hello to Herb."

"Mr. Dixon, the girl on the front desk said you were in the office," the woman said in a reproachful and cutting tone of voice. "You were asked to wait up front!"

Turning, he came face to face with the stern visage of Lorraine, in the doorway. From her short cut, gray hair, to her severe business suit, to her practical lace up shoes, she was all business. He had known it was her approaching with her squeaking shoes. He didn't know if she bought real cheap shoes or what, but the thought always crossed his mind that he'd like to tell her, *you need to oil your shoes, you old bag of bones*, every time he saw her. However, tempted as he was, he knew he'd better keep his mouth shut because she'd probably not forgotten their run-in several years ago and most likely still held it against him.

It had been a minor infraction on an order he had sold. He'd made a simple omission of information on the contract, but she had created a major flap about it. Clay had had enough and challenged her not to make such a federal case about it. He recalled the old bun-head had not appreciated him talking back to her. Clay justified in his mind it had been a minor mistake at the time and she needed to be made aware that he didn't answer to her. Of course, she didn't appreciate that at all, he remembered, and it had been an unspoken standoff ever since with her looking for an opening to castigate him.

In a subtle rebuke, he replied, "Yes, Lorraine, that's correct. I decided to visit a few of my friends before I checked in with you." It was a backdoor attempt to throw an underhanded insult at her by differentiating between his friends and her. She obviously didn't miss it because he saw her left eye twitch a bit.

"Sir, you were not supposed to be in the office until four-thirty," she said with an edge to her voice.

Clay was surprised with her use of the word "sir" in such a manner, but said nothing. "Yes, so I recall and I believe I'm beginning to understand why," he retorted, not quite able to control the edge in his voice. *Don't try to push me around, you old, gray haired martinet, he thought. I don't give a damn anymore if you do hold a grudge, I'm not going to take this kind of shit from you!*. His reply caught her by surprise and before she could make a snappy comeback, he beat her to the punch saying, "By the way, what happened to Herb Sanders?"

"He retired."

"Why wasn't I notified?" He became highly annoyed at the autocratic, old fart. "I've known him a long time and I'd have liked to been here when he left!" He had a very good picture in his mind of the real story, but was just laying down a smoke screen to see what Lorraine would say. "By the way, was there a party?"

Chapter 4

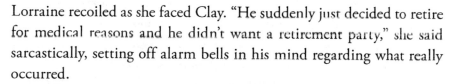

Lorraine recoiled as she faced Clay. "He suddenly just decided to retire for medical reasons and he didn't want a retirement party," she said sarcastically, setting off alarm bells in his mind regarding what really occurred.

"I see," he said in a non-committal tone of voice. He didn't let it show, but his stomach started to roil, suspicion starting to cloud his mind. Looking steadily at the boss's "gunslinger", he thought bitterly, *My ass! There was no party because it sounded like they ambushed him and forced him out! Probably he was making too much money and with twelve weeks of paid vacation, one week every month that he had earned over the years, they thought they were losing money. Sad thing was, the stupid fools had forced out the best thing that had every happened to them, one of their biggest assets!*

"If you'll follow me, Mr. Campbell will see you now." It was not a request, but an imperious command from the boss's "palace guard dog". *Yeah, I'll follow you, you old croaker,* he thought, *with my size ten foot up your tightly puckered ass!* However, as he followed her, he managed to keep his dark thoughts to himself, not letting them show on his face, but only just barely.

He trailed her up the corridor with somewhat of a hang-dog look, creating the impression of a disobedient student following a schoolteacher to the principal's office for detention. There was no question, he was depressed about what he had just learned and as each minute passed, he became more so. The longer he was in the office and the more he found out about recent events, he realized that things had been deliberately kept from him. He could feel the small, but growing snake of panic uncoiling in his gut as he unconsciously became increasingly tense. He also felt the hideous monkey of paranoia crawl up his spine and perch itself on his shoulder. It was difficult to keep it inside and it couldn't be helped if it was transmitted to the way he carried himself.

Moving along the corridor toward Campbell's office, he glanced inside a few of the cubicles, but either they had overheard his exchange with Lorraine or someone had cracked the figurative whip over their heads. Everyone had their nose to the proverbial grindstone; they were too busy or intent with their work to acknowledge his presence, or too scared. He knew the signs because he had seen them before. They were avoiding an old friend and coworker as if he were a leper and afraid some of it might rub off on them if they dared speak to him. They're afraid for their jobs, he instinctively knew, frightened that if they were seen talking to him by the wrong people, they would be in trouble by association. He truly pitied them. What a way to go through life… scared for your job, scared of your own shadow! Disgust for them rose in his throat like bile. *Run, you bunch of little chicken-shits, and keep running until they don't need you anymore, then they'll chop off your heads, he thought contemptuously*, as he glanced quickly at them one more time.

They approached the outer railing of what he had always characterized as Lorraine's little fiefdom. It was portioned off by the waist-high railing and contained her desk and the hard chair sitting in front of it where she sat her victims while she interrogated them. It was essentially the outer reception area to Campbell's huge corner office and also contained a modern leather couch and coffee table where people could wait before being ushered in to see the great man. The immense, ornately carved door to Campbell's office stood open in silent invitation. *To a lynching,* he now thought.

"Please go right on in, Mr. Dixon," she said in a syrupy, phony voice.

Yeah, right into the lion's den he thought, with a cynicism he hadn't felt a little earlier. As Clay entered the office, he glanced back at Lorraine, out of the corner of his eye. She was standing by her desk like a member of Caesar's Praetorian Guard, with a stern, no-nonsense look on her face. For a brief moment, he looked into those cold, gray unemotional eyes; there was something hateful there. He didn't like what it portended.

Entering the plush office, he saw there was a very uncharacteristic, friendly smile on Campbell's pudgy, florid face. He also noticed that his short, balding boss had gained quite a bit of weight. It didn't look good on a short person, even with the custom made suit. Now who in the hell are you trying to fool with that phony smile, you sneaky old bastard, Clay thought, as he displayed his own phony smile in return.

"C'mon in, Clayton and have a seat," Campbell said, apparently in a forced effort to be cordial, although his eyes betrayed him. "Can I get you anything? Coffee, tea, soft drink?"

"No thanks, Mr. Campbell. But from the impression I've been getting since I've been here this afternoon, maybe you might feel better serving me a cup of hemlock!"

For the briefest moment, surprise registered on Campbell's face, but he quickly covered it up and ignored the statement, trying to conceal it with a short bark of a laugh. Clay also didn't miss the slight flare of irritation that he caught in his boss's eyes.

Clay couldn't help noticing the tenseness in the air that was almost like static electricity crackling just before a thunderstorm. He recalled that Campbell had always been a demanding taskmaster in the past, rarely cracking a smile, rarely courteous and always wanting more out of someone. *He's really restraining himself today, instead of bolting forward and shouting like he's done in the past, Clay reflected. He must have a real chocolate-coated poison pill ready for me! So now the fencing begins, he thought.*

Reflecting back, Clay couldn't forget that because he had needed the job so badly in those early days, he had conveniently ignored the blatant arrogance and rudeness of the man. As time passed and he started gradually to move up in the company through his own grinding self-sacrifice, he realized one day it had become too late to leave and go anywhere else. He accepted the fact he'd become trapped because of his age. He knew, because of that fact, he'd be automatically classified with that phony euphemism of being over-qualified for any other jobs outside this company. *Who's kidding who with that B.S. line, he often thought.*

Campbell recovered his composure smoothly saying, "I was surprised to learn that you had arrived quite a bit early for our appointment."

"I had some old friends I wanted to say hello to first." Clay took a seat in the red leather, straight back chair facing Campbell's massive desk where the boss issued his imperial-like edicts to his subordinates. It could be intimidating to anyone and for a brief moment, Clay almost felt like a new job applicant about to be interrogated.

"So how have things been going for you in your little office out there in the sticks?"

Now there's a switch, Clay reflected. In the past, Campbell always used to say, "Your office is one of the brightest jewels in the corporate crown." Plus he knew exactly how well the office was doing, down to the last penny! Clay was very surprised by the off-the-wall negative comment, but he didn't let it show.

"I'm very surprised you refer to my branch in that way. You must agree we've all made it one of the most profitable for you out there," he said respectfully, but firmly.

"Ah, yes, that's true, but times are changing and it *is* the smallest branch we have…what with the economy the way it is…" Campbell let the last hang heavy in the air like an approaching rain cloud.

Clay's mind went into overdrive. *What is he leading up to, he wondered. Is it a pay cut?* He didn't like the rapid direction the discussion seemed to be taking, but in defense, he said, "But again, it has always been one of your most profitable, even more so than some of the larger offices, you must admit."

"Yes, that's true, but with the costs of running it increasing…"

Clay's whirling brain went on automatic as he numbly listened to Campbell drone on, churning out all sorts of facts and figures regarding overhead and business projections. He only half heard all the information that Campbell seemed intent on churning out. It was all smoke and mirrors, Clay thought, excuses for something possibly and probably underhanded. The promotion started to look further and further away by the minute. He suddenly woke up and came to full alertness when his numb brain heard the hateful word his boss uttered. *Downsizing*, a current buzzword being tossed about by many.

His mind abuzz, nearly missed it when he heard Campbell say, "So we're going to have to pull in our horns and regroup."

I hope that doesn't mean what I think it means, he thought, as the icy chill of fear stated slithering up Clay's spine. After that comment, Clay skidded into total shock when Campbell informed him they were going to close down his office.

I'm not going to take this lying down, he calculated inwardly, then voiced his concerns. "How can that be? It doesn't make sense! My office has consistently been one of your more profitable offices!"

"But that's not the point, my boy," Campbell said in a grandfatherly way, "It's the overhead. Since you have the smallest office, and even though you are profitable, the income you've been generating just doesn't compare to..."

Clay angrily cut him off, not caring about the consequences. "Wait! You just can't do that to those people who've been so loyal to you over the years!" Before Campbell could reply, Clay continued, now in desperation. "Can't I bring them with me to *this* office? I know we can work them in here at this office, assuming they all still have jobs."

His boss leaned back in his luxurious, throne-like, high backed chair, interlocked his fingers and placed them on top of his ample belly. His manner abruptly changed from the hearty-good-fellow approach to a steely-eyed businessman facing an adversary. His cold eyes bored through Clay like two swords. "Well now, that's another subject we'll get to shortly..." he said, subtly reverting into his phony, folksy voice. "But there's something else we have to address first and that's you!"

Clay remained silent as Campbell elaborated at length on how much of a loyal employee he'd been and on and on. Clay ignored all of it, waiting to go beyond the sugar-coating, to the point. While his boss droned on, he thought about what appeared to be happening. *The worst it can be he figured, is that I won't be able to bring my people up here, but I'll fight hard to include them. Or maybe I'll have to take a pay cut…I can live with that, especially after I sell the house.*

When the ax finally fell, he refused to believe what he heard. Not after all these years, he thought, in shock. He sat there in stunned silence as though in a hypnotic trance, as Campbell embellished the alleged necessity of downsizing and all the other bullshit excuses. Then he got to the whole crux of the meeting. "So it is very unfortunate, but because of the current economic climate, we are forced to let several people go." When Clay heard this, the cold fear from earlier, returned in a rush and wrapped its icy tentacles around his gut, squeezing it in a vice-like grip.

"There is no way possible that we can fit you or your staff into this office here," Campbell said, a distinct coldness to his voice.

Am I dreaming? Clay thought. Is this some hideous nightmare I'm going to wake up from shortly? He felt like he was leaning over the edge of a precipitous cliff, looking down at the razor sharp rocks below, waiting to destroy him. It figuratively felt as if someone kept nudging him slowly, closer and closer toward the edge, to his ultimate demise on the waiting rocks below.

"Just wait a minute! Let's back up here because I'm not quite sure I understand you correctly," Clay said with an edge of anxiety in his voice. Like a drowning swimmer, he grasped at anything to keep his head above water.

"Certainly, my boy," Campbell purred, as if he were a cat playing with a frightened mouse.

"Downsizing! Letting people go! What the hell are you talking about here? What about *my* people?"

"I guess I haven't made myself quite clear," he bluntly said. "We're closing your office down. That's it!"

"What? You can't!"

"I can do anything I please! It is no longer profitable. All the numbers have been prepared and given to me." Clay just sat there stunned as Campbell continued. "The larger offices, while they have not been as profitable as yours, generate larger sums of money. With some small cutbacks there and with some people carrying more responsibility, they'll be more profitable."

"I can't believe my ears! Whose stupid idea was this?" Clay said in a stunned and subdued voice. "I can't believe you would do this...you, the person who has always promoted yourself as a father figure to all these people!" Suddenly it became clear to him and he knew who had engineered this whole thing. That scumwad Jacky had manipulated this, he reasoned, gritting his teeth! "And just who was it that came up with these so-called numbers?"

Campbell did not rise to the challenge. Instead he mumbled, "Sorry! I'm not at liberty to discuss it at this time."

Throwing any small iota of caution to the wind that he might have had at this late juncture, Clay forged ahead with his true thoughts. He knew now he had nothing to lose. "You're sorry!" In desperation he put words to what had been hanging heavy on his mind since the conversation started. "But my promotion to Herb's post. What about that?"

"That's not going to happen. I'm sorry, but your job has been eliminated. There is no way we can fit you in here at this office!"

Clay found himself in mental shock, past believing what Campbell said about anything. "Sorry! Like hell you are! I know better now!" he retorted angrily.

"Now don't go getting all upset, my boy. We have a nice severance package for you. You'll be well taken care of."

"I'm not your fucking boy!" he said in a low and menacing tone of voice. Campbell missed the ominous inflection, or chose to ignore it. Repeating himself and in a cold, measured tone of voice, Clay said, "But what about my promotion to Herb's job? I earned it with my sweat and blood and you know it! What about that?"

Campbell looked at him silently for a few seconds, then said, "Well, that's what I have to talk to you about..."

Clay cut him off. "What do you mean talk to me about! I was long overdue for a promotion! I performed for you above and beyond and I deserve that job!"

"Yes, you did and I can understand how low you feel, but there are other considerations."

"Other considerations! What other considerations? What the hell are you talking about?" Campbell tried to say something, but he cut him off. "No one is more qualified than I am for that job!" The fencing was over and he had thrown all caution to the wind.

"I'm not in a position to discuss that with you."

"You mean you're giving the job to someone else?" he practically yelled, half coming out of his seat, although his mind already had flashed him the answer who was behind this. "My job! That is my job! It should have been my job, I fucking-A well earned it with my sweat and tears, God-damn it!"

"Sorry", Campbell uttered, momentarily thrown off balance by the outburst.

"So who gets it? As if I didn't know already!"

Campbell recovered quickly and shot back viciously like a deadly viper, striking an unsuspecting victim. "Sorry, but that's confidential information. The subject is closed. Drop it!"

Clay exploded, "What kind of bullshit is this you're trying to palm off on me? What the hell has been going on behind my back?"

In a cold tone of voice, Campbell said, "You had better get control of yourself or I'll be forced to call security and have you forcibly removed!"

Still extremely angry, but getting his emotions under control, Clay said, "So this is how you reward your people after all their years of loyal service! I gave my all to this company, putting it above even my family."

His boss remained silent as Clay vented his anguish.

"Have you any idea of how many times I've had to miss important family occasions because I had to work late or be out of town because of this stupid-assed job? Because you told me how important it was to my career and that the big reward would come in the future! That's certainly some reward you're giving me after my unstinting loyalty after all these years! No longer useful…dump'em in the trash bin! Is this what you did to Herb?"

Campbell listened to the outburst in stony silence, a cold, impersonal look on his fat face. The only giveaway to what churned inside the man was that his face was now florid. Campbell was not used to being spoken to in this manner and he appeared to be working hard to control his seething anger at the outburst from his underling. Ignoring the potentially explosive question, he said, in a totally cold, hard, impersonal voice, as if he were talking to a stranger he disliked, "Mr. Clayton Dixon, you will be taken care of!"

"Yeah? How the hell am I supposed to find a God damned job at my age? Doing what? Flipping burgers for minimum wage at some fast food chain?" As he said this, his voice went up a couple of octaves. "Yeah, I'll bet you'll take care of me! Based on what's happened so far, I don't have a helluva lot to look forward to!"

Campbell snarled, "Get yourself under control now or I'll call the police and have you arrested!"

Clay just stared back, cold hate, for his boss and his cronies, radiating from his eyes.

Reaching behind him to the top of the highly polished walnut credenza, Campbell carefully picked up a large, brown manila envelope, as if it held a hand grenade. He then slid it across his desk to a spot just out of Clay's reach. It was labeled, "Severance Package, C. Dixon".

So! Clay thought with disgust, this has been planned well in advance! He rose to the bait and came half out of his seat, reaching for the envelope.

A slight curl of a malicious smile crossed Campbell's lips as he looked Clay in the eye and jabbed his index finger down on the envelope to hold it in place.

Seeing this, Clay froze, almost ready to fly out of his chair, fury seething in his eyes at being purposely suckered in this manner. Clay had not been this angry in years and now it had taken hold of him and was growing. *He wants me to lose it so he can call the cops and screw me out of everything, including this so-called severance package, he calculated furiously.*

"Not yet, Mr. Dixon!" Campbell maliciously purred, confident he was in full control. "Not until you give me all of your office keys."

Standing up straight and towering threateningly over his boss, he reached into his pants pocket and pulled out a key ring with several keys on it. Slowly, extending his arm at shoulder length over the highly polished walnut desktop, he let them fall carelessly out of his hand. They landed, making a heavy metallic thunk on the bare wood of the desk.

Reaching forward, Campbell snatched them up and dropped them into his top desk drawer, acting as if he thought Clay might steal them back, slamming it closed angrily.

In doing so, Clay couldn't miss the marks that had been created in the beautifully finished desk, much to his satisfaction. *Little things do mean a lot, he thought*, glancing at the fresh nicks, and smiling in satisfaction.

Campbell said nothing about the insubordinate act, but Clay could see the fury in his eyes. He took his finger off the envelope and shoved it hard at Clay. It slid across the desk and would have fallen to the floor had he not reached down and stopped it with his open palm, near the edge of Campbell's desk.

"There's your severance package, Dixon! It's more than generous and more than you deserve after this little performance of yours. I would have gone over it with you, but considering your unjustified actions, you're lucky I'm even *giving* it to you! Now get the hell out of here! Now!"

Clay came out of his chair slowly and in an almost arrogant way, as if taunting Campbell to make a move on him or try to shove him toward the door, or take a swing at him. He was mentally begging for Campbell to touch him or try something physical. In his murderous mood, he would have smashed his former boss to the floor without thinking. For the first time, he let a mocking smile cross his face and said, "You'll be hearing from me, you miserable son of a bitch! You can't get rid of me by shoving me in the garbage can-like you did to poor, old Herb!"

"Herb is ancient history and so are you!" Swiftly, reaching across the desk, Campbell snatched up the thick envelope and flipped it wildly at Clay, probably hoping to miss so Clay would be forced to bend over and pick it up off the floor. He had done it intentionally, Clay knew because Campbell looked so furious that he wanted to reach out and grab his former manager around the throat and choke him.

The move was intended to be an insult, but Clay's reactions were instantaneous and he opened his hands like a football player catching a lobbed pass and closed his fingers around the package when it came toward him. In a momentary flash of memory, the time in the Philippines when he had been playing football with his pals came back to him. He recalled how he had been, so full of life then. Not the shell of what he once had been - the myriad emotions, feelings and the fear in isolated moments. It had been a special time in his life until that one time near the end, when everything just fell apart on that terrible morning. He still carried it with him, weighty baggage that he figured would be with him forever.

Looking over at Campbell, with the envelope clutched firmly in his hands, Clay felt a minor triumph. He was rewarded by a slightly surprised look on his boss's face, that immediately turned to red-faced rage.

Campbell's angry reaction to his instinctive catch took Clay back many years. He recalled in a flash of memory, that he had always had swift reactions. The recollection of it all suddenly flooded his mind like a vivid black and white TV picture. That soul-searing moment on Mindanao in the Philippines, when they'd been under heavy attack in the dark of the early morning hours. It all came back, the surreal and shattered ground before him in the burning light of the parachute flares, swinging and slowly drifting toward the killing field below. It was like a moonscape, all torn and roiled up with shell craters dotted everywhere.

It had been a major attack by a large splinter element of the Jabul Gobai terrorists, a particularly vicious offshoot of the Jemaah Islamiyah group imported from Indonesia. They were determined to penetrate the defensive perimeter and get at the helicopters and supplies, safely protected in temporary revetments behind the line. A dozen or more, he could never quite remember during those frantic seconds, had spread out and were rushing his position. As they scrambled up the slight rise, stepping on the numerous dead bodies lying on flattened barbwire, rushing toward his fighting hole, he fired off his last few rounds, dropping two of them. But the rest continued relentlessly coming toward him like an unstoppable wave from the ocean.

Suddenly, unexpectedly, his weapon clicked on empty. He searched in a panic for a full magazine. Oh shit! he had thought at the time, I'm going to be dead in the next couple of seconds. In the flickering light of the flares, he could clearly see that they had bayonets affixed to the barrels of their assault rifles. He knew exactly what they would do to him before they finished him off with a shot, even if he raised his hands in surrender. He could almost feel the cold steel crunching into his body.

Clay recalled that at that moment, something came over him and he decided not to go down without a fight to the bitter end. He lay his rifle down on the low, flat dirt berm in front of his hole and was reaching for his own bayonet when he had a brief intuitive thought. He turned toward his left where his buddy, Scotty held his own in another fighting hole. Scotty fired short bursts with his M-16, but also had a Winchester Combat Model pump shotgun laying within easy reach for use against anyone who got too close. The proof - the two bodies lying on either side of his hole less than ten feet from his position.

Clay remembered yelling as loud as he could, to be heard above the sounds of firing, "Scotty! Ammo!"

Scotty turned and acknowledged him with a brief bob of his head, lay down his rifle and instantlly reached down to a small shelf in his hole, coming up with a full magazine of ammunition.

"On the way," he yelled, as he flung the fresh magazine in Clay's direction. The magazine floated lazily in an arc through the air. As he reached up to catch the magazine, he saw an enemy soldier rushing Scotty's hole from the left. He screamed a warning, even as he snatched the magazine out of the air. In a flash, Scotty had reacted. With rifle almost out of reach, he snatched up the shotgun, pointed it in the direction of the bayonet-wielding guerilla and fired point blank, catching the man in the chest. The stopping power of the double "Ought" buckshot was such that the terrorist's feet kept going out from under him even as the man dropped like a boneless rag doll, the AK-74 slipping from his dying hands and clattering to the ground.

Clay grabbed his weapon and slapped the magazine home, charged the weapon, chambering a round, point-sighted it on the nearest attackers and fired a quick burst, taking down two of them. It was a purely instinctual shot based on experience. He now had a little more time to stop the rest of them and enough ammunition for the moment.

He recalled in a flash, what if I'd missed catching that magazine. I guess I wouldn't be here now. Thank God for blessing me with quick reactions, he thought, coming back to reality. He would never forget that fateful moment in time and then today catching that flung envelope had brought it all back to him.

With the envelope in his left hand, he moved toward the heavy oak door. Stopping for a moment, he turned toward Campbell. "Go to hell, you fat bastard! And when you die, I'm going to come and piss on your grave, count on it!" Campbell opened his mouth to say something, but Clay over-rode his voice angrily. Raising his arm, he pointed his finger at his old boss, while raising the envelope so Campbell would get the idea. "Don't try to fuck with me over this paltry settlement! If you do I'll take you to court and win ten thousand times what you're pawning off on me! Trust me, I'll win, one way or another!"

Fury covering his florid face, Campbell remained speechless, as if the violent encounter had put him into shock.

When Clay reached the door to the office he angrily pulled it open, stepped through, and slammed it closed as hard as he could, hoping he'd break the hinges. This instantly caused heads to turn. They immediately dropped their eyes back to their work. In reality, he figured most of them wanted to clap their hands, but kept quiet in fear of retribution from Campbell's enforcer.

Stopping just outside the office, Clay turned toward Lorraine. She stared silently back at him with a cold, venomous look, like a rattlesnake sizing up its victim.

"Go choke on a chicken bone, you skinny old, harpy bitch!" he snarled loudly at her, so those closest to her couldn't miss what he said. He knew it would be around the whole office in minutes.

Her eyes flared wide at his words. She was so used to being kowtowed to by all the office underlings and never snarled at in this manner, that it shocked her momentarily. In another moment she recovered and spit out in a venom filled voice, "Good riddance," almost under her breath, as if she was now slightly frightened of this wild man and definitely less sure of herself for the moment.

Clay heard a tittering behind him and caught the girls at their desks grinning. They quickly bent back to their work as Lorraine snapped around like an aroused viper, looking for something to strike.

"Up yours, you old bag of shit! Been wanting to say that to you for so long, I can't remember!" Without waiting for her to say or do anything more, he purposefully strode out of the waiting area toward the center aisle, leading through the office, and to the entrance. Determined to leave this hateful place with his head high, he walked down the main aisle, concealing his ripped, torn emotions. Inside, his whole world crumbled around him, but he never let them see it.

Chapter 5

Striding confidently down the center aisle, Clay couldn't help but notice the overwhelming dead silence in the office. The idle thought crossed his mind; you could have heard a feather hit the floor. It was as if everyone were momentarily frozen in time or waiting for a bomb to go off. Of course, the bomb had already gone off big time. In the blink of an eye, the spell was broken, the normal office clatter started up again as all the wage slaves went back to their duties. He knew they all had to have heard some of his clash with Campbell and Lorraine or at the very least, the loud, muffled, angry shouting.

He left the gray haired, bun-head standing behind him with a kind of stupefied shock written all over her prune face. His final sarcastic recommendation had temporarily stilled the old harpy's wasp-like tongue, he assumed. He strode purposefully, unhurriedly down the center aisle to show everyone that he was leaving voluntarily, with his pride intact, not that anyone really gave a damn, he figured disgustedly.

He realized how totally wrong he was in his negative opinion about most of his former associates when one of the guys he knew looked up at him, gave him a big smile, and a thumbs up that none of the others could see. The simple gesture meant everything to him and reinforced his belief that he was right.

At the end of the aisle, an arm came out of a cubicle, to catch his attention. The hand held an envelope with his name hastily scrawled on it. Taking the envelope, he stuck it in his pocket figuring he'd satisfy his curiosity as to the contents back at the hotel. Glancing into the cubicle, he gave the woman a strong smile, remembering her as one of the staff who had helped him when he had done his stint here when Herb had been on vacation. She also gave him a warm, supportive smile and he received another thumbs up. It bolstered him.

Reaching the fabric-covered wall at the end of the aisle, he stepped around it and went through the entryway into the reception area. The receptionist arrogantly stared at him, not smiling. Looks like she got the word to make sure I leave, he thought.

Clay just couldn't let it pass. Controlling himself and not letting his smoldering anger show through, he said, "Listen to me carefully, you stupid little gatekeeper!" Her lips twisted into a snarl as she began to say something, but he stopped her cold. Putting his finger up to his lips for silence, he said commandingly, "Be quiet and pay attention. You've got a lot of manners to learn! Just remember, your time will come too, and you'll be history around this place just as quickly because you're nothing to them! They'll chop your head off just as fast!"

He was through the front door and gone before she could make the smart-ass retort that he knew would be forthcoming. The temptation to slam the huge door hard, hoping to ruin it, was high on his mind, but the minor satisfaction it would bring just wasn't worth it and he headed for the elevators. His mind swirled at how fast his whole world had tumbled down around him.

Getting off the elevator on the ground floor, he stepped through the large glass entrance doors to the building, pausing for a moment on the sidewalk. *The negatives are coming one after another, he thought, no wife, no family, now no job! Damn, what the hell is next!*

Trying to push out the depressing thoughts clouding his mind, he headed for his car, half-humorously expecting it to have been stolen.

Getting in, he pulled out the envelope from his jacket. He started to tear it open. Curiosity had him wondering what kind of information she would pass on to him at the possible risk to her job. On second thought, he slipped it back into his jacket, and started the car, needing to get away from this hateful place. He decided he would open it up in the privacy of his hotel room, just in case.

Pulling out of the parking lot, he thought, what the hell, I've still got a night at the hotel on the company and the miserable bastard forgot to get the company credit cards back from me. Sooner or later Lorraine will surely remember and check with Campbell, so if I need anything, I'd better use the cards as soon as possible.

At the hotel, he immediately went into the bar and ordered a scotch and water. He'd had a big lunch on the way up from his old office, so he wasn't hungry. There were only a few people in the bar and he decided he didn't want to sit there alone, get depressed all over again, then totally sloshed, till they'd have to carry him up to his room. *No, I don't want that, he thought.*

Instead, he summoned the bartender. When the man, who recognized him from previous trips came over, he asked, "Tell me, Tommy, what is the very best scotch that you stock here?"

The bartender thought for a second and replied, "Johnnie Walker Gold Label, eighteen years old. Need to know how much?"

"No, that's okay."

"Are we celebrating?" Tommy asked.

"You might say that," he replied. "Sort of." Pulling out his wallet, he handed Tommy one of the company credit cards and said, "Would you mind having a bottle with ice and a glass sent up to my room?"

"No problem," Tommy replied and left to ring up the sale.

Clay had no idea how much the hotel charged for the scotch, nor did he care. He did recall seeing it locked behind glass in a grocery store a while back and vaguely remembered that it cost in the neighborhood of $70 a bottle. He also knew that the hotel would most probably charge considerably more. So what! After signing the charge slip for his drink and the bottle, he made sure he left Tommy a generous tip.

Tommy looked slyly at Clay and winked, saying, "Would you like an additional glass and would you need anything else?" The inference as to female companionship went without saying.

"That's okay, Tommy, but thanks for thinking of me anyway."

Leaving the bar, Clay walked over to the front desk in the lobby. He explained to the clerk he'd be checking out early in the morning, and if he ordered anything else, to just add it to his bill. That done, he headed for the elevators just off the lobby. In actuality, he had originally planned on spending the whole weekend with friends, but clearly there was no need for that now, nor could he face them at this point.

Back in his room, Clay had an idle thought. *Maybe I should have taken Tommy up on his offer of a high priced hooker. Maybe that would take my mind off what had just happened to me.* He recalled someone saying that they now took credit cards these days. But he decided against it in the end because he didn't really feel in the mood for something like that, considering the circumstances. Besides, he laughed to himself, he hadn't done anything like that since he was in the Philippines.

A few minutes later he heard a knock at his door. He knew it was room service bringing up his bottle of scotch. He waited patiently while everything was set up, then signed the bill and wrote in a generous tip. The young man thanked him profusely and left. He knew this would be added to the bill and hopefully cause Campbell to have something akin to a coronary! And what the hell! Why not, he thought, those back-stabbing assholes at the company could well afford it!

The waiter had set up the bottle, bucket of ice and carafe of water on a small breakfast bar by the tiny convenience kitchen. Clay sat down, *thinking he might as well relax. I've got nothing but time on my hands now.*

Getting up for a minute, he pulled off his jacket and folded it, laying it over the back of the couch. He noticed the envelope, sticking out of the inner pocket of the jacket, that he'd been slipped on his way out of the office. He pulled it out and propped it on the coffee table in front of him, preparing to open the mysterious message after making a nice, healthy drink.

Stepping over to the small bar, he mixed himself a very ample double scotch and water, stirring the ice cubes around the glass with the plastic stick the waiter had left. Before taking a drink, he raised his glass and proposed a toast out loud. "Here's to all you back-stabbing, hypocritical sonavabitches! And here's hoping and praying you all get your nuts cut off sooner than later!" Taking a big swallow of the amber liquid, he savored the rich taste. There was no bite to the scotch and it went down smooth as a snowboard slicing down a whipped-cream mountain.

Setting down his drink, he picked up the envelope and sat down on the couch. Opening it up and unfolding the single page, he began to read the few, neatly typed lines. *This information comes from an impeccable source,* the words began. *Prenotsky was the one behind all the backstabbing and undermining done to you and others. He is very vulnerable because of some of his disgusting habits. This can be addressed at a later date should you decide to pursue this matter.* The note ended with the challenge to not give up. And the words, *Give this same serious thought, you are in the right and can prevail.* There was no signature, nor did he expect one.

Staring at the page, he asked himself, why didn't I see this before? I should have been smart enough to pick up on it. The very least I can hope for, he thought, is that those responsible will eventually get theirs in spades, if I have anything to say about it. Do somebody dirt and sooner or later, it will come back to bite you hard in the ass when you least expect it, he reasoned, dearly hoping it was true. Crumpling up the note, he stood up and tossed it and the envelope in the trashcan. He finished his drink and went over and mixed himself another, then slumped back down on the couch. Taking another sip, he stopped for a moment to enjoy the taste of the high priced liquid. Thinking about the message it conveyed, he changed his mind and pulled the note out of the trash. Smoothing it out, he folded it, placing it in his inner jacket pocket, thinking he might pursue the matter later.

Sinking back onto the couch, his mind wandered. Sipping the drink brought back many memories in a rush. It took him back to his tour in the Philippines, remembering the first time he had ever tasted scotch. They had run out of water and been forced to use the local streams, adding those terrible tasting purification tablets. Nobody wanted to drink it, nor did they fully trust the tabs supplied to neutralize all the bad stuff they knew existed in the local water. It had a strange taste that none of them could stand.

They'd all been sitting around their small camp in the mountains, sipping on some of the locally bartered brew nicknamed "Koo Koo Juice", the name implying what you felt like doing after a few of the raw, throat searing distillation. In the midst of their imbibing, one of their buddies had shown up with something suspicious in a large, rubber coated laundry bag. The man had made an emergency trip down to a permanent Philippine Special Forces base several miles away to get some spare parts for one of their Hummers that was giving them problems with the compressor that raised and lowered the pressure in the tires for travel over soft terrain.

Setting the mystery bag down in the middle of the circle, with a mischievous smile, he slowly reached in and like some kind of magician, carefully pulled out a bottle of Dewar's scotch whisky, to the total surprise of everyone. Where or how he had managed to get his hands on the scotch, no one asked or cared. No one had obviously given it to him and beer was the only thing available at the club miles away at the main base, for a dime a can. They were rarely there, so they all had to get very creative when it came to getting their hands on anything alcoholic. He wouldn't say, but their best guess was apparently he had liberated it from the back of a supply truck or some big-shot officer's tent.

He ceremoniously set one bottle on the ground and then pulled out two more, like rabbits out of a hat. It was the "good stuff", as they liked to say. Everybody held out their canteen cups as their buddy opened the first bottle and started pouring. Clay had never had scotch before and when he took his first hesitant sip, he noticed it had a unique taste to it, different from any of the other bourbons or whiskeys he had drunk in the past. The amber liquid had a somewhat smoky taste to it - an acquired taste. After ordering scotch in bars after he returned to the states, he decided he liked the taste and that's what he always drank thereafter.

Now, here he sat in the present, sober as a judge, not feeling the booze at all with nowhere to go and nothing to do. He had turned on the TV with the remote and stared at it but did not really see the program, a talk show. His mind reeled.

He refilled his glass several times, but because the scotch was so smooth, he didn't realize he was getting totally plowed until the last trip to the bar when he weaved a bit and stumbled against the edge of the couch and almost fell down. "Oh, boy! Am I getting hooty," he said out loud, using an old word he used to use in the Army for getting totally smashed. "I better watch it or I'm gonna' get really, really stinkin' drunk! Then again maybe I ought to!" Every time he got up to refill his glass, he weaved or staggered a little more.

Deciding he needed some fresh air, he weaved over to the sliding glass door to the balcony and slid it partially open. A cool, refreshing breeze floated softly over him and into the room. It had grown dark and the lights of the city sparkled magically before him from eight floors up. It dazzled him and drew him forward.

Stepping through the opening, he tripped on the bottom guide rail of the sliding glass door, causing him to lurch unsteadily forward. The drink in his hand threw him off balance as he clumsily tried to stop any of the precious amber fluid from spilling. Hazily, through the cloud of liquor, he felt his body lurch toward the black metal railing that surrounded the small balcony.

Hanging onto the heavy, cut-glass drink tumbler for dear life, he staggered up against the metal railing and felt his upper body start to tip over the top. He felt no fear, just a kind of matter-of-fact feeling that if he went over, so what, he really didn't give a damn at this point.

As his upper torso leaned precariously over the rail, an instinctual inner force of self-preservation automatically kicked in at the last deadly moment. As he slowly started to roll over further, his left hand flashed down and grabbed one of the wrought iron vertical bars and held him in check from tipping all the way over the top rail. This halted his forward motion and allowed him to regain his balance. It was an automatic gesture.

Pushing himself upright, he realized what had almost occurred. Sweat beads broke out on his forehead as the implications of what could have happened to him penetrated his alcohol-fogged brain. His mind went off in several directions at once. Realizing he'd almost gone over the rail, but didn't seem to care, or wasn't frightened out of his wits, caused him to pause and think about it. Maybe this was the solution to all his problems, present and past. Just do it, a harsh voice in his mind screamed at him! *The mental hurt and pain will all be over in seconds and I'll be back with them, he thought. That where I should have been in the beginning,* his mind berated him with self guilt, I should have died with them. Involuntary tears flowed freely down his cheeks in his anguish.

Random thoughts kept swirling through his befuddled mind. Staring out at the city lights before him, his head started to swim and he felt himself sway again. An instantaneous message from his mind told him that it was the effects of the scotch and he needed to get back in control of himself, if only for the next minute or two, till he got out of this situation.

Ignoring the inner warning, he took another big gulp of his drink and in a comical *Charlie Chaplinesque* type gesture, like a puppet on strings, he slowly bent over and very carefully set the cut crystal glass of scotch on the concrete floor of the balcony. Straightening up, he leaned against the thin, wrought iron rail for support. He took a long look at the city, sparkling like a precious jewel before him, and up at the stars twinkling in the jet-black sky above.

"Maybe this is the best way after all," he said to the stars. "Why not! All my problems will be over in the blink of an eye!" His vision reeled as he unsteadily swung his right leg over the rail and hung there for a moment. His mind swirled along with his vision and he thought he could see his buddies again. They silently voiced the words to him, "Do it! Do it! End it!"

His alcoholic induced vision spun around him like a kaleidoscope as he lost his balance and felt himself going over the rail again. *No! I can't let this happen now!* His inner consciousness screamed at him. *It's not to late! No! There has to be a better way!* These conflicting thoughts raced through his mind, as his body arched over and downward.

Without thinking, he stuck his other leg between the vertical rails and hooked his foot around one of them, halting his rapidly gaining momentum. He could still feel himself going over. In a dying man's desperation, his hands gripped the upper rail in a claw-like manner that would never let loose.

Hanging halfway over the rail and looking straight down, he saw the inner courtyard three stories below. A mind numbing, immobilizing fear embraced him. With crystal clarity, he could see the swimming pool in the center of the courtyard, with guests sitting around it, totally oblivious to the drama that was transpiring three floors above them.

Momentarily he thought back to his days in the paratroops. This was nothing like then, when he eagerly looked out of the aircraft's door at the purple, early morning's dawn on the horizon and eagerly anticipated the jump. When he went out the door of an airplane in those days, he felt no fear. He knew the training had programmed his mind not to think about the fall back then. But this was far different.

Looking downward, his muscles froze and he could not move to even save himself. Reason took over and he slowly, physically forced himself to overcome the crippling terror that gripped his body. Gradually he began to carefully pull himself, inch by painful inch, back over the rail. He could feel the perspiration running down the sides of his temples and forehead and into his eyes, burning them. His moist hands weakened his grip as he felt himself beginning to slip loose. At this moment he came to the conclusion that he was not ready to die, but now it appeared to him to be beyond his control.

An inner survival instinct took hold of him and he tightened his leg hold tighter on the rail till the muscles burned and he wanted to scream with the pain. The grip of his hands became so desperate that he could feel his nails cutting into the heels of his palms. In excruciating slow motion, Clay worked his way back over the rail and safety.

When he was fully back on the balcony, in a psychological reaction, he felt his legs literally collapse under him as he slipped to the floor of the balcony. His clothes were soaked from his perspiration. He sat that way for several minutes and stayed motionless, physically unable to move himself, slowly mulling over in his numbed mind the near death experience that had just occurred.

Knowing he couldn't stay like this all night, he laboriously rolled over onto his hands and knees, crawled over to the doorway in an agonizingly slow manner, very aware that he was still totally drunk, even after the close encounter with death on the balcony.

Gripping the edge of the doorway, Clay carefully pulled himself up to a standing position. He was afraid if he lost his grip and fell, he wouldn't be able to get up again. Slowly and deliberately he worked his way inside the doorway a laborious inch at a time. Looking at the bed, he tried to guesstimate his chances of making his way to it without falling flat on his face. It looked to be only around eight or so feet, but in his condition, it appeared like eight miles.

Accessing his chances again, he launched himself from the doorframe toward the bed. In his alcohol-induced state his legs felt weak and wobbly, but he managed to stagger to the side of the bed.

When his legs came up against the hotel bed he felt himself fall forward into a sprawl. Laying still for a few moments, he felt uncomfortable with his face pressing against the coverlet, so he rolled over on his back. He realized belatedly this had been a very bad move moments after he did it.

No sooner had he rolled onto his back, than the ceiling and room started spinning rapidly around him, going faster every second, like he was on some kind of crazy carousel. It made his dizziness worse than it already was and he immediately became sick to his stomach. Sweat beads rapidly started to break out on his forehead all over again. He knew the symptoms, having had the same stomach roiling experience in his younger days. He knew he was on the verge of having to run to the toilet to throw up.

Doubting that he could even make it to the bathroom without upchucking his stomach, he rolled onto his side and curling into a fetal ball, willed the dizziness to disappear. He closed his eyes tight, hoping that would help, but everything kept swirling around him. In this state, he eventually fell into a drugged, dreamless sleep.

Chapter 6

Around two in the morning, a cooling breeze wafted in the open patio door and gently caressed Clay's sweat drenched forehead. He remained unaware of the invigorating draft, finally falling into a deep dreamless slumber. Curling into a fetal ball, his last conscious thoughts had been of desperately willing his mind to stop the stomach churning and the spinning in his head, letting him descend into blessed oblivion. Before finally dropping off, one last thought had penetrated his feverish mind. It had clearly let him know that he would most assuredly regret his rash reaction of getting stone cold drunk out of his idiotic mind. "Stupid, stupid, stupid," his mind kept repeating until he slid off into his alcoholic induced hibernation. There was an unspoken awareness that his hangover would be blindingly crushing.

Having slept several hours, his subconscious mind unaccountably brought him up to an inner awareness, as if he were awake and fully cognizant of what was going on around him. He found himself in a dark room surrounded by an opaque, black sheet of fabric. His mind responded to this by sending rapid signals that this had to be unusual.

He realized he was floating upright above a floor he couldn't quite discern in the murky darkness.

Suddenly he registered a ripping, tearing sound, like a bed sheet ripping, but more pronounced. The black curtain steadily parted down the ripping seam, revealing an eye-watering brightness beyond the tear. His eyes focused on the dazzling light behind the dark sheet.

The split opened further, pulling widely apart, revealing full daylight and open ground. Numerous clumps of tropical foliage dotted the terrain. The large clearing, somewhere in the tropics, looked vaguely familiar, from his younger days in the military.

In the distance, his eyes caught movement, but could not quite make it out. Clay did not have long to wait. Things were still blurry, and he couldn't quite see clearly yet, but there was no doubt that these were figures of a group of men slowly moving purposely toward him. The figures drifted closer, as if floating on air and Clay began to focus on them, his heart thudding harder in the slow beginning of recognition. His memory cells flashed him rapid warning signals that there was something definitely familiar about the approaching group.

The distance swiftly closing, he could make them out with more clarity, even though they were still a little way off in back country. Their images remained slightly fuzzy and distorted even as they drew nearer. One thing left no doubt in his fevered mind, they definitely were heading directly for him and not just wandering.

All the past images and memories suddenly flooded his fevered mind. *Not that all over again? Please! No!* His first reaction was to run, but felt himself powerless to do so as if he were chained in place. He tried to scream, but nothing came out.

He immediately recognized their chilling identity. Looking at each of them individually, one at a time, he instantly recognized the faces of his best friends. Clay also couldn't help seeing once again, their bloodied and mutilated bodies. Mere yards away now, Clay knew the horrid apparition from the past, but somehow did not mentally connect that he was in a dream world. He was there in their reality, rooted in place, and facing them as they moved ever closer. Reaching for him with their bloodied and slashed arms, they began speaking to Clay, but no sound came from their mouths. It was uncanny, but his feverish mind knew what they were saying. They kept beseeching him to come join them in their journey of death. That his rightful place was with them they assured him.

He lost all control and let loose a spine chilling shriek of terror. The scream carried through to his conscious mind and his eyes snapped open to the deep darkness of his hotel room. In a mindless panic, still seeing the images before him, he continued to scream as he crawled and groped around on his bed in the darkness. He still could see the bloodied apparitions of his buddies trying to grasp him.

Groping sightlessly in the stygian blackness of the room, he tumbled off the edge of the bed and landed in a painful pile. Panic overwhelming him, he vainly tried to flee on his hands and knees, from the gruesome reflections of his former compatriots. The grisly spectacle still haunted his delirious mind as he scrambled blindly away. He ran smack into the low coffee table that still contained the expensive, half empty bottle of scotch and the cut crystal glass. Dazed, he reached out for anything to protect himself. His hand closed on the bottle and without realizing what he was doing, he grabbed it as a weapon and threw it in the direction he visualized his tormentors were approaching. The wildly thrown bottle smashed with a loud crash against the adjoining wall of the room next to Clay's. It briefly registered on his mind that he had probably awakened the room's occupants, but he could care less because he was so totally frightened out of his mind

In the darkness, Clay continued to grope around for anything to protect himself against the horrid specters coming after him. His fingers touched the heavy drink tumbler, and wrapping his hand tightly around it, he heaved it in a futile gesture at where he visualized his tormentors were coming at him. The heavy lead crystal glass thudded against the wall with a hard bang and immediately shattered into a hundred pieces. In the back of his mind Clay was vaguely aware that his erratic actions might cause problems for him, but at this point he was beyond caring.

Clay continued to drag his lethargic body along the carpet, trying to get away from the ghastly phantoms. Completely disoriented, he continued to crawl around, not knowing where he was, until he ran head-on into an end table. Reaching out with one hand, he touched the large, ceramic vase lamp sitting on the small bed table.

His heart beat faster as he balanced himself on his knees and using the end table for support, shakily stood up. By feel, he took hold of the lamp by the neck with both hands and lifted it up. Still being confronted by his demons, he faced them with the lamp, one hand grasping the neck, the other supporting the bottom and holding the whole thing like a spear. Screaming at the images, he said, "No! No! Get the hell away from me! I won't go with you!"

They still kept moving toward him in a threatening way. Drawing back the lamp to heave his weapon at them, he moved toward the images, unknowingly moving in the direction of the open patio door.

The cadaverous phantoms still continued to entreat him to come with them, but as he moved toward them, threatening the group with the lamp, they slowly moved backward until they were floating just above the patio railing, baiting him.

"Come! Come! Come with us!" Their silent lips seemed to be saying. *"You deserve to be with us."*

In a totally, irrational act of terror, Clay raised the lamp over his head as if he were going to throw it at them. This seemed to amuse his buddies, as he saw them all start to laugh, though they had to realize that there was no way he could hurt them anymore than what had already been done to them. Like a brittle, dry stick snapping, Clay lost it completely. In a fit of rage at the apparition of his former friends and with a strength he didn't know he possessed, he heaved the large lamp at them with his whole being.

They continued to laugh at him as the lamp sailed right through them and over the edge of the railing, dropping like a large, lethal bomb to the pool area below. Still feeling shaky and unbalanced, Clay turned wildly, looking for something else to throw, when he banged the side of his head hard against the open patio door. It was the catalyst that jarred him out of his nightmare world and back into reality.

His eyes blinked at the brief jolt of pain and he found himself now fully and painfully wide awake. Looking out over balcony area where he had tossed the lamp, the first thing he noticed was the macabre images had disappeared and no longer taunted him. He could have sworn he had momentarily heard derisive laughter, could it have been them as they disappeared like smoke in the wind? Trying to clear his head and think reasonably, he figured he was just hearing things and it was just a strong breeze.

Taking stock of his situation and taking a good look around him, Clay could see the stars twinkling brightly above him in the inky blackness of the sky. Gazing up at the pitch-black galaxy brought him to the sudden realization that he was out on the small balcony of his room overlooking the pool area. Remembering what had almost occurred earlier in the evening, a rapid chill raced up his spine. Bare moments later, he distinctly heard a distant, crashing sound resound from below, followed seconds later by a shrill, female scream and a loud bellow of rage.

It hit him face on like a cold bucket of ice water as to what had occurred. Clay knew he should not chance to see what had happened, but morbid curiosity, more than anything, drew him over to the black, wrought iron railing to look down. Soft lights lit up the pool and lounge area below. Staring at the scene below, a chilling shock slammed into him like being hit by an onrushing bus, in the middle of a street.

Loosely arranged in a row around the pool were chaise lounges for the guests to sun bathe. Below his balcony were two loungers situated about three feet apart from each other. A young woman sat on one with her face in her hands. She appeared to Clay to be crying hysterically. Standing next to her was a beefy, bull of a young man who looked like he played halfback for the Oakland Raiders.

The lamp had apparently hit the cement deck between the two loungers, near the headrests. It was also obvious to him that had the vase landed one foot or so to either side of the two it would have smashed down on one of their heads. Clay also had the instant realization that the sound of the lamp vase slamming down between the two of them had to have scared the living hell out of the pair. Clay could see the couple had been enjoying a late evening drink together when the lamp had landed, totally spoiling their quiet evening.

The big guy looked upward probably trying to figure out where the lamp had come from. Spotting Clay who looked down at the scene over his railing with guilt written all over his face, the man must have detected the culprit immediately. Pointing an accusing finger directly up at Clay, he roared, "You! I'm gonna kill your fucking ass, you stupid son of a bitch! You almost killed us!" A few moments later he disappeared into the hotel.

Stepping back into his room with an urgency, Clay recalled he hadn't done anything this asinine since he had gotten plastered when he was with the special training command in the Philippines Islands.

The inside of his mouth felt and tasted like it had been coated with gray plumbers putty. His sinuses were clogged and his nose had the sensation that several Q-tips were jammed up each nostril. On top of that there was a dull throb in his right temple that felt like a miniature native was sitting on his shoulder and poking it with his razor sharp spear. He knew it was the beginning of a monumental headache, brought on by his stupid, emotional reaction the previous night. He would have preferred to stay curled up into a nice safe fetal ball, he thought, but the urgency of the situation he had inadvertently created forced him to get moving and get out of there as soon as possible.

Staggering into the bathroom, he flipped on the light and took a brief look at himself in the mirror. Disgusted with his disheveled appearance, he quickly splashed cold water on his face to get rid of the dried sweat and to refresh himself. Wetting his hair, which was a mess he combed it back. Drying off with a towel he took another look in the mirror and felt a little better about his appearance, but not by much. As an afterthought he fumbled around in his toilet bag and found the small container of extra strength Bufferin he rarely used, but kept in there for emergencies. Filling a plastic glass with water, he threw down the pills, hoping and praying they would stave off the impending hangover headache that he had begun to experience.

He took one last fleeting glance in the mirror at his rumpled visage and thought, *Who the hell is going to see me at this hour anyway! And who the hell cares, for that matter! I'll never see this place again in my lifetime, at least I hope so!*

Clay knew the clock was ticking down dangerously and soon he could expect a nasty surprise banging on his door; he had to get a move on now. His gut reaction, ringing in his ears, told him to get himself together immediately and out of the room immediately before it was too late. He just couldn't let them catch him at this point, he thought desperately. That bastard Campbell and his bitch henchwoman would absolutely love hearing about his idiotic mistake, and he wasn't about to let that happen.

Clay ripped off his tie and threw it carelessly into his overnight case. Aware that time was critical, he left on his soiled clothes from the previous night, figuring he'd change when he got back home. Feeling totally grungy, Clay accepted the fact that unfortunately now even a brief shower was out of the question.

Tossing his belongings into his travel case, he slapped it shut and put on his suit coat. Since he had paid for his bill earlier, he dropped the magnetic room key on the nightstand, grabbed his garment bag and after a quick glance around the room to make sure he hadn't left anything, stepped over to the door. Through the now throbbing headache, he had a momentary, mirthful thought. At least he'd had the last say in a way by sticking Campbell with the hotel bill and the booze. That ought to really piss him off when he got the bill. That bottle of scotch was not cheap change!

As the door to his room closed with a solid click behind him, it crossed his mind that this hurtful chapter of his life was closed forever, with the closing of that door. He wondered what the rest of his life held in store for him as he began to navigate down this new, unknown and very uncertain path of life. One thing for sure, he thought, this was definitely a very different and bizarre beginning than he could have possibly envisioned for himself. He wondered in what direction fate would take him next. The only thing he knew for sure was he had to get the hell out of there before they came after him.

Chapter 7

He moved swiftly along the hallway toward the elevators, hoping to get to the lobby, and out of the hotel before anyone reacted to that big, pissed off gorilla's complaint. Nearing the cross hallway next to the elevators, he heard the distinctive chime of an elevator arriving at his floor. Not wanting to run into anyone, especially that wild man who threatened him, or someone connected to the hotel, he looked around in a minor panic for someplace to duck in and hide quickly. He mentally chastised himself for acting like some kind of a fugitive or criminal, even though he realized the stupid thing he had perpetrated most likely put him in that category.

Spotting a small alcove where the hotel kept the ice, snack and soda machines, he found a temporary hiding place. He heard the elevator doors open and someone getting out and then moments later he heard the loud slam of the stairway door closing, running feet and the voice of someone talking and out of breath, by the elevator. The voices got louder and seemed to be heading in his direction. Panicking, he tried to hide behind one of the big drink machines.

Expecting to be discovered any second, he literally froze, held his breath and tried to become invisible, wedging his body as tightly as he could into the corner. After a moment, he heard the voices receding down the hallway in the direction of his room. He hazarded a peek around the edge of the alcove to see who they were. He recognized the big, husky one in the tweed sport coat with a graying, close-cut military type haircut, a security guy – he'd seen him before roaming the halls. The other individual, an older man, graying, a big and beefy individual, with a pot belly, and wearing a dirty set of dark blue coveralls with the hotel logo patch on his left pocket. This had to be the maintenance man, he guessed.

Watching them, they went almost all the way down to the end of the hall. Clay noticed with a twinge of alarm that they stopped at his room and the security guy knocked on the door. When there was no reply, he knocked again, this time louder and more persistently. He did this several times and when there was still no answer, he saw the guy take out a plastic room key, insert it in the door slot and pushed open the door to his room. The man entered carefully and alertly, as if he was expecting to be jumped or find a body. After a moment, he nodded and the other man followed him inside, the door clicking shut behind them.

Not wasting a moment, Clay knew time was critical and he had to get out of there now. When they found him gone, they'd come storming out of the room and the alarm would instantly go out. Immediately thereafter they'd be turning the hotel upside down searching for him. But now what to do? How to exit from this trap without being caught? Clay felt a certain degree of shame, but still needed to escape their clutches desperately. The elevator was definitely out, as he just knew that everyone in the lobby on the lookout for him. Taking another quick peek to make sure they had not come out of the room, he stepped out to the alcove.

Moving swiftly, he stepped around the corner, past the elevators over to the duplicate, parallel hallway on the other side of the building. Turning right, he rapidly walked down the corridor, forcing himself not to panic and headed for the lit exit sign at the end, leading to the stairs. As quietly as he could, he opened the emergency exit door, stepped through and gently let it close. His shoes slapped hard and fast on the concrete steps as he tried to fly down the musty smelling, dimly lit emergency exit stairs, to the ground floor. He breathed a momentary sigh of relief that he had made it without anybody spotting him. So far so good. He was almost home free, he confidently felt, just a few more steps and he'd be gone.

On the ground floor leading to the parking lot, he rushed over to the exit door and had started to push down on the release bar, but was stopped at the last moment. In the poorly lit landing, Clay read the red aluminum sign prominently attached to the door release bar. The words jumped out at him - *Emergency Only. Alarm Sounds When Door Opened.* This is the dilemma, he thought, I press the bar and open the door, the alarm sounds and they know *exactly* where I am!

A little bit of panic welled up in him as he looked at his surroundings in apprehension for any other avenue of escape. To his right, he saw another set of steps leading downward that he'd originally missed in his rush. They had to lead to the fire door exit from the underground garage. Grabbing his bag, he flew down the short flight of stairs figuring he'd sneak out the parking garage entrance. Without giving it another thought, Clay grabbed the long handle and turned it downward to open the fire door. To his disgust, the handle just turned a scant inch and stopped. It was obviously locked, and only someone exiting from the garage would be able to open it. He pushed and banged against it a few times, but nothing gave way. The steel door was solidly locked.

Shit! Shit! Shit! He thought tensely, *now what?*

Taking two steps at a time, he flew back up the steps to the landing on the parking lot level. In a quandary, his eyes fell on the short staircase leading up to the lobby level. *Maybe if I'm careful I can sneak out the front door and make a run for it, he thought.* He figured the lobby might be deserted at this hour, as he was pretty positive they were combing all the floors for him, like a fine-toothed flea comb on a cats fur.

Reaching the top of the small landing, Clay grabbed the long door handle and started to turn it downward to open it when he heard approaching voices on the other. Letting go of the handle like it was red hot, panic overwhelmed him once again. He felt like a trapped rat on the end of a long tree branch. Clay didn't know which way to turn now. If he let them come through the door, they'd have him cold. Trapped!

Knowing he couldn't allow that to happen, when the voices came right up to the door, he grabbed the handle and held it hard in the upright position before they tried to open it, putting it in a locked position on the other side. He felt the downward pressure on the handle as the man tried to turn the handle down to open it.

"It's locked," he heard a muffled voice say through the metal door.

"It can't be - not from this side," another voice replied in irritation.

"Maybe it's jammed or something else," a third suspicious voice said.

Clay realized a third person had joined the group. He could only guess. Perhaps the bell captain had joined the hunt. He knew it definitely wasn't the football linebacker individual. He would have instantly recognized that voice.

This new development made Clay hyper aware of his dangerous predicament. He did the only thing he could think of and got right up flat against the door to give himself better leverage, bracing himself with his feet and held the handle jammed upward now with both hands.

He could tell the men on the other side suspected something because he heard one of them say, "When I give the word, you two push down as hard as you can on the handle."

"Keep holding the door handle down, I'll take a run at the door and throw my shoulder into it. If that doesn't do it, I'll get a damn fire ax!" he heard another shout.

I'm dead meat, Clay thought, wildly looking around for anything, and not knowing what to do next. Glancing down at the dust-covered floor, he noticed a small, dark object up against the wall near where the door was hinged onto the doorframe. Focusing more clearly on the object he recognized it. This could be my salvation, he thought with a tiny bit of renewed hope, if it works.

The downward pressure was off momentarily as Clay figured the big guy got ready to rush the door. In the blink of an eye he bent down and grabbed the dusty object. To his great relief there was no mistaking what he held in his hand - a hard rubber wedge used to hold a door temporarily open. Maybe, just maybe this will do it, he inwardly prayed like he'd never prayed before.

He had just pushed the dark rubber wedge into the tiny crack of space between the bottom of the metal door and the cement floor when he heard one of them yell, "Get ready!"

Kicking the rubber wedge as hard as he could with the heel of his shoe and forcing it to wedge solidly under the door, he grabbed the door handle and held it upward, just as he felt the downward pressure from the other side.

One of the others yelled, "I just heard a sound. There's got to be someone on the other side!"

"No shit, Sherlock!" one of the others said in disgust.

"Okay, stand back!" Clay heard another one say, thinking it might be the big security guard, "I'll take a run at the door the first time. If that doesn't work, all three of us will hit it the next time around. One way or the other we'll get that sonavabitch open!"

Clay knew what was coming and braced himself for the impact, hoping he wouldn't get knocked down the stairs.

When the guy slammed into the metal fire door like a cold slab of beef, to Clay it felt like, and sounded like an explosion going off next to his head. The teeth-jarring vibration and ear shattering noise, transmitted through the door, echoed through his body and the staircase. *Holy shit! I know this door can't take too many more of those heavy hits, nor can I, he thought. Next time around I might not be so lucky.*

Thinking on his feet, knowing he had to do something before the next hit on the door, Clay reacted. Allowing the handle to return to the normal position so the others wouldn't hear, Clay grabbed his bag and leaped down the stairs two at a time.

His feet smacked the bottom stair landing at the same moment he heard one of the group slam against the door again. The hard rubber wedge was holding, just barely, but the door creaked and groaned agonizingly, coming partially open a tiny crack.

Clay thanked his lucky stars that the wedge was still mostly jammed under the door, but he doubted it would stop them the next time around. He knew he only had seconds and dared not look back up the stairs. Hitting the landing and wildly propelling himself toward the emergency exit, he heard another loud bang and then the tormented metallic screech of the door finally giving way. He didn't have a moment to lose. With those three beef-balls throwing themselves at the door, he knew the wedge had finally given up the fight. A second later his super attuned ears heard the clamorous bang of the door opening, flying around on its hinges and slamming resoundingly against the wall. The pursuers paused for a moment, as if they couldn't believe they'd finally opened it. A blink of an eye later, they all tried to crowd down the steps together, falling all over each other, and unwittingly gaining Clay a couple of vital seconds of time.

"There he is!" one of them yelled. "Get his ass!" he screamed angrily.

At that moment Clay punched his hand down hard on the emergency door-opening bar, pushing with a strength brought on by his adrenalin rush. In his mind, his escape and freedom was just beyond this door.

The raucous, earsplitting sound of the emergency alarm instantly assaulted his ears with a loud, deafening reverberation in the confined space, blotting out all other sounds from above. Clay threw the door open, leaping onto the small, cement landing, with a short flight of steps leading down to the parking lot.

Not hearing anything beyond the deafening din, Clay knew the pursuers were coming fast down the stairs. Clay jumped off the last few steps, and ran like the devil himself was hot on his heels, toward his parked car. His breath rasped out of him in huge gasps, knowing and regretting he was so sorely out of shape.

Halfway across the lot, he heard angry shouts behind him ordering him to stop. A minor thought flashed through his mind while he ran. You've got to be kidding if you actually think I'd be stupid enough to stop and get myself murdered by you assholes! Ignoring them, Clay knew he had it made now, no way could they reach him before he got to his car.

He was a little surprised by the feel of the much colder than normal night air against his cold, sweaty forehead. He recalled it wasn't this chilly earlier in the afternoon. Maybe a front had passed over, who knows. Clay also couldn't miss the obvious fact that the ground was wet, and there were a few small puddles dotted around the lot. There had apparently been a brief shower sometime during his alcohol-drugged sleep.

Hearing the unmistakable sound of pounding feet on the wet pavement behind him, he knew they were closing the gap fast. Spotting his car, he raced toward it with renewed energy. Several yards from it, he started to splash through a wide puddle of water. With no time to avoid it, he continued on through, not noticing the oily film that floated on top. The water on top and the oil patch below combined to become slick as ice on a frozen lake in winter. One moment his left foot stepped on one of the hidden oil spots, the next his foot was uncontrollably skidding out from under him.

He experienced the awful feeling of losing his balance as his foot skidded out sideways as if it had a mind of its own. In a desperate attempt, he leaned back slightly to regain some semblance of balance and thrust his semi-hard clothing case down into the puddle. The hell with getting his clothes wet, he thought. So what! Better they get soaked than to get caught, he rationalized. He knew they could always be cleaned, but he had no one to bail him out of jail if they got him.

In a split second the case hit the puddle with a big splash, but found solid ground. In the next instant Clay felt himself regain his balance. Staggering up, he sprinted the short distance to his car with the shouts of his pursuers getting too close for comfort.

Dropping his case by the car, he grabbed his keys out of his pants pocket, thankful he hadn't lost them in his drunken stupor. Hitting the alarm button, he heard it reassuringly chirp off. Yanking the driver's door open, he grabbed his case and heaved it onto the passengers side and dove into the driver's seat. The angry, excited shouts were almost on top of him now, like predators closing in for the final kill.

Thrusting the key into the ignition, he turned it, feeling great relief as his faithful old Mustang kicked over immediately. Seconds later, out of the corner of his eye, he saw that one of them was suddenly at the side of the car, reaching for him. It looked like the maintenance man in coveralls. Reaching in through the door, he roughly attempted to grab Clay's shoulder. At the same moment, in one fluid motion, Clay threw the control lever into drive and hit the gas. There was no one in front of him and the car lurched forward immediately into the aisle. The door was still partially open, as the man, in an attempt to stay with him, grabbed the edge of the door and hung on, still trying to get at Clay, as the car gained speed and pulled out of the parking slot. In his rear view window Clay saw him eventually give up.

Slowing down, Clay made a left turn going around the last of the parked cars and headed back toward the exit and the street beyond. Turning left, around the end of the aisle, the pull of gravity, and the angle of the turn, caused his door to slowly swing closed. Reaching out, he grabbed it and slammed it shut.

Giving it the gas, he hurriedly aimed the Mustang for the nearest exit. Movement to his left caught his eye. Coming out of a side door of the hotel, heading into the parking lot, he was shocked to see the gorilla in the Hawaiian shirt, headed in his direction. *Jesus! Doesn't that guy ever give up? I really didn't intentionally mean to drop that lamp on them!* Seeing the contorted, angry face, it was clear the giant slab of beef had serious intentions of pounding him into dust. He worriedly observed that the guy was practically leaping his way between the parked cars, determined to cut him off. Sizing up the angle, Clay knew it was going to be close. Apparently the big, ugly, beefcake must have figured he'd head for the parking lot. Clay figured that as soon as the monster came out of the door, heard the shouting and saw the running figures, he knew immediately his quarry was in the car trying to get out of the hotel lot.

Getting close to the exit, Clay kept a wary eye on the beefcake, headed for his aisle. It was going to be tight, and he didn't know how he'd react if the guy tried to block him. The big guy put on a burst of speed, as if he were running to catch a touchdown pass. Seconds later, he jumped into the middle of the aisle facing Clay, wildly waving his arms up and down, thinking that would actually stop him. He came across, determined not to move from the center of the aisle, no matter what. There was no way around him, nor did he have the time to turn around and try another exit.

It was now or never! *What to do? What to do?* Clay repeated mentally. *No way, you nasty pile of shit! You're not going to stop me this close to getting the hell outta this God-forsaken hole!* Ramming his foot down hard on the gas pedal, the car leaped forward heading right at his blocker.

Putting on a brave front, the beefcake kept waving his arms up and down, refusing to budge an inch. Just as determined, Clay bore down on him, hoping beyond hope the fool would chicken out and get out of the way. In any case he was in too deep now, and had no intention of stopping.

In seconds, the view of the man filled his windshield - his car was virtually on top of him when Clay turned the wheel sharply to the right, in the end, not wanting to hurt the stupid fool. He came a hairs breath away from slamming against the cars parked to his right. Clay's Mustang just barely missed the burly linebacker as the guy leaped aside, a terrified look on his face, hopefully scaring the living shit out of the big guy, creating a few new gray hairs on his head and probably wetting his pants in the process, Clay thought.

Clay blew out of the lot like the devil himself was on his tail, making a screeching left turn, his tires loudly protesting the abuse, and left the hotel behind in his rearview mirror. He was lucky, there was no traffic on the surface street at that hour.

Driving as fast as he could, without speeding excessively, he wanted to put as much distance between him and the hotel. The streets were well lit from the streetlights and he hoped the city police were all parked in donut shops, and not in the vicinity at this hour.

A few blocks further up the street, he encountered a vehicle moving very fast in his direction. Well lit as the streets were, as the car approached him, Clay's heart fluttered and then started thumping in trepidation. It was a city police cruiser. No lights were flashing, but it couldn't be a coincidence the way the patrol car was flying down the street in his direction. Clay held his breath and looked straight ahead, his heart wildly pumping, as the two cars approached from opposite directions. He figured that he'd hear the screeching of brakes in a moment or two. *My God!* He thought, *Won't I ever get this miserable episode behind me!*

****

Chapter 8

Like a zombie, with both hands on the steering wheel, Clay stared straight ahead, doing his very best to act nonchalant, ignoring the rapidly approaching squad car. He let up on the gas, and let the speed of his car glide down to the city speed limit without hitting the brakes moments before the other vehicle was upon him. Clay held his breath and prayed, his hands starting to tremble at the thought of this new threat.

That's all he needed, he thought, to be thrown in jail for the whole world, including his wife and Campbell to find out about it. How totally embarrassing, because of his one stupid, unconscious act, he thought. He felt like wishing the whole disastrous series of events out of his life immediately. But he knew in reality it wouldn't happen.

The other car was just passing when Clay risked a peek out of the corner of his eye. As they flashed by him, it was clear the two officers were totally intent on getting somewhere fast. Probably the hotel, he guessed. They were staring straight ahead and essentially didn't even see him. One second they were next to him, the next they were past and up the street.

He was temporarily relieved, but it still wasn't over as he thought about it. If indeed the hotel had called the cops, and he had to assume they had, the security guy would tell them in what direction he was headed, and the police would immediately give chase. He was still in deep trouble and didn't at this point know what he was going to do. He began to feel his options were limited.

Heading in the direction of the interstate freeway, Clay reflected back over the whole chain of events. He now wondered if possibly his former employer had finally realized, in retrospect at this late hour, that he still had the company credit cards, and even though Clay had been able to use them, had called the hotel and somehow tried to make trouble for him, adding to his problems. Clay couldn't be sure, but he wouldn't be surprised if this might have happened, although that's about all Campbell could do about the cards. As far as the hotel was concerned he didn't feel bad, as he knew that when the cards were run they were approved, and the hotel would collect their money. The card had been valid when he put his room and the other things on it, so Campbell Enterprises would be forced to pay for the charges. That thought made him feel a tiny bit better, but not much. *Stick it up your nose, you bunch of bastards!* He thought for the umpteenth time. Anyhow – he was aware hotels were insured for possible damages by guests – that's why the hotel charges were so high!

Concentrating on his driving, he noticed that the rainstorm, which apparently had passed over the area, had been brief and light, but the outside air seemed noticeably chillier and the scudding clouds above, partially blocked out the moon. This seemed to be a harbinger of something else he hoped to avoid. He prayed it wasn't snow flurries. They were the last thing he needed at this point.

Nearing the city limits, he spotted the large green and white sign giving directions for the Interstate in north and south directions. Taking a left turn, he headed for the southbound. His immediate intentions were to get away from this place of bad memories as soon as possible. He figured if he drove straight through he'd be back home in a few hours.

He kept telling himself he shouldn't worry about it, but he thought there was always that rare chance that the police might possibly be coming up behind him, or radioing ahead to the Highway Patrol. Clay didn't think the ruckus he had caused at the hotel would warrant the intervention of the police, but he just never knew for sure and couldn't take any chance. Approaching the entrance to the southbound Interstate, he noticed a sign for the old alternate route. Having traveled it on weekend outings, he knew it to be a twisting and winding, sometimes hair-raising route. It was especially dangerous at night. He recalled that it was the old, original highway that wound through the mountains before they'd built the faster and more convenient, straight north-south interstate. He had rarely used the old road over the years. It was the scenic route, with lots of sharp switchbacks, heavily forested and not very heavily traveled now as most people used the newer, faster Interstate highway.

Clay had always taken the main highway in the past, but this time he chose the old road which did not have a lot of sharp curves in the beginning until it started to descend to the lower elevations in the mountains. Then the sharp turns and switchbacks began. He tried to think what the police would do, if they did anything. He guessed they'd figure he was headed for the interstate.

He was not concerned, as he'd been this way before, but not in the recent past. He needed the time to think through the problems now facing him, regarding his future life. Alone with his thoughts, on this quiet, little traveled road, he knew he could do his best brainstorming and problem solving behind the wheel of his car. It was the solitude, with few if any interruptions, plus cell phones didn't work in these mountains. In any case he'd turned it off, having no desire to speak with anyone right now. He assumed anyone calling might be trouble.

He also figured this was a better route to follow, as the state troopers patrolling the interstate might view him with suspicion at this time of the night and pull him over on some phony infraction.

Entering the old route, he found himself passing through a rolling foothill area. The road, relatively straight with few curves, gradually started a gentle increase up to the summit on this, the northern side of the mountains. There were no streetlights and the wet road ahead, in his headlights, looked like a sheet of black glass. He drove a little faster than he should have, ignoring the fact that it had recently rained. He considered himself to be a better than average driver and remembered that this end of the old highway had very forgiving curves and fairly long stretches of straight road. He still carried that fatalistic notion in his mind that if he died, so what, no one was going to miss him anyway. Now in the dark and quiet, his mind began to think, plan and review.

Clay had been driving for close to an hour when the stresses of the previous day and everything else caught up with him. Feeling exhausted, he just wanted to pull over and go to sleep. The next moment, his eyes involuntarily dropped shut. He blinked them open in surprise a second later, wide-awake for the moment.

"You're gonna manage to get yourself killed if you keep this up," he said out loud to keep himself alert and awake. "And maybe that's what you're trying to do."

He tried to move around, slap his face and talk to himself, but nothing helped. He'd be driving, staring at the road ahead when his eyes would unintentionally slip shut. He always blinked them open a moment later and remained wide awake for a short time, but then in a little while the whole cycle started all over again. Clay didn't know what to do. He tried turning on the radio, but the only thing he could pick up was an all night talk radio show that had a lot of static and kept drifting in and out. He finally gave up and shut it off because the noise from the static started to get to him.

There were no towns along this road and he didn't want to turn around and go back to the city, so he kept going. Finally, he got desperate and against his better judgment, pulled to the side of the road. Shutting off the engine, he leaned over on the front seat and closed his eyes. He drifted off to sleep and it worked for a short while when suddenly he came wide awake again and sat up. His subconscious sent him the message that if he did fall into a deep sleep and the wrong people driving down this lonely stretch of road saw his car and stopped, he might get robbed or worse. That was enough to bring him wide-awake again.

Sitting up straight, he started up the car, rolled down the window, and began on his way again, still very fatigued. He inhaled a large lung full of the night mountain air. The breeze along with the fragrant smell of the pine trees briefly invigorated him. Clay noticed that it was considerably chillier than he'd experienced at the hotel. After driving for a distance, the cold night gusts blowing into the car got to be too much, so he closed the window. He was not overly concerned as he felt wide-awake once again.

Clay, in retrospect, now understood he'd made an emotional miscalculation. He realized it had been very stupid to drink so much. He rebuked himself, thinking that if he'd been more clearheaded he would have left the hotel and found a smaller businessman's motel on the other side of town. After a good night's sleep, he could have left in the morning.

Stupid, stupid, stupid! He rebuked himself. He knew he had reacted irrationally because his whole life had come crashing down around his ears and those horrid lifelike nightmares just kept returning.

The deeper he drove into the mountains, the more heavily forested it became. The trees were closely spaced, coming right down to the edge of the road, giving him a closed in feeling. As the elevation slowly increased, the curves and turns in the road became noticeably sharper. He recalled that the foothills he had just passed through were the gentle, sloping side of the mountains. Once he reached the summit and began his descent down the southern side, he knew that it dropped down to the lower elevation a lot faster then his ascent up this side. He also knew that the other side of the mountains had much sharper curves and switchbacks for him to contend with.

As he slowly worked his way up the mountain, Clay became lost in his thoughts and went through the motions of driving automatically. Among other things, his mind mulled over the fact that he had given so much of his time and self to his job so that he could provide a better life for his family and now he'd lost both in the blink of an eye, it appeared. Was there a reason, he wondered, why all this had happened? He knew deep down in the darkest part of his heart there was that unfinished business in his past life that continued to haunt him. If only there was some way to resolve it, he thought hopelessly.

Nearing the summit, as his headlights pierced the blackness of night on the road ahead, he noticed something and thought for a moment that his eyes were deceiving him. At first he didn't recognize it for what it was. It looked like fluffy, tiny bits of cotton were hitting his windshield. Suddenly, with dread, he recognized what those minuscule white bits were, sweeping past the beams of his headlights. Snow! After the rain it had apparently turned cold enough at this altitude for snow flurries. He again rolled down his side window, letting in the chilly night air. Momentarily, sticking his hand out of the window, he felt the sensation of the snow touching it and melting.

The air that flowed into the car was brisk, but it invigorated him again, as he went over the summit and began the laborious descent down the other side of the mountain. Now he slowed down as he began the twisting and turning trip to the lower elevation. In the daytime it was an area of magnificent beauty, but in the blackness of this night it was forbidding, with hidden dangers lurking around each tight curve, with numerous switchbacks of the narrow road. Heading downward, the mountains were to his left and came right down to the roadbed. To his right, out the passenger side, he glimpsed the bone-chilling, steep drop-off almost perpendicular down the mountainside.

Clay took his time, working hard to control his speed in the hairpin turns. Any mistake could cause him to skid onto the slippery shoulder of the road and go over the side, especially with a light coating of snow on the ground. In the past, he had stopped in the daytime and looked down the slope into one of the steep gullies that always awaited the unwary traveler. On several occasions he had seen vehicles lying at the bottom. If he went over the side, it was at least a one hundred foot drop and a guaranteed trip to oblivion.

Close to another hour of careful driving passed and he was beginning to come out of the upper part of the mountains. It was less heavily forested and the slopes became more open with smaller pine trees. He noticed the curves were not quite as tight and the sharp switchbacks were now behind him, he hoped and prayed. He began to feel like he was home free the worse was behind him.

It was still forested in pine trees as he began the descent into the foothills, but not as dense as up on the higher slopes of the mountain. In his headlights he could see clear stretches of road ahead of him, moving further into the lower foothills.

Clay also started to run into small wisps of fog, coupled with the continuous snow. He figured there must be a small river or stream nearby that was contributing to the fog, or perhaps the cold rain hitting the warmer ground at the lower levels had brought it on. He didn't know or care where it came from, just that he became more careful, because when he was in it, his headlights would only pierce a few dozen yards into the descending white blanket. It was enough to bring him wide-awake and fully alert. The road improved, just a tiny bit wider now, even though it remained just two lanes, but there were still several miles before the end of the foothills.

Clay began moving to the left around a wide blind curve, slightly faster than he should have been. His view was momentarily blocked by a sharp upward slope to his left that came right down to the shoulder of the road. His mind, occupied with other thoughts, he didn't ease off enough on his accelerator as he went around the curve. It didn't appear to be a sharp curve, but the image that filled his windshield on the other side caused him to gulf in shock.

Out of nowhere, it seemed, a heavy patch of fog totally obliterated the road ahead. Headlight beams only penetrated less than a yard or two ahead of him. He stuck his head out of his side window, trying to get a better view and saw, reflected in his headlights that the pavement in front of his car looked like a flat, shiny sheet of black obsidian glass. Ice? It had to be! "Damn!" he exclaimed in anger and panic, "I'm in deep ass trouble now!"

He was moving far too fast for the curve and the situation he realized too late. In a typical reaction, he applied too much pressure on his brakes and failed to realize the temperature had dropped low enough in the frigid mountain air and a thin crust of black ice had formed on top of the smooth pavement. An eye blink later, he was in the middle of it.

Moving into the turn and hitting his brakes at the same time caused his wheels to lose traction and slowly he slipped across the icy surface. He turned his wheel sharply into the direction of the skid, but inadvertently overcompensated, causing the car to go into an uncontrolled spin.

He frantically turned the steering wheel this way and that, trying to bring his car under control. It seemed like it was happening in a slowly moving dream and for a brief, frightening second it appeared as if he was on an amusement park carousel, revolving around in a circle at a slower than normal speed. But the effect was heart numbing and totally frightening.

In a momentary flashback he recalled the time years ago, when he was in college and returning to school from the Christmas holiday with some friends. It was late at night and he was driving west on the Indiana Turnpike. There was a fire truck a few hundred yards ahead of him. Suddenly he saw the truck go into a wild, uncontrolled spin down the highway and run into a bridge abutment. Why did he have to think of things like this now, he thought with trepidation.

The wild spin increased, as he desperately and vainly tried to compensate for this out of control situation. In his present predicament he felt encapsulated in an entirely different world; one mistake here and he was dead, he knew.

As the car gyrated through the spin, the wheels hit a rough spot in the road that did not have the sheen of hard ice covering it. It enabled him to gain control of his vehicle and get it going straight again, but his forward motion was still too fast.

Moments later, he burst out of the fog bank, into the clear, dark night air. His view through his windshield almost caused his heart to leap into his throat. Coming out of the fog, instead of following the direction of the roadway, he realized in horror that he had come out of the spin headed straight for the outer rim of the curve and the vehicle killing mountain slope.

In a gut reaction he slammed down hard on his brake pedal and then realized what a big mistake he had made as his front wheels hit the loose soil and gravel of the shoulder, and his brakes locked up. Instead of slowing down, the car couldn't help but go into a forward slide, picking up speed as it headed for the edge. It was like being on a child's sliding board, once you started down the slippery metal, there wasn't any way of stopping. The shoulder acted like slick grease as the car unerringly slid toward the edge of the road.

Frightened out of his wits, he suddenly took notice that the state highway department had not seen the need to install guardrails around the curves at this slightly lower elevation where the turns and switchbacks were not as extreme. Without the corrugated metal guardrail to stop his forward motion, he knew he was headed for the edge of the precipice.

Clay felt the hair-raising sensation as the car's front end left solid ground and went airborne as the out of control vehicle skidded, beyond control over the edge. He automatically clamped his eyes tightly shut, figuring the next thing he would see was that bright tunnel of light that told him he was dead. Keeping his eyes closed, he waited for the car to clear the edge and begin the precipitous drop down the incline. It flashed into his mind like a giant billboard that this would be his drop into final oblivion. He didn't have time to think, or be any more terrified. Everything happened so fast. He grimly hung on, accepting his fate. His last thought as he felt his beloved Mustang skid over the edge - he had spent all this time restoring his classic beauty of a car, only to have it totally wiped out in one reckless moment.

Clay expected a few moments of silence as his car passed beyond the edge, then started down what had to be a sharp incline. Then he expected the blackness to suddenly envelope him when he hit the bottom of the canyon. That, he knew would occur when he passed from this life to the next.

Instead, the front end of the car slammed down on hard crusty earth with a loud metallic clang, which shook the front end like a terrier shaking a dead rat. The shock of hitting solid ground caused him to snap open his eyes in total surprise. It rudely shook him and almost threw him out of his seat when the front wheels slammed down on solid earth. He began to hear a painful, metallic screeching coming from the underside of his car as it started to roll downhill, passing over small boulders and outcroppings. In hindsight as he headed downward, he knew this was the one time he should have done something he always hated to do, fasten his seatbelts. He'd been in such a panic to get away from the hotel that he'd let it go.

A split second later, in the headlights of his car, he saw to his utter amazement that he was instead on a fairly gentle downward slope. The ground all around him had been partially cleared sometime in the past, for whatever reason - perhaps to park and store road building equipment.

He didn't know or even care; all he felt was a total relief wash over him like a warm shower, celebrating that he was actually still alive, and in one piece. Still the car remained beyond his control.

The Mustang began to pick up considerable speed, barreling down the hill like a giant, snowball, leveling everything in its path. He continued to hear loud metallic screeches coming from the underside of the car as it passed over protruding rocks and high points in the ground. A few thin, new-growth, saplings appeared in front of him, but the car just mowed them down like wheat. In a panic, his foot pounded the brake pedal, but it went all the way to the floorboard and did nothing. Apparently some of the rocks he had passed over had damaged part of his brake lines and now he had no brakes, nor any way of stopping. He felt utterly helpless.

Blind terror overwhelmed him as he grabbed the steering wheel in a death grip, attempting to gain any kind of control of the car, but to no avail. It picked up speed like a roller coaster at the top of the downward slope, going faster and faster until he felt like his heart now throbbed in his mouth.

In an act of desperation he tried to turn the wheel of the car to the left, and to steer it off to the side, hoping to bring it out of its downward roll and stop the vehicle. But every time he did that, the front wheels of the car started to go into a skid, and the side of the vehicle tilted dangerously down the steep slope. He sensed if he even tried to turn too sharply he'd roll the car, so he just let the car continue on its own, as he tried in desperation to bring it to a stop.

Ahead in his headlights, he could see what appeared to be the bottom of the hillside. Reacting, he sucked in his breath because of his view out his windshield, which closed the distance, at breakneck speed. He noticed that the trees on the upper slope near the bottom were not the new growth, thin saplings he'd been passing over. Two larger trees, thick enough to cave in the front end of the Mustang, loomed close apart in his path, like malicious twins. He knew if he hit either one, the vehicle would come to an instant stop, caving in the whole front end of the car and badly injuring him. There looked to be the tiniest bit of space to pass between them. In an attempt to avoid ending his downward journey on the trunk of a tree, he muscled and honked the steering wheel to the right, his power steering long gone.

He missed hitting the trees, but as his car passed between them, to his complete surprise, he saw something that had been obscured by the growths and other concealing overgrowth, lower on the slope.

Like a horrid monster leaping out of nowhere, a huge, black, rock protrusion, about waist high, loomed in his windshield. He couldn't avoid it, at his accelerated speed. A second later his car slammed loudly into the pile of rock and dirt with an ear-splitting, metallic reverberating crash, and echoed throughout the forest. Steam immediately burst from the blown radiator while the headlights remained strangely on.

The force of his vehicle hitting the obstruction propelled Clay forward. His head slammed against the steering wheel hard, there was a split second of intense pain and then everything went to blackness and oblivion for him.

Chapter 9

Clay felt his body floating and drifting in a kaleidoscope dream world. Everything that had happened in his past life flashed around him with the speed of light. This dreamlike state caused him to experience a strange sensation, a kind of ethereal feeling throughout his body. His mind flooded his senses with a chilling message, telling him he was on the verge of crossing over to the other side. *The other side? Am I dead?* His mind flashed the terrible question.

In the blink of an eye, he found himself floating scant inches above a white field of snow, but looking down he could see it wasn't snow. *What is this?* He thought. *Where am I?* The brilliant, eye-watering white made him want to involuntarily blink his eyes. It seemed to emanate from way faraway. Moments later he thought he saw a figure far in the distance, at a spot where the radiant whiteness formed into a huge cone-like substance. The figure seemed to be moving toward him. Beginning recognition bloomed in his brain cells as the person approached closer.

A man waved at him. Then all of a sudden Clay realized that he recognized him. His father! He had died several months before of colon cancer. As his father came steadily closer, Clay felt dismayed because his dad had a frown on his face. Instead of waving to him, he now understood – the man tried to wave him *away*. Then his father appeared right next to him. He didn't walk, just glided toward Clay. *Very strange*, Clay thought as he watched unhappiness spread all over the old man's face. Clay wondered what he had done wrong to anger his father. He loved him very much and mourned his loss deeply.

Facing Clay, his father began to push him harshly backward as if to send him back, speaking to him at the same time. No sound came out of his mouth. He mouthed the words, *Go back! Go back!*! Clay felt himself pushed harder and harder. His right hand kept pushing on Clay's left shoulder, then unaccountably, a bright white light flashed in front of his face. Clay didn't know where it came from and he thought he heard a muffled voice, as if his ears were plugged with cotton.

It now began to grow darker and his father turned to walk away. Stopping once, he turned back around and waved to Clay, a smile crossed his face and clearly said, *"Go back, it's not your time yet!"* But the sensation of pushing and shaking continued and other words penetrated his foggy mind, from what appeared a great distance away, they were strangely clear and distinct to him.

"Hey, buddy, are you okay? C'mon, wake up! You gotta come out of it. Wake up!

C'mon, you've got to come out of it or you'll die!"

Clay's head hurt like hell. He let out an involuntary groan as he rolled his head to the side. His mouth felt like someone had stuffed a big wad of cotton in it and on opening his eyes a little, they hurt and everything turned fuzzy around him. As his vision slowly began to clear, he realized that he his head rested against the steering wheel. The last thing he remembered, he had flown forward, and the steering wheel came up at him before he blacked out.

Looking over toward the driver's side window, he saw the shadowy head and shoulders of a man leaning in the window. One hand held Clay's left shoulder and the other around his back and right shoulder. He attempted to lift him away from the steering wheel column.

"Still feeling groggy?" Clay heard him say. "That's it! Good! Now, c'mon, help me to lean you back in your seat, so I can check you out for injuries."

Clay managed to lean back against the car's headrest, rolling his head to the side, his eyes on the mysterious stranger. When the man stood back a little, Clay observed him to be in a white uniform with no identification patches, somewhat like a hospital or ambulance attendant. Because of the man's attire Clay briefly considered the idea that he might be dead, but quickly discounted the idea because of the reality of the situation and how banged up he felt. He knew he wouldn't feel anything if he was in reality, dead.

When Clay spoke, his voice came out in a dry croak, "Who are you? What are you?"

The man smiled and said, "Just somebody who happened by at the right time. Let's just say, someone you desperately needed."

"I'll say!" Clay again noticed that he wore white, and his clothes looked more like a finely tailored suit, than an ambulance attendant's or hospital garb. The stranger looked clean-shaven, had salt and pepper hair in a very close cropped, military style haircut. The strong, weathered, leather-like features of his face also caught Clay's attention. It didn't really appear to be the face of an everyday ambulance attendant.

"Am I dead? Am I in some kind of limbo?"

"No, Clay, you're still very much alive. Just a little banged up."

"How did you know my name?"

The stranger smiled, but didn't answer. Reaching into the car, he plucked a black wallet off the dashboard and opened it, showing Clay's driver's license. Clay hadn't noticed it sitting there when he returned to consciousness.

"This apparently came out of your coat pocket when you had that argument with those rocks." Showing it to Clay, he then set it back on the dashboard and said, "It was next to you on the seat."

Somewhat satisfied by the answer, Clay said, "Oh, okay. Who are you anyway? What is your name?"

"Hang on a minute while I get some stuff from my vehicle. Then I'll answer your questions."

Turning, the man walked back toward his vehicle. Clay took a closer look and now could see it clearly. Some kind of 4 wheel drive SUV by the position of the headlights, plus a pair of off-road lights mounted on the roof that helped illuminate the area which seemed unusual for an ambulance. *"Nothing like being prepared,"* Clay thought, impressed.

Inclining his head to watch, Clay noticed the man stood fairly tall, and while he didn't appear to have a muscular build, he looked to be in superlative physical condition. Clay watched as the man opened the passenger side door and pulled some things out of the vehicle. Clay pushed and attempted to get his door open, but it seemed to be solidly jammed shut.

A minute later the man returned, setting a few things on the ground nearby. "Here, let me open that door for you, then I want to clean up that scratch on your forehead."

"It won't open. I think it's jammed shut."

"Oh? Here, let me give it a try." Reaching down, the man lifted the door handle and pulled out on the car door. The door wouldn't budge. He stopped for a few seconds, looked up at the sky for a moment, as if he was summoning up some hidden strength, then down at the door again and gave it another pull. With ease the door swung open, with a metallic groan, much to Clay's surprise.

"Hey! How'd you do that? I know that door was sprung and jammed tight."

The man flashed the same smile again and said, "Guess I'm just lucky! Plus the first time I tried may have loosened up the jam."

Clay looked doubtful, but remained silent.

"Besides, I've got better leverage on this side than you on the inside."

"You seem to be in awfully good shape for an ambulance attendant who sits around watching TV, eating donuts and waiting for calls."

The man gave a short laugh without confirming or denying his job description, "I try to stay in shape. Now c'mon, grab my hand and swing your legs out. I'll help you to stand up. You need to get your head together."

Taking hold of the man's hand and forearm, Clay carefully brought his legs out of the vehicle and slowly stood up. He felt very wobbly.

"Let me help you over here to the fender. You can sit on it while I clean out your cut."

The front tire of the car had blown and Clay easily sat down on the fender. The stranger set down what looked like a military type first aid kit. As he cleaned out the superficial scratch on Clay's forehead, Clay asked, "So what do I call you? What's your name?"

"You can call me Gabe."

"Gabe?"

"Yeah."

"Gabe, as in the angel Gabriel?"

Again, the short laugh, "Yes, that's really my name, but the rest doesn't apply to me. And by the way, before you say it again, no, you're not dead! As I said before, you're very much alive."

Gabe efficiently finished cleaning out the cut, and applied a gauze bandage. As Gabe put the first aid kit back together, Clay looked up at the sky. A full moon had broken out from behind the clouds, and now illuminated the area in a brilliant white glow.

"I'm going to turn off your headlights for right now. We will need all the battery juice we can muster to start it up again," Gabe said.

"Start up my car? I seriously doubt that. Have you taken a close look at the damage? Besides the tires, no brakes and the radiator is blown."

"Yes, I understand that. In any case I've got a cable and winch on the front end, so I should be able to pull you out of here. At least get the car up to the road where it can be picked up later. Trust me!"

"How about calling a tow truck or something?"

"Not a chance, my friend. I've already tried."

"Oh?"

"Yeah, I tried my CB but got mostly static. Heard a couple of truckers talking, but their signal was bounced off the ionosphere. They were way out West somewhere on Interstate 40 near Flagstaff, Arizona. There was no chance they could hear my signal"

"Okay. Do you have a cell phone?"

"Yeah, I tried that and again nothing. I seriously doubt if they bothered to install transmission towers for this little used, back road.

Majority of people use the Interstate. We're apparently in a dead zone in these mountains."

"Shit!" Clay said. "Might as well be dead!"

"Don't ever talk like that again!" Gabe said, a hint of anger in his voice.

Gabe reached down to the ground and picked up a canteen, "Here, take a good drink of this." Gabe handed the canteen to Clay.

Clay noticed it to be a military type, the same kind he had carried in the Philippines with the Counterinsurgency Training Command. He undid the cap and took a short sip, stopped for a moment, then slowly took a long drink. The water tasted cool and refreshingly like spring water. Like nothing he had tasted before.

Remembering back, Clay recalled that the tepid water he carried in his canteen, back in that fetid jungle, never tasted like this. He was about to comment, when Gabe said, "Look Clay, you need to move around a little to get yourself feeling better. Let me help you up and let's take a short walk. Get circulation going again."

He didn't argue as Gabe helped him.

"Just a minute," Gabe said and sprinted back to his vehicle to turn off its lights. When he returned he said, "Wouldn't do to drain my battery. Then we'd both be shit outta luck!"

"Yeah, guess you've got something there."

"Besides, with that bright, harvest moon it's almost like daylight out here!"

Looking up at the moon, Clay said, "Yeah, guess you're right about that."

"Why don't we take a walk along that dried streambed, down there," Gabe suggested, "It's a lot flatter and easier to walk than this slope."

Gabe took Clay's arm and helped him down the slope a short distance to where it joined the streambed. Once they were down in the flat, sandy area they began following the dried-up watercourse. There were few obstructions and they moved along side by side with ease, in silence.

Clay glanced at his savior for a moment, saying the question on his mind. "Why are you here?"

Gabe took a few moments to digest that statement and frame an answer. Then he said, "I don't know the answer Clay. Maybe because I needed to be here to help you."

"That doesn't tell me anything."

"I know. I think it would be best to just drop the subject for now. Agreed?"

"Okay. But I just find it hard to believe that you just happened along. Very few if any take that road, especially at night. Almost everyone takes the interstate highway. It's quicker and safer."

Clay suddenly stopped, grabbed Gabe by the arm and said, "I've got it!"

"Got what?"

"I know what he said now!"

"Who? Said what?"

"My father."

"What about your father? When?"

"I don't fully understand what happened, but I may have had a near death experience. I've read about it and I believe this is what may have happened."

"Why do you say that?"

"Because my father died six months ago, and before you revived me, he came to me and said something I didn't understand until just now."

"Yeah, well, I've heard of this sort of thing happening."

"The way things have been lately, I was ready to go with him!" Clay said.

"Go where?"

"Die! Leave this lousy life behind for good! But he didn't want me to go."

"Surely it can't be that bad!"

"You don't have a clue! I almost went, back at the hotel, but something stopped me." Sitting down on a large rock, Clay leaned his elbows on his knees, deep in thought.

Gabe said, "Look, is there anything I can do to help?"

He thought for a moment, then looked up at Gabe, laughed cynically and said, "Sure, you can give me a new life! Let me live my life over!"

"Wow! That sounds pretty grim. Things can't be that bad, can they?"

"They can and they are! I screwed up a long time ago, and my life has never been quite the same since. Everything has turned to dust and ruin, no matter how hard I've worked. My wife, children, job, everything, gone!"

"You still have your life, surely there must be a way out of this?"

"If there is, I'd sure like to know about it."

"Well, a good place to start is at the beginning. What say we start walking again, as you explain to me."

"I'll try, but I just don't know if I can. Are you sure you really want to hear everything?"

Gabe said, "The answer is yes. But first, you said you knew what your father said to you."

"Right. He said…Go back! It's not your time yet!" And he waved and pushed me back the way I had come."

Gabe thought about that for a minute, then said, "I think he really did come to you. There had to be a very good reason."

"Why?"

"Maybe there are some things that you still have to do yet, that you don't know about at this point. Unfinished business."

"I know of one thing I'd sure like to set right!"

"Why don't you tell me about it."

"I just don't know if I can."

"Try me," Gabe replied.

Clay had no idea why he was even opening up to this man, but for some reason he felt comforted by this unusual savior, who had helped him and probably saved his life. He realized now that this man had brought him back from the brink of death, but for what reason?

As the words began to flow, bitter tears coursed down his cheeks. "I screwed up very badly, a long time ago. It's haunted me all these years. Probably contributed a good deal to ruining my marriage."

"Uh huh. Well, don't be too hard on yourself. Remember, it takes two to make it work!"

"Well anyway, I let a lot of people down, big time! My very best friends in this world! Now they're all dead! Because of me! Stupid, stupid me!" He coughed, the tears started to flow freely down his dust-covered face.

"How can you be so sure?"

"I'm sure!"

"Why?"

"Because they never came back! They were never heard from again! Not even after we were pulled out of the Philippines. They just disappeared!"

"Go on."

"I'm not sure that I can. It has torn me apart for all these years."

"Look, see this streambed in front of us?"

"Yeah."

"Think of it as sort of the highway of your life in front of you and you are once again traveling back along it from the beginning. Start where you want and take your time. Take all the time you want. Time is something we have a lot of."

"What are you, some kind of roadside psychologist or something?"

"Thanks for the compliment, but no. Just someone who has seen a lot, done a lot and lived a lot, nothing more."

They started walking along the wide, sandy, dried-up streambed while Clay began to slowly unburden himself of the guilt he had carried on his shoulders like a backpack full of bricks for so many years. As the pair walked along the streambed, Clay backtracked the events in his life, starting with his recent close encounter with eternity on the hotel balcony.

"So you see, deep down in your subconscious, you really did not want to die. What happened proved it," Gabe said.

"Yeah, I guess you could say that," Clay admitted.

"But you were damn lucky, you know that now, don't you?"

Reluctantly, in a subdued voice, Clay replied, "Yes, you are correct. It was very close."

"As far as your job is concerned, you were obviously blindsided. You didn't and couldn't have seen it coming. It is not your fault. There's nothing much you can really do about it and keep in mind, you weren't the only one! Sounds like they pulled the same thing on your friend Sanders first."

"That's true," Clay said.

"Sounds like the age old game of office politics with a heavy dose of nepotism thrown in. Nothing you really could have done about it, but..." Gabe left the last word hanging.

"But what?"

"You should have had your ear closer to the ground! You know, the old rumor mill! Maybe cultivated enough friends and contacts at the home office so you could get reliable information from the employee grapevine. When you showed up, you didn't know it, but you were already kaput, finished. They had already done the knife job on you, and cowed the others into towing the line, or else. Scared people will do a lot to save their asses, and loyalties go right out the window!"

"True, but..."

"A little lesson, a little late in time, but if you had, you could have beaten them to the punch!"

"How?"

"Told them to stick it! Go piss up a rope! If you'd really thought about it you, could have easily gone to work for one of the competitors and gotten your due that way, or even started your own company. From what you told me, a lot of the other employees would have followed you. Something for you to think over for the future."

"That thought never crossed my mind."

"That's unfortunate, because most people never realize that they are expendable."

"So?"

"Give it some serious thought. Look at all the hard, practical experience you gained over the years. Try to understand just how valuable you are because of your hard earned knowledge. You're a dangerous man to them and they don't even have a clue yet! All they can think of right now is to gloat over how cleverly they stabbed you in the back. Given time, they will realize their mistake, but if you're smart, you'll have a head start on them and they will end up paying dearly for *their* mistake."

"Never even thought of it that way before."

The streambed had started to narrow until it ended in a jumble of large boulders. When they reached the boulders, they noticed that the streambed took a sharp drop downward and there remained no way to continue in that direction.

"No use going any further. Guess we need to backtrack," Clay said.

"Not necessarily," Gabe said, pointing to the side of the bank on the same side as their vehicles. "Looks like what could be a trail over here that crossed the stream here. See those large, flat, evenly spaced rocks in the streambed?"

"Sure."

"Well, somebody took the trouble to probably position them down here when the stream was active, to cross over it."

"Not bad, Sherlock!"

"Let's see if the trail continues on the other side of that growth of bushes over there," he said, pointing toward the far side, which contained an overgrowth of heavy brush.

They both pulled themselves up the steep bank. Using the bushes to haul themselves up the bank, they reached level ground. At the top, they saw a wide trail through a growth of young pine trees. The moonlight illuminated the area brightly around where they stood. It had been cleared of any vegetation a long time ago, perhaps for pitching tents and a shallow pit with small rocks around it with the remains of an old campfire.

"Let's see where this trail goes, just for the hell of it, okay?"

"Sure, why not," Clay said.

As they started off, Clay noted that the trail wound through a very sparse growth of young pine trees. But as they moved further along the pathway, he noted the underbrush and growth of trees started to become heavier with the pathway disappearing around a long bend. However, the trail remained wide for the time being and well lit by the moon and he did not become overly concerned.

Walking side by side, he pair picked up their discussion where it had been left off. Moving through the forest, it seemed like hours as Clay hesitantly related the recent upsetting events, in both his job and marriage. He remained surprised that Gabe listened with such a sympathetic ear to what he had to say. He couldn't figure it. *Was this some sort of test?* He wondered.

Time had passed, so it seemed and as he started to relate what had occurred while he was attached to the Counterinsurgency Training Command all those years ago, he happened to glance at his surroundings. He noticed with surprise that the forest appeared to be getting denser, and for a moment he could have sworn that it felt definitely warmer, and much more humid than it had been back on the hillside near his car.

Must be my overactive imagination and perhaps a mild concussion from when I hit the steering wheel, he reasoned with himself about what appeared to be happening. He passed it off as the denser forest retaining the heat of the day longer than the hillside. But one thing he couldn't quite figure out, even though the forest growth had seemed to increase, and the top cover appeared to close out the ambient light of the moon, the illumination did not become dissipated. As if someone or something lit their way. *But to where...?* He wondered. The thought gave him a momentary chill.

He could still see the trail ahead clearly as if something was inviting him to move forward. The moonlight appeared to be an unnatural twilight and a little unsettling. Clay dismissed the spookiness he felt, attributing it to the recent turmoil in his life, causing him to think irrationally. The unearthliness gnawed at him. Something was just not right, his mind kept repeating. An urge to turn around and get out of there kept clawing at him. Was he being drawn into some kind of hell, he wondered?

Chapter 10

They had moved beyond the bend in silence, each apparently deeply lost in their own thoughts. Clay noticed that the trail they were following now had begun to narrow. Glancing to his right to comment on this to Gabe, he also noticed he wasn't beside him anymore. Bothered about this, he stopped, turned around in a minor panic and bumped right into him.

"Relax, I'm still here! I'm not going anywhere."

"The trail is narrowing down, maybe we should be heading back? This is kind of spooky in here; the forest is closing in around us. It also appears to be getting warmer," Clay said.

"Will you calm down and relax? We'll be okay. Trust me!"

Reluctantly Clay nodded his head in agreement.

"Okay, so why don't you tell me about your time over there."

"You mean when I was in the Philippines?"

"Yeah."

"Not a lot to tell really. I was just over there doing my job."

"Somehow I find that hard to believe. I think there was more to it than that, or you wouldn't be going through what you have been all this time. So tell me, what did you do over there?"

"Well, it was sort of an unusual group. We were a catch-all type outfit. Kind of a bastardized lash-up."

"Yeah, and what in hell is that supposed to mean?"

"Hah!" Clay gave a short, derisive laugh. "I meant that we caught all the lousy jobs no one else wanted, or else squirreled their way out of! They kept bullshitting us, telling us we got those jobs because we were so good! What a fucking joke!" Clay reined himself in for a moment, surprised at his expression. He had not used these kind of words, in years, since he'd been in the military. Then it had been common for everyone to use these four letter forms of expression and punctuation. Yet, strangely, right at this moment it just rolled off his tongue naturally, like he was used to saying it all the time. *What in the hell is happening to me? Am I reverting back to my younger years?* He wondered?

"So tell me a little more about this unit you were part of," Gabe said.

"We had some unusual types of anonymous characters, constantly filtering in and out of the unit on a regular basis. You couldn't miss it because it was a very small unit. Highly secretive type shit."

"Unusual types?"

"Yeah, like special operations guys. Some were civilians, no doubt of that, and that could mean a lot of things, but our best guess at the time was "Christians In Action"."

"Christians In Action, what in the hell is that? Some missionary group?"

Clay gave a short derisive laugh and said, "Yeah, sure! Spell it out!"

"C.I.A.? Oh yes, crystal clear!"

"Right. But there were other things going on too."

"Figures. So what was your job?"

"The unit was known as the C.I.T.C., which stood for the Counter-Insurgency Training Command, but the designation covered a lot more ground than that. It had somehow become a very proactive combination of long-range patrolling, forward observers and rapid reaction teams. If you have the right equipment, it could be a very lethal combination."

"Right equipment?"

"Yeah, we seemed to be always testing out new types of long range radios, some updated weapons and other gear. Like maybe they were getting ready for something serious, like another Nam."

"And you?"

"Primarily a forward observer and one of the gunslingers on our team, meaning a small arms expert, familiar with using any kind of firearm. What would happen is the intelligence section, and that's a misnomer if I ever heard one, would pick up some hot information about a large group of Islamic terrorists in a particular area, a hidden weapons cache, or either terrorists or supplies coming ashore in the gulf of Palawan. We would be sent into the field to check it out, verify the information to see if it was authentic, and if it was critical, to take action."

"Go on."

"If it checked out and was valid information, one of us would communicate with the base camp and call in the special operations people, whoever was part of the rapid response team. Usually the Philippine Special Forces, often operated with our guys as armed advisors. Or if we were short of time and the suspected terrorist infiltrators were not large, we would be tasked with handling it ourselves. If we knew their direction we could set up an ambush and wait for them to show up."

"When you say authentic, how do you mean?"

"Well, sometimes this hot intelligence turned out to be a couple of abandoned thatched huts, or maybe a small tunnel that might or might not have held any weapons. Sometimes it turned out to be an outright lie. The so-called reliable intelligence information turned into a trap, they'd be waiting for us. It was very touchy work because we were usually always operating in Indian Territory, you know what I mean, where the bad guys owned the turf. Naturally there was always a degree of uncertainty in that situation."

"By that you mean areas controlled by the terrorists?"

"You got it pal, totally! Very definitely and carefully, pussy-footing around in the bad guy's back yard! The terrorists moved freely throughout their area with no problem. The local populace were generally totally cowed, and would say nothing for fear of brutal, and inhuman reprisals.

"I understand."

"Do you?" Clay said, his voice taking on a tense tone. "Most people don't have a clue what it's like when it suddenly starts happening. Normal guys are scared out of their wits, but they continue doing their job. They begin praying that they will just get through it alive, in one piece."

"Maybe I might understand more than you realize!" Gabe replied calmly.

The statement surprised Clay and caused him to wonder about his strange benefactor a bit. Finally Clay continued, "And that's what I think happened to my buddies. I can only guess, but I think they walked into a big fat trap. It should have been me with them!"

"Why?"

"Look, they were my best friends and I let them down. They never came back. Nobody knows what happened to them. They just totally disappeared…into thin air! If I had been there maybe I could have helped pull all of us through whatever happened. If not, at least I could have died with them!"

"Maybe the circumstances were different than you imagined."

"No!" Clay said adamantly. "I just cannot believe that.

"So what you've been telling me is the reason you've been on this guilt trip for all these years."

"It's not a God damn guilt trip! I deserve to be dead. I should have been there for them!"

"Have you ever considered the possibility that even if you were there it might not have made a difference?"

"I don't give a damn, period! I should have been with them!"

"You'll never know. Maybe somebody had something else in mind for you. Ever thought about that?"

"I doubt it. Maybe they'd all be alive today if I'd been with them."

"So what happened?"

"Forget it! I don't want to talk about it."

"C'mon! We've come too far for you not to get it out of your system. You agreed you would talk about it. Besides, it goes no further than the two of us." Gabe gently pressed a little harder. "Let me ask you one question before you continue. How about your wife? Did you ever try to explain it to her?"

Angrily Clay retorted, "Soon to be my ex-wife! Many times I tried, but she never was all that interested enough to hear about it."

"Anybody else?"

"She got me to go to a shrink for a while, but I couldn't bring myself to tell the whole story and the nightmares wouldn't go away. Besides the pencil-necked, four-eyed geek had never been even remotely close to combat, much less gunfire. He would have undoubtedly pissed and shit his pants! He didn't have a clue of what it was like!"

"So why don't you get it out of your system now, once and for all. Now what happened!"

Why not, Clay thought. *It might help to get it all out.* He glanced around him. It had definitely turned warmer and the air felt more humid. "Strange," he thought aloud. Then he noticed the forest around them had become much darker and the pine trees had been replaced by something else. Some kind of broad-leafed type of tree that he vaguely recognized dominated the woods on both sides of the path.

He tried to peer into the denseness of the underbrush, but couldn't make out anything. The large trees seemed to part at the upper level and the path remained well lit by the moon. *Very strange*, he thought.

He brought himself back to reality and continued his story. "It all started with a party in the small town, not far from the Philippine Special Forces base we were attached to at that time. See, we had a party because my tour would be ending shortly. A short-timer, that's what they called guy's like me. Do you follow me?"

For the first time Gabe smiled knowingly. "Sure do!"

Clay thought it a little odd because Gabe had never said anything about a military background, but he continued anyway, "I had only a few weeks left in country. Then I would be sent to Davao to be processed for my return to the States and reassignment elsewhere. I figured I'd be going to a training command because this thing over there grew bigger every week. Sound familiar?"

"Yes, So go on."

"We had a long range patrol scheduled for early the next morning, my last patrol. We were going to a place up in the mountains near Bungulu, a very dangerous area."

Gabe said, "I'd heard a lot of guys get real squirrely near the end of their tour, and don't want to tempt fate or take any chances."

"True, but that wasn't me. These were my friends and I'd do anything for them, just as I knew they'd do anything for me. Besides, we'd always had a run of good luck together, so why would this last patrol for me be any different? It was a job and it had to be done."

"I like your attitude. It apparently carried over to your civilian job. You did well."

"Yeah, till I got shafted by the boss and his fuckin' son-in-law!"

"So continue…"

"Well, we all got pretty drunk. I know I did, and the next thing I know I'm waking up at dawn, in the bedroom of this girl's apartment, and the guys are all gone!"

"What did you do?"

"I freaked out. I asked the girls, but they told me that the guys had said I should sleep it off and left."

"Why'd they do that?"

"I guess I'll never know now."

Gabe looked at Clay for a moment silently, as if he was appraising him, and then said, "So what happened next?"

"I got dressed, practically ran all the way back to the base. There were no cabs around at that hour."

"I see."

"When I got to our unit I found out, they were gone. I'd missed them by only about fifteen minutes."

"So close! And you've carried around that fifteen minutes on your back all these years?"

"Yeah, I guess so and the worst of it - everybody else thought I was some kind of lowlife piece of garbage because I didn't make the mission with them. They figured I'd done it purposely."

"Did you ever try to explain?"

"Oh, I did, endlessly, but nobody listened or believed me. Even though I had to leave shortly, I became the unit leper. They figured I'd done it because I didn't want to take any chances of getting killed in my last days. Nobody would have anything to do with me!"

"That's pretty sad. I'm beginning to understand what's been going on in your head."

"The accusations were not true! Absolutely not! They were my best friends. I would never do that to them!"

"So what happened when you first got back to the base?"

"I immediately checked over at base operations. The original plan called for our team to spend a couple of days trying to find a large suspected terrorist training camp. We had a pretty good fix, but we were sent out to confirm it."

"So the chopper was supposed to just drop them off and return?"

"Yeah."

"Then how would anybody know when it was time for them to be picked up again?"

"A daily radio check, giving their coordinates and updates, in code of course."

"So what happened?"

"They just disappeared. The chopper and the whole team were never heard from again!"

"No distress calls?"

"None. I had a rough idea on the time frame for the chopper's return. So I waited by the flight line, to find out from the pilot where they'd been dropped off exactly. I waited until well after dark. They were never heard from again."

"That's pretty sad."

As they continued walking along the pathway, Clay fell silent, lost in renewed, miserable thoughts of his guilt filled past. He had been concentrating on the trail ahead, but now he took a look around him.

He observed the ambient light from the moon which strangely lit up the pathway directly in front of them, but otherwise the darkness of the night closed in on all sides of them.

There were a couple of other things he recognized. He knew that the air had risen a few degrees and become very moist and humid. He thought his mind played tricks with him, because he could have sworn it felt almost jungle-like. Beads of sweat had begun to form on his brow. He also found it odd that Gabe had no comment on these conditions, and didn't appear to be sweating a drop.

Clay noticed the vegetation had also changed. It seemed heavier, and if he didn't know where he was at the moment, he could have sworn it looked tropical now. He ignored it and figured he might have a mild concussion that he had received when he hit his steering wheel.

"Yes, it was sad. I'd let my best friends down."

"How can you be so sure?"

"Because as I said before, all of them were never heard from again. They mounted several aerial searches, but couldn't even find evidence of the wreckage of the chopper."

"So what do you think?"

"I'm just guessing, but I think they accidentally blundered into a terrorists' trap."

"What do you mean? Explain!"

"Well we had begun to hear that the terrorists had managed to get ashore heavy machine guns, and shoulder launched missiles, like the Russian Strela or the American Stinger. They would put out false intelligence, then set up the trap in or near likely landing zones that they knew either had been used or looked likely for a landing. Then they would try to sucker us in with "red herrings", fake intelligence. We were wise to the ploy most of the time, but not always."

"And you've lived with this on your back all these years?"

"Yes."

"Why?"

"Because maybe I could have made a difference. Another pair of eyes that might have spotted something suspicious."

"Be realistic! How can you be so sure?"

"I can't help it. I let them down."

"No you didn't!" Gabe said, iron in his voice.

They continued on in silence. Clay couldn't help but notice now that the pathway started to gently slope downwards. At the bottom of the slope, when the ground leveled off, Clay felt his shoes squishing in mud. He looked around him, finding that the ambient light had dwindled and it had become dark. The area surrounding them appeared to be swampy in nature, and the heat was now cloyed, like a heavy wet blanket on top of them. They had not spoken as they came down the slope. The trail had narrowed, so Gabe so followed him to the rear and slightly to his right.

"So let me get this straight, Clay. You've been carrying this guilt on your back like a three hundred pound gorilla all these years, correct?"

"Hey! You've already asked me this same question five times! I'll answer you one last time. Yes, I feel responsible. Why do you keep asking me that same question?"

Gabe fell silent for a moment, then said, "There's a reason. Now bear with me, if you would. Let me ask you this… Let's just say, for the sake of argument, if you were actually able to go back and live those particular moments of your life over again, knowing that you are alive, and in one piece today, could you really do it? Be totally honest with me, okay?"

"What kind of an asinine question is that?" Clay asked. "In the blink of an eye I'd do it! I'd make sure I wasn't stupid enough to get drunk and I'd make that mission."

"Even if there was a good chance that you might have disappeared with your buddies on that mission?"

"Absolutely."

"Why would it be so important to you?"

"Because it was my duty! I've already been over this with you several times! Now stop asking me over and over again, damn it! Are you satisfied?" Clay said tensely.

"Yes."

The heavy foliage obscured the path ahead when they reached a bend in the trail.

The whole surrounding area appeared soaking wet, as if a tropical rainstorm had just passed over. Because of the heat, a heavy mist drifted upward from the ground and vegetation. About twenty-five yards ahead, a break appeared in the darkness that surrounded them. It looked to Clay that the heavy undergrowth ended because now there was a brightness he couldn't fathom, almost like daylight showing through. The whole situation now had him completely spooked and he was ready to get away from this strange place.

Uneasy already, he couldn't be sure, but the opening in the undergrowth, where it became brighter appeared to be the rough outline of a small arched doorway. He couldn't believe his eyes. This couldn't be true. Maybe he really was dead or he had to be hallucinating.

That was it! He couldn't handle anymore of this shit! When he stopped and turned around to ask Gabe about this strange phenomenon he received the shock of his life. Totally speechless, Clay discovered the whites on Gabe that he believed to be an ambulance attendant's uniform was gone. They were replaced by a jungle camouflage fatigue uniform, with no insignia of rank or name tag.

"What the hell is going on?"

Clay's clothes also had been replaced by a camouflaged utility uniform. He had no idea how or when it happened and hadn't noticed it before. It was as if they had passed through an invisible portal and had changed their clothes. Stranger still, he immediately noticed it was not a new uniform, but well worn and over his left pocket, his name tag was neatly stitched. He didn't know what to say. Maybe that mist they passed through back around the bend had something to do with messing up his eyesight or brain? He had no idea, only that it had happened. "What the hell am I in, some kind of latter day Twilight Zone," he said.

"Let me show you something," Gabe said, bringing him back to reality and motioning him forward.

Clay felt a small knot of fear of the unknown, but couldn't stop himself. An archway appeared in the mist. The bands around the archway pulsed as if it were alive, in a bluish-green color. He felt a pull beckoning him forward like a moth to a light bulb. He stopped a few feet from the archway. Beyond it there was something, but he couldn't quite make it out because the image across the archway was blurry, and inundated in and out like a heat wave on a hot day, on a desert highway. What he could see of it, he could tell that it was a large open area, broken by trees and high clumps of brush or vegetation. He also could have sworn that he was hearing popping sounds that he distinctly remembered were the sounds of automatic rifle fire.

He twisted around and looked at Gabe with the unanswered question still on his lips.

Gabe held up his hand for silence, then said, "Clay, I know we've talked about this a lot as we came this way. Would you be interested in finding out the truth, once and for all? I mean it, this is no joke or hallucination."

"The truth? What are you talking about? Who the hell are you, really!?" He demended tersely. Is this another dream and I'm going to wake up in my bed in a few minutes?"

"In answer to your question, no, it is not a dream. Okay I'll repeat it one more time. If you had the chance to live that particular part of your life over again, would you really do it? Or is this just a lot of rhetoric and bullshit so that you can continue to wallow in a self-pitying guilt trip?" Gabe challenged.

Clay grew visibly angry at the insinuation. "Just who the fuck are you? And how did you get involved?"

Ignoring Clay's questions, Gabe just said, "Someone who can help you. Now, did you really mean what you said?"

His eyes boring into Gabe like steel rods, Clay answered firmly, "Yes I did. So let's get on with it!"

"If you change your mind, do it now. Last chance, because there's no going back once you commit. Think about it. Do you want to go back to your old broken up and messed up life? Or do you want a real shot at possibly changing things for the better?"

"What do I have to do?"

"All you have to do is step through that *Doorway* over there," Gabe said pointing to the pulsing light.

"Doorway? Is that what that thing is?"

"That's right, it's a doorway of opportunity, a portal to a past life, where you can possibly make things right. That is, if you really want to. But you must understand, there is no ironclad guarantee. It will be totally up to you."

Clay remained silent as Gabe continued.

"You must try to understand one vital point. Everything that happens, once you walk through that *Doorway*, will solely be up to you, for good or for bad. If you screw up this time, it will be permanent."

"What about you?"

"I'll always be with you, watching over you, even if you can't see me. It's decision time, Clay! So what do you want to do?"

Half of Clay wanted to run as fast as he could, all the way back to his car. The other half drew him, unerringly forward, to the unknown - like a train, heading downhill and gaining speed. As each moment passed, the stronger the pull - to take those irreversible steps Into an uncharted future. The opportunity - totally beyond his comprehension.

Gabe challenged him again saying, "If you decide that you can't handle it, we'll just go back to your car and you won't remember anything that happened here. All you will have to worry about is that someone finds you before you die of your injuries and exposure."

It hit him then, exactly what his father was trying to tell him. "What are you, some kind of guardian angel?" Clay asked.

"Hardly! Let me put it this way, I have been given this rare opportunity to help you. I really can't discuss the details of why I have been chosen.

Clay mulled it over for a few moments, then made his decision. Looking Gabe in the eye he said, "You coming?"

"I'll be right behind you."

Turning back to the Doorway Clay moved forward until he stood almost in the Doorway, then stopped. Looking through the portal, he saw the tunnel-like entrance. Also, what he saw on the other side were very distorted, what appeared to be shimmering heat waves. Nothing was clear, except that it appeared to be daylight just beyond the opening. *Now or never,* he thought. Holding his breath, he stepped forward toward the pulsing light of the Doorway, into a different future, he hoped. The sensation in the portal became preternatural and on the edge of terrifying - a light show with flashes of steam having an unusual flowery scent and cool air washing over his face and body, as though his body and mind were cleansed of the previous life he was leaving behind. The archway turned out to be more along the lines of a short tunnel leading up to a blurry, pulsating opening at the end.

He forced himself to keep moving, more than a little spooked, as to what he would find on the other side of this possible extraterrestrial Doorway. Maybe another planet. He hesitantly continued to carefully step along the tunnel-like portal, when he suddenly felt someone or something grab his right arm. Already more than a little bit skittish, he jumped, and then snapped his head around, expecting to find a fire-breathing dragon behind him.

Un-nerved, he saw it was only Gabe. "Here, you're going to need these," he said, without further explanation, handing Clay two pairs of full canteens, each pair tied together at the belt hooks with green nylon parachute cord.

Looking at the canteens Clay asked "What the hell is this all about? Where did you get four full canteens? Who are you, the incarnation of Houdini?"

"You'll understand fully, after you pass through that," he said, pointing at the opening ahead. "Hopefully you'll make it back to your friends alive."

"What? Are you serious?"

"Never more serious in my life. You better get a move on. Time is of the essence!"

"What about some kind of protection like maybe an M-16 rifle or at least a pistol?"

"Sorry, but I can't do anything about that right now, but we'll get that worked out. Trust me."

"You're sorry? Yeah, you really look like it!" Glaring at Gabe, he continued. "Trust you? I'm beginning to wonder what my chances of survival are if I do so." Angered by the latest situation, Clay flipped one pair of canteens over his left shoulder and hefted the other pair by the cord in his right hand a couple of times. He moved with renewed purpose toward the Doorway, now anxious to continue this strange sojourn.

Stopping just short of the blurry, opaque, shimmering barrier, Clay felt as if he were in some Sci Fi epic. "It just couldn't be for real," his mind kept repeating, but he knew otherwise. Everything he had experienced, from the revival by Gabe, to this moment in time, finally convinced him this was his reality and not just another crazy dream.

Willing himself to move, Clay stepped up close to the opaque apparition in front of him, took a deep breath and bravely stepped into it with a wildly beating heart. The ephemeral moment in time he experienced, in stepping into that shimmering void, felt nothing like anything he had been through in his life, or ever would. One moment he stood in front of the opaque, pulsating exit, with the blasts of air and small clouds of cool steam with that strange sweet smell in the tunnel, the next moment he found himself in a whole different world, a kind of dark kaleidoscopic enclosure. Images and sounds whirled all around him from all directions, at dizzying speed. Voices coming from the images sounded familiar.

Focusing on the images, he found them to be tiny bits and pieces, like short clips, of his previous life. He began to experience a feeling as if every molecule and cell of his body had become disassociated from the rest of him. "No time to think, just keep moving," his mind commanded him.

A second later he stood in bright, eye-blinding sunlight. For a few seconds, he felt a chill wash over him at the unnaturalness of it all. Suddenly, an unexpected heat intensity enveloped his body as if he'd been body slammed in a football game. A lot like stepping out of a nice, cool, air-conditioned car, into the blast furnace heat of a mid-day Phoenix, Arizona summer day, but worse, because the instant humidity caused his sweat glands to start pumping overtime. In moments, his forehead covered in perspiration and flowed freely down his face. It stung his eyes. He could feel the sweat rolling down the rest of his body, soaking through his clothes.

"*I've been here before,*" he thought, "*I know this land.*" As recollection washed over him.

In the dead still air enveloping him, he experienced a frightening silence about this different world to which he had somehow been transported. The momentary silence was suddenly shattered by sounds of running, splashing, metallic sounds, beyond a growth of high underbrush, several dozen yards to his front.

"*From the sound of it,* he thought, *I don't think I'm on some strange planet.* "Those are human sounds," he said aloud. "On the wild chance, could it possibly be my buddies I'm hearing out there?" Excited about the thought and without stopping to think it through, he started to move toward the sounds.

Chapter 11

Common sense and caution prevailed and Clay froze in his tracks. Dropping to one knee in the dirt, he let both pairs of canteens quietly slide to the ground. Carefully checking his surroundings to the front and sides, he took stock of his situation, pondering his next move. Scared and unsure as to his location, his imagination started running wild. Vivid pictures blossomed in his mind, recalling the old movie he'd seen years ago, *Jurassic Park*. A chill ran up his back as he recalled the vicious, razor-clawed Raptors that stood upright and ran in wolf-like packs. He wondered if he was hearing some of those hideous creatures on the other side of the trees? *You just never knew,* he thought worriedly.

Running through everything that had happened, he idly wondered what was Gabe's reasoning for the canteens, which were oddly already filled? Why had Gabe appeared to try and hurry him through the forest and portal near the end? They were imponderables he could not grasp at this point or maybe ever, he thought. Whatever happened, he rationalized, life would never, ever be quite be the same again.

All his physical senses continued on overload from the glaring sunlight and sweltering heat. He dearly wished for a sweatband or hat and a pair of dark sunglasses. He continued surveying the terrain 180 degrees left to right. Long buried memories started to slowly resurface.

He recognized he'd ended up in a large clearing with rotting vegetation on the ground and clumps of low tropical plants dotted throughout. Apparently a small stream flowed to his right front as he could hear the faint sound of the water. The foliage continued to be high and obstructed his view of what lay beyond, except for a small, well-used, animal path that cut through it.

Kneeling there, quietly cycling all these odd bits of information through his mind, it all chillingly clicked into place. If this wasn't some kind of crazy dream, then he'd been transported back to the "Wild West of the Philippines", the nickname for the island of Mindanao. *Surely this couldn't be true,* he thought. But based on his old memory, the terrain looked vaguely familiar. Clay knew he had to be somewhere in the Maguindanao-Lanao Del Sur region where his group had been operating.

The long conversations he'd had with Gabe all came flooding back in a rush. What had been on his mind for all those years, the dreams, everything! He'd broken down and explained his deep desire to Gabe at length. Now, he realized in horrifying amazement, it had actually happened, he'd been granted his wish beyond his wildest dreams. But now, in retrospection, he wasn't sure he could go through with it. The old, overused, words, *be careful what you wish for, you just might get it,* kept ringing in his mind.

Spooked by the whole situation, Clay stood up and started to turn around, ready to head back thru the Doorway. *That's it! This is too much! I've had enough of this crazy shit,!* He thought, *And I don't think I want any part of it! I think I'd rather take my chances back at the wreck of my car!* But when he took his first step and looked toward the portal he had just come through Clay received another shock. It was as if a bucket of ice water had been tossed over his head. Unfortunately he'd forgotten what Gabe had carefully explained to him.

Where once has been the pulsating light of the Doorway from his other reality, it had disappeared. Nothing there, that is, except a solid green, impenetrable wall of jungle foliage, with no way through it. No sign whatever that the gateway from his previous life had ever existed. *This is turning into a damn nightmare before my very eyes!* He thought. *Am I just in the middle of one of my recurring nightmares, or is this for real?* Clay felt caught in a trap, with no escape in this new existence. He had to do something and quickly, but what? He immediately thought of his mentor, his security blanket.

He knew he had to talk to Gabe, like right now! Snapping his head around, he looked for Gabe anxiously, but the man who had been with him a few moments ago was gone! Totally disappeared! In a panic, he swiveled his head around in all directions, but it was as if his new friend had just evaporated into thin air. A distinctive and unmistakable sound of an assault rifle on full automatic sent him running for cover. The sound dredged up old, long buried memories, never quite forgotten, buried in the recesses of the mind that had instantaneously become chilling reality. He knew what it was, could never forget that killing sound, the trademark reverberation of a Kalashnikov assault rifle.

Listening to a few long bursts of fire, Clay realized that whoever fired the weapon had to be inexperienced. *Whoever the hell it is,* he thought, *they're burning up ammo at a fast rate and if they keep it up, they'll be tapped out pretty quickly.*

But Clay had other pressing matters on his mind at the moment. "Gabe! Where the hell are you? I need your help!" He called loudly. Hearing stealthy steps on the mushy ground behind him, Clay jerked his body around, ready to face the new threat.

It happened so swiftly, he didn't have time to think. About to yell for Gabe again, he turned when a big hand clamped firmly over his mouth, silencing his yell. Looking up, he saw Gabe's angry eyes burning down at him in reproach. Whispering angrily, in a low, threatening tone of voice, he said, "Quiet fool! You're going to get us both killed!"

"Christ almighty! Where'd the hell you disappear to? You scared the livin' shit outta me!"

"I said keep it down! I don't want to attract any unwelcome attention."

Speaking in a whisper, Clay said, "Where in the hell were you? I turned around a minute ago and you weren't there! I began to think you had been feeding me a line of bullshit and deserted me."

"I would never do that. Absolutely not true! I was only gone a few minutes. I had to check out the situation and can travel better alone."

"What situation?"

"You ought to know the answer to that. You've been praying for that for years, follow me!"

"Okay, yeah, I understand, but still find it hard to believe. So what's the deal?"

"First, do you remember what I told you earlier?"

"I don't recall. So many things have been happening, so fast."

"Don't you remember that I said I would always be with you?"

"Yeah, I guess so."

"Well, I will. Just that sometimes you won't see me. As I said, I had to check out the present situation. Now I know a little bit better."

"Okay, so now what?"

"Now we have to find your buddies as quickly as possible. Then you'll be on your own." Pointing toward the opening at the far edge of the clearing, Gabe said, "Now that I've checked it out, I know your destiny lies in that direction, but it isn't going to be a cakewalk."

Clay digested this thought. He now heard increased automatic weapons fire from more than one rifle.

"This is the only option open to you, the only direction you can take. We gotta get a move on now! Timing is critical," Gabe said.

Clay suddenly felt very much alone. He fearfully turned around, half expecting Gabe to be gone again, but was relieved to find the man right behind him. What completely shocked him was Gabe now appeared to be decades younger than the man who had come to his aid on the hillside. One other thing caught his eye, in all this exertion, Gabe did not sweat a drop. *What gives*, Clay thought. Gabe looked cool as a spring breeze in April, in both appearance and manner. *That man looks like he is totally in his element, like he was born to this.*

Clay again looked beyond Gabe, hopefully to where the doorway had previously been, but he saw only jungle. Focusing back on Gabe, he uttered the primary thought that came to mind. "You've been here before, haven't you?"

Gabe smiled and said. "You could say that. Remember, I'm here to help you on your way. Always keep in mind, that no matter what happens, this is your decision. The fewer questions, the better." Pointing at the canteens, Gabe said, "Better pick those up and let's move it!"

Reaching down to pick up the canteens, Clay glanced at the back of his right hand and he saw that the age marks, he often referred to as liver spots, were gone from his hand. The color of his hand and forearm were a healthy, sun-darkened tan. He glanced back up at Gabe with the obvious question on his lips.

"That's right, you are now at the same age you were, when you were here the first time. Also, you are in the same perfect physical condition once again."

Clay said nothing further and slung one pair of canteens over his left shoulder and moved forward with the other in his right hand. They were nearing the opening when Clay saw the small stream bisecting a corner to their right, where apparently the mysterious canteens had been filled.

In the distance he could see a column of smoke slowly rising up on the sluggish air currents, but not its origin. He could hear increased gunfire coming from that region, but he couldn't quite see the exact spot because he was too far away, his vision obscured by trees and low hills.

"C'mon," Gabe urged again. "We must hurry! Time is short!"

The whole thing still bothered him, but the pieces started to fall into place. At this point, in what appeared to be this new chapter in his past life, it had suddenly become reality. Clay found it scary on one level and highly exciting and exhilarating on another. He suddenly felt live living life to the fullest once

Carabao in distant field

again. And maybe, just maybe he might be able to help out his old friends - and come out of this in one piece!

"Which way?" Clay asked.

"There's only one direction," Gabe said, indicating the rising smoke.

Realization dawned on Clay. "So this is where I am! And that smoke is coming from the chopper that contains my buddies. Yes? True?"

"You got the picture! Remember, this is what you wished for, now here, put this on," Gabe said, tossing a cartridge belt with a K-Bar jungle knife, in a used leather sheath at Clay's feet. "You might just need it!"

Picking it up, Clay looked it over, then automatically strapped it around his waist and buckled it on, securely tying the green parachute cord lace at the bottom of the sheath around his thigh.

"Where'd this come from?"

"Let's just say, at this point, it was a necessity, like the canteens of water. Trust me."

Gabe flipped a soft, camouflaged, wide brim jungle hat to Clay, saying, "Here, ya look like you could use this."

"So, I'm back in the Philippines, in Indian Country, right?"

"Yep, you could say that, but they're not Indians, nor are they Moros anymore, as you might recall. They are now members of a splinter group of the MILF. If you remember some of the history of this island, everything blew up in violence when the Philippine Armed Forces launched a huge attack on Camp Rajamuda, one of the Moro Islamic Liberation Fronts most important bases in the late 90's. Since those years, the situation has simmered and gone steadily downhill from there, like tossing matches near spilled gasoline. Sooner or later there had to be a flare-up!"

"Think back to your last time here. If you recall, there is an ultra-violent splinter group, that broke away from the MILF, called the NMIFM, for New Moro Islamic Freedom Movement. They are getting lots of modern weapons, funding and organized by their international friends from al Qaida." Gabe nodded toward the direction of travel and concluded with, "Let's move."

"But I don't have a weapon!"

"Sure you do."

"The knife? You've got to be kidding! I mean an M-16."

"We'll get to that. Trust me."

"Trust you? I don't know if that's such a good idea for my continued health!"

Ignoring him, Gabe said, "Follow me," and without waiting to see if Clay followed him, led off setting a brisk pace.

He moved fast and with a fluidity that amazed Clay. Clay found himself hard pressed to keep up, even though he felt in better shape than he had in a long time. Reaching the narrow game trail, they moved in single file. Once they negotiated the pathway through the high brush, the layout of the terrain changed considerably. Like through a pass in the mountains, everything seemed different. The first thing that entered Clay's mind was the word *Danger*. This looked like ambush country to him. After the relative openness of the clearing, he did not want to cross this kind of country, especially with only a knife for protection.

**Accidental confrontations with an angry
Carabao can be very dangerous**

While the area spread out like a wide plain, it had numerous gullies, some deep enough to hide a shooter. In the distance where the smoke came from, his vision beyond seemed obscured by a low hill, not quite head height. Interspaced at odd intervals, like a big maze were large sections of heavy brush and closely spaced trees that could hide anything from a platoon of men to a tank. There were also several large sections of high, thick bladed grass that could conceal anything from a Carabao to a terrorist. While Clay felt he could deal with a terrorist, he had serious doubts about dealing with an angry, and unpredictable wild water buffalo.

The word uppermost in Clay's mind was *"ambush!" This would be like running through a gauntlet of killers, bare naked, with only a nail file for protection!* He thought cynically.

Catching up to Gabe he said, "This is real ambush country."

"Yes, so it is. But there's no way around it. If we go the long way to avoid this, we'll be too late." Without further explanation, Gabe moved on. Clay knew what was left unsaid…his buddies were in imminent danger of being killed.

They moved rapidly like this for several minutes until the sharp, rapid, popping sound of rifle fire came closer. Gabe held up his hand in a silent halting motion. Then he lowered his hand and with the palm facing downward he gestured up and down a few times, a signal to get down. When they were both crouched in the brush, he slowly motioned Clay forward with a wave, touching his index finger to his lips in a sign of silence. Slowly and as quietly as he could, Clay scooted up to Gabe's side.

With his eyes boring into Clay with a deadly calm not seen before, Gabe tersely whispered, "Okay, we're very close now to the opening act of this little play. We've got to move forward in complete silence to try our best to avoid any of the terrorists, if we can. We're not here to get into a big assed fight with these guys, the way we're armed. We just need to get past them. Do you copy?"

"Got It."

"From here on in - you lead."

"What! No fuckin' way!" Clay said, surprised at the command.

"It's your show from here on in!"

"No way! With what you gave me to protect myself? Who the hell do you think I look like, John Wayne?"

"You heard me, God-dammit! You do as I say! No arguments from here on in. Understand? You're acting like you're having second thoughts."

"Okay, okay!" Clay replied in a controlled tone, his anger to the reprimand showing only in his eyes. "You don't have to rip me a new asshole! It's just that I'm not used to the sudden change to this reality. I'm doing my best to acclimate myself to the situation."

"Okay. Be sharp and be ready for anything! I mean it! Anything! Let's move."

"Shit!" Clay tersely whispered, "What the hell is going on here? I'm gonna get my miserable butt drilled fulla holes!"

Snapping a sharp reply back, Gabe said, "No, you won't if you pay strict attention to what I tell you!"

Following orders, Clay silently started to move forward into the brush country, shocked at how all his training started to fall in place once again, all of what he had learned by hard experience. *It is all automatically coming back to me*, he thought ironically, *from what I've learned in another life. That old, overused cliché about riding a bicycle one is sure as hell true!*

He carefully worked his way through the brush-choked gullies as silently as he could, figuring any one of them could be a possible ambush site. Moving around a short bend of the shallow wash, he followed, he suddenly found himself facing a dilemma he had hoped to avoid at all costs. Standing near the far side of the shallow gully a dozen yards in front of Clay, in the process of ejecting a spent magazine from his weapon, stood a young Islamic Terrorist guerilla. Short, but well muscled, his uniform consisted of a patch-work of a new camouflage blouse, worn out, patched and faded black jeans, sandals and a scarlett headband, with markings, that Clay guessed might mean were connected to the NMIFM. The guerilla left no doubt as to his intentions. He held a new AK-74 assault rifle, griped in his hands, with fold-back stock. Clay recognized it immediately because of the trademark, long muzzle-brake at the end of the barrel, much different than the older AK-47. *This must be the jackass who had been blazing away nonstop like he had all the ammo in the world. Inexperienced, but still deadly,* Clay thought.

The terrorist heard the sound of Clay breaking through the brush, his head snapping around in surprise. A startled look appeared on his dark, sweat-stained face. Their eyes locked for microseconds, as if they were both frozen in time. Recognition and reaction hit both of them at the same instant.

The guerilla had been reaching for a fresh magazine from a pouch on his chest when he heard the noise. In that second of threat recognition, Clay knew that the thoughts that certainly were crossing both of their minds had to be, *Where in the hell did he come from?*

Attached to the front barrel of the terrorist's assault rifle was a mean looking, razor sharp, bayonet. The brief look that Clay saw reflected in the eyes of the terrorist left no question that he fully intended to use it or the rifle on him. But it was the rifle that Clay was most concerned about. Hard experience and training from his past appeared in his mind as if it had never left. In that split-second of time it all flashed through his mind…the long muzzle-brake required less marksmanship training because it reduced muzzle climb when fired. So, an inexperienced shooter could learn faster and become highly accurate. The smaller 5.45mm high velocity round, highly accurate, did more damage to its victim. So, what it came down to, Clay recalled chillingly, the increased accuracy essentially equated greater first-hit probability even from an inexperienced shooter. The conclusion flashed in his mind like a bright neon sign… he had to do something, and fast, or he was dead meat!

Clay had only been a dozen yards away when he had burst through the brush that covered the wash. While he had been momentarily astounded at seeing an enemy guerilla for the first time in many years, the shock was gone the moment he heard Gabe yell, at the same time, in his ear, "Take him down!"

The terrorist whipped the magazine from his pouch, flipped it around, starting to slam it up into his empty weapon. Clay realized that once in the weapon, it would be only second for a round to be stripped off the magazine, chambered and ready to kill. But the terrorist was young and his weapons training had been fast. In his haste, he caught the back of the loaded magazine on the edge of the magazine housing. It took only a second to correct, but…

Clay's instinctive reaction, ingrained from his previous life, was a nanosecond ahead of his brain to the deadly threat. He did the only thing he could in that eye-blink of time, to save his own life. His mind and body on full automatic, he ripped the pair of canteens from his shoulder in one fluid movement, whipped them around once over his head like a bolo, to gain velocity, and let fly at his adversary.

The magazine slammed home in the weapon and the man charged it a second later. He desperately tried to bring his loaded rifle up and to bear on Clay's chest, his finger squeezing the trigger. Wildly thrown through the air, the canteens luckily hit the barrel of the rifle, deflecting it just as the trigger was pulled. On full automatic, the guerrilla managed to get off a long burst of several rounds, but they luckily impacted harmlessly in the dirt next to Clay, barely missing him and far too close for comfort.

A second later, Clay launched himself through the air and body slammed into the guy before he could recover and fire again. In the initial scuffle, he managed to knock the rifle from the man's grasp and they both hit the ground, kicking, scratching, biting and fighting like a pair of crazed cats in a fur ball.

Both rolled around on the ground tearing at each other, oblivious to their surroundings and only intent on coming out the winner. The terrorist might have been smaller than Clay, but he more than made up for it in strength and was an experienced, dirty, street fighter.

The brutal fight went on for several minutes. Clay fought like a wild animal, with a ferocity that came from an inner core that he had never known before. He knew that only one of them would walk away alive from this violent encounter - and the outcome was very much in doubt at this moment.

In a mindless fury, they rolled over in the dirt several times, the guerilla managing to pin him to the ground. Reaching behind him, he pulled out a short, wicked looking knife that Clay knew was a Kris, from underneath his camouflage smock and slashed for Clay's throat. He would have connected had not Clay, in a desperate move, grabbed the man's wrist in his hand and held it back with all his might. But it was a losing battle because the terrorist was a little stronger and gradually the wicked little blade moved inexorably toward Clay's throat and the certainty of an agonizing, bloody death.

Clay held the guerrilla's other hand tightly at the wrist, but the wiry fighter twisted and managed to break free and slammed his hand under Clay's jaw pushing it backward, opening up the throat area more for a knife thrust. At the same time, his fingers pushed down on the lower part of Clay's face.

Before Clay could reach up with his free hand and pull the man's hand away from his face, the terrorist's small finger came to rest on Clay's lips. In a move of desperation, Clay moved his head sideways as much as he could, which wasn't much under the constant pressure, and the man's little finger slipped between Clay's lips.

In the brief moment that the guerilla realized the danger he was in, it was already too late for him, even as he attempted to pull his hand away from Clay's mouth.

Clay opened his mouth, ignoring the dirt and felt the little finger slip between his teeth. Reacting instantaneously, Clay bit down as hard as he could, feeling the skin part to the bone and the hot coppery taste of blood gushing into his mouth.

The man let out an unearthly scream and tried to pull out his finger. But Clay clamped down as hard as he could and hung on tight like the bite of a snapping turtle. The terrorist, now crazy with pain, went berserk, only wanting to finish off this American and get away. He pushed harder to ram his knife into Clay's throat. The deadly little blade touched and nicked the soft skin, producing a thin trickle of blood. One harder thrust and it would rip into the vulnerable soft skin below his jaw.

Clay, now on the edge of panic, blindly groped around the ground beside him with his free hand for anything to smash into the terrorist. As he ran his hand across the ground he came back in contact with his leg. He suddenly felt the jungle knife strapped to his leg that he had totally forgotten about, so engrossed was he in just surviving this brutal life and death encounter. Now in one swift motion, he unsnapped the clasp and ripped the knife from the scabbard.

The hand holding the Kris knife vibrated violently. The terrorist had pushed Clay's hand down to where the wicked little stabber was again practically touching Clay's throat. One last, hard, quick thrust and it would be *in* his throat.

Clay operated strictly by gut survival instinct now. He swung his blade in a tight arc and slammed the K-Bar as hard as he could into the side of the guerilla, entering between the ribs. He strained and pulled it out, then rammed it home again with renewed strength. Then, one more time for good measure, he slammed the blade home, held it there and twisted the blade.

The reaction from his adversary was instantaneous, almost like a balloon deflating. One moment, he was fighting, hard as nails, the next, a strangled burble escaped the guerilla's throat and he went limp, his eyes glazed over in death. Clay pushed the body off of him and rolled away. Unable to move a muscle, he gazed up at the cloudless sky, puffing and breathing harder from the exertion than he had in many years. With almost total exhaustion consuming him, he contemplated his deadly surprise encounter. *This has got to have been my worst experience. Even in my previous existence, when I was here, nothing like this had ever happened! I hope there will be no more surprises like this!*

Chapter 12

His body drenched in sweat, totally drained from an encounter he had not expected or trained for, Clay dragged himself away from the lifeless remains, which oozed its life's blood into the sandy ground.

Rolling onto his back again he stared up at the clear blue sky in a kind of stupor. Funny, the idle thought crossed his mind; I've never really noticed before how blue the sky is. Perhaps this harrowingly close brush with death enabled me to appreciate these simple things in life a little more. That is, if I ever survive!

For an iota of a moment he questioned his decision to go through the Doorway. Did I really do the right thing, he pondered? I really want to help my friends, but am I capable of it?

The face of Gabe leaning over and examining him closely from head to toe, suddenly blocked his view of the sky.

"Well, you seem to be okay, only a few scratches and bruises," Gabe said in an impersonal tone. "Better get up, we need to get going." He didn't congratulate, nor mention the fact he'd just witnessed a brutal life or death fight.

Clay was surprised at the seemingly detached way Gabe spoke after the violent fight. Speechless for a moment, he then allowed his anger to boil into his throat.

"Look, I realize this is a new experience for me! But in a tight spot I'd never experienced before, why didn't you help out?" When Gabe didn't answer right away, Clay continued, "Where in the hell were you? I almost got killed!" Gabe remained cool and impersonal in the face of Clay's angry outburst. "Yes, that's true, you could have been killed, "Gabe said. "That was the risk you took when you chose to undertake this journey. I am truly sorry but it was totally out of my hands. I had nothing to do with it. It was your choice and you were completely on your own. There should be some consolation on your part that you succeeded. It was something you had to experience if you are to survive. Look, I really want to pass on my experience, but this is not going to be a cakewalk!"

"So what the hell does that line of crap you just handed me mean?"

"Briefly, it means I was not allowed to intervene or help you on this one."

"Oh really! And just why is that? Look mister! I'm no coward, and I really want to find and help my buddies, if they're still alive. But you're gonna to have to cut me some slack, friend! I've gone from out of shape, middle-aged office lizard - to John Wayne and Rambo in one night! Follow me pal?"

"Okay, I get you! However you are back to your original youthful health and strength from that time period. But as I've tried to enlighten you, the fact of the matter is, once you made the decision to commit, my role from that point forward is to just provide you with helpful guidance when you are truly in need of it. I'm limited to a certain degree. I could not interfere, such as help you fight that al-Qaeda terrorist." Offering his hand, Gabe said, "Here, let me help you." Clay reluctantly grabbed the proffered hand while Gabe pulled him to a sitting position.

"Let me explain again so you are totally clear on this. Coming back to this moment in your life has been solely your decision and your responsibility. I did not force you. No going back now. You're here and that's it, whatever way it turns out, for good or bad, it's all up to you now. Why can't you seem to get it through that thick skull of yours? You've been given this chance to go back and change things from the way you perceived they turned out in your nightmares. Maybe they didn't end the way you think in that other life you left behind, who knows? You are either very blessed or lucky by being given this chance to go back and live your life over again and attempt to change it for the better. Am I getting through to you yet?"

Clay was silent for a long time, deep in thought. "Okay, I understand, but what about you? What's your story?"

"That's a whole different situation and I'm not at liberty to discuss it with you at this time, maybe later."

"Who are you trying to kid? I can plainly see you've got a military background."

"Well, let's put it this way. I was given an unusual opportunity and I decided to take advantage of it. I have a debt to pay, that's all I can tell you. I'm here to guide you on your journey. Look, just let it lie. Remember I will always be with you, no matter what or wherever, clear?"

"Okay," Clay said. He knew Gabe would not clear up the mystery-at least not at this time, if ever.

"Right," Gabe said, getting back to business. Now first you need to do is check the weapon to make sure no dirt or crud got into the action or barrel. I have a definite feeling you're going to need it real soon! It should be coming back to you."

Clay went over to where the AK-74 lay on the ground and picked it up. Again, as with other things, the familiarity of holding the weapon slowly resurfaced in his mind. Releasing the magazine, he first worked the action, pulled back the bolt and checked the chamber for dirt. It appeared clean, except for a small amount of dust that had gotten on the exterior when the rifle had fallen to the ground. With the action open he lifted the stock end of the rifle toward the sunlight and looked down the front of the barrel. Determining that it had not become plugged with dirt, he swung the weapon around, grasped the handgrip and inserted the magazine in the housing, then slid the bolt forward, putting a round into the chamber; he left the safety off. Now he was ready.

Clay didn't have the foggiest notion why he did it-an automatic reaction from out of his past and he never gave it a second thought. Reaching into his pants pocket and without thinking about it, he pulled out an olive drab handkerchief. Looking at the cloth for a moment, he realized he didn't even know he had it, but he automatically knew what to do with it. Very carefully, he wiped off the outside of the rifle until he had it clean of dirt and dust. He found himself doing what every rifleman in the infantry did to make sure his weapon proved to be serviceable.

Still continuing to perspire heavily in the muggy, humid heat, Clay leaned the rifle up against some stout tree branches. He then took the kerchief, snapped it in the air a couple of times to get rid of the dust, then carefully folded it several times to make a sweat band and tied it around his damp forehead. He knew this would help keep the salty perspiration from running into his eyes and burning. Old habits died hard, he thought.

Picking up his soft jungle hat where it had fallen during the fight, he slapped the dust off on his leg. He then folded it a couple of times, stuffed it halfway down into the small of his back between his shirt and pants. He knew it would be secure there until he needed it later on.

"Okay, I'm ready," he said.

"No, you're not. Get the ammo pouches off him," Gabe said, pointing at the body. "You're going to need them and then some!"

Stepping over to the dead terrorist, Clay unhooked the buckles and pulled off the harness holding the spare magazines of ammunition. He put it on, but found he was too big to close the fasteners, so he just let it hang loose around his shoulders.

Motioning toward the body, Clay said, "This is one al-Qaeda trainee that didn't pay attention too well in class!"

"Don't become overconfident, you're not "bulletproof," even if you're beginning to think you are! They're not all like that. You were damn lucky and don't you forget it!

"Yeah, you've got a point there. I respect your knowledge and experience."

"Now we gotta get going! I'm going to set a fast pace so I want you to keep a sharp eye as we move through this country, we're not out of the woods yet. This terrain is perfect for ambushes and we can't afford to be slowed down. Time is running out!"

"What in the hell does that statement mean - Time is running out? You keep repeating that and it's driving me nutso!"

"Let me enlighten you! We have a small window of opportunity in this present reality. If we don't make it on the timetable, all is literally lost!"

"Here we go again! What the hell do you mean, in this reality and all is lost? And what's all this crap about a timetable you keep hammering on?"

"I mean that if we get there in time, your friends might have the opportunity to live. If not, well..." Gabe let the last words hang in the air like a dense fog at night.

"If not...you mean they'll all be tortured, killed and mutilated like in my nightmares?"

"Well, no time like the present to bring this into the open. Those nightmares you were having weren't quite just bad dreams. Because of your close friendship with your buddies and the guilt trip you've carried over all these years - the dreams were actually a dose of reality about them. That's why I keep telling you to move because we're close and there's still is a small window of opportunity to save them from that very fate!

Totally shaken by the statement, Clay said, "Oh, m'God! Let's get our asses moving! Now!"

"You lead off," Gabe said, "And do keep a sharp eye out!"

Clay moved off, feeling an urgency he had not experienced previously. Gabe's earth-shattering words hung heavily on his mind. It wasn't that he was scared. Anxious, that's the word he would best describe his concern for the safety of his buddies. The nightmares that he had suffered through over the years were still very vivid in his mind. He automatically moved forward with a renewed exigency, bordering on the reckless. He had to get there before the nightmares he had endured became his present reality predicted by Gabe.

A new feeling developed in his mind. He now felt no fear of death. He only wanted one thing now-to get to that downed helicopter as fast as he could. He moved rapidly through the broken terrain, dodging from cover to cover, using whatever kind of concealment he could so that he would not reveal his position as he moved forward. Old habits resurfaced fast and he felt very natural doing what he was doing.

Glancing over his shoulder a few times, he saw Gabe, right in step behind him, a set, determined look on his face, his eyes darting from side to side, looking for any kind of threat. Clay observed Gabe in wonderment as not a drop of sweat appeared on Gabe's deeply tanned forehead, as if he had been doing this all his life. Maybe he had, Clay momentarily considered.

What is this guy? Or is he some kind of superman or real John Wayne Green Beret from another life?" he thought as he rushed through the undercover and heavy brush.

Clay recalled that military people called it situational awareness, in essence meaning being totally aware of what is going on around you at all times. Clay did his best to keep abreast of any threats to his front and sides. Though he had been very good at this game in another life, he wasn't quite up to speed yet, but it was coming back very fast, he noticed. He also became aware his previous life was gradually fading from his mind, as the new reality took its place.

Rapidly covering about one hundred yards, without running into any resistance, Clay started to believe that this was going to be a cakewalk and he became a little careless. He tried hard to believe the hopeful fairy tale that he wouldn't encounter any more problems and would be able to avoid the rest of the guerillas. Dashing from cover, a clump of dense brush, he started to rush across an open area of sparse growth, when he heard Gabe yell, "Your left!"

Snapping around that way and bringing up his rifle to bear, all in one fluid motion, he saw a green camouflaged uniform and an assault rifle pointing in his direction. The grizzled old terrorist must have been as surprised as he was and slow on the uptake, because it cost him seconds he could not afford to lose. The fleeting thought crossed Clay's mind that the man had not expected anyone to appear from his rear.

Sniper catches Dixon by surprise

Before Clay could aim his AK-74, the guerilla managed to get off a few panicky shots. Clay felt a momentary burn on his right thigh and felt something tug the sleeve of his left arm. He knew the soldier had obviously been surprised first by his sudden appearance, but then Gabe's warning yell had surely contributed to throwing off the man's aim and thus saving Clay's life.

Not even thinking how lucky he was, Clay point aimed his rifle at hip level and fired a long burst on full automatic. The sound of the AK-74 going off temporarily deadened his hearing, but he was lucky and the volume of fire did the job. Enough of his wild rounds caught the terrorist in the upper body, killing him before he collapsed to the ground.

Clay relaxed a second and was about to turn around and make a comment to Gabe, when his mentor yelled again. "Behind you!"

Because of his hearing being momentarily deadened by the sound of his AK, Gabe's voice carried as if it came from a distance, inside a tunnel. Reacting, he whipped his head around. A strangely shaped bush suddenly took on a life of its own and separated from the surrounding brush. In the next split second, Clay saw the barrel of an assault rifle start to rise up.

"God damn! It's alive!" He yelled, as he tried to swing around and bring his own weapon up to fire. Too slow, the terrorist had him dead cold he knew. Pivoting around, trying to dive for cover, his left foot struck an exposed root sticking out of the ground. As he collapsed, Clay realized he'd lost control. His momentum of dropping and turning, pulled him over to the left.

Clay anticipated feeling the hammer-like strike of the enemy's rounds slamming into him at any second. His ears detected that frightening, familiar sound, like the buzzing of angry hornets, as the guerilla's bullets parted the air all around him. He realized how lucky he was in accidentally tripping. It just might have saved his life. His adversary, realizing he had missed his golden opportunity, and anxious for a quick kill, hastily tried to correct his aim. Landing on his side, Clay had the presence of mind to hang onto his rifle.

Clay knew the guerilla would be carefully lining up a sight picture of him as soon as he hit the ground. He also knew he had to move. Reacting on hitting the ground, he rolled sideways a few times hoping to temporarily spoil the terrorist's aim for a vital second or two.

Throwing himself into the prone position, face on to his adversary and presenting as small a target as possible, he slapped the butt end of his AK snug into his shoulder and lined up a fast sight picture of the guerilla in his sights. It was a split second situation; a case of whoever could get off the next shots would live.

The terrorist proved to be faster and managed to get off the first, few wild shots. Clay heard the bullets tear up the ground where he had been moments before, but he was still not out of the woods. His adversary still had the jump on him and if he got lucky, Clay would be history.

His training took over as Clay let all thoughts leave his mind. The guerilla's upper torso filled his sight picture. Holding his breath for a moment and letting a little out, he squeezed off a short burst, being careful not to panic and jerk the trigger, thus throwing off his aim.

The enemy jerked sideways, but he was still stood, a lethal threat, as the man, not giving up, managed to bring his rifle back up to bear with determination. Clay could tell this soldier was no amateur, as the enemy took aim at him once again.

Having gained those precious few seconds, Clay again took careful aim and squeezed off several shots. This time he was rewarded with seeing the man go limp, collapsing to the ground, his rifle sliding from his limp hands.

In the moments after it was over, Clay rested his right hand on the upper stock of the rifle and leaned his sweat soaked forehead against it. All his energy and emotions were drained by the frenetic, life changing seconds that had just passed.

Gabe trotted over and asked, "Are you okay?"

"Yeah, I'll be okay. I think one of the rounds grazed me on the thigh."

"Let's have a look."

Unbuckling his belt, Clay pulled his pants partially down to expose his thigh and a minor flesh wound. The bullet had just grazed the skin enough to break it and a small amount of blood had welled up to fill the slight wound. Gabe applied antibiotic ointment, and taped gauze over it.

"You'll be okay. This ought to be enough to get you a Purple Heart, pal!"

Clay looked Gabe straight in the eye and said, in a dead serious tone, "I'm not here to win medals, I'm just here to save some friends."

"Good! That shows me you've grown a lot, in a very short time."

"I feel like I've lived a whole lifetime at this moment."

"Yeah, I imagine you have!"

Clay stood up and dusted himself off, checked his rifle and started off in a trot in the general direction of the downed helicopter. Gabe followed at a short distance behind Clay, acting as a rearguard, a small smile of satisfaction on his ruddy face.

In this manner, the two men gradually worked their way closer to the downed aircraft. Their approach would be, to a certain degree, a classic attack, Clay figured, flanking the enemy and then coming at him from where he least expected it, the rear.

From their actions the guerillas appeared to be overconfident. They believed that this was their undisputed territory. Under normal circumstances this was true. They never expected to be attacked at all, or for that matter, least of all from the rear.

Clay moved as fast as he was able, crossing the difficult terrain. Each time he came upon and surprised a terrorist, he attacked with a renewed ferocity, quickly dispatched the surprised guerilla and moved on quickly, after removing the man's ammunition and weapon. Gabe took up the laborious task of lugging the extra equipment with no complaint and without missing a step. Clay figured that sooner or later his buddies would run out of ammunition and the extra weapons and ammo would help solve the problem.

Sometimes the terrorists would spot him, but Clay was seconds quicker and getting better all the time. As he drew closer to the downed chopper, because of his actions of dispatching the enemy one by one, the volume of fire started to drop off a little. He wondered if either side in the firefight would notice the difference and then wonder what was going on and in the case of the Islamic terrorists, come looking for him.

Breaking through some brush in a shallow draw, Clay surprised three guerillas laying down murderous fire with an American M-60 machine gun, obviously captured from the Philippine Army. One of them must have heard his rapid approach, because he turned toward the sound. A surprised and fearful look crossed his face on seeing Clay, saying volumes. "Where in the hell did he come from?" The question was plain on his face.

Yelling his alarm, the gunner and his assistant turned, clumsily tried to swing the M-60 in Clay's direction. Knowing he was no match for the weapon, Clay reacted, firing an ammo eating burst from his hip, in their direction, his assault rifle clicking on empty. He was lucky, as the long burst got all three.

Inserting another full magazine in his weapon, Clay went over to the bodies. Before he could pick up the M-60, Gabe, next to him, had hefted it in his hands in front of him and said, "Well done, you're getting better. You're learning! What I suggest you do is hide this close by and come back for it later. This, plus the ammo is too much to carry right now. We've got to move!"

Clay felt extremely pleased at the unexpected compliment. He picked up an extra belt of ammunition out of a metal box and wrapped it around his neck and followed Gabe to where he had concealed the weapon in a shallow, brush covered draw.

"That M-60 just might come in handy later on," he said."

"Yeah, just might," Gabe said knowingly.

Just before they started off again, Gabe halted Clay and added, "We're almost there, but the danger is still very real and not over yet!"

Clay couldn't quite figure out how or why Gabe was cognizant of this information, but he knew now from recent experience, not to question what his mentor said and accepted it as gospel. Clay nodded and they moved out once again.

Clay guessed that they were now within approximately a little over three hundred yards from where he could get a good look at the wreckage. From where he stood, the aircraft looked like it had come down relatively intact, which told him that whatever had occurred, it had forced the pilot to make a hard emergency landing. At least they appeared to have landed in one piece, he thought. Most of the chopper was in view, but he couldn't see anybody and figured they were well concealed.

The area, broken up by dense brush, tall grass and clumps of low hanging trees, afforded the enemy good cover. By now Clay noticed the firing on both sides had dropped off, with sporadic firing hopefully due to his efforts. He guessed a few small pockets of the guerillas still remained. He figured the Americans were holding their fire, because they were probably very low on ammo about now. Good thing he had saved the extra weapons and ammo. Clay figured the terrorists were up to something and didn't think they'd give up that easily on their own turf.

Rapidly maneuvering himself forward toward where his buddies were bottled up, he suddenly came upon what he realized Gabe had been cautioning him about. It hit him hard in a brutal flashback, the memory of the horrid nightmare for just an instant. What he saw answered the question about the dream. Well hidden under some dense, low hanging trees and covering brush, two Islamic guerillas squatted. One of the men stood, an RPG sitting on his right shoulder, in the process of taking careful aim at the helicopter. The other man, his loader, carried the spare rounds for the gunners rocket propelled grenade launcher. The pair had apparently very carefully, infiltrated themselves closer to the Americans while the furious firefight was in process. Now they were in a position where they couldn't miss.

"This was going to be like shooting fish in a barrel if I don't do something" he thought, "but what can I do?"

Clay knew that the RPG, a merciless killer, would devastate what was left of the helicopter and all the men around it. He just couldn't let this happen. He had to act now, as he could see the guerilla was on the verge of firing.

Starting to bring his rifle up, Clay yelled at the top of his voice in an attempt to distract the attention of the gunner and throw off his aim. The man was like a rock and the yell had no effect on the gunner, his concentration was solely on aiming and firing the RPG, no matter what.

Time stood still for Clay. His movements seemed to be in slow motion. In actuality they weren't. Clay knew that if the man was able to fire the grenade launcher it would devastate the crash site and it would be all over for his buddies and this whole journey would be for naught. Life would be over for all of them and as far as he was concerned, also for him. If they succeeded, the end result of the RPG attack had to be what had triggered the horrid nightmares, made him miserable with guilt and plagued him for years, partly helping to ruin an already shaky marriage. He realized, at that moment, that somehow, across time and space, a desperate, urgent message had been conveyed to him. How, he didn't know, but he was here now and it was up to him. It began to appear they were scant minutes too late. Seeing the events in motion, in desperation, Clay did the only thing he could think of; strictly a gut reaction.

Chapter 13

Making his last desperate move to distract the gunner, Clay knew that this was one of those minute bits in time, when lives are unalterably changed and hinged on a single event. Would he live to go beyond this or would his past nightmares become his reality, his mind flashed to his consciousness. Mentally it appeared his actions occurred in slow motion, but in reality every movement was fluid, automatic and at hyper speed.

He shook the distraction from his mind and concentrated on what he must accomplish. In that blink of an instant it was crystal clear in his mind he had one and only one chance, so he'd better get it right as he wouldn't have a second chance.

Like a robot, without thinking, he lined the rifle up, sight picture filled with the gunner, butt tight against his shoulder, and squeezed off the shot, his only shot. A rapidly aimed headshot had to be virtually impossible at this distance, but if he could hit the RPG launcher, that might be enough, giving him that extra few seconds he needed. Rolling the dice, he took the gamble.

Too late! His gut instinct told him the gunner was already depressing the trigger with his finger. At that instant, a large clod of dirt flew through the air, out of nowhere it seemed, smashing against the terrorist's neck and part of the launch tube. It disintegrated into a cloud of dust and small pieces just as the weapon fired. *What the hell!* He thought, totally surprised as he watched, everything happening in rapid-fire sequence. At the very moment the gunner fired, the hard dirt clod slammed against him, causing him to flinch in surprise and shock, causing the tube to buck slightly upward. It was enough, for when the grenade ignited and rocketed out of the tube on its upward trajectory, it passed harmlessly over the chopper, exploding harmlessly moments later in the jungle. The gunner's assistant was a fast take on the situation. With a quick scan, he spotted Clay, dropped the spare grenade round and swept up his AK-74, pivoting in his direction. The guerilla's fluid movements were that of an experienced military man, possibly a deserter from the Philippine Army, Clay guessed.

Clay's mind was totally concentrated on getting the gunner. It took only a moment to realize the gunner was no longer the threat to them with the empty launch tube. In that brief second that could be fatal to him, he saw the movement of the loader out of the corner of his eye. Seeing the barrel of the AK swinging in his direction, Clay realized he was behind the game and attempted to react to the danger. Totally absorbed in dealing with the attack, the butt of his rifle jammed snug against his shoulder, Clay lined up his sights on the loader, held his breath for a moment and squeezed the trigger-all in the same motion as though he'd been doing it all his life. Surprising himself at how easily everything seemed to fall back in place. Still he didn't know if he had been faster than his opponent, and could only hope he survived another hair-raising moment.

At the same time, Clay felt his weapon buck into his shoulder; he felt the slight tug of something near the intersection of his neck and shoulder. A moment, later the sound of his adversary's weapon reached him. He knew his enemy had beat him to the draw and the thought crossed his mind - any closer and he would have taken a serious hit.

Staring through his rifle sights at the terrorist, he saw the man drop to his knees. Still not out of the game, Clay could see a red blossoming of blood on his upper right shoulder.

Determination on his face, the man clumsily tried to raise his weapon with his right hand. Clay fired a double tap and hit the terrorist center chest. Dropping toward the ground, the loader started to fall forward. The gunner reacted like lightening, grappled the AK from his assistant's dead hands, dropped to his knees and took aim and fired.

The wildly fired rounds buzzed around him like angry hornets. Reacting to the new threat, he quickly took aim and fired a short three round burst at the camouflage clad guerilla. The bullets caught the man in a diagonal from lower right to upper left on the man's torso. The shock of the hits caused the gunner to tip backward, the AK-74 slowly slipped from his dead fingers and slid to the dirt, unfired.

Clay leaped and ran toward his two adversaries, on full alert, worried another might be hidden nearby and would try to reach the launcher. Dashing across a small clearing, he caught a brief glimpse out of the corner of his eye of a small portion of the site where the helicopter lay. Gunfire from the direction of the copter suddenly increased in intensity. He was shocked to realize that his buddies were firing in his direction, hearing the angry whine of bullets passing over his head and landing nearby. *Geezus! They think I'm one of the terrorists*, he thought in a minor panic, *And the crazy idiots just might get lucky and nail me by accident!*

Hitting the ground in full stride, he saw Gabe already down there hugging the orange dirt like it was his security blanket!

"What'll I do?" Clay yelled, over the gunfire.

"Jump up and yell to them." Gabe cynically offered in jest. "I'm sure they'll believe you!"

"You're such a big help! Are you outta your gourd! With those trigger happy assholes?" Clay yelled back.

"What else are you gonna do?"

"Wave a white flag?" Clay asked.

"Do you have anything white?"

"No, how about you?"

"No, but I'll tell you what I do have," he said. Gabe reached into his cargo pocket on his cami pants and pulled out a small triangular, dark green plastic wrapped packet and handed it to Clay. Unfolding the packet, he noted it was about eight inches across the bottom and sides.

"Try this!" Gabe said, offering the packet.

Clay took it and looked at it quizzically.

"Go ahead, open it."

Hastily ripping open the plastic, Clay saw a dark blue nylon cloth. As he opened the packet further he saw white stars on a field of blue. Pulling the rest from the plastic he carefully unfolded a small sized American flag. "What the?" Clay said, surprised.

"Think that might do the job?"

"Can't hurt to try with those trigger happy assholes. They're probably scared out of their wits. I was just surprised that you had a flag."

"Been carrying that around for a long, long time and hoping to use it some day. Never knew when it might be needed. Like in this situation." Gabe replied.

"Amen to that buddy!"

Gabe grabbed a long bamboo shoot and chopped it off at the base with his jungle knife, then trimmed off the small branches. Handing the pole to Clay, he dug around in his pocket and came up with a spare pair of shoelaces, which Clay recalled most savvy soldiers carried, in case a bootlace broke out in the field.

Clay took the laces and put them through two small brass rings sewn into the small flag. He roughly estimated the size to be about 18" by 24". After threading the laces through the flag he tied that to the bamboo pole.

"Now what?" Clay asked.

"Stick it up where they can see it and wave it side to side so they'll recognize it"

"They might think it's a trap."

"That's the chance you'll have to take." Gabe replied.

Clay stepped over near the clearing without exposing himself to his trigger-happy buddies, stuck the flag above the covering brush, and waved it side to side. At the same time he yelled at the top of his lungs, "Hey guys it's me! Stop the damn firing!"

His efforts were greeted by a renewed burst of firing from the vicinity of the chopper. "Shit! They think it's a trap like I said."

"Forget it." Gabe said, "they can't hear you. You're too far away. Just keep waving the flag."

Clay noticed the firing continued with some of the rounds piercing the flag itself.

Taking a huge chance, he leaped into the middle of the clearing, with the flag pole in his right hand and literally started jumping up and down, while wind-milling his left arm and waving the flag with his right. Literally at the top of his lungs he screamed, "Stop it you stupid fools! It's me, Clay! Cut it out!"

All of a sudden the firing ceased and he could see someone standing up and looking at him through what he figured were binoculars. A few seconds later Clay saw the man wave his arms to him in a gesture to come toward him. Clay noticed that the man had brought up his rifle and pointed it in his general direction.

Still, greatly relieved, Clay turned around and stepped over to where Gabe stood guard over the extra rifles, ammo and RPG.

"Here, let me take some of those." Clay said.

"Sure, no problem."

Clay slung a couple of the assault rifles over his left shoulder and the canteens over his right. Then he picked up a pair of spare ammo harnesses in his left hand.

Gabe stood watching as Clay loaded up, next trying, with no success, to pick up the RPG.

"Forget the RPG for now," Gabe said. "You can get it later. Are you ready?"

"Yeah, and thanks to you, I'm still alive. You saved my ass more than once out there. Thank you my friend." Clay said with genuine appreciation and renewed respect for his mentor and benefactor.

"Pleasure's all mine. It's not over yet, so watch out."

"One thing though."

"Sure, what is it?" Gabe asked.

"What would have happened if that gunner had gotten off that RPG round and actually killed my buddies? Or if I had been shot by that terrorist?"

"Then, unfortunately, it would have all been over." Gabe replied very seriously.

"Over? What do you mean?" Clay said, puzzled.

"Your life would have ended. Your buddies would have been really dead and you would have been spirited back to your car, fatally injured and dead of exposure sometime before dawn, when someone finally happened on the wreck by chance the following day."

After a long pause, Clay said, "Are you serious?"

"Yes, I've never been more serious! That's how it all would have really ended."

"Oh, my God!" Clay said in a stunned voice. Now a changed man by events, an idea started to germinate in his mind. The thought came to him that he was leading a charmed life. In this new life he began to convince himself that maybe he was immortal-bulletproof!

Gabe seemed to have read his mind, because he said, "I know what you're thinking! Don't go rogue on me, thinking you're immortal and bulletproof! You're flesh and bone pal, and don't forget it. You're a good guy for what you're trying to do for your friends, but if you stop a bullet, you'll be just as dead and anybody else!"

Clay was silent as the dark thought sank in and hit home. Then Gabe said, "Look I think it would be a good idea if you get going and make contact with your buddies, before they get nervous. Don't forget for a moment this is al-Qaeda and Moro Islamic Liberation Front controlled territory. You and your buddies are in luck for the moment. It's only a matter of time before somebody in their command structure realizes that the patrol they sent out has not reported in and they come looking for them. It's not a good idea to stick around here."

"Great! But where the hell are we supposed to go. I have a feeling that no one knows where we are, if my memory from the past is correct."

"True. But think, man! Think! Use your head. You know from past patrols, that the helicopter was not supposed to land in this valley. Think about it."

"I'm trying to remember. It's coming back slowly," Clay replied.

"The chopper could have been headed for the landing zone you had used before, but instead appeared to have blundered into a well laid trap. Who knows what drew them into it? Could have been a bogus radio signal, hard to say? Anyway, that's my best estimate. Somebody must have tipped them off that your buddies were on the way. It looks like some of the terrorists jumped the gun because they didn't manage to shoot the chopper down and it somehow made its way a few valleys over, to this location and made an emergency landing. Only problem is - no one knows where you and your pals are and chances are better than average the radios are out. Now, is it coming back to you?"

"Yes, I do remember. How could I ever forget? They launched a big search, but no trace was ever found."

"Okay, that's in the past. This is the present for you now. If you recall, there were some active and safe landing zones a few valleys over near the mountains, toward the coast. Your group used them before as a jumping off place. It's safer because it's closer to some of the larger Philippine Army outposts and al-Qaeda doesn't totally control the whole area."

"Tell me, how the hell do you know all this?"

"I just do. Let it go at that. Maybe somebody above gave me a good briefing before I got temporarily stuck with protecting your clumsy ass!"

"Gee! Thanks for the compliment."

"Hey! What happened to your sense of humor? Anyway, I didn't really mean that and don't be so sensitive. You're the one who wanted this to happen, remember? You'd better live every minute you have here to the fullest, because in your past existence you apparently didn't, and let time slip by you like sand leaking through your fingers. Savor it, because when it's over, all you'll have is the memory!"

"Now what?"

"Okay, apparently your memory is not quite up to speed. It appears you hit your head when the chopper was ambushed and you were knocked out. Your buddies will explain what happened. Feel that bump on the right side of your forehead?"

Clay hadn't noticed it before but now touched it and yelped, "Ouch! I didn't even know it was there!"

"Yeah, it was there all along. In reality, you got that bump from your steering wheel. But in *this* reality, you picked that up when your head hit the bulkhead of the chopper when it made a hard crash landing."

"Amazing. Any other good news?"

"No. No other surprises. So you better get moving and make your way over to them. You've got to get organized and get out of this area fast. It's too hot!"

Clay tried to pick up the RPG, but couldn't quite make it. Looking over at Gabe he said, "What about all this other stuff?"

"Don't worry, I'll be right behind you as soon as I get loaded up. I'll take what I can and stash the rest under the brush." he said, cracking a rare smile.

Stepping into the clearing, Clay moved off as fast as he could with the cumbersome load. He balanced the pole with the flag high so his buddies wouldn't mistake him for the terrorists. He assumed Gabe was right behind him with some of the other equipment. Hiking across the distance to the chopper, Clay soon broke out in a heavy sweat, loaded down with all the gear. Getting closer to the chopper, he recognized who had waved him in his good buddy Rick Latozi, who was also their squad leader.

Clay was up to shouting distance and was about to say something to him, when Rick suddenly got an urgent look on his dirt stained face. Suddenly Rick yelled, "Down! Get down!"

It didn't take much. Clay, now spring-loaded to react to any threat, just hit the dirt. Out of the corner of his eye he saw two guerillas pop up out of the tall, hip high grass and take aim at him and Rick.

Expecting something like this, two of Rick's buddies, who had also lain hidden in the tall grass, to keep a sharp eye out on the perimeters, popped up with rifles already aimed and fired on full automatic. Both guerillas went down without getting off a shot.

Struggling back up to his feet, Rick yelled to Clay, "C'mon! Hurry up and get your dead ass over here, soldier! Where the hell have you been? We were about to give you up for dead."

Grateful at having his life saved once again, Clay struggled back up and shuffled over to Rick, with his overload of gear. "Yeah man, it's really great to be back with you guys! You have no idea!"

Rick gave him an odd look and said, "Are you okay? You act like you've been away for days or weeks instead of a few hours to get water. Maybe that knock you took on the head in the chopper is more serious than you think."

"In any case, I'm just glad to have made it back to you guys."

Before Clay could say anything further Rick took notice of the weapons and said, "And where in the hell did you get all that stuff?" He referred to the AK-74's, AK-101 and ammo pouches. "I send you out to get a little water for us and you come back with a damn arsenal!"

"It's nothing really much. Just some stuff I picked up along the way," he replied.

"Oh yeah, sure! What the hell are you, the king of understatement now? Holy carimety!" Rick said in disbelief. "Well, I tell you what pal, that was good timing on your part, whatever you did. We're just about out of ammunition and figured we were goners." As an after thought Rick added, "We were worried about you short-timer! Got to keep you alive so you can make it back to the good old U S of A!"

With a familiarity created from long and steadfast friendship, Clay automatically replied in the typical macho banter that was a hallmark of close buddies, "Yeah, well maybe I just got lucky! Figured I'd probably have to save your scroungy asses sooner or later!" They all had a good laugh about that one.

"Okay, let's get going," Rick said as he turned and started to head back to the others at the chopper.

"Whoa," Clay said. "Wait a minute."

"What?"

"I nailed an RPG gunner just moments before he was about to fire a grenade into the group."

"No kidding? Anything else?" Rick asked, with surprise in his voice.

Finding it impossible to explain away the presence of Gabe, Clay decided to color the truth a little, saying, "By the way, I also ran into a straggler. Must have gotten separated from his patrol."

"Are you serious? American?"

"Yeah, plus he saved my ass a few times and I've got some more gear back there," he said, pointing "He's guarding it for me."

When they arrived back where he and Gabe had stashed the extra gear, Clay called out to him, "Hey Gabe, c'mon out. It's me, Clay - with my buddies."

The team all looked at Clay strangely and then at the extra gear. Rick was the first to comment. "So what the hell did you become - Sly Stallone and Arnold Swarzenager - all rolled into one? Some kind of *Rambo-Commando*?"

"Naw, just collected this along the way. Can't figure out where Gabe went though."

"Look, Clay, you must have hit your head harder than you thought. You're apparently hallucinating about this fictitious guy. Gabe? What is he - the angel Gabriel?"

"Don't laugh, man! If it wasn't for him I wouldn't be here right now" Clay said in a dead serious tone. "I left him right here when I went forward to meet with you guys."

"Yeah, well, let's just forget it, okay?" Rick replied, dubiously.

"Good idea!" Clay said in a slightly tense tone, not able to figure out what happened to Gabe, but keeping quiet about it. He didn't say anything further because if he did, they'd probably think he'd gone totally off his rocker. But one thing he did know, he wasn't crazy. Gabe had been with him, because he could see his boot prints in the dirt in front of him. *Didn't Rick see them? I wonder if he could? He thought.*

Suddenly, he heard a low, hoarse whisper in his ear. Looking around, he could see no one. The words hit home hard, "Just remember, I will always be with you."

Clay said nothing further, but knew he wasn't crazy and he knew he was totally happy. He had made it back where he belonged. No matter whatever else happened.

They had gathered up all the gear and were headed back to the downed chopper when suddenly the sound reached their ears. The broken echo of aircraft engines reverberating off the walls of the distant valleys reached their ears.

"Quick, back to the chopper...we've been able to get the emergency radio working!" Rick yelled, as they all took off, lugging their bulky loads.

Chapter 14

Rushing back to the crash site, Rick urgently said, "Everybody quiet! Listen up!"

"What?" one of the others said.

"Quiet! Can you hear it?"

The sound was there, faint for a moment, then disappearing for a second or two. A wind change at elevation or the shape of the distant valleys could easily affect the echoes, Clay knew. But there was no mistaking what they heard. It was definitely the faint noise of an aircraft somewhere in the distance. Still a long way off, it seemed to be increasing a little and appeared to be headed their way. They all turned and faced in the direction of the reverberation.

"If that's a search aircraft, then the search and rescue helicopter can't be far behind," Rick said.

"How about the radio in the chopper?" Clay asked.

"No good," one of the others said. "It took a couple of hits in that firefight we were in just before you got back. It's dead."

"Damn, of all the luck!" Clay said.

Still, they were all very excited at the prospect of possible rescue and their hopes were up once again.

"Okay, let's get ready. Get out a smoke grenade to mark our location and get that emergency radio transmitting,." Rick said to the others.

"Will they be able to hear us beyond those hills?" Clay asked, nodding toward the winding, steep hills in the distance that could possibly block weak radio transmissions.

"The signal is not very strong, but it's all we've got," Rick replied. "It should work."

They all gathered where the rest of the team waited by the open door of the chopper and started pulling out what was needed to mark their location and get in contact with the aircraft. Fortunately, the small emergency radio had not been damaged in the crash. It was their last hope.

Clay, the most excited of all of them, once again felt part of the team. After all of those years, it had come to an end. Enduring the nightmares, imagining awful things happening to his buddies because of his own actions, it had finally reached the ending. Maybe – if they were lucky – a good ending.

Another thing – he couldn't just go back to his other life. Did he *even want* his other life? The marriage gone – the job – out the window. He looked over at his buddies and felt their presence again – they were real, alive and he had walked back into their lives as though he hadn't been gone, but for a moment in time. The battle to live surrounded him and he felt unafraid, fearless, strong and full of life. He could endure anything with them beside him and Gabe nearby. He could even feel Gabe's presence although now he realized he would be the only one of them who would be able to actually see Gabe. An excited chill raced down his spine. *God must care for me,* he thought. He looked again at his team. *God must be on our side to care so much.*

The aircraft appeared to be growing closer as they all prepared to make contact. From the sound of the engines, while at altitude, the plane seemed to be in the next valley. It was very hard to tell, it could have been further off because echoes bouncing off the walls of the distant valleys, caused distortions. It seemed as though it was in the vicinity of the landing zone where their helicopter had been ambushed.

Gazing out the side window of the cockpit at the jungle choked valley below, the copilot felt very vulnerable. He remembered the joking between pilots when they were over hostile territory and there had been a possibility of attack by a missile, and how it puckered up their rear-ends. He felt that way right now and was grateful for the armor plating under his seat.

He wasn't real pleased with having to fly in this older, two-engine reconnaissance aircraft. He'd much rather be flying over this dangerous terrain in one of the newer, faster recon planes, but he and the pilot were stuck with an ancient, Vietnam era, Sikorsky search and rescue helicopter. It had been the only one available and now slowly followed them a short distance to their rear. The older chopper, while reliable, was incapable of keeping up with any other than their own, older twin-engine recon craft.

The drone of the heavy engines even penetrated his earphones, along with an incessant, irritating static that had started up the deeper they penetrated this god-forsaken terrain. He recalled the pilot had commented that possibly somebody had picked up their frequency and was trying to jam their transmissions. It was certainly a possibility, he thought. He continued calling out the missing helicopter's call sign as they traversed the winding jungle valleys. "Grasshopper zero four, this is Ridge-runner, come in."

He repeated the call sign several times, hesitating for a few seconds after each transmission, hoping to pick up some kind of signal from the missing aircraft. Then a moment after his last transmission, he thought he heard a weak reply.

"Grasshopper zero four, this is Ridge-runner, can you read me?' His transmission broke up by a burst of loud static that irritated his ears. "Damn it to hell, I think some sonavabitch is trying to jam us!" Then a second later, he got part of a reply, "Hopper zero four," then he lost it. He switched over to the cockpit frequency and told the pilot, "I think I've got somebody! Sounds like our guys!"

"Be careful, it could be a trap. Make sure," the pilot instructed his partner.

As they approached closer through the winding valley, the transmission from the weak emergency radio cleared up a bit.

"Ridge-runner, this is Grasshopper zero four, we hear your engines." The pilot cut into the transmission and said, "Get an authentication before we commit."

"Right," the copilot said, and then transmitted the request to the downed helicopter.

"Look, you dumb ass," came the terse reply, "our pilot has been badly injured and the copilot is dead. We don't know where to find the damn code!"

"Sorry," the copilot replied, "there've been too many traps that have downed aircraft. We can't take the chance without that authentication!"

"Look, paisone!" came the sarcastic reply. "I was raised in South Philly and I will even give you my street address! If you don't come and get us, I'll have some of my big brother's mob buddies look you up if and when I get outta this shithole! Trust me pal, you don't want that to happen!"

Another voice cut into the transmission. The copilot recognized it as the pilot of the helicopter following them. "It's Rick Latozi okay, and he still has a mouth on him!"

They all heard a hard laugh from Rick, on the ground, "Damn straight I do, Cavanaugh, you dumb Mick! And I owe you a case of San Miguel Light for that favor you just did us!"

They all heard the laugh from Cavanaugh. "Okay Rick, I am gonna collect on that! Count on it, pal!" Then he continued to the copilot, "I know this guy. He's the head of the recon mission and an old pal. He's legit."

The copilot thought about the comment from Rick and wished he could be back at the airstrip with a frosty, chilled bottle of San Miguel right at this tense moment. That delicious, dark Philippine beer was always the highlight at the end of a hot and sweaty day for him.

"Okay, that's good enough for us," replied the copilot for him and his pilot. "We'll go and find them."

As the rescue team flew deeper into hostile territory, they all became increasingly tense and jumpy. Both pilot and copilot kept scanning the terrain on all sides for any kind of a threat. They recognized they needed to get a definite fix on the location of the downed chopper. "Ahh, Grasshopper, this is Ridge-runner. If we're going to come to you, we're going to need the coordinates of your position. The automatic locator beacon in your aircraft is apparently not functioning."

"Ridge-runner, Grasshopper, that is not a good idea." the copilot heard Rick say. "We give you our location and every goddamn al-Qaeda operator who has their ears on, listening to our transmissions will know exactly where we are and come arunnin. Bad idea! Very bad idea!" We're already in hot water with Clay-John Wayne-Dixon knocking off all those guerillas, not that we don't appreciate it. But when they don't report in soon, somebody's gonna come alookin' for them!"

"Roger that," the copilot replied, "You went down way beyond planned landing zone, so there's only one option left."

"We're listening, Ridge-runner." Rick replied.

"Grasshopper, Ridge-runner, it's going to have to be a line of sight approach. When you see us coming through the valley, put up a flare. When the chopper is on final for the pickup, pop colored smoke and we'll identify."

"Ridge-runner, Grasshopper, that'll work for us. Out."

The pilot communicated to both his copilot and the SAR helicopter following them at a distance, "Keep a sharp eye out for anything strange, or out of the ordinary. I don't want to fall into a trap." Everyone rogered back their replies. The deeper they went, the tenser they all became.

Coming out of the deep valley, the copilot noticed the terrain in front of them opened up onto a wide, broken plain. He could see it was essentially pretty much flat, but dotted with numerous low knolls, and rain washed gullies. Knowing they had to be close, both he and the pilot strained their eyes trying to pick out the site of the wreckage on the ground to their front.

Suddenly the radio came alive, "Ridge-runner, Grasshopper, I think I now see you just above the broken clouds, coming out of the valley. We are approximately halfway across the plain, close to the intersection of a low valley and the flat terrain, to your left front. You should see our flare in a moment. Thank God you made it!"

"Done deal, guys," the copilot radioed, "the SAR following us should be on the ground in a few minutes. Then we'll get you the hell outta there!"

Both copilot and pilot started to relax. It was almost over. They concentrated hard, through the cockpit windscreen, on scanning the terrain ahead looking for the crash site and the rescue flare. Suddenly, a half dozen miles to their left front they saw a bright, burning orb of light arc up a few hundred feet and at its apex, slip over and begin its brief journey back to earth.

"There it is!" the pilot shouted into his mike.

"Got it," the copilot replied, pleased at how this was turning out. It would soon be over.

"Roger that," the pilot said, relieved that they had found the team.

"Did you copy that Rescue Seven?" the copilot radioed the Search And Rescue helicopter following. He received two clicks on his microphone in reply, signifying they had heard the whole transmission.

"Okay, we're going in for a pass" the pilot said, dipping the plane over into a gentle descent.

At that precise moment, out of the corner of his eye, the copilot's peripheral vision caught a momentary flash of light to his right. Snapping his head in that direction, he was shocked to see a long, thin, trail of smoke rising in that area. It wavered a bit as if it had corrected itself, then headed dead on for them. *"Holy shit!"* was all he thought, but in the blink of an eye he knew what it was.

"Missile launch! Break left! Break left!" he screamed into his microphone.

The pilot reacted automatically and snap-rolled their aircraft steeply to the left and dove straight down toward the ground to gain speed. A few seconds later, he leveled off and whipped the plane around in a hard G turn to see if he could break the missile lock and to keep the missile away from the vulnerable, slow-moving helicopter

The radio crackled from the chopper, "Probably a fucking Strela. We'd heard they had some, but this is the first attack." The copilot knew he was referring to the Soviet version of the shoulder fired Stinger missile used by American and allied forces, used so successfully in Afghanistan and the Middle East conflicts. It was difficult to defeat, especially at low altitudes and close range.

The missile was like a hound dog on a coon hunt. Once that dog picked up the scent of the raccoon it kept its nose to the ground till it treed the coon. The seeker head of the missile was in many ways the same as the hound, it locked on to the heat of the aircraft's engines and locked on till it accomplished its mission.

The pilot put their aircraft through all types of maneuvers trying to defeat the missile and break the lock-on, but the missile, just like that hound dog, persistently stayed on their path, moving closer and closer. He fired off bundles of chaff, thin pieces of tinfoil, designed to confuse and throw off the seeker head of the missile, but it ignored the chaff, flew right through it and continued after them, slowly closing the gap. The pilot knew he had only one desperate option left.

Chapter 15

The men on the ground scurried about getting the wounded and all of their equipment ready for the expected extraction. Clay and Rick stood transfixed watching as the approaching recon aircraft came out of the broken clouds. The helicopter, which had hung back for reasons of safety and self-preservation, was still not visible to them. Clay quietly observed Rick as he worked the radio to establish communications with both aircraft. Both men had their eyes on it as Rick provided information for the safest line of approach for the pick up. Several of the other team members had stopped the preparations to evacuate, to watch in excited silence as the aircraft became fully visible to them.

One of the other men yelled to Rick, "Shall I pop the smoke now, Rick?"

Rick thought about it for a moment, then said, "Sure, we're practically out of here! It shouldn't be a danger." The man heaved the cylindrical smoke grenade into the clearing and it fired, spurting a bright purple cloud of smoke that drifted up into the humid sky.

A profound sense of satisfaction came over Clay. He had done it! He'd returned and accomplished what he needed to do, rescue his buddies before they were brutally annihilated. There would be no more nightmares. He repeated his thoughts with a certain satisfaction. *He was done here. Did he want to return to that other life? He knew the answer now. This life held so much more excitement. He had never felt more alive in his life. The further he became involved in this strange journey, the better he liked it, savored it! No! He would not return, ever!* He continued to feel a distinct rush from everything he was experiencing.

Suddenly he heard shocking, vulgar exclamations from the others around him. "Damn! Will you look at that!"

"Sonavabitch! Where did that thing come from?" Somebody else said.

Clay and Rick looked up and in the direction of the aircraft. Rising rapidly out of the brush in the distance, like an angry Cobra, a thin line of white smoke headed for the lead aircraft. The thing weaved and dodged, making corrections as it steadily drew closer to the plane, like that deadly snake as it prepared to strike its prey. Barely perceptible at this distance, he could see at the tip of the smoke that it was a shoulder-launched missile. A moment later the aircraft sharply banked over and dove, executing a series of rapid dodging and weaving maneuvers in an attempt to break the lock of the seeker on the missile.

The aircraft continued through a series of abrupt attitude changes, banking, rolling, climbing, then diving unexpectedly toward the deck. As it approached closer to the ground, it would suddenly pull out and start climbing again as it continued its evasive moves, Clay thought. Clay also realized what the pilot was doing. The helicopter, a big, fat, slow moving and hot target for a missile would have time to distance itself from the imminent danger. The plane continued its series of wild gyrations.

"What the hell is he trying to accomplish?" Rick asked. "Why doesn't he just run?"

A low voice, next to Clay's ear sounding unmistakably like Gabe, gave him a quick rundown of what the pilot was doing. Apparently, only he could hear Gabe's voice.

In reply to Rick's question, Clay answered, "Okay, here's what I think he trying to accomplish. The pilot is playing a dangerous game of cat and mouse. What I think he's trying to do is keep away from the missile long enough till it runs out of fuel."

"Okay, sounds logical, but will it work? Will he be able to keep his distance long enough till that happens?"

"Well, you've got to figure that if the guerillas had another missile they would have fired it by now to finish off the plane. Looks like they don't, so I figure his strategy is, if he's real lucky, and the missile peters out, he'll lead the way for the helicopter to come and rescue us."

"That pilot's one ballsy, brave hombre!" Rick said.

"Yeah, I sure as hell agree. Especially considering he's putting his life and that of his copilot on the line to try and save us. He could just as easily cut and run at the first hint of trouble!"

Rick said, "I think I already know the answer to this, but I'll ask it anyway. How could the terrorists have possibly known?"

Clay thought about it for a moment, and then the voice was there again, giving him the answer. "It's pretty clear there obviously were others tuned in to our emergency frequency. Wouldn't be too difficult to do with the right equipment. They could buy it anywhere. They certainly have become more sophisticated as they must have a scanner to pick up radio transmissions and a radio. What is bothersome to me, is they appear to be going beyond the standard guns, RPG's, bombs and ambushes."

"I figure they had obtained an emergency radio from a crashed aircraft," Rick replied.

"That's a very good possibility. Clearly aircraft have gone down in this area of operations and many of the wreckages were probably picked clean before anyone got to them."

"The other possibility is the black market." Clay said.

"Yeah, that stands to reason. Yeah, I've heard it happened all the time in Vietnam, from the Vietnamese Generals on down to the lowest ranks!"

"Right you are buddy, there's your answer."

"So what do we do about it?"

"We hold our breathe and hang in there tight and hope that recon aircraft survives."

The pilot realized he could do little else. He knew this particular aircraft, extremely fast and maneuverable, was running out of time and airspace. The missile should have run out of fuel by now, but it kept dogging them. Both he and his copilot grunted and strained as the pilot tightly rolled, banked, turned, dove and put the aircraft through every conceivable maneuver he ever knew, but the missile continued to creep inevitably closer by the second.

"Okay, Rickenbacker, I'm starting to get a little nervous!" the copilot grunted as the pilot went into yet another high G roll and turn, "Time to get us the fuck outta here now!"

The pilot managed to grunt back, "The almighty Iceman nervous? You're bullshitting me, right?"

"Nope! I'm not. This is not looking good at all. We're in deep, deep steer manure!"

Rickenbacker just grunted his acknowledgement.

"Okay," the copilot said, "now's the time for you to show me all those hot moves you keep bragging about, the ones you inherited in your genes from your famous namesake!"

"Truth time!" The pilot managed to get out.

"Truth time?"

"Just in case, you're entitled to know."

"Know what?"

"I'm no relation to the famous World War 1 ace."

"I don't care! Just get us out of this! The copilot said. "You are the best damn pilot I've flown with! Now prove it!"

"Okay, quick! I got an idea. Where's that fucking antique flare gun you keep dragging around?"

"I have it."

"Well, partner, get ready to use it!"

"How?"

"Okay, I'm going to make a couple of quick turns to try and confuse that little bastard, then go into a power dive. That'll give us some extra speed. At the bottom I'll take this bird straight up, full power, till she stalls out. The dive should give us an extra second or two; we'll need it! At the top of the stall I'll drop her over on her right wing and that's where you come in. How many shells you have?"

"Four."

"Quickly! Load it and open your side window. When the she stalls and starts to drop to the right you'll have a face on view of the approaching missile. You only have a second or two. Fire the flare right at the missile and keep reloading and firing till you run out of ammo. Hopefully the burning magnesium from one of those flares will fake-out the missile."

"I knew you'd think of something, pal."

"Yeah, well, if this doesn't work, we're gonna be a smoking hole in the ground in short order!" the pilot replied. "Here we go, Iceman!" He threw the plane into a sharp bank.

Stiles groaned and strained against his safety harness, as the pilot broke left, rolled and then dove straight for the ground. The missile, an electronic robot, had a little difficulty keeping up with the instantaneous attitude changes of its human controlled target, but it corrected quickly, and even though it lost a few seconds, got back on track to the aircraft.

Under the strain of these abrupt maneuvers, the copilot reached into the side pocket of his seat and pulled out the flare gun and shells. It was difficult for him to do this under the turns and banks. He could hear the groan of the fuselage at each wild, erratic move that Rickenbacker made.

Stiles jammed the shells tightly between his legs so they wouldn't fly off his seat onto the deck of the aircraft and out of his harnessed reach. Cocking open the old pistol, he reached between his legs and pulled out a shell. Quickly inspecting it, he shoved it into the breach of the gun, slamming it shut. Getting ready, he slid open the small window to his right and jammed the loaded flare gun between his legs. The copilot knew his partner would need all the help he could get when they bottomed out of the dive. Keeping a sharp eye out the window, looking for the approach of the missile, a terrible thought pushed its way into his mind as he waited. Those were old shells he'd been dragging around for a long time. Suppose when he took aim at the missile, the gun misfired? Or, suppose it did fire, but the flare, composed of old material, had deteriorated to the point that it might not burst into a bright magnesium flare and just might sputter weakly. The thoughts gave him an involuntary chill, even though he was sweating profusely under the strain.

At the bottom of the dive, still going full power, the pilot yelled for help. The copilot grabbed his yoke and both men strained, pulling back hard on the plane's steering mechanism, trying to manhandle the aircraft out of its breakneck, downward dive.

At the bottom of the dive, grunting, sweating and struggling, the two men slowly pulled the aircraft out of its downward attitude and headed upward, the engines screaming mightily. With the giant push from the dive, the plane rose swiftly toward the heavens above, as though the banshees of hell were on its tail.

The aircraft rose upward as if on an express elevator, pushing both men backward in their seats. Up, up, up it flew with the momentum of the dive and the powerful radial engines pulling it upward into the thin air. Gradually it started to run out of impetus as the propellers clawed at the air, but then started to have difficulty pulling it further into the sky. The pilot knew what he was doing and kept the throttles jammed to their stops. At the apex of the climb, the plane ran out of the power to take it further upward and hesitated in its upward position for a second. Both men could hear the strident screech of the stall horn going off, even through their headphones.

"Get ready!" The pilot yelled.

A second later, at the top of the stall, the pilot pushed the controls to the right. He knew this would put his copilot in a good position to spot the missile. The aircraft rolled to the right and the copilot had a good view out his side window, as the plane rotated over toward the side, then the earth's gravity started to pull it toward the ground.

There it was, tracking them relentlessly like a bloodhound and getting closer by the second. *But I've got a surprise for you, you merciless bastard.* Knowing he didn't have a second to lose, the copilot pulled out the flare gun and wedged it hard against the sill of the window to steady his aim. There was no mistake that the dot rapidly approaching them was the Strela. Cocking the pistol, the copilot took a rough aim at the missile and squeezed the trigger. He heard a short pop and felt the light recoil of the flare gun as it fired. The flare arced out toward the missile, but there was something drastically wrong. The flare was not burning hot and bright as it was supposed to be doing. The sonavabitch was a dud! Holy shit! he thought. Of all times, just my luck! The flare flew through the air toward the missile, and the copilot hoped beyond hope that the missile would take the bait. He felt his heart drop as the missile ignored the flare and continued on its way to the stronger heat source, the planes engines.

"Sonavabitch, we're dead meat!" Stiles muttered. If he'd stopped to think about it, which he didn't, Stiles would have been surprised at himself that he was so able to do what he was doing with no conscious thought. Faster than his mind could think, he had the flare gun out of the window, slapped it open and grabbing another shell, threw it into the barrel and slammed it shut. Poking it back out the window, he took hasty aim at the incoming angel of death and quickly pulled the trigger with not a microsecond to lose; the missile had locked hard and was almost on them. He squeezed his eyes tightly closed, not wanting to see if this flare was a good one, praying and bracing himself for the inevitable impact of the missile.

Chapter 16

Clay, Rick and everyone else stopped what they were doing and watched in shocked silence at the wild maneuvering of the recon aircraft.

"Do you think he'll manage to evade that missile until it runs out of steam?" Clay asked.

"Hard to say," Rick said, concentrating on the wild aerial display above them all, "Only time will tell."

"Holy shit! Look at that," Clay said, as they watched the aircraft reach the top of its climb, begin its stall, then slowly drop on its wing to the right and head for the ground. "He fired a flare! But the damn missile is ignoring it," Rick said. Moments later they both saw a second flare fired from the aircraft. Both wondering if this would do the trick.

When the missile impacted his aircraft, the copilot prayed that he wouldn't feel any pain, and it would be over quickly. Squeezing his eyes shut tight in anticipation of the missile slamming into their starboard engine, the copilot was unprepared for what happened next. A tremendous explosion rocked the plane back on its wing. The plane shuddered like a big dog shaking off water from a bath, and continued flying. At the same moment, he heard the sharp, metallic patter of shrapnel, from the missile as it peppered the fuselage, but did no damage.

Opening his eyes, the copilot looked out his window in awe. The engine had suffered no outward damage and continued its solid, heavy, reassuring drone. Turning his head toward the pilot, Stiles saw Rickenbacker was struggle to pull the aircraft out of its dive and an inadvertent spin after the stall. Stiles grabbed his wheel and duplicated the pilot's movements. A few moments later they had gotten everything under control.

"Holy shit in heaven!" The pilot said, "We actually made it! And without a single scratch! Okay, time to get this show back on the road. Contact Rescue Seven and get'em back here." As he said this, the pilot was already steering the aircraft back on course, and headed out over the broad, brush covered plain for the location where Clay, Rick and the rest of the men waited anxiously on the ground.

"Roger that." The copilot replied as he changed radio frequencies and contacted the rescue helicopter.

Clay felt a strong sense of relief as he, Rick and the rest of the team watched the plane alter its course and begin once again, to move in their general direction.

"Where's the chopper?" Clay heard one of the men ask.

"I'm sure it won't be far behind, now that the way is clear again." Clay replied.

"Yeah," Rick said, "We better get all our gear together and get ready to get out of here, like pronto when that chopper gets here! If they didn't before, the guerillas sure as hell must know our location now. That smoke grenade we popped had to have been like waving a big, red flag at a bull!"

A few moments later their emergency radio crackled to life. "Grasshopper zero four, this is Ridge-runner. What is your status?"

"We have wounded and need a pick up ASAP." Rick replied.

"Okay, the search and rescue chopper is only a few minutes behind me."

"Affirmative."

"I have your coordinates and will fly top cover when Rescue Seven arrives at your position."

Rick depressed the transmit button and replied, "That's a roger, Ridge-runner. We're ready. Out."

The copilot carefully scanned the plain ahead of them as they moved in the direction of the coordinates they had been given. "Okay," He said, "I've got them. I see yellow smoke on the heading of 322 degrees. He could feel the plane change direction as the pilot corrected to the proper heading in response to the information from his copilot.

Contacting the team on the ground, the copilot said, "Grasshopper zero four, this is Ridge-runner. I see yellow smoke. Confirm."

A moment later Rick transmitted, "Ridge-runner, Grasshopper, affirmative, we have yellow smoke." All knew they had to go through this procedure to confirm they weren't flying into a smoke signal set up by the enemy as a trap.

"Roger, Grasshopper." The copilot replied. Immediately without further prompting, the copilot automatically contacted the rescue helicopter requesting they contact the team on the ground at the frequency he gave them.

"Grasshopper, this is Rescue Seven!" All heard the rescue helicopter, on the emergency radio.

"Seven, go!" Rick replied.

"We'll be there in five. We have your sitrep from Ridge-runner. Have your wounded ready to go. We'll board them first while you maintain perimeter guard, okay?"

"Okay, Rescue seven, we're ready for you. Good luck! Out," Rick replied, clicking off the microphone.

In the recon aircraft, the copilot felt a sense of relief. It was almost over. Just a few more minutes out here in Indian Country and then they would be back, safe and sound, at their base. He was already daydreaming and anticipating that first, frigid bottle of San Miguel, when the sky lit up in front of him. It looked like brightly lit, green ping-pong balls, slowly waving across the sky and moving toward them, trying to seek them out.

"Break left!" He screamed into his microphone, but he was an eye blink behind the pilot who had already rolled the plane over and was already starting to dive away from the approaching deadly menace.

"Jesus Christ! What did we ever do to deserve this warm reception?" the copilot shouted into his mic above the cockpit noise.

"Bastards have been laying low, probably figuring we'd continue on toward the bait once if we survived the missile." The pilot replied.

Diving away from the deadly wave, trying to make contact, the copilot watched as the bright green string moved closer and closer. He knew the bright green ping-pong balls were tracer rounds and in between each one was ten bullets, some armor piercing, some perhaps incendiary, from a heavy machine gun. They had to somehow get past this obstacle and come in from another angle to the crash site. Maybe the door gunner on the rescue helicopter could help. They were packing a small mini-gun aboard. That thing could probably crank out six hundred rounds a minute.

The pilot quickly put his aircraft into a ninety-degree turn in an attempt to avoid the pulsing menace trying to touch the plane with its deadly sting. As he did so, another heavy machine gun opened up below to their left, and they only got a glimpse at the last moment.

The pilot tried his best to evade this new threat, and he almost did, as the death-dealing string of lethal pearls converged with the right engine nacelle just as he dove away. It appeared that only a round or two had connected with the engine, but it was enough and the engine immediately burst into bright flames, black smoke from ruptured hydraulic lines poured out of the cowling, to the rear. Both men reacted automatically, activating the fire extinguisher while struggling to get the plane, now straining on one engine, under control. They had to take evasive action to get them away from the two heavy machine guns trying to converge and finish them off.

Chapter 17

Ambush!

"Damn! Did you see that?" Rick breathlessly said in shock.

"Yeah, the bastards! Sonavabitches were probably laying for them all along - which means, in my mind, they also know where we are, but are going for double their money!"

"Right, it's clear now what they're up to, they heard the emergency radios, figured a rescue team was on the way, waited to nail them first. Then they headed over to us and get payback for what we did to their other patrol that was attacking us."

"Nice people! But I wouldn't want them for in-laws!"

"Yeah, well there goes our ride, it looks like," Rick said glumly.

"You could be right, but I hope not. Let's see how this plays out. Those guys of ours still may have a few tricks up their sleeve."

Both men, along with the rest of the team, watched with rapt attention as the recon aircraft continued a series of evasive maneuvers, in its attempts to get past the guerillas' heavy machine guns. They also noticed something out of the ordinary. As the plane, on one engine, kept dodging the ground fire and kept the gunners' attention, the helicopter had subtly drifted closer to the danger zone without the terrorists, concentrating on the aircraft, taking notice.

"What the hell is the chopper trying to do?" Rick asked.

"Haven't a clue," Clay replied.

All eyeballs were glued to the drama unfolding above them in the sky. The rescue chopper continued to move closer and closer into the danger zone while the machine gunners, oblivious of this, concentrated on converging and connecting with the wildly maneuvering recon plane. The helicopter slowed in its forward movement, then stopped and drifted almost sideways. Moments later, to everyone's surprise, what appeared at first to be a pulsing red beam of light, erupted from the open doorway in the middle of the chopper and in the direction of the terrorist machine gunners.

Rick, Clay and the whole team watched with rapt attention, as the beam from the chopper seemed to concentrate on the terrorist's machine gun to their right. Neither gunner seemed to recognize the threat and didn't react until it was too late. Seconds later, a high-pitched racket reached Clay and the rest of the team that sounded remotely like a super fast chainsaw. A few seconds later, they witnessed an angry, black cloud of smoke slowly rising up into the air. Moments later, the reverberation reached their ears of a large explosion and the secondary sound of ammunition cooking off.

"Heard a lot about them, but never saw one in action, until now," Rick said with a touch of awe in his voice at what they were all seeing.

"I don't recall a lot about them, except they were used extensively in Vietnam and Iraq," Clay said, his memory from his past still a little foggy.

"Don't tell me you don't recall when they had that session and what was available to us for fire support?" Rick said, surprised.

"Yeah, I guess so." Clay said, not really remembering some things from his past life there, to which he had now returned. "Refresh my memory, why don't you?"

"Okay, what you saw was an upgraded version of the Gatling Gun used in Nam and elsewhere. But with a difference. It has been upgraded to an increased rate of fire and a few other bells and whistles!" Rich paused for a few seconds.

"Okay, don't keep me in the dark," Clay said, wanting to have the blank spaces filled in.

"It's used in other weapons platforms besides the AC-130, as you can plainly see with the chopper. Plus they have added more tracer ammo for the psychological effect. That solid red stream and the eerie buzz saw sound are specifically designed to create the impression that indeed it is a death ray in the eyes of the enemy. If you are on the ground and you see that solid band of red coming at you, it's hopefully enough to put the fear of Muhammad in you!"

"Looks like it achieved its goal, the other machine gun has gone silent and probably has high-tailed it out of the area or ducked into some gully to hide."

"Hopefully yes, so they can come in and snatch us up without any further problems. I had heard rumors that this crop of guerrillas had taken a page out of the book from Mogadishu, Somalia, and were mounting their heavy machine guns on the beds of Nissan and Toyota pick-up trucks. The call them "Technicals" for God only knows what reason. Very cheap, down and dirty! Bolt the gun to the bed of the pick-up and you've got a cheap, mobile weapons platform, serviced by just two men – and easily replaceable."

"That could very possibly be what we witnessed here. The only thing I'm really worried about is I have a feeling those bastards want that fat target real bad and they'll go to any length to get it!"

"The helicopter?"

"Yeah."

"Let's hope not, or we are totally and completely screwed!"

There was the sound of static on their radio, then the voice of the copilot in the recon aircraft. "Grasshopper, Ridgerunner, come in."

"Go Ridgerunner," Rick replied.

"We're on one engine, but I think we can still guide Rescue Seven to you. Then we've got to RTB due to damage.

Both Clay and Rick commented to each other that they were immensely impressed with the bravery of the two pilots in the recon aircraft with their willingness to continue the mission and not return to base immediately.

"Roger that Ridgerunner, and sincere thanks from all of us. Out."

The team had gathered their wounded and all the gear they could carry, ready for a rapid load into Rescue Seven. They all watched with anticipation as the recon aircraft again headed in their direction. All noticed the helicopter followed cautiously at a discreet distance with the knowledge that the other truck mounted heavy machinegun was still lurking out there somewhere, in the heavy brush, like a rattlesnake ready to strike at a moments notice.

The recon plane was closing on them fast. Clay could see that the fire in the starboard engine had been extinguished and it looked like the pilots had regained almost full control of the aircraft. Staring upward as the plane passed overhead, it then began a large, lazy circle around them, observing the surrounding terrain for danger. The rescue helicopter began a gradual sloping descent in their direction. Being the big, fat, juicy target that it presented, the crew was extremely wary of the missing heavy machine gun.

Suddenly, off to the team's far left, in the distance, an evil string of green tracers from the other lurking machinegun arced up toward the helicopter. All were aware that a hit on one of the vital controls, such as the tail rotor, would cause the aircraft to lose control and possibly crash. They watched in horror as the green ping-pong balls of the tracers converged on the chopper, all well aware there were ten rounds in-between each tracer, some armor piercing, some incendiary.

Before the gunner in the chopper could react, the team heard someone frantically yelling into the radio, "We're taking hits, we're taking hits!" The helicopter rocked back and swung to face the threat at an angle, giving the gunner an unobstructed field of fire. Moments later he opened up with the Gatling gun, homing in on the source of the machinegun. As if the other gunner had anticipated his move, it immediately ceased firing. A red stream of hell raked the area, as the gunner searched for his elusive tormentor, but to no avail, the elusive snake-in-the-grass had slithered away. The gunner in the chopper stopped firing, but continued to search the area for any kind of movement.

They all listened as the radio on the ground crackled to life again as Rescue Seven communicated with the recon aircraft. What began to unfold before their eyes chilled them to the bone, even in the heat and humidity of their jungle location. A small, evil looking stream of black smoke started trailing out of the exhaust ports of the chopper, more than normal. It was clear, something vital had been hit, even though the craft continued to fly.

"Ridgerunner, this is Seven."

"Go ahead, Seven."

"We've taken a couple of nasty hits where it hurts. I'm experiencing control problems. I'm afraid we can't take the chance of landing and taking the team aboard, and getting in the air again. Sorry, but we're going to have to abort the mission and RTB."

The team on the ground listened with trepidation, their hearts in their mouths, their hopes dropping into a deep, dark hole.

"Understood, Seven. We will fly cover for you." Then the copilot of the recon aircraft addressed the men on the ground. "I'm very sorry, Grasshopper, but we can't take a chance. Without sufficient air cover and that machinegun still out there, we can't take the chance. If the chopper lands and takes the team aboard and then gets off the ground with that heavy load, it will be an even bigger target. We can't afford to lose both the chopper and your team. Understood?"

With a heavy heart, Rick replied, "We understand, Ridgerunner."

"We will have another team back out here at first light with air cover."

Rick looked at Clay and the rest of the team and shook his head in the negative, before replying. "Thanks, Ridgerunner, appreciate the thought, but we can't take the chance. This is an open channel; they already know we're here and they will be coming for us soon. We can't hang around. We will try to re-contact you from wherever we are. Thanks for trying and good luck to both of you on your return."

Both aircraft commanders rogered back to the team on the ground and began to egress from the area with a great deal of caution. The team watched with heavy hearts as the sounds of the aircraft faded, and the rescue craft disappeared into the distance in the canyon.

Clay could see the hopelessness and despair of the situation they were now in, reflected in their dirty, exhausted faces. He was surprised to see the same expression of defeat on Rick's face. He had always thought of him as being stronger of will.

"*This can't be allowed to happen,*" he thought, angered at the terrorists that had snatched salvation away from them. It has been so close. He had to come up with something to resolve their critical situation, so he walked away from the group to think and get his mind straight. He verbalized his thoughts out loud as he walked. "There's got to be a way out of this mess," he said. "We just can't roll over and give up. I've seen the consequences of that in my dreams."

A familiar voice behind him said, "That's right, Clay. You've come too far to let them give up now!"

"Gabe?"

"Yes, it's me. I told you I'd always be with you, remember?"

"Yes, now that you mention it, I do. So, now what the hell are we gonna do? We can't wait for the morning and the rescue aircraft. It will be too late then. The terrorists are sure to come at us tonight."

"Count on it, if you and your team stick around."

"Okay, so...?"

"I want you to use your brain and think. You've got a good head on your shoulders. Think! Push it hard and a solution will surface. It might not be exactly what you had in mind, but it will be better than doing nothing and waiting for your fate."

"Okay, Gabe, I'm thankful you are here to help. I'll give it my best."

"No, Clay, you've got to give more than that. You've got to pull them back together and give them hope. Now, go do it!"

"Okay, I will." Turning, Clay headed back to the group.

When he reached Rick, his buddy gave him a funny look and asked, "Are you okay, good buddy?"

"Yeah, fine, why?"

"I was watching you out there by yourself. I could swear it looked like you were having a conversation with the invisible man!"

"Oh, that! No I'm fine. I just do some of my best thinking by verbalizing it out loud. Kind of like having a conversation with myself."

"Oh? Really!" Rick said doubtfully. "I've never seen you do this before. You sure you're okay?"

"Yeah, man, I'm fine as frog's hair. Now let's talk abut getting the hell outta here as soon as possible. Well, before nightfall at the very least."

"Okay, so what do you have in mind?"

"Let's chew on this for a minute and get creative. There's got to be someplace else where they can get in a heavy chopper, like that big Sikorsky they used, into a landing zone, without those murderous bastards waiting to knock it down!"

Rick pulled out the map and spread it on the ground. Both men knelt down and looked closely at the map. "It's an old map, left over from when the Japanese occupied the island, but it has been reproduced with a number of changes. There are still a lot of errors because the Japanese copied the maps from the old Spanish ones of the area. Plus rivers and streams change course and a host of other irregularities," Rick explained.

"That's just wonderful! Just what I needed to hear!" Clay said, as a way of understatement. "Any other good news?"

"Sure, now that you mention it. Along with everything else I've heard on the grapevine that there are still some Japanese soldiers left over from WW II, still hiding on Mindanao, maybe even in these mountains. Rumors say they think the war is still going on! We've had reports from other patrols of odd sightings and strange occurrences, rations being stolen in the middle of the night, claims that they were followed, but never seeing anything but tracks, momentary glimpses of raggedy, old individuals disappearing into the brush carrying what looked like old bolt action rifles. This was certainly not some local Philippine villagers, we can be sure of that, kind of scary in a way."

"Any other uplifting news?" Clay asked.

"No, that's about the size of it," Rick said. He touched a spot on the map with his index finger, "We're right about here."

"In all this area, there's got to be some place that's safe for us to use," Clay said, closely scanning the map. He moved his finger across the map, almost as if an invisible finger was on top of his and guiding it. *"Gabe, it's you, isn't it?"* he thought. His finger came to a stop at a small, open area between the mountains with some strange coded markings on it. He had almost missed it and neither one would have seen it if not for the bits of guidance he was receiving.

"What about this place? It looks promising. It's a little bit of a trek, but I think we can make it fairly quickly."

Rick looked at where Clay had his finger. "I would have missed it if you hadn't pointed it out to me." Rick told Clay.

"Do you know what these coded markings are?"

Rick took a closer look and thought about it for a few moments, then said, "Yeah, I think I know about that place, but it still might be dangerous."

"Why?"

"It's an old Japanese garrison and airfield that the Philippine Army used occasionally in the past. They were using the landing field as an LZ, but the rebels found out and it got too hot, from what I heard.

There was a lot of gossip on the grapevine about it. The place hasn't been used in a long time and is abandoned, from the stories."

"Stories?" Clay said.

"Yeah, according to the grapevine, the Philippine Army walked into a big, hairy ambush there by the rebels and barely was able to fight there way out of it."

"So what happened afterwards?"

"After that, they totally abandoned the place as being too hot a landing zone to land their troops. Now nobody goes there, supposedly, not even the terrorists, or so we've been led to believe. There have even been stories that it's haunted."

"That just might be the ticket!" Clay said. "A haunted LZ that maybe even the terrorists might hesitate approaching!"

"But if we head off in the direction of the airfield, they'll figure it out immediately or sooner, and they'll be waiting for us! These are not stupid people we're dealing with here." Rick cautioned.

"Right. But if we feed them a red herring, as the saying goes, and head for a more obvious destination, they'll hopefully buy it. Then we figure if we divert to the abandoned LZ - by the time they've got their heads together, we'll be long gone!" Clay replied.

"Not a bad idea. It just might work. Let me take another look at that map," Rick said, bending over the map.

"It better work!"

Closely scanning the map, Rick said, "Okay, here's an LZ that has been used, but I wouldn't recommend it because I think they have a spotter living nearby and as soon as he hears helicopter engines, he gets on his radio and the bad guys come running."

"Okay, but they don't know that we know. So we'll do a ruse like we're heading for that location." Clay offered.

"But, when we head out of here, they're sure to be right behind us!"

Clay thought about that for a few moments, then said, "Not if someone stays behind to slow them down and gives the team a good head start."

"Yeah, and who do you have in mind?" Rick looked unhappy at the thought.

"Me, old buddy!"

"You? Bullshit. I know what you're going to do. You're going to sacrifice yourself for us. I won't have it! End of story! Besides, it's my job. You saved us once. Now you lead the team out of here," Rick said, iron in the tone of his voice.

"So when did you get this martyr complex, asshole!"

"Up yours. You're out of line."

"Bullshit! You're the patrol leader and I'm just an appendage! I owe you guys that much! Besides, I'll catch up with you after I slow them down. I promise!"

"Yeah, sure you will! What the hell are you thinking with talk like that? Are you bucking for the CMH?"

"Are you kidding me? Do I look like Congressional Medal of Honor material to you?"

"Yeah, asshole you actually do after that stunt you pulled getting back to our lines."

Clay thought about it for a moment, and then said, "Look, my life is not important. It's my job to see that you all get back safe and alive."

"Since when did you become our keeper? We can take care of ourselves."

"Okay, I'm not going to argue with you. I'm staying, that's it, period!"

"Where in the hell are you coming from with this line of hero crap?"

"Look, just leave it be. Okay? This is the way I want it. Besides I can handle myself. You know that now!"

Rick gave Clay a strange look and said, "This is not at all the same Clay I remember. Yes, I can see that you can, from all the trophies you brought back with you, from your little excursion to get the canteens filled!"

"They aren't trophies. We're gonna need these weapons and ammo because you said we're close to being tapped out on out regular M-16 ammunition."

"Okay, if that's the way you want it?"

"It is." Clay said.

"Right, now let's put our heads together and come up with a decent plan of action." Rick finished.

After discussing their options for a while, studying the map, both men stood up and looked at the rest of the team. It was clear on the faces of the men. Everyone was despondent, as if their one and only chance of escape had evaporated before their eyes. It appeared that most everyone had gone back to believing that the chances of survival were once again about zero, unless some kind of miracle happened. They also seemed to feel that any miracle would not be forthcoming soon enough to save them from a vengeful enemy, who would have no compunction whatsoever about killing them all, after torturing and mutilating them before hand.

Clay looked at them with a mixture of pity and anger. He turned to Rick, "Would you mind if I said a few words to them?"

"Not at all, be my guest."

"Hey, guys, listen up. Let me have your attention," Clay said in a commanding voice he didn't even know he had in him. "We don't have time to sit around here moping. The terrorists know where we are and for sure, they'll be coming for us in force, loaded for bear! We can't possibly hold them off until the rescue craft gets here in the morning. So Rick and I have come up with an alternative plan that may save our asses! Or at the very least, give us a fighting chance. All yours, Rick."

Sitting down, he listened for a moment as Rick explained the rough plan. Looking at their grimy faces, he could see a small seed of renewed hope. Examining the map again while Rick talked, Clay's mind started to turn over the series of events that had led to this moment. He was surprised at the change in him. He'd never been this aggressive in the past. He recalled with disgust, that in his past world he just went with the flow and let other people take the lead; he had been a follower, just putting his time in, treading water and waiting to get out of the service. Now, when he thought about it, he realized a subtle change had occurred in him, he was experiencing a rush from all the excitement. "*Is this really happening to me? Am I turning into somebody I don't know? Is this the real me?*" he wondered. Clay realized he had become a different person along the journey to this moment in time. While he had been extremely self-confident in his old job, this was a different kind of self-confidence. It was physical and he felt very much in control of his destiny. In this new beginning he began to feel overconfident, as if nothing could harm him. His old persona cautioned him subconsciously that this was dangerous thinking, just as Gabe had, but he still let it grow within himself.

After Rick finished talking to the rest of the team, he and Clay studied the map again. They discarded several alternate routes that were too plainly obvious and where the terrorists would be watching for them. They finally settled on a winding route, through the mountains. They traced the meandering route, which avoided areas where terrorists might have easy access to them and small villages. The local villagers were known to have questionable loyalty to the government in Manila, due to mistrust dating way back to the days of the Moros. Clay knew they didn't call this island the "Land of Broken Promises" for nothing.

When both men stood up and faced the rest of the team, someone in the group said, "Okay, so what's the plan?"

Rick looked at Clay and said, "You pulled us out of the pickle we were in, so why don't you go ahead and explain how you plan to get all the extra weapons, gear and wounded co-pilot out of here?"

Grabbing a machete from one of the packs, Clay looked at the men gathered around him and Rick, waiting in anticipation with renewed hope, for answers to the primary question on everyone's mind…escape! No one said a word as they waited for Clay to speak. The silence was deafening and unearthly after the departure of the aircraft. There was a shift in the mild breeze that had come up as Clay was about to speak to the group. He stopped, raised his index finger to his lips and whispered, "Quiet! Listen!" He swiveled his head around trying to get a fix on the sound he was sure he had just heard, drifting in on an errant gust of wind. Straining hard, they all listened. From the direction that they had last seen tracer rounds rising toward the aircraft, they faintly heard the distinctive sound of a heavy engine.

"We've run out of time!" Clay said, with urgency in his voice. "Those are not friendlies we're hearing. Looks like intelligence may have grossly underestimated the capabilities of the guerillas. I don't know what that is, but it could be anything, even a tank! We've got to move, fast! They're coming!"

Chapter 18

With a renewed sense of urgency, Clay continued explaining what needed to be done and started assigning tasks. While he deferred to Rick as the leader of the patrol, Clay assumed the job of a sort of operations manager, no doubt a throwback from his successful organizing ability in his previous life. He felt good that he was doing something productive to help the team and no one, including Rick, questioned this new role he had assumed.

"Okay, I know I'm repeating myself," Clay said to the group, "but this is the way Rick and I see our situation. We've got to put as much distance away from this place, as soon as possible. We are rapidly running out of time!"

Rick added, "Whatever's out there, it's headed our way and I guarantee you, it's not a rescue party! We're not in any position to take on a heavily armed force, so we've gotta get outta here ASAP!"

"What about the wounded man, he can't walk?" One of the others added.

"To leave anyone behind is a sentence of death! Those bastards take no prisoners, especially wounded. No one gets left behind, you're all coming home, one way or another! Count on it!" Clay said, surprising everyone.

Clay took over again, saying, "There's no way that we've ever going to be able to disguise our tracks with the wounded guy and all the essential gear we need to take with us. But we can make that work to our favor."

"Oh?" One of the men said.

"You'll see," Clay replied, "But first we have to get everything we can use out of the chopper. We'll leave the M-60 door gun mainly because we have less than a can of ammo left, I understand. Get rid of the bolt and firing pin in the jungle. Next I want to put our demolitions and booby trap artists to work. Who're the best at that?"

They all looked at him in surprise as if he'd lost his marbles. Two of the guys raised their hands and said, "Shit Clay, you know that!"

"Yeah, guess I did. Musta banged my head harder than I thought. Memory is a bit hazy. Just wanted to confirm that you were still the best at it." he said, covering up his mistake.

Turning to Rick, he said, "I think the best thing to do is booby trap the remains of the chopper. When they get here, they're sure to go poking around inside of it. Perfect situation."

"I get it," one of the demo men said. "The whole thing will go up and if we're lucky, take out a few of the bastards at the same time."

Rick said, "Agreed, let's just hope they don't have a talented booby trap expert along with them and find our little surprise."

"True. There's a sure fire way around that," Clay said.

"Tell us, we're all ears." Scotty, one of the other team members said.

"I'll explain shortly, but right now let's break out the blocks of C-4 and the detonators."

Clay recalled that they usually brought along several blocks of the C-4 plastic explosive, in case they had to blow a bridge or something. Then inspiration hit him when he remembered that they always brought along a couple of Claymore Mines. He had an idea that would put one of the nasty explosives, containing thousands of tiny ball bearings, to very effective use and maybe slow down the pursuit that was sure to occur. He knew that anyone in the kill zone of the Claymore would be literally shredded. Calling over one of the demolitions guys, he said, "Okay, this is where I want you to conceal a Claymore, so it will cover this area." He pointed to a section near the open side of the chopper.

After the demo men set to work, Clay took a machete and joined a small work crew in the nearby brush. "Okay, here's what we need to do. Cut down the longest pieces of bamboo you can find. Try to get at least ten to twelve feet. Get at least twelve pieces."

"What the hell are you going to do with those?" One of the others asked.

"Make a different kind of litter, like you've never seen before."

"Yeah, but bamboo is so flexible and bends."

"True, bamboo is actually a grass, but it grows in some parts of China to timber size. It is extremely strong and in some parts of the orient, they make scaffolding out of it. It also makes extremely hard and beautiful hardwood floors. So how about that?"

"Shit, that's amazing. Never thought of it that way. Always thought of it as a pest that popped up all the time in my parent's backyard."

"There are many different species of bamboo. With what you cut down we're going to make a travois for the wounded man and another for our extra gear."

"A what?"

"You'll see. I'll explain in a few minutes, but first let's hustle and get the pieces cut. Time is short," he said as he lopped off a nice long length of bamboo.

After they had dragged all the cut pieces the short distance to their site and dropped them to the ground, Clay said, "Okay, next, before I show you what to do with all these lengths of bamboo, I want you to give me all your ponchos out of your packs. Just drop them in a pile here."

After the men had deposited all the ponchos next to the pile of poles, Clay said,

"Okay, let me show you how I want these poles put together. I'll give you all a hand, to get you started." Stepping over to the pile, Clay selected three similar lengths of bamboo poles of similar length. "Take three lengths of bamboo like these and tie them together with nylon parachute cord," he said, as he demonstrated how he wanted it done. "Bind them together at three or four different places along the length of the poles. One man holds the poles, while the other wraps and ties. Make them as tight as you can get them because they will be carrying a heavy load.

When all the poles had been tied in this fashion, he had them lay the poles down side by side lengthwise, each pair about twenty-four inches apart. "Okay, now lay the ponchos, overlapping them from top to bottom on top of the sets of poles. Make the overall length of the ponchos about six and a half feet. Leave about three feet near the top of the poles and about two feet near what will be the bottom."

When they had finished doing this, Clay took a long piece of olive drab colored parachute cord that they all carried with them for emergencies and cut it into smaller sections. Next, he laid down a length every foot or so on each side of the ponchos. "Okay, here's what we're going to do next. Take each pole out from under the poncho and lay them lengthwise on top of the overlapped ponchos at the outer edges."

After they all performed this step he said, "Now, roll the lengths of bamboo poles around the ponchos several times until the wrapped poles are about two feet apart. This will give strength to the sides."

When this step was done, he stood back and said to the team members, "What you have now are what looks a lot like overly long stretchers, but that is not what they are going to be. As I said before, leave a few feet open near the top of each pair of wrapped poles."

Finishing this, Clay quickly moved on to the next step, knowing time was critical and the terrorists might be better organized than they thought and start arriving shortly. Time was of the essence. Demonstrating the next step as he explained, Clay showed the team members how to cut a small slit in the poncho near the poles at each spot where the nylon cord was laid out. Then he had them insert the cord into the hole and wrap it tightly around the pole several times at each location and tie it off.

"I know what you're thinking. It looks like an overly long stretcher, right? But it isn't. What you've just put together is an old Plains Indian method of transporting loads over long distances with a minimum of strain. As I told you before, it's called a Travois. It will beat having to carry a regular stretcher along the trail we will have to follow."

"So what were you, some kind of Boy Scout? Never would have believed it of you, crazy man!" one of the team said.

"Hey Scudder!" Clay said, addressing the man who had just commented on his creation, "Don't go knocking it until you've given it a trial run! Guaranteed, no pain, no strain, no shit, I kid you not!"

"You are shitting us, right?" Claude, the big boned kid named from Georgia commented sarcastically.

"No, really! It's going to make it a helluva lot easier to transport the wounded copilot and all the extra gear and weapons I collected along the way. We may well have dire need of all of this stuff before this little party is over. And, by the way, yeah, I was a Boy Scout, you cracker asshole!" Clay threw back at the trooper.

Claude took the reference to being called a cracker well, instead of getting pissed off at Clay, at the old Yankee derogative aimed at Southerners, he said, "Okay, Clay, no offence intended. Just not used to this sort of thing."

The other team member, a strong looking black guy from Chicago named Roscoe said, "So okay, how are we supposed to use these *Rube Goldberg* devices you had us put together?"

"What I believe is best is for all of us to take rotating turns in shifts, carrying the upper end of the poles. Here, I'll show you how this works." The men gathered around the finished litters in a group as Clay continued. "Scudder, can you step over here and give me a hand?"

"Sure boss." he said laughing.

"Look, I'm only trying to make things easier for us! I'm nobody's boss."

"Okay, just kidding you."

"All right, here's the best way. Scudder, step over here by the left side of the upper end of the poles and face forward, okay?" When he had done this, Clay said," The man on the left lays the pole over his right shoulder, the man on the right lays the poles over his left shoulder. Everybody understand?" There was a chorus of yes's and Clay continued. "Okay, here we go, reach down and pick up the poles." Both men reached down and raised the poles and set them down on their shoulders.

"Next step. We need cushioning for the poles, so take out any excess clothing or any kind of blanket that you might have or might be in the chopper. It needs to be cut into strips, wrapped and tied around the upper ends so you will have decent padding for your shoulders. The men went to work on this chore quickly, instinctively knowing time was growing very short. When this was done, they loaded the essential gear on one Travois and the wounded copilot on the other.

"Time to move out," Rick said to the assembled men, "Clay and I have discussed this. There is no way we can hide our tracks, so the only thing we can do is slow them down and discourage them." Nodding at Clay, Rick added, "Clay has chosen to stay behind temporarily to make certain the demolitions go off. We just can't take a chance of the guerillas discovering where we set the charges. The two demo guys will show Clay the set-up and then catch up with us. Clay will follow after he blows the demolitions when the bad guys get to the clearing. Let's move!"

The litter bearers shouldered their loads and slowly trudged after the rest of the team out of the clearing and onto the old game trail. Passing by him, all his buddies acknowledged him with nods of their heads and quick hand shakes. Clay watched them depart with a touch of sadness, hoping that the odds were with him and he'd get to see them again in this world.

The two demolition men stood close by, waiting in anticipation for instructions. Clay gave them a quick smile of confidence that he didn't altogether feel and said, "Show me what you've done and how to control it and then I want you both to hot-foot it outta here and catch up with the team."

"What about you, Clay?" one of the men asked.

"I have to see this through. It's the only way we can be sure that everything goes as planned."

"First, let me show you how we've rigged the chopper and the M-60 machine gun," the senior of the two said. After showing how the explosives were arranged to be the most effective, they moved to where the Claymore mine was disguised in some high grass.

"Where are the controls to set all this off?" Clay asked.

Both men nodded toward a ditch that had the look of a streambed for runoff during the monsoon season. He immediately saw it was deep enough to conceal him nicely. "The electric detonating wires are well camouflaged, buried in the sand and terminate at a small, hand held controller over there. That's your spot. The gully is deep enough for you to hide in when the main body gets to the clearing. No one should find the wires, even if they have a booby trap expert looking, before you're ready to set them off. At least that's what we're hoping. But of course you never know!"

"Sounds good so far."

"We left a lot of stuff laying around and in the chopper to draw the scavengers in. The explosives are rigged so when you blow them, everything including the chopper will be destroyed. The Claymore is angled out into the clearing like the base of a triangle. The pattern should finish off anyone not standing close to the chopper. We are guessing, but there will probably be quite a crowd since they are probably thinking they've got us cornered."

"Right," Clay said, "And it also means they will come in force as they know we're not going to just roll over and give in. They smell blood and they'll be coming for the kill! Now, you two better go."

"Okay, man and good luck to you. Hope to see you soon."

"Right!" Clay said as he watched the two men trot off. After the departure, a feeling of being all alone in the middle of nowhere clouded his mind. While he hadn't heard anything, he hoped Gabe was close by watching over him. Clay had watched sadly as his teammates had put the dead pilot in a rubber body bag and carried him into the jungle for burial, marking the spot for later retrieval. *There would be no defiling or mutilation of their dead soldier by the enemy,* he thought, recalling the incident years ago in Mogadishu, Somalia.

Jumping down into the ditch, Clay uprooted several large clumps of dead bushes and created a temporary hiding place surrounded by them. He made a guess based on what had occurred when the helicopter tried to land and assumed the enemy would be coming from the surrounding area to his right front. He positioned himself on the slope of the streambed, facing the clearing behind some foot high dead grass and ground hugging brush. From this vantage point, he had a good view of the clearing and felt well concealed.

Stressed out by the continuous and rapid-fire series of events that had occurred in such a short period of time, a heavy blanket of fatigue finally overwhelmed him, now that he was totally alone. Laying there, scanning the clearing through the dead weeds and grass to his front, Clay felt his eyelids unconsciously begin to droop. He caught himself several times, shook his head to clear it and even slapped his face to get him out of this creeping stupor, but the strong desire to close his eyes always came slithering back. Finally, against his better judgment, he convinced himself, that the guerillas wouldn't be here all that quickly. He needed to refresh himself, if only for a few minutes to be fully alert when the enemy did arrive, so he gave in to the urge.

Lowering his head, he rested his forehead on his folded hands in front of him, and gratefully let his eyes close. Only for a few seconds, he kept saying to himself. He was aware that his body was not used to the exertions he had been experiencing in this new world he had found himself thrust into, but was experiencing changes occurring in his system that had him feeling he was that same age again when he had first visited this island.

Within seconds, exhaustion caught up with him and he dropped off into a deep, dreamless sleep. It was a blissful feeling with no cares or worries. While his conscious mind slept, his subconscious acted as a guardian and stayed alert.

When it happened, it was like a lightening jolt, the simple snap of a dry twig, very close to where he hid. The sound brought him fully awake in a microsecond and he was about to react when strong hands clamped over his mouth and held his body in place. His instinct told him that the next thing he would experience would be the feeling of icy cold, razor sharp steel slicing across his throat.

Chapter 19

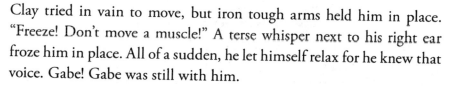

Clay tried in vain to move, but iron tough arms held him in place. "Freeze! Don't move a muscle!" A terse whisper next to his right ear froze him in place. All of a sudden, he let himself relax for he knew that voice. Gabe! Gabe was still with him.

"I'm going to remove my hand from your mouth, don't talk, only whisper!" Gabe instructed.

"What the hell is going on?" Clay whispered urgently when the hand was removed. Releasing his tight hold on Clay and easing to the side, Gabe said, "Ever so slowly turn your head to the right. Now, closely watch the row of brush on top of the far bank at the edge of the ditch about fifty yards away."

As he focused his eyes on the area, Gabe pointed out, Clay noticed the long shadows. It was now late afternoon and dusk would be here soon. Seeing this, Clay realized he must have been more exhausted than he thought for he had fallen totally asleep. Dangerous in this country, he cautioned himself.

Clay continued to strain his eyes on the spot. Something peculiar caught his attention; the large piece of brush in the middle of the row seemed to move slightly in an unnatural way. Clay strained his eyes because he thought he was seeing things. Then, ever so slowly, it appeared the brush was growing, as it slowly rose. When it rose to man height, Clay knew. It was one of the guerrillas attired in what the American Military called a *Gilly Suit,* an all-encompassing camouflage suit with hood and various pieces of the native vegetation attached to it to enhance the image that looked literally like a pile of dry vegetation. But there was no mistaking the long and lethal weapon wrapped in camouflaged burlap that the terrorist carried. The man carried a first class sniper rifle. Clay immediately recognized it as a Russian Dragunov SVD, highly accurate and one of the best rifles around for this purpose, although he realized someone would argue this.

Sniper that almost got Dixon

The sniper must have crawled into place while he was asleep, Clay thought. "When did he show up?"

"While you were having your beauty rest, Tonto! Good thing you don't gab in your sleep!" Gabe whispered back sarcastically.

"What's the story? What do you think he's doing here?"

"My best guess is that he's an advance scout to see if your team is still around, check out the overall situation and maybe add a couple of scalps to his belt, while causing confusion."

"So, that would probably mean the rest of the group is not far behind and will be showing up shortly, correct?"

"Right, so stay sharp! No more naps! I'm going to go and check out a few things myself."

"Do you have to go?" Clay asked in a concerned voice, as his confidence ebbed a tiny bit at the thought of facing the unknown once again.

"Yes, don't worry, I'll be around if you need me. I'm sure you've got the ability to handle the rest of this situation with no problem."

"Gee, I wish I had your confidence in me!" Clay said, half jokingly.

Winking at Clay, Gabe silently crawled away, while Clay steeled himself for the coming confrontation, telling himself that he could handle the situation.

He carefully watched the movements of the terrorist sniper as the man slowly worked his way down the gentle slope of the ditch. When he set foot on the streambed, the canny sniper paused and suspiciously scanned his surroundings, for being careful like this is what kept him alive, Clay recognized. Clay could see from the man's actions that this individual was a professional and not some wild-eyed radical terrorist.

Clay watched with interest, knowing the man was meticulously checking one-hundred and eighty degrees for any slight movement, disturbed ground or wilted foliage – a sign that he was not alone. Satisfied, he started to move toward the stream, then curiously he stopped and turned to look down the streambed to where Clay lay, tensely hidden among the pile of dead brush.

While Clay knew the sniper could not hear him breathing, he still held his breath. The terrorist knelt down, lay the deadly rifle across his knee for a quick response and pulled the camouflage back from the upper part of his face. It was as if the man had a sixth sense, Clay thought, feeling exposed as if he were laying there with no cover. As the terrorist focused on his hiding place, Clay stared into dark, steely eyes that were more like the eyes of a venomous snake then that of a human. Clay was afraid that making eye contact with the killer would somehow tip his hand. Bothered by what might happen next, he felt a droplet of sweat roll down his forehead and go into his eye, causing it to burn. He froze in place and focused his eyes downward, trying to imagine himself invisible.

When he looked up again he saw the sniper standing, slowly advancing in his direction, the Dragunov pointed out in front of him at waist level and at Clay's hideaway. As the man moved toward him, Clay slid his hand down his leg, undid the snap and pulled his fighting knife out of its sheath. At the same time, he brought his right leg up to a position like a loaded spring so that he could leap up and attack the sniper if he got any closer. He gauged his chances because he knew that this sniper's rifle was very unusual. He recalled that most special rifles made for this purpose were bolt action for greater accuracy, but this was not the case here. The Dragunov was semi-automatic and a sniper could get off more than one shot at him from that short distance when he went after the man.

His odds were not very good, but it was all he had, should the man get any closer. He steeled himself for what was on the way. Examining himself again inwardly, Clay realized again there had been a subtle change in him mentally and physically since he had found himself in this situation. He wondered a little about himself because subconsciously he had become almost eager to take on the confrontation.

Clay tensed and readied himself as the man warily moved in his direction. Then unaccountably, the man stopped, put his hand up to his ear cuplike and appeared to be listening to something. That's when Clay realized he and the team were in more trouble than anyone had realized. It looked like this guy was wearing what appeared to be an up to date digital radio. That meant to him that all the terrorists were in communication which would make their bid to escape much harder. The sniper listened for a few moments to his earplug, then spoke briefly, in a low tone into the lip microphone by his cheek. Clay obviously couldn't hear what was being said, but it appeared the terrorist had received his orders from his higher up somewhere nearby. The man stopped his forward progress toward Clay's hideout and abruptly changed direction, working his way up the forward slope of the streambed. Reaching the top, he carefully moved off, taking a path that crossed Clay's line of sight to the helicopter about fifty or so feet out. He watched as the guerilla warily moved over the sand and weed choked ground, angling back and forth, but generally moving in the direction of the aircraft. The man had his head bent over, as if he looked for something. Clay figured the conversation with his superior might have had something to do with this behavior. At first Clay thought the man might be looking for land mines, but it turned out to be worse than that.

About fifty feet or so from the ditch, at a slightly oblique angle from where he lay, Clay saw the man stop and start moving his foot back and forth over the sandy ground as if he had discovered something. Clay got the distinct feeling that their little explosive surprise party for the enemy had possibly been found out. The electrical wires attached to the series of explosives did not go in a direct line of sight between Clay and the chopper, but branched out at angles.

The guerilla stopped what he was doing and bent over. He appeared to be closely inspecting the dirt at his feet. Kneeling down, he carefully placed the lethal sniper rifle by his side and got down on both his hands and knees. Some stupid little thing must have raised his suspicions, Clay thought, but he'd never know for sure. Maybe the man was just a suspicious type. Whatever it was Clay, knew he had to do something, and soon, or all would be lost if he wasn't able to carry out his mission of slowing down the enemy.

Kneeling in the dirt, Clay watched with trepidation as the sniper dug his hands into it and probed around. Suddenly, he stiffened as if he had encountered something. Pulling his right hand out of the dirt, he held a length of wire in his fingers. He dragged an extra few feet of wire out of the dirt and began to closely inspect it. The man had found one of the wires buried in the dirt and connected to several C-4 charges laid out in and around the crash site. Clay didn't know which particular charge the electrical wire was attached to, but he couldn't allow the terrorist to damage it or disconnect it in any way.

The sniper glanced to his left, in the general direction of where Clay lay in concealment. He tensed when he saw the terrorist inspecting the area where he was hidden. For whatever reason, the guerrilla chose not to follow the wire toward where Clay lay hidden and turned his attention to the wire to his right. Clay felt his body relax and let out a low sigh of relief.

Standing up, the terrorist roughly started pulling up the wire out of the dirt until he could clearly see that this particular section of wire led directly to the helicopter. He had exposed about eight feet of the wire as Clay watched the man with horror. The sniper reached his hand inside his Gilly suit and came out holding a wicked-looking fighting knife. Clay knew in a flash what the man was about to do.

Clay knew he had to act immediately or all was lost. Rising from his hideout in a blur of movement, Clay shot up the shallow slope and over the lip at the top with his feet pounding as hard as he had ever known, as if his very life depended on it, running toward the preoccupied guerilla. A multitude of thoughts flashed through his mind in a jumble, as he charged the sniper. He knew that perhaps not his own, but the lives of the team depended on his stopping the terrorist from cutting the electrical cord in his hand. In the brief seconds that it took to cross the distance to where the guerilla stood, poised to slice through the connection, two options stood prominent in Clay's mind. The first was now history, but he still thought of it. He realized he could have prematurely blown all the charges in that first moment when the guerilla had found the wire, then hope that he could eventually escape the full force that would be howling and hot on his tail. Or, option two, now in motion, and the most dangerous - take out the sniper, clearly a military professional.

Energized as if he had a double dose of vitamin C and a large syringe of vitamin B-12, Clay sprinted across the dirt with a virtual velocity that was not unlike a comparison to a baseball pitcher's fastball. It was a physical and unthinking moment of life and death.

The sniper, still engrossed, pulled up the wire and did not hear the approach of Clay. Halfway to the man, Clay's foot landed on a dry twig that made a brittle snap. Even though it wasn't overly loud, the wary sniper's keen ears must have picked up the out of place sound. Without even looking, the sniper dropped the wire and knife and whipped around to face the threat. As the sniper did so, he dropped to his knees, with his hand automatically grabbing the Dragunov. Flicking off the safety, he started to swing the long rifle around to bear on the rapidly approaching adversary. He knew it would be a pointblank shot, he couldn't miss, all the more better than to fight it out with the knife. The snipers confidence level appeared to be such that he felt confident he was in a win-win situation because he glimpsed the man running toward him held the knife at waist level, like a spear. It was a fatal mistake, not keeping the knife and choosing to use the rifle.

Seeing the long rifle swing in his direction, Clay could feel the kinetic energy from the adrenalin release, pump through him as he redoubled his efforts to almost super-human lengths to cover the short distance between him and the terrorist. He knew he had to close on the sniper before he could get off that, pointblank fatal shot.

Clay body-slammed the guerilla in full motion, like a fully loaded semi-tractor trailer going down a hill. The momentum caused the sniper to fall backward out of control. They slammed into the ground with Clay on top of his adversary, then rolled over and over. The fight was as vicious and deadly as two feral alley cats fighting, clawing and scratching in some dark back street. Clay had to stop the guerilla from firing a shot of any kind and alerting the main body that would soon be there.

Clay viciously slammed his left forearm against the man's right wrist, and was satisfied to see the rifle drop from the man's hand without that warning shot being fired. Going down hard, Clay slammed his right hand, holding his jungle knife thrust outward, upward and under the Gilly suit. He felt the knife stab the man under his lower sternum. The sniper groaned in guttural pain, struggled and fought for his life, even though mortally wounded. He flailed his hands like claws at Clay's face. In defense, Clay raised up his left forearm to try and stave off the outstretched, lethal, claw-like fingernails from reaching his face and tearing out his eyeballs.

He pulled the knife out a fraction and slammed it home all the harder, trying to finish off the fiercely struggling guerilla. Clay, in a fury, his anger at this terrorist out of control, his mind told him that in his dreams, this was one of the faceless murderers that would have killed and mutilated his teammates with no mercy. This seemed to stun the guerilla and in that brief moment, Clay leaned up and over and slammed down the sharp point of his elbow into the man's nose. A second later, the man deflated like a balloon with the air rapidly escaping. Totally exhausted, Clay rolled off the dead body and lay next to it for a few moments.

A few minutes later, after getting his wind back, Clay got to his knees and pulled the Gilly suit off the sniper, planning on using it himself, picking up the rifle at the same time. He rationalized that time was not on his side. Thinking that someone might try to communicate with the dead guerilla or that the man may have had regular check-in periods, Clay figured he'd have to get the body out of sight immediately. No sooner did he have this thought, than he heard a slight crackling noise, not unlike static. Someone *was* trying to get in touch with the man. Picking up the earphone and lip mic combination, which had been torn loose during the fight, Clay put the earplug next to his ear and listened. The strident, angry words, in a language he didn't recognize, coming into his ear, could only be orders by the dead man's commander to answer immediately. He was out of time.

Clay didn't know how close they were, but he figured that if their man did not check in, his superiors would take no chances, figuring he was in trouble or dead, and then quickly send a rapid reaction team to investigate. He didn't know where to start, but he knew he had to get it all done before they arrived, if he was going to pull this off.

He had to get the dead terrorist into hiding quickly, but the problem was the dead weight. He pulled the man up to a sitting position, then he struggled to get the man into an upright position by wrapping his arm around his chest and pulling him upright. It was like trying to get several strands of cooked spaghetti to stand straight up on their own. He knew he could easily drag the body to the ditch, but that was sure to leave a very obvious telltale sign that would be difficult to conceal in the short time remaining to him.

After several frustrating, sweaty attempts to try and get the dead guerilla on his back in a fireman's carry, Clay gave up. Every time he tried, the dead terrorist just collapsed into a pile on the ground. Disgusted, Clay grabbed the sniper by the back collar of his camouflage uniform and proceeded to unceremoniously drag the man across the ground to the edge of the ditch. At this point, he didn't give a damn that he had left a clear trail in the dirt leading back to the ditch, he just wanted to get the sonavabitch under cover.

Lining up the sniper on the lip of the ditch, he gave the body a shove with his foot and the man rolled down to the bottom of the gully. He trotted back to the scene of the vicious fight, Clay knelt down and rapidly reburied the electrical wire, doing his best to conceal it. He scuffed his feet across the ground repeatedly where the fight had occurred, to cover up the clear splotches of blood already soaking into the earth. Grabbing the Gilly suit and rifle, he ran back to his hideout and deposited them so that he could get his hands on both quickly.

Taking his jungle knife, he chopped off a couple of long, full leafy branches from a large overhanging bush several yards up from his stakeout position. Hurrying back to the spot where the vicious fight occurred, Clay knew he had to make the dirt around the area look as natural as possible. He immediately went to work using the long leafy piece like a big broom, brushing away any traces of what had taken place on that spot. After this was accomplished he worked his way backward, erasing as best he could any sign of his footprints and drag marks. When he reached the dry streambed, he threw the branch to the bottom and hurried down the slope to the body.

First he checked the sniper's body for any kind of identification, but found none. He was not surprised when he found a copy of the Quoran. After checking it, he put it back in the dead man's pocket and continued his search. Rolling the body over, he made an interesting discovery he had somehow overlooked. Tucked into the terrorist's back waistband, in a special holster, he found the man's apparent backup weapon. A Beretta 9 mm pistol was nicely concealed, attached to the belt, along with a pouch containing two spare magazines. The pistol was covered with dirt from when he'd dragged the body to the streambed. Taking out a handkerchief he'd acquired as a sweatband at the crash site earlier, Clay carefully wiped away all the dirt. He released the magazine and found it to be fully loaded. Pulling back the slide part way on the pistol, he saw a round in the chamber. Releasing the slide on the weapon, he pushed the magazine back in, put on the safety and slid the Beretta into his front waistband.

He pulled off the man's belt, slipped off the ammo pouch and waistband holster figuring he'd put them on later. Grabbing the body, Clay dragged it down the wash, looking for a likely spot to hide it. The best he could find was a small section near a curve of the streambed that had apparently been eroded during the last monsoon. Unfortunately the alcove was not deep enough, so the body stuck out like a sore thumb, he could see with concern. With no other solutions in mind, he ran back to his hideout and grabbed the Gilly suit. Laying the camouflage suit over the body, Clay felt satisfied that it covered the body sufficiently, so that it would not be discovered prematurely. It now looked like a natural part of the streambed.

Trotting back to his hideout, Clay loosened the sling on the Dragunov to enable him to carry it on his shoulder when he left this place. At least he hoped he'd be able to walk out of here, he thought, but then again, maybe not. He hated the thought that perhaps this might be the spot where *his* life came to an end.

Getting himself situated and comfortable, he prepared for the arrival of the main body of the guerilla band. A little fatigued from all the strenuous efforts he had put out, Clay lay against the forward slope of the gully with his eye level just above the top of the slope, and checked out the landscape in front of him.

From his viewpoint, Clay figured he had a good half-pie-shaped panorama of the complete area around the crash site with the chopper approximately in the middle. Continuing to keep his eyes glued to the locations he expected the guerillas to come from, he was a little worried by the blind spot off to his right periphery, concerned he might not see the approach of anyone coming that way. He cautioned himself to keep a sharp eye out.

He strained his eyes, looking for enemy movement. After several fruitless minutes of this exercise, his fatigue caught up with him and his eyes slipped shut, as he napped off. He didn't know how long he'd drifted off, but he snapped fully awake at the distant sound of an engine.

He was shocked to see the main body had arrived and several people were grouped near the downed chopper, inspecting it. He noticed there was even one man in the pilot's section and feared one of them might find the booby trap wires if he didn't act immediately.

He was in the motion of clapping together the electrical contacts to set off the explosive charges when he almost missed the soft crunch of a foot on dead leaves nearby. He dropped the electrical igniters and snapped his head to his right, moving a branch to see better. Clay was shocked to see a burly, hard faced individual with the dark-lined facial features of someone having spent a life in the sun. The guerilla was crouched over and moving stealthily toward his hideout. The man, dressed in coarse looking peasant clothing could have easily passed himself off as a farmer. In the man's hand, held at waist level, he saw a long and sharp looking jungle machete.

Clay had no idea of how he had been detected and didn't care at the moment. Moving to face this new threat, the thought raced through his mind, *Sonafabitch! Things never seem to happen the way you want them to!* Realizing the man has spotted his sudden movement, he watched as the man stood upright and started running toward him from several yards away. The machete was now raised above his head as the man ran, screaming loud but, unintelligible invectives. Clay shoved himself up off the slope and into a half crouch as he hurriedly groped for the pistol in his waistband. Grabbing the handle, he thumbed off the safety and started to yank the gun out, but it accidentally caught in his shirt as the screaming terrorist closed in on him.

Chapter 20

The terrorist was practically on top of him, scant yards away when Clay ripped the Beretta free from his shirt, in a state of utter panic. The guerilla raced toward him with the machete held high over his head, murder in those black eyes, an animal scream on his drooling lips. There was no question, the terrorist clearly intended on chopping that lethal looking machete down on his head. Clay didn't even have to think about it, knowing he only had less than a second to act. He point aimed the pistol and squeezed the trigger. Feeling the sensation of the pistol buck in his hand, he held the gun rock steady and kept on pulling the trigger. It didn't seem to have any effect on the guerilla as he continued to charge at him. Clay didn't know if his shots were hitting home or not, the only image that filled his mind was the wild terrorist coming at him.

The pistol rocked in his hand three more times and then time ran out. The terrorist was right on top of him. Without a thought, Clay dove to his right, rolled once and came up on his elbows, gun pointed at where he had last seen the terrorist. With his adrenalin pumping, he looked for the enemy, ready to empty the rest of the magazine into him if necessary. He saw a bloody heap on the ground, just beyond where he had been kneeling.

Leaping to his feet, Clay rushed over to where the guerilla lay and took a careful look at the man. He saw the machete still tightly gripped in his hand. He had to be sure the man was down permanently. Suspicious that the terrorist could be playing possum, Clay edged closer to the body, the pistol aimed down and ready for any sudden move. He gave the terrorist a couple of quick kicks in the ribs to be certain the man was finished. Rolling the body over, Clay saw he'd been very lucky, the guerilla had taken four solid hits in the upper torso.

Hearing yelling in the distance, Clay leaped back to his brush hideout and quickly scrambled up to the top, of the forward slope of the streambed. With his eyes just above the level of the top, he scanned the area around the crash site first and then the surrounding area. The whole location crawled with al-Qaeda terrorists in various modes of half and full camouflage uniforms. Many were in rough peasant attire; all carried AK Kalashnikov automatic assault rifles of one form or another. There were many more than he had anticipated. Obviously, they had been expecting to make an all out attack to take out his team. *Sorry to let you assholes down!* He thought cynically. *Guess I got their unwanted attention1*

He saw the man, their apparent leader, issuing orders and was tempted to grab the Dragunov and take him out. Everyone at the crash site appeared busy searching the area, many moving in his general direction from which the shot had been heard. A few of the terrorists, with AK-74's held at the ready, were moving cautiously toward his hiding place. Taking all this in, Clay voiced his thoughts out loud, "Looks like I'm going to have to accelerate my plan a tiny bit!"

Clay glanced to his right, near the top, where he'd cleared a small shelf in the dirt, where he had positioned the three pairs of electrical contacts. Laying neatly in a row, ready for instant access without looking, he picked up the first set he knew to be connected to explosive charges under and in the helicopter. Shifting his eyes back to his front, there was still a small group around the downed aircraft and a man working to release the door gunner's M-60 machine gun from its pedestal.

"*Show time, assholes!*" he thought. Clapping the first pair of contacts together hard, as if that would somehow make them work better, an electrical impulse was sent speeding along the hidden wires, to the detonators pushed into the blocks of C-4 explosive at the crash site. Clay kept eyeballing the chopper, waiting for something to happen. For a second or two, the thought that there might be a cut in the wire somewhere or a faulty detonator crossed his mind.

Suddenly, the craft literally rose into the air about a foot, followed by a huge fireball which engulfed the whole chopper. Seconds later, like an earthshaking clap of thunder, the explosion reached his ears, causing him to involuntarily flinch.

"Holy Shit!" he said out loud without even realizing it. He instantly knew the demolition guys had put a block of C-4 explosive next to the fuel tank, which contained the remaining fuel and vapors. All contributed to the humongous fireball which disintegrated everything inside and in close proximity to the chopper, into thousands of bits of metal and shredded bloody flesh.

A couple of minutes later, when the smoke and dust had dissipated a bit, he could see the crash site was no more; the area had been leveled and any trace of the chopper had become history. The smart ones, further away from the site, had immediately thrown themselves to the ground to reduce their chances of being hit by shrapnel from the explosion. They were all now getting up, examining themselves for injuries and in general, acting like a nest of Africanized bees that had been disturbed. He could see the anger in their faces and knew they were out for blood, his blood! The guerillas quickly recovered and fanned out, looking for the perpetrator of the death-dealing attack.

He had to try and level the playing field a little bit more in his favor. Clay immediately initiated his next step of the plan. He realized the guerillas would shortly be beyond the lethal range of the hidden Claymore mine and grenades that had been covertly placed just beyond the crash site. Grabbing the other two electrical igniters, Clay hastily slapped them together. The charges went off, but he didn't nail as many of the terrorists as he had hoped. They had spread out and were searching for their tormentor with a vengeance. He could only speculate on what kind of long, lasting torture they would put him through, if they got their hands on him, and before they finally killed him. *Time to boogy on outta here!* he thought, satisfied with the outcome.

Ducking back down, Clay shoved the Beretta into his waistband. After putting the spare magazines for the pistol into the small backpack, he shouldered it and loosened the leather sling on the Dragunov sniper rifle. *Don't think I want to leave you behind. You might come in handy.* he thought, looking at the lethal killing machine. Slipping it securely onto his left shoulder, he picked up the AK-101 he had previously acquired in his fight to get to his team, in his right hand and got ready to get out of there, post-haste. Hefting the rifle for a moment, he just happened to like the feel of this version of the famous AK assault rifle; it was well balanced in his hands. Clay was also pleased because it fired the very same round as the M-16, 5.56 mm, which would make it easy for him to get ammo.

Ducking low, just in case one of the terrorists might spot his head above the top level of the dry streambed, Clay took off with as fast a pace that he could, with his cumbersome load. The ditch made a lazy curve to the right, in the general direction he needed to escape.

Two hundred yards further up the gully, it petered out to a flat, eroded area where the wash began. Knowing he was very close to the old animal trail that his team had taken, Clay kept running hard, hunched over, trying to make himself as small and inconspicuous as possible. It was not to be. Looking straight ahead as he ran, Clay heard an angry shout, then sounds like angry bees buzzing by his ears, chipping off bits of vegetation near him and furrowing the dirt in his pathway. The distinctive flat crack echo of numerous assault rifles followed immediately. He knew he had to react instantly or the terrorists would quickly get the range in him and finish him off, now that they'd spotted him.

Fearing they'd pick him off before he was able to get under cover, up the game trail, taken by the team, Clay knelt down and brought his AK-101 up to his shoulder and started to take aim. Snapping his sights on the nearest terrorist, he squeezed off a short, three round burst. Satisfied to see the man collapse in mid-stride, he moved to pick his next target.

Squinting through his sights for another guerilla closing on his position, Clay continued to hear the angry buzzing of the enemy's bullets slicing the air around him. Suddenly he felt as though he'd been slapped on the skin of his upper shoulder, above his collarbone. It started to burn and sting, and he knew he'd been hit. Knowing he'd been very lucky and it appeared to be only a superficial wound, he continued to scan the terrorists moving toward him. It could have been worse, he thought, the shot might have hit his collarbone or some other vital area. Clay knew he was rapidly running out of time and had to do something drastic to hold them off long enough for him to effect his escape, but what?

Angling from his left front, about two hundred yards out, he spotted two men moving to cut him off. One held a shoulder launched grenade launcher. Seeing a serious problem, Clay chose to deal with the threat immediately. The enemy rifleman let loose a long burst from his AK-74 to keep Clay's head down and cover his partner. The terrorist holding the launcher, knelt and began to get his range, taking aim.

If you can't nail'em with a fly swatter, then hit'em with a sledgehammer! "Clay thought cynically, referring to the terrorists using a rocket grenade to get one man - him.

With no other choice open to him, Clay took careful aim, first at the guerilla with the grenade, fired, then immediately switched sight picture to the other terrorist. As he squeezed the trigger he felt the shock of a tremendous explosion at the very spot and the two men ceased to exist. One or more of his shots had accidentally hit the grenade itself. *Tough break, assholes! Risks of the job,* he thought.

Everyone else on the field seemed to be momentarily stunned at the explosion. Clay took the opportunity to make his break for cover before they recovered and closed in to finish him off. With almost a full magazine, he sprayed the whole area to his front with short bursts from his AK- 101. He was gratified to see everyone hit the dirt.

Grabbing both of his rifles, one in each hand, he jumped up and sprinted the several dozen yards to the game trail, running like he had the very devil on his heels. With bullets buzzing by his ears and all around him like yapping dogs, he ran up the trail, looking desperately for any kind of cover. The foliage rapidly changed as he traveled deeper along the path. It had been sparse, like the plain area at the very beginning, but gradually had become heavier jungle growth. Clay kept going until he was almost out of breath, his shirt soaked thoroughly through with his sweat. He realized he was overdoing it and only then did he come to a stop, his lungs pumping like an old steam engine in the oppressive heat and humidity that enveloped him like a dark cloud. He'd made it around a sharp bend and was temporarily under cover for the moment. The guerillas would soon be in hot pursuit and sooner or later with relays they'd wear him down and catch up to him. He pulled two of his precious grenades from his pack and pulled the pin on one, keeping his fingers tightly wrapped around the spoon. For the briefest of moments he remembered why they called it spoon, and how an ingenious U.S. Army Infantryman in World War Two had taken his spoon from his mess kit, bent it and somehow attached it to his grenade so that when he threw it, the spoon popped off after a couple of seconds, giving him extra seconds before exploding. He recalled it had worked so well, it had become standard issue.

Clay had played outfield in school and in pick-up games at the base, so he felt he could put the baseball like grenades where they would do the most good and slow down the pursuers. He didn't have long to wait. In the distance, a half dozen guerillas came trotting up the trail in his direction. He let them get within throwing distance, then arched his arm back and lobbed the first one high, toward the front of the group. Pulling the pin on the second one, he pitched it, aiming for the middle of the approaching group, as if he were trying to throw the ball to home plate.

The first grenade hit the ground and bounced once, several yards short of the lead terrorist. The man yelled the alarm and they all dove off the trail as the first one went off harmlessly. The second one landed to the left of the trail, bounced off a log where some of the guerillas had chosen to take cover. It was not exactly where he had wanted it to land and Clay felt displeased with his lousy aim. It went off on the other side of the log providing a small degree of protection and apparently inflicted only minor injuries, but not enough to stop the pursuit. He was somewhat mollified to hear a couple of screams, and was thoroughly disgusted that he'd not accomplished his objective of taking them totally out. He knew it wouldn't be very long and they'd be hot on his trail again.

Reaching in his pack, he found only two more grenades and the Claymore mine. Deciding to save the grenades for later, he picked up his gear and trotted up the trail, leaving the momentarily bloodied terrorists behind. He hoped this would make them a whole lot more careful and slow them down until the rest of their main body arrived. This was the group that he needed to give a serious "bloody nose" to, so they would be put out of action for enough time for him to link up with the team and get out of the area.

Trotting another four hundred yards or so up the trail, Clay stopped again where the jungle had become dense. He was in a shaded area, in a small depression where the trail dipped slightly. Setting down his pack, he pulled out his last two options. Should he use the Claymore or one of the grenades? He didn't have the time to make elaborate preparations he felt were needed with the Claymore, so he chose a grenade. His options were getting slim, so he had to do his best to get it right.

Stepping over to a small tree, close to the trail, but hidden from view, he took his roll of olive drab duct tape and taped the explosive securely to the tree at waist level. Attaching the camouflaged trip wire to the ring on the pin, he carefully unrolled the wire from his spool, looped it through a fork in a root near ground level and slowly strung the wire in a direction up from the trail. Taking a turn around another small tree, he crossed to the trail and on the other side placed the wire low, near the dead brush. On the far side, he found another small sapling and pulled the wire tautly around it, finally securing it in place. The wire across the trail was now tight and he felt confident of his handiwork.

Crossing back to the grenade, he loosened the pin in the spoon enough so that anyone stepping on the wire in the trail would pull it out the rest of the way. He'd positioned the explosive so that it would go off in the middle of the group, or so he hoped. On the trail he checked his handiwork. The tripwire, coated in a camouflage finish was virtually invisible, even where it was stretched across the trail, a little over an inch above the ground. He next placed some ground debris and dead leaves around the wire to hopefully conceal it.

He picked up his pack and weapons and moved on up the trail a couple of dozen yards. Having wasted two grenades and only inflicting minor casualties, he needed to be absolutely sure that he had done major damage to the pursuing column this time around, to discourage pursuit. Moving further up the trail, he carefully stepped off of it and into the heavy foliage, working his way in around fifty yards. When he felt he'd gone far enough, Clay backtracked his way back down, paralleling the trail, looking for a good observation point.

On a small, upward rising slope he found what he looked for adjacent to the section of trail where he had set the booby trap. Carefully concealing himself in a prone position, he prepared to observe the approach of the terrorists in a well-concealed vantage point. He had a fairly good view, mostly unobstructed, almost like a small picture window between some small trees and brush. He felt very confidant it would go off as planned and then he'd be able to make his escape without lingering thoughts of eminent pursuit.

Waiting for the guerillas to make their appearance, Clay wondered. A myriad of doubts raced through his mind. Was the trap good enough? He didn't have long to wait. Suddenly, he brought his mind back to reality and focused his attention on what appeared to him to be an advance scouting party, silently, stealthily emerging close to the shaded part of the trail near the tripwire.

What looked like a grizzled combat veteran of the guerrilla wars, who might have fought in the old Moro insurrection, appeared in the middle of this small group. The man acted as their leader, and they all deferred to him. Clay knew the type from his uniform and appearance. The guerilla leader had a leather-tough-deeply tanned and stone-hard face with lines that looked like a badly eroded hillside after a heavy rainstorm. A faded, worn-out camouflage uniform that looked like it had been repaired numerous times was worn like the badge of authority that it represented.

The leader had purposefully moved to the head of the column as they entered the shaded depression in the trail, mere feet from the camouflaged trip-wire. Clay held his breath in anticipation, knowing one careless step would pull the pin, setting off the grenade, causing maximum casualties. Clay fully focused on the old guerilla warrior as the man closely observed this shaded portion of the trail. Clay could almost see the suspicion in the guerilla's wizened eyes by his facial expression. The leader grunted a quick, guttural command and everyone immediately froze in place, much to Clay's disgust.

The guerilla chief held in his hand a long, thin twig, taken from a dead bush. Moving cautiously, with the twig extended in front of him, he guided the tiny branch lightly along the ground in front of him, light as a feather. Clay could see the guerilla was a pro and knew what he was doing. Halfway through the depression, the man stopped and uttered something to his men. From his actions, Clay knew from his own training that the leader had felt the twig encounter resistance to the forward movement. Freezing in place, while holding the branch, he slowly knelt down and worked his way on his knees closer to where the branch was hung up. When he got to the place where the twig was hung up, a brittle, knowing smile cracked across the weathered face. Leaning close to the ground, he reached carefully with a dark and gnarled hand lightly brushing his hand across the top of the tripwire without causing any pressure. Allowing a short, guttural laugh, he motioned two of his devil's apprentices to join him. Clay was thoroughly disgusted with himself, knowing he'd been so easily found out. He racked his brain, knowing he had to somehow come up with a solution to counter this wily old guerilla fighter who seemed to have a sixth sense and anticipated his every move.

As Clay watched, he saw two men detach themselves from the group. They stood there, observing the leader with the kind of awe and apprehension a younger, inexperienced man would pay to a high priest, while the two moved hesitantly to the man's side. For them, Clay could almost read their minds, as he knew that they realized this was what was euphemistically called OJT, on the job training with potentially lethal consequences. One small mistake and their training was over in a burst of explosive shrapnel. He remembered a saying during his own training in demolitions, "Experience is a hard teacher because she gives the test first, the lesson afterward."

Showing them the tripwire, the leader instructed them on how to carefully clear away the leaves and follow the wire in both directions from the trail. Realizing they were losing precious time and their enemy was gaining valuable ground on them, Clay figured the leader was resigned to making sure there would be no more casualties for his followers.

When the two men each reached the spot where the wire originated on each side, he tersely whispered to them. He instructed the one at the place where the wire was tied off at the sapling, to cut the wire and release the tension slightly. Then he had the one who knelt by the tree where the grenade was taped, to check around for any other booby traps. When none were found, he commanded his apprentice to push the pin back into the spoon of the grenade. Then he instructed the soldier to cut the wire and the tape away from the explosive and bring the baseball like explosive to him.

When both men returned to where their leader knelt, he took the offered grenade and carefully inspected it. Clay watched as the terrorist stood up, then with studied, casual slowness, looked up into the surrounding foliage with his wizened eyes, as if to say to his adversary, *I know you are up there somewhere.* For a brief moment Clay could feel the old guerilla's eyes brush past him. It was a chilling sensation. The man pocketed the explosive, and Clay could guess with certainty the guerilla had plans to return it to him, minus the pin and spoon. The terrorist stood up and scanned the jungle surrounding them very slowly and very carefully, uttering words that Clay could not distinguish. It gave Clay an eerie feeling. He could only surmise the guerilla said words to the effect, "I know you are out there watching me! See! I found your trap!"

Clay realized he had to do something immediately to slow down the pursuit. He still had the Claymore mine and one grenade. In this difficult position he didn't want to waste either foolishly. Thinking quickly and desperately, he had one solution to slow them down. The guerilla leader had to be on the same wave-length because as he was about to act, the guerilla gave a quick command and they all dropped to the ground, disappearing from his sight. Clay could only guess that they might have spotted him or suspected his location and were about to counterattack in his direction.

Flipping off the safety on his AK, he stood and fired several long bursts from his rifle in the general direction of where he'd last seen the terrorists, emptying the magazine and hoping he'd hit someone. The answer he received in return told him everything he didn't want to know. He had acted rashly and emotionally and gave himself away, stupidly thinking this would slow them down. It didn't happen. A fierce return fusillade, chipped of pieces of branches and leaves all around him and told him they were headed toward him. Time to get out of here!

Releasing his empty magazine, then turning and inserting the other taped magazine into his rifle on the run, Clay rapidly worked his way back through the jungle the way he had come. Puffing and huffing through the heavy foliage, he hadn't come very far when he heard two grenades blasts behind him. If he had stayed, they would have got him, he knew. Now a new problem dogged at him.

They were far closer than he wanted them and something had to be done to give him time. Reaching the spot where he had cut in from the trail, he worked his way back and then began running up the trail as best he could under his load. The heavy sweat he had worked up soon thoroughly soaked through all his clothes and ran into his eyes, the salty tears burning them. He brushed it away and kept going, knowing they would be on him like a hound dog on a June bug if he even stopped for a moment.

The exertion began to wear on him and he needed a breather. Clay took a chance and stopped a couple of hundred yards up the trail, to revive himself a bit. After his rash and foolish move he felt his confidence return as he began to think rationally again. Listening intently for the pursuers, he finally heard them puffing hard as they approached. They were still out of sight, on the other side of a slight rise in the pathway when he grabbed his last grenade. Pulling the pin, waited a second, and then heaved the grenade up and over the rise, hoping the old guerilla was leading them. Not waiting to see the results, he turned and began running. Moments later he heard the blast of the grenade, but couldn't be sure if it had done any good.

Now, practically out of options to slow down the terrorists, he decided to take a chance and try an idea that had popped into his desperate mind. Several hundred yards further up the trail, he stopped at a likely spot and strung the tripwire in the same fashion as before, across the trail, but attached no explosive, since he had none to spare anyway. Carefully camouflaging the tripwire, he then hurried on his way. Clay stopped after another few hundred yards and did the same thing, then once more. That ought to frustrate the bastards, he thought with relish, and maybe, just maybe give him some extra minutes.

Clay followed the trail and indentations made by the litters his team were dragging. At an unexpected fork in the trail, the drag marks disappeared and he didn't know which direction to take. What the hell were these guys doing? Didn't they know he was behind them, or did they think he was dead?

Half-guessing that the path to the right was probably the correct route in the eventual direction of the old, deserted Japanese air base and also the direction his team had hopefully taken, he headed off to the right. He wanted to make contact as soon as he could because it was late afternoon and dusk would soon be upon him. Clay did not want to even think of approaching his trigger-happy team members after dark.

But it didn't work out that way for him. He kept moving further and further up the trail, but there were still no signs that his team had put down the litters and were dragging them once again, or had even come this way. He began to become very concerned as he moved on in silence, tiredly placing one foot in front of the other. It was now dusk and soon the jungle night would be upon him, like someone switching off a light bulb in a room, plunging it into inky blackness.

The trail had narrowed down to virtually a tiny footpath at this point. He realized, beyond a doubt now, that he had made a very bad choice when he took this branch of the fork. Did he dare take the chance and backtrack, he wondered. That's all he needed, he rationalized, to go back and run smack into the guerrillas. *I'm literally between a rock and a hard place*, he thought digustedly, repeating the old, overused adage.

Continuing to move up the narrowing pathway, Clay couldn't help but notice the foliage had grown considerably heavier. It seemed to be closing in on him and he felt claustrophobic.

He stopped for a moment to catch his breath in the heavy, humid air. Positive that he had heard stealthy movements in the heavy foliage to the right side of the track, he forced himself to think rationally and get control. He started to move forward when his ears, now attuned to the slightest noise, heard a slight rustling sound again from the heavy brush to his right. His mind whirled with questions. Had the guerillas outflanked and gotten around him? Was this an isolated, lone guerrilla, who'd heard him coming and had leaped to concealment in the undergrowth? He didn't know what to think, but it could be a threat He had to seriously consider that.

Clay was compelled to find out, one way or other, he just couldn't avoid it. Un-slinging the sniper rifle, he carefully set it on the ground. Laying his AK rifle down close to him, just in case, he pulled off his small backpack. In one of the side pockets of the pack he had stashed a heavy duty, angled military issue flashlight, before the team departed. He knew the dependable flashlight had a sharp, direct, piercing beam. It was what he needed in this situation. He picked up his rifle and crept forward.

Darkness was just about upon him when he began to push his way with a lot of apprehension through the heavy foliage. With his heart trip-hammering in his chest, he hesitantly moved toward the rustling sounds. He held the flashlight in his left hand, the AK-101 in his right, the safety off and his finger lightly wrapped around the trigger. Parting his way through the heavy, green underbrush with both arms, he pushed his way through until he detected what appeared to be an open area just ahead. He stepped out of the underbrush when his flashlight picked up a pair of red, glaring, angry eyes in the beam, staring menacingly back at him. A moment later those fearsome eyes were accompanied by a ferocious growl that roared forth with a life threatening sound that would instantly chill anyone's blood, as the thing leaped at him.

Chapter 21

Clay recoiled backward in shock and fear, as if he had just stepped into a nest of rattlesnakes. Totally unhinged, his flashlight came close to slipping from his hand as the thing lunged at him. His arm shot up to protect himself. He barely recovered when his heel tripped on an exposed root, coming dangerously close to losing his balance. It probably saved him as the beast was practically at his throat.

His finger tightened on the trigger in an automatic reflex on the verge of spraying the place with a long, wild burst from his rifle. The fearsome, angry eyes and hellish growling sound made him want to turn and run and never look back.

Something inside him stayed his hand and he didn't fire. Why hadn't this raging beast landed on top of him and ripped out his throat? It could have been so easy! Playing his flashlight beyond the fearsome eyes and on the body of the animal itself, he saw it to be shorthaired with a mixed coat of a black - brown and a cream color all blending together. It rang a responsive bell in his mind and looked familiar. Where had he seen colors like that? At the base, he wondered? The animal's body appeared to be heavily coated with mud, dirt, grime and what looked to be dried blood.

He saw the heavy chain, securely attached to the animal and tied off somewhere, allowing the beast very limited movement. It ended in a heavy, leather collar, and a dog tag, the same kind that soldiers are issued for identification, attached to a small ring on the collar. Playing the light back and forth over the animal, he suddenly knew why it looked familiar. A dog, but from outward appearances, a barely recognizable one, but still a dog, he thought! Not just any one either, but a highly trained K-9 patrol dog, a German Shepard. The poor animal appeared to be chained up and attached to something, and that's what probably had saved my life, he realized with a sense of relief. He had heard rumors that there were K-9 units stationed somewhere near his base, so maybe this could be where it had come from.

Finally, finding his voice, he hesitantly spoke for the first time, croaking the words out from a dry throat. "Whoa, buddy! I'm not going to hurt you!" At the sound of Clay's voice the dog stopped growling for a moment and looked at this intruder just beyond his reach. It occurred to Clay that clearly the animal recognized his language. Yet, it continued to strain at the chain and Clay knew with certainty that if the chain ever broke or came loose, the dog would be on top of him in an eye blink.

Trying again, Clay said, "Take it easy now, buddy! I won't hurt you. Where's your master?" Clay took a small step forward for a closer look, eliciting a low, menacing growl, deep in the dog's throat. It grew in intensity as the seconds passed. It appeared to be a serious warning to come no closer, and Clay stopped dead in his tracks.

How am I going to figure out what's going on, what happened here? There must be something, he thought. How in the devil did this dog get here? Not knowing how long the poor animal had been chained up in this overbearing heat and humidity, he figured that the dog had to have a raging thirst. Maybe that was the way to get around the problem, he hoped - with a gesture of kindness.

Slowly pulling off his soft jungle hat, so as to not alarm the dog, Clay gradually lowered himself to a kneeling position and laid the hat upside down on the ground, at his feet. Reaching behind him, he pulled out one of his two canteens of water attached to his web belt. He knew water was vital to survival in a climate like this and had made sure he had plenty of if before the team had departed. He had no idea how vitally important the water would become until this critical moment.

Opening up the canteen, he carefully poured the tepid water into the hat, making sure the dog could see what he was doing. *Even though it's warm*, touching the water with his finger, *it's still better than nothing at all, he thought.* When he had filled the hat a quarter full, he slowly edged it over to where the dog stood. The animal remained stiff and ready, in the attack stance, eyeing the hat and Clay suspiciously. Bending its dark head down and sniffing the air above the hat a couple of times, Clay knew the animal had sensed the presence of water. After a few moments, the dog sat back on its haunches and alternately stared guardedly at the intruder and then down at the water, as if trying to make some kind of decision.

When the growling ceased, Clay felt emboldened, and continued to carefully edge the hat closer to the dog. Its ears twitched a few times as the dog stared at the hat with what appeared to Clay to be a look of interest.

Holding his breath, Clay finally pushed the hat closer to the animal, up to its feet. The animal looked from Clay to the hat, but did not make a move. Finally Clay took a chance and said, in a soft voice. "Go Ahead, buddy! I know you're thirsty! Drink up!"

With those soothing words, something appeared to be released within the dog, as it relaxed its guard a little. Bending over the hat, the dog sniffed it a few times and then looked up at Clay with questioning eyes, as if to say, *can I trust you?* Apparently satisfied, the dog dipped its muzzle into the water and lapped the fluid up hungrily. Clay watched, not making any sudden moves while the dog drank.

The poor, thirsty animal drank until it had consumed all of the water. Bending forward, Clay added a second helping. "There you go, pal, have some more," Clay said in a soft, soothing voice. The animal hungrily lapped it all up, and then sat in place staring at Clay curiously, as if to say, *Okay, what's your next move?*

With his light, Clay examined the dog's body. A lot of dried blood covered a good portion of the dog's coat, but the animal didn't appear to be seriously injured.

Talking to the dog soothingly, Clay asked, "What happened here, buddy? I know you can't talk, but I'd sure like to find out how you got here? The animal stood up, looked Clay in the eye, made a long, sad, whining sound as if to say it had lost someone special, then it started to pace back and forth at the end of its chain.

Clay slowly stood up, trying not to alarm the dog and shined his light over the clearing in an attempt to determine how the dog had made his way to this place in the jungle.

His light passed over a piece of camouflage green, fatigue uniform, under the heavy ground cover in the clearing. Clay froze and snapped his light back to the spot; and then he saw the body, almost hidden in the foliage. He moved the light further around the clearing to discover two more bodies laying there, half-hidden in the ground cover.

The dog seemed to sense Clay's dismay because it turned and walked over to the closest body. Whining with a note of longing and sadness, one more time he lowered his head to the body and sniffed, slowly wagging his tail back and forth, gently touching the body with his nose.

The way it looked to Clay, it was as if the dog was trying to arouse his master, asking him to get up. On the other hand, it appeared to Clay with a deep throb of sadness, that the dog sensed his master was gone. The poor animal then sat down next to his master and lay its head on his paws, its eyes trained on Clay.

Not knowing quite what he should do and afraid to approach the body, Clay worried that the dog would protect his dead master and try to attack. Clay did the next best thing he could think of under the circumstances. Skirting around the outer edge of the bodies, Clay did his best to inspect them. They had apparently died in a fierce firefight as he could see empty shell casings littered all over the ground. He had no way to tell if they had walked into an ambush or had been pursued. It looked like everything was there, including their weapons and their gear which was highly unusual.

He picked up one of their assault rifles and checked it out. It was empty and scattered near the body were several empty magazines for the weapon. Shining his light around the area, he noticed it was the same story for all the others. Again, he wondered what had happened here.

The oddity here, he thought could have been that the enemy, had not taken their weapons or looted their personal belongings. That alone seemed very unusual. Also he noted, none of the bodies were mutilated as the terrorists relished doing to spread more terror or killed the dog, which was really surprising. They hated the war dogs with a passion, so what was the story?

He noticed a large opening in the jungle clearing at the opposite end from the way he had blundered into his strange place. In the beam of his flashlight, he couldn't help but observe that the bodies of the men were all facing in this direction. Curiosity drew him as he stepped over to the open outer edge of the clearing.

Training the flashlight over this area, he saw that it was much larger than the small area where the bodies lay. Moving his light over the field, he guessed it to be more the size of the infield of a baseball diamond. The ground was covered with an ankle high growth of wild grass and low ground cover. He theorized the area lay open like this as a result of a lightening strike that may have caused a fire, sometime in the past. Several dead trees nearby had charred and blackened trunks, as his beam passed over them, confirming his guess.

To Clay, the most shocking fact of the clearing were the numerous dead bodies. There had to be more than a dozen of them, all in the violent contortions of death.

Stepping into the clearing and moving among them, Clay noticed that they too, still had their weapons and gear. From their rough attire and half-uniforms, he quickly came to the conclusion that this had been another guerilla patrol. Making a guess, he thought that the three dead soldiers behind him had unluckily run across the enemy patrol somewhere nearby. It appeared to have been a running battle that had ended where he now stood with no one the winner. The only survivor appeared to be the German Shepherd.

Clay stepped gingerly out among the bodies, noting that many of the assault rifles still had ammunition in them and all their personal gear remained intact. Then he stopped his inspection for a moment and stood up. Silence surrounded the area. It was as though the animals and birds of the night that inhabited the area, were avoiding this charnel house of death.

From all appearances, it looked to have been a savage, no-holds-barred fight to the bitter end with everyone paying the ultimate price. Then something else came glaringly to his attention and senses. He quickly covered his nose with his handkerchief. He noticed for the first time the distinct, nauseating, stomach turning odor of death. Clay knew the putrefying flesh, in the hot, humid air hanging over this clearing like a black, somber cloud, decayed at a rapid rate. The stench began to roil his stomach and he had to get out of there as soon as possible.

Turning and moving quickly back to where the three soldiers lay he looked at them again. Everything about them, from their carbine-like assault weapons, to their hi-tech gear, pointed to the fact that these had been special operations troopers. Why had they been here? Going from body to body, he removed one of their two identification tags, leaving the other behind for when recovery people from the base could get in here to collect their remains for interment. Taking three quick compass readings, he pulled out his map and made a quick mark with his pencil. He would ensure they kept true to their motto of "no one left behind," if he survived. He left the dog's handler to the last.

Clay expected the dog to leap at him in a rage, but it didn't happen. It appeared the dog had accepted the fact that his beloved master was gone. The big German Shepherd did nothing when Clay approached. "Take if easy, boy!" Clay said as he approached the body. The dog just stared at him and didn't move.

Going through the man's pack, Clay found several foil packets of dry dog food and a couple of small, collapsible containers for food and water. Opening up both, he put them near the dog, then opened one of the packets and poured the dry kibbles into the canvas bowl. Next he poured some more water from his canteen into the other container.

The dog got up and moved to the bowls, eating hungrily and drinking more water.

While the dog ate, Clay went through the pack and piled all the foil packets of dog and human food he could find on the ground next to him. He methodically worked his way through the packs of the other two men and pulled out everything he could use.

Opening his own pack, he loaded it up with all the packets of food he had discovered, knowing they would be needed. Of the canteens on the men, only one was near full which he attached to the outside of his pack as a spare, having no more room to hook it to his belt.

The dog finished and sat down once more to stare at Clay curiously. Packing up the two containers, Clay asked the dog, "So what's your name boy?" Moving for a closer look at the animal, he noticed, as he shined his light over the dog's coat, that the animal appeared injured. From the dried blood, he guessed it could have been from a bullet grazing his body or from a machete narrowly missing and leaving a long, thin, surface cut from the top of the shoulder to the hindquarters. He was concerned about the dried blood on the dog's coat.

"If you'll let me, I'll help you," Clay said soothingly to the canine. He pulled out a small first aid kit and removed a tube of antibiotic ointment and a roll of gauze bandage. Kneeling down next to the dog, he squeezed out a large dollop of ointment on his index finger and let the curious dog sniff it. "Okay, pal, I'm not going to hurt you." Taking a chance, he carefully moved his hand over to the wound and gently began to spread the pain-relieving antibiotic along the length of the cut. He was well aware in this jungle environment, that infection would occur fast in an open wound. The animal slightly flinched at the first touch, but otherwise stayed still while keeping its eyes glued on Clay.

Clay gently coaxed the dog to stand up after he was finished. While the animal stood there docilely, he carefully checked over the rest of his body for any other wounds or cuts. Looking from the animal's blood covered coat to the body of his handler, Clay made a guess that most of the blood had come from the handler after he had been fatally wounded and the dog had lain down next to him to be close to his master. That would explain the excess blood.

Inspecting the animal, he applied bandages along the length of the wound and wrapped the roll of gauze around the dog's body to hold them temporarily in place. He knew it wouldn't last, but it would at least give the antibiotic and pain reliever time to work.

While the dog stood there, Clay leaned over to the animal's collar and checked for some kind of identification. He found a dirt-encrusted tag attached and when he cleared it away he could see a name. Spelled out on the tag, he read out loud, "Stryker". Looking at the dog, Clay thought, some name. *I bet you're hell on wheels*! "Okay Stryker, we need to get outta here." At the mention of its name, the dog's ears twitched and he wagged his tail back and forth a couple of times.

Looking at the chain attached to the dog, Clay traced it to what looked like a lightening-shattered, tall tree trunk. The chain had become solidly wedged in a split part and then the dog had complicated matters by wrapping itself around the stump a couple of times, locking himself in permanently. Might have happened during the chaos of the firefight, he guessed. That poor animal would have died here, if I had not taken the wrong branch of the trail and shown up here, Clay thought. Fate or something seems to be guiding my hand, he mused.

Carefully, so as to not alarm Stryker, Clay gently removed one of the dead handler's I.D. tags, commonly called dog tags by the military, he recalled. Pocketing it, he stood up and took the loose end of the chain and worked his way around the stump and pulled it out of the tight wedge of the split wood.

Having checked all of the packs and weapons for anything useful, Clay got down on his knees again and taking a wild chance for the first time, reached out to gently pat the dog on its back. The dog didn't growl or make any moves to stop him. Softly, as if he was whispering in the dog's ear he said, "Okay, Stryker, you have to make a decision." Saying it as if the dog could understand him, he continued, "You can't stay here or you'll die. You are going to have to come with me if you want to survive. Can you understand?"

The dog looked up at him with a look on its brown, intelligent face, as though he fully understood. Clay picked up the chain and pondered about it and the dead men for a moment. There must have been a reason to have the dog on a chain, he thought, but what was it? And the special operations patrol, what had been their mission?

Thinking about the three bodies in the clearing, Clay began to guess at a couple of possibilities. The likelihood that they may have been choppered in to a site close by and were part of an intensive search for his lost team seemed plausible. Maybe they had been one of several search parties looking for his team.

Could they have been part of a long range, counter-insurgency operation and just had the very bad fortune to stumble into the guerilla patrol? Clay could only theorize, but he figured that being overwhelming outnumbered, good judgment predicated to avoid and run to fight another day. Unfortunately, the guerillas had pursued and managed to catch up with and corner them. They had clearly stood and fought bravely while one of their numbers may have been trying to call in air support or help of some kind. Clay recalled seeing a ground to air radio near one of the bodies. He had picked it up, hoping he might get lucky, but it had been penetrated and made unusable by several bullets in the case. Poor guys, he thought. They'd been trapped, with nowhere to go, so they'd fought it out to the bitter end.

"Okay Stryker," he said. "It's time we make fast footwork outta here! We've gotta go all the way back the way I came in, and that's going to be the rub, because we're going back toward the bad guys!"

Getting up with the chain in his hand, Clay said again, "Okay, buddy, we have to go now!" But the dog didn't budge. Clay had taken a couple of steps and when the dog did not follow, he turned back to see what the problem was. Stryker seemed completely undecided from the way he acted. He looked from Clay to the body of his handler and back again, giving a long, pitiful whine and didn't budge.

H had figured that he would have to coax the dog to come with him for its own sake. "C'mon, boy, we gotta get the hell outta here now! We can't wait any longer!" The urgency rang loudly in the tone of his voice. After a few more moments, the dog appeared to have made a decision, because he stood up, took another long, soulful, look at his dead master, then walked over to Clay and stood alert at his side, gazing up at him expectantly. Glancing down at the dog, Clay thought, *are you reading my mind?* Then he said, "Okay, new partner, let's hit the road!"

They made good time, backtracking down the trail. Night settled in, but a huge, brilliant harvest moon had risen up in the heavens and provided a ghostly illumination of the game trail they traversed. Having come this way earlier, Clay knew what to expect and they both covered the ground rapidly. He worried and it continued to gnaw at him. He hoped and prayed they could make it to the branch of the trail before the terrorists got there or they'd be in big trouble.

Approaching closer to the branch, Clay slowed down, and moved as silently as the narrow trail would allow them. The dog sensed the change of attitude in Clay, becoming much more alert.

After leaving the clearing, as a precautionary measure, Clay had brought them to a halt, every few minutes to listen to the sounds around them. The dog seemed to understand this, because he did the same, twitching his ears around at any nearby disturbances. Clay tuned his ear for any noise that was out of the ordinary, anything that wasn't natural. The normal rustlings and noises of the jungle had returned. This had a calming effect on Clay, just to know that the jungle would go silent at the approach of a threat. They were safe for the moment.

Reaching the fork in the trail, Clay stopped for a moment before starting up the other branch. The moon had momentarily drifted behind a small bank of clouds making it a little harder to distinguish things, but he was not overly concerned. Closing his eyes, he turned his ear, listening intently down the trail, for he knew the guerillas must come from this direction. He could hear nothing, other than the normal jungle sounds. Then out of the corner of his eye, he saw Stryker stiffen, his ears alert, intently staring down the pathway. The slight breeze had apparently shifted, bringing a scent of something that Stryker didn't like with it. A low, menacing growl emanated, deep down in his throat and the hackles on the back of his neck rose. Clay knew unquestionably, the dog had sensed a threat he would have missed. The tension was so thick; he could have walked on it.

Seconds later a slight sound drifted in on the breeze - not a part of the normal jungle noise. He almost missed it, but knew that it shouldn't have been there. A tiny, metallic click like a loose piece of equipment...

Snapping his eyes upward and peering down the ghostly - lit trail, Clay knew he was out of time. He didn't know what, if any options were left. Freezing like a statue and trying his best to become part of the jungle foliage, Clay felt an icy chill race up his spine as three ghostly figures slowly emerged as if they were floating from the surrounding shadows. He figured they were around fifty to seventy-five yards away, but extremely difficult to separate from the jungle brush. With their camouflage uniforms in the spectral, diffused light of the moon they were practically invisible.

Clay realized he'd walked right into a hopeless situation, but he prayed anyway, harder than he'd ever prayed before that the terrorists had not yet seen him. He watched them, in horror as they slowly raised their assault rifles and took careful aim. In a flash, he realized that they had probably spotted him a mere second or two before; they had him dead to rights. He figured he was a dead man - there would be no missing him with the three of them firing, from that short distance. Clay knew beyond a shadow of a doubt, he'd never be able to get his AK assault rifle off his shoulder, up and aimed in time. At the same moment, Stryker went absolutely berserk, straining at the leash, growling and barking furiously. In the brief moments that the dog diverted their attention, Clay did the only two things he could think of at the time. He started saying his Hail Mary's, and hoped that there would be a last and only option to gain him the few seconds he desperately needed.

Chapter 22

Without having to think about it, Clay knew they had him dead cold. There was no earthly way he could pull his assault rifle off his shoulder, bring it up and fire, before the three terrorists fired at him. Stryker continued to strain at the chain, trying to get at the guerillas, growling and barking in a rage; Clay had difficulty reining him in. He could only guess that the dog associated the scent of these three with the others that had killed his master. He couldn't let the dog get loose, because he just knew the minute Stryker charged at them, they'd shoot him.

Without a thought and in one fluid motion, he transferred the chain to his left hand and wrapped it once, tightly around his fist. It was a spur of the moment idea, but he knew he needed something, anything, to give him a tiny, extra edge, if only for a few seconds. It was as if some unseen hand guided him he felt.

Whipping his right hand down to his belt, he yelled at the top of his lungs, "Stryker, stop! Sit!" Frustrated at not knowing what commands the dog trained to respond to, he had said the first things that came to his mind. For whatever unknown reason, the dog immediately responded to him. Perhaps it was the tone of his voice, he didn't know, but the dog stopped straining at the chain, remaining alert, staring straight at the intruders.

Grasping his heavy duty, angled flashlight in his hand, Clay literally ripped it off his belt in one motion, aimed it at the guerillas and flicked the switch on. It was so dark the beam seemed to light up the stygian darkness of the night like a football stadium. Aiming the strong beam right at their faces, he shined it into the eyes of all three, back and forth several times before they could get off a shot. The surprise of the beam of light in their eyes had a couple of potent consequences for the men. Clay could tell it caused them momentary confusion at the unexpected surprise and knew that it caused instant night blindness with the strong beam hitting their eyes. It gave him just enough time to react. Keeping the beam in their eyes, he knelt, presenting a smaller target and let the flashlight slide down his leg to the soft, moss covered ground. Swinging his right arm around, he had his AK-101 off his shoulder and in his hands in seconds. Bringing it up to fire, he flicked off the safety, roughly point aiming his weapon toward the guerillas.

They reacted as he had hoped they would, immediately firing their weapons. Clay expected to feel the burn of one or more bullets as they fired wildly in his direction. Knowing by kneeling he'd made his profile a smaller target, near the ground, he also recalled that shooters sometimes had a tendency to aim higher then they should. He was counting on that idiosyncrasy.

Aiming low, Clay let loose a long burst with his weapon, traversing all three terrorists. Taking no chances, he fired another long burst, lower to the ground, until his AK clicked on empty. Pulling out the taped, twin magazines, he switched them around and charged his rifle, ready for the next round.

Listening intently for a minute or two that seemed a lifetime, he heard no movement or anything, except the ringing in his ears from his gunfire. He picked up a slight sound from the location of the guerillas, the painful groaning of a wounded man.

Not waiting to press the issue and knowing this had probably been a fast moving, advance scouting party, Clay made a snap decision. He knew the main body had to be strung out some distance behind these men, but how far he had no idea and didn't care to find out. In all probability, they'd heard the gunfire and a backup reaction force could very well be rushing in this direction.

Realizing he had no time to waste, he shouldered his rifle, reached down and picked up his flashlight and shut it off. He checked it out, but there was no damage from when he'd dropped it. Clipping it back to his belt, he thanked his lucky stars one of the guys in the team had put in fresh batteries, insisting he might need it. His buddy had practically twisted his arm to take it with the rest of his gear. He was going to shake that's man's hand when he got back to the team. He knew it had helped to save his life.

Switching the chain to his right hand, he said to the dog with a touch of humor that he knew only he understood and would be lost on the dog, "Well, Stryker, it's time to get the hell outta Dodge! There's going to be a lot of unwelcome and very unhappy guests here very shortly!" Looking at Clay, Stryker twitched his ears a couple of times and stared at him with anticipation in his intelligent eyes. The dog appeared to be on Clay's wave-length because he trotted up to Clay, stopping next to him, then looked expectantly up at his new sidekick, as if to say, *okay, boss, lead the way.*

While the dog didn't understand a word he said, Stryker had an uncanny way about him in that he seemed to understand what Clay wanted. He wagged his tail a couple of times, looked down the trail, toward where the enemy would soon come from, looked up at Clay, and gave a short, sharp bark. "You're right pal, time to boogy outta here!" Clay said.

He was keenly aware that now they must run hard and fast, putting as much distance as they could between them and their pursuers. Clay knew the terrorists were going to be after them with a bone in their teeth, murderous vengeance in their heart, after finding the remains of their advance party. He squinted his eyes as he shined the light in the guerrilla's eyes, hoping he wouldn't lose his night vision, but he had lost most of it anyway, plus the flash from his rifle hadn't helped.

Taking a few moments and getting himself under control, Clay closed his eyes tight. He tried to keep them closed for as long as possible, knowing it had probably been only two minutes, even though it seemed a longer time. The urgency of their situation kept eating at him and kept him on edge.

Slowly opening his eyes, he noticed a usable portion of his night vision had returned. That coupled with the bright moon above, lit up the pathway better than he had hoped. Moving forward up the left branch of the trail, Stryker automatically took the lead.

Clay trotted along in a steady ground eating pace in what he remembered to be called the paratrooper shuffle. He wasn't running, nor was he walking, but the stride allowed him to eat up distance without being winded. His mind wandered momentarily back to those training days and all the miles he had racked up running.

He only theorized, but the appearance of those three guerillas at the branch had to be the doing of that cunning old guerrilla leader. Clay had to assume that he was pushing his men hard to catch up with him and the team. The problem was that if they had gotten their hands on the kind of Hi-tech communication system like he'd found on the sniper, then it was beginning to look very dire and dangerous for all of them. He began to wonder what else he or the team might run into by accident or otherwise.

The all-consuming heat was oppressive and felt like a heavy, damp blanket enveloping him. It just sapped the very energy out of him and it even took away any desire to eat food. One hopeful consolation - he didn't think the others behind him could keep up a hard, steady pace either. He had to slow down a bit and take a short breather for a few hundred yards or he would drop in his tracks from exhaustion. He couldn't even remember how long he'd been on the move, from the first step into this other existence to now. It was catching up with him fast.

Clay guesstimated he had probably covered around a mile from the branch of the trail when he finally forced himself to slow to a walk. Common sense told him he couldn't keep going like this or he'd eventually fall over into a dead sleep as he walked. He let out a short chuckle at the thought and Stryker turned in curiosity to see what was up with his new pal. Clay prayed he could catch up with his team soon, as he was in dire need of sleep.

His mind wasn't the most alert when Stryker suddenly stopped cold, staring at a spot off the trail just ahead. Moments later, he bared his fangs and a low, menacing growl began deep down in his chest. Clay, instantly, wide awake, and fully alert thought, *Now what? More terrorists?*

Quietly un-slinging his rifle, he took a couple of steps toward Stryker, standing frozen like a statue, intent on a nearby section off the trail. "What is it, buddy?" He said, not knowing what to expect at this point. "Whatcha got there?" Stryker gave no response, remaining frozen in place, the growl rapidly becoming stronger.

Mere seconds later he heard something very heavy, from the sound of it, crashing through the jungle and moving fast in his direction. It gave him the shivers, making loud, grunting noises, like some beast on the attack.

"God damn!" He said aloud, not realizing it. "What in the hell is that?" Stryker immediately leaped forward, almost tearing the chain out of his hand, barking furiously. Keeping a steady hold on the chain, Clay lowered his AK to waist high level, slid off the safety and prepared to fire. Not recalling if there were any dangerous animals in this southern jungle, he felt on razors edge. He couldn't figure out what moved through the jungle like an out of control express train, but his heartbeat had started trip hammering, his imagination running wild.

It moved toward him, making loud, angry grunting and snorting noises. The possibility that it might be a rogue Carabao bull gone wild momentarily flashed in his mind. He would never, ever want to mess with one of them, avoiding it at all costs. He knew that the local populace had for many decades domesticated this breed of Water Buffalo. Normally docile, a renegade one gone wild was a completely different matter.

His attention concentrated on the side of the trail about twenty-five yards ahead. In the shadowed moonlight a large, bulky beast burst through the jungle brush and stopped in the middle of the trail blocking his way. It clearly challenged him and the dog. He did his best to focus on the animal in the weak glitter of the moon. Huge and intimidating, about waist level height, it stood on short, stout looking legs. Clay couldn't miss the tiny, angry eyes confronting him in the moonlight. *Oh, shit! We've got big trouble here!* he thought.

Giving Stryker a terse command, the dog stopped the barking but stayed tensely on alert. All three froze, staring non-stop at each other and creating a highly volatile and dangerous standoff. Recognition suddenly registered like a bright neon sign in Clay's brain. *Geezuss H! That is the biggest damn wild pig I've ever seen in my life! I wouldn't want to mess with him in any way, now or ever. Okay! So how in the hell do I get us out of this in one piece? Gabe, where the hell are you when I need you?* He thought with genuine concern for the safety of both the dog and himself. Clay knew he had to keep the dog from tangling with this beast or the dog stood a good chance of getting badly hurt, no matter how brave Stryker had proven to be...

The beast gave an angry snort giving Clay the jitters, as he wasn't sure if or when the unpredictable animal would charge them. The monstrous beast pawed the ground in obvious agitation and defiance, seemingly trying to make up its mind as to what to do about these two intruders on its territory. Clay got ready, anticipating the irritated animal would charge them at any moment. Trying to defuse a clearly threatening situation he tersely said to Stryker, with special concern for the dog's safety, *"Back up, buddy!"* as he gently, but firmly pulled backward on the chain. *"Give that mean looking hunk of pork plenty of room!"*

The dog seemed reluctant but when Clay kept gently pulling on the chain and started to back up himself, the dog slowly complied. Clay and dog both continued to stay on the alert not knowing what was going on the tiny brain, of this irritated beast. He kept his rifle pointed at the animal in case it decided to take them on.

Moving back a half dozen feet, he stopped to see what the wild pig would do next; hopefully deciding to go on its way. The animal seemed ambivalent in the presence of the two intruders on its territory. Finally it stopped pawing the ground, its agitation appearing to slack off a bit. Turning slightly, back the way it had come out of the brush, it made some other kind of noises that Clay couldn't begin to figure out. Suddenly there was a distinct juvenile squealing noise, three young piglets burst from the concealing brush and swarmed around their mother.

Clay surprised by their appearance, realized what he had thought was a he, turned out to be a she, protecting her brood. He should have known better by her very attitude and behavior. She acted just like a momma Grizzly protecting her cubs, and just as dangerous. *Don't ever get between a momma and her kids, or you put your life at risk!* he thought.

Stryker apparently saw the whole thing with different eyes. The dog strained at the leash, whining and clearly wanting to get loose. Clay could only assume the dog was thinking what great sport this would be - chasing after a bunch of piglets. Sensing this could turn around and become a disastrous confrontation, Clay ordered in a low, stern voice, *"No Stryker! No! No!"* hoping the mother guarding her offspring, didn't hear him and panic. The dog continued to strain at the chain for a few moments longer, then obeyed his command and slacked off, sitting down and facing the mother. Clay kind of chuckled to himself, guessing the dog had accepted the fact he wasn't going to be able to go after the tasty looking piglets.

Clay continued to watch as the mother ministered after her tiny brood, wondering what was going to be her next move. After a few more moments, she took one last, disdainful look at Clay and the dog, made another nasty grunting noise and crashed off into the brush on the other side of the trail. Clay watched in amusement as the piglets took off after her in hot pursuit.

Greatly relieved that the confrontation had gone no further, Clay and the dog resumed their trek up the moonlit path. The tenseness of the situation had shed off him once they got moving, but fatigue rapidly caught up with him. He had an overwhelming desire to lie down and drop off into a deep sleep. Clay was well aware to do so had to be dangerous at this point. He was already thinking of other things, such as where could he set up the Claymore mine in a suitable location to insure it would not be discovered by that wily old guerilla leader.

He knew it had to be good because it was his last chance to stop and discourage the resolute pursuit of the enemy.

Pushing himself hard, Clay had two primary goals on his agenda. It was important to find an ideal location that his cunning adversary would not detect to set up the last ambush. Without a doubt, he knew this would be the biggest challenge in light of his enemy's extensive experience. Secondly, he hoped to catch up with his teammates before he totally ran out of steam so he could safely get some protected rest from his growing fatigue. Clay realized the two were closely tied together. If he could bloody the pursuing terrorists good enough with the Claymore, he was hoping they'd be discouraged and just turn back, thus relieving the pressure on him and the team. If only…he wished, in frustration.

He had traveled a little less than a mile by his estimate, when the ground began a gentle slope downward. Each side of the trail had low banks coming up to a little above his calf. He was surprised to see that the trail widened out a few feet. He became curious because it appeared to be a point of convergence by many animals. Shortly he found the reason why, the trail widened, ending in a shallow, sluggish moving stream. Obviously this was where the local animals came for their water. He guessed the waterway to be about twenty or so feet across. Stepping into the creek, it felt warm, coming up to just above knee level. In the moonlight, he could see almost nothing below the inky body of slowly moving water. Inspiration struck him as he stood there staring at the brook. *No little twig trick is going to work here!* he thought.

He'd been racking his brain, trying to figure the best location for the Claymore that the wily old guerilla, because of his apparent vast experience, wouldn't detect. This place was about as good as he was going to get in the limited amount of time he felt he had left. Clay knew he couldn't stick around this time to see the results so it had to be his best shot. While he wasn't exactly feeling confident that he'd nail them, after his last frustrating failure, he had to put as much distance between himself and his pursuers so he must set up this ambush with a great deal of care.

In the moonlight, he could see where the pathway resumed on the far side of the creek. Moving upstream about ten or so yards, he spotted what looked like a rock outcropping just breaking the surface. Moving over to the far bank, he carefully lay both rifles down, setting his pack down next to them. Pulling out the tripwire, he slung the pack back onto his shoulders and sloshed through the water to the small rock outcropping. He meticulously unwound a long section of tripwire and dipping his hands below the surface, wrapped it around the rock several times at about mid-calf height, tying it off securely. With the wire spool in one hand, he worked his way diagonally back downstream to the other bank. Moving carefully in the sluggish stream so as to not roil the bottom silt unnecessarily, leaving a telltale trace, Clay carefully inspected the bank, looking for just the right spot he needed.

Stopping about five yards beyond where the path entered the creek, he spotted what he had been looking for sticking out from the bank, angling down into the water. The small, sturdy root enabled him to loop the wire underneath to act as a very rudimentary pulley. Reaching under water, he looped the tripwire under the root and moved to the bank, which had a gentle, foliage covered slope rising from the stream. Exiting carefully, disturbing the underbrush as little as possible, Clay moved inland parallel to the trail, backtracking the way he had originally come earlier.

Moving away from the stream, he looked for just the right tree with a crook at the correct height, but couldn't find one. Using his head, he took a small, screw-in metal eyelet, with a tiny open slot at the end of the loop and searched in the dim light, looking for a suitable sapling. Finding one, he screwed the eyelet into the small tree and slipped the wire through the tiny gap, which allowed the wire to move smoothly. After disguising the shiny eyelet with some moss, he unwound the wire, moving parallel to the game trail. He kept looking for a good spot near it to set up the Claymore.

A short distance further, he found what he had been searching for, a close location, concealed from the trail, at a slightly higher level then the worn down trail. Setting down his pack, he removed the Claymore and opened up its three-pronged stand. Momentarily looking at the lethal mine in his hand he marveled at the lethal simplicity of the weapon. It looked somewhat like a fat, slightly convex rectangle. He knew the interior of the mine contained several hundred tiny, flesh-shredding ball bearings. The raised letters on the convex side, *FRONT TOWARD ENEMY,* left no doubt as to the proper positioning of the weapon. *Well,* he thought to himself, *I can only hope this lethal hunk of hardware works and slows the terrorists down; the last booby trap was a total failure.*

Clay set the mine at an angle aimed down the trail in such a way that when it was tripped it would fire in a wide, pie-shaped pattern outward. At this distance, the blast pattern would hopefully have the greatest coverage, catching as many of the terrorists on the trail as possible. He felt this was his last chance.

After tightening up the wire and meticulously wiring up and arming the device, he worked his way back to the creek, crossing over to where his rifles lay, careful not to trip his concealed wire. Stryker waited patiently for him on the other side. Clay was pleased when the dog stood up as he approached, and wagged his tail a few times, giving a short welcome yip, as if to say, *Glad you made it back!* "Okay, buddy, I'm done and we're outta here!" he said to the dog.

Picking up the trail again they set a steady pace. After traveling, by Clay's rough estimate, about a mile, he heard a sharp whump of an explosion behind him in the distance. He instantly knew the Claymore had been tripped. Feeling it had not been a smart idea to stick around to check out the situation, as he had done foolishly before, Clay kept up the steady, ground eating stride. He just hoped the mine had caused enough causalities and damage that the terrorists would have second thoughts about continuing the pursuit and maybe back down. Now that this final effort had been accomplished, he could concentrate all his efforts on catching up with the team. It gave him a little peace of mind at the same time knowing he may have slowed or stopped the enemy so he and the team had a better chance to escape and return safely to their base.

Checking his watch Clay, noted he'd been on the run for more than a few hours. The fatigue had begun to take its toll on his body and he felt he had finally reached the end of his rope. Totally exhausted from the continuous physical and mental tension he didn't feel he was capable of taking ten more steps.

Knowing he had to stop soon, he started looking for a suitable spot where he could get off the trail, conceal himself, and get some desperately needed rest. He figured ten or twenty minutes would revive him. Several yards up the trail, he spotted what looked like the overgrown remnants of another narrow game trail that bisected the main pathway that he traveled. Smaller than the track he was on, it looked like something rabbits or other small game would use. Deciding to investigate, he carefully pushed his way through the light brush overhanging the tiny track, vividly remembering his recent experience with that ill-natured momma pig.

Moving several yards along the trail, it opened up on his left to a tiny clear area, dominated by medium sized, umbrella like tree that gave a small degree of shelter. A quick look around the area convinced him he'd be safe and secure here long enough to get his needed rest. He couldn't tell in the darkness, but underneath the tree was a soft looking bed of leaves from the tree. Of course, his active imagination warned him of what venomous thing might be waiting for him under that inviting soft looking carpet. As a precaution, he told Stryker to stay then walked around the whole leafy carpet, shuffling his feet to disturb the leaves, seeing if anything scurried out from underneath. Gratified, after his inspection that nothing had made a home beneath the dead leaves, he made himself at home.

Glancing again at the small trail in the dim moonlight, it looked to him to be unused and he felt that nothing had come this way in a long time. He didn't want to be surprised in the middle of the night by some uninvited, four-footed guest. Satisfied he laid his AK101 on the ground, within easy reach. Slinging the Dragunov off his shoulder he gently set it next to his other weapon. Pulling off his pack, Clay put it on the leaves by the softest looking spot. Speaking to Stryker, he said, "Okay, pal, it's time for a short snooze." Not wanting to take a chance of losing the dog that he had become very attached to, he took a small, extra precaution. He hoped he wouldn't regret doing this, but he had to be sure the dog wouldn't wander off to chase wild game and possibly get in trouble. He wrapped the chain around the small tree several times and tied it off.

Clay gratefully lay down, resting his head on his pack. Moments later his eyes involuntarily slid shut. He drifted off into a deep, dreamless sleep, the nightmarish images of his buddies long gone. Stryker made himself comfortable near his head and laid his muzzle on his front paws, his ears continuing to twitch around at the jungle sounds of the night. In moments he also closed his eyes.

Clay's dreamless sleep had seemed like days had passed, it seemed so deep, but it wasn't, as his subconscious mind alerted him to a new and alien disturbance. So exhausted he could hardly move his leaden body, he tried to pull himself up from his deep slumber. As the seconds ticked by, the low growl of Stryker immediately caused his sleep clouded mind concern. His brain kept repeating to him, over and over again, *Why is Stryker growling? Why is Stryker growling? Something is not right!* A second later a shrill, panic feeling coursed through his body with the speed of light. He knew in an instant tht he was no longer asleep and this was not a dream. *Had the terrorists caught up with him?* His mind screamed at him in panic. Stryker's growls became more strident.

Feeling a tapping on his boot, he struggled to raise his leaden eyelids and didn't even begin to raise them till the next moment when he'd experienced a slight sting to the sole of his foot. His groggy brain kept telling him that it felt like some insect or reptile had bitten him. But it didn't make a bit of sense, it repeated logically, how could something like that bite him through the sole of his boot? He just wasn't thinking in this state and he'd better wake up fast, his brain cautioned, because he had the unmistakable feeling he was in trouble. Stryker had started to growl louder, breaking out in angry barking, the chain rattling, where he was secured to the tree.

Snapping open his eyes in panic, the first thing he noticed it was foggy and it looked like early dawn. The thought flashed through his mind, he'd slept way longer than he had intended. A moment later when his eyes focused, he found himself staring down the barrel of an old bolt-action rifle with a razor sharp looking bayonet attached to the end. The hole at the end of the barrel looked as big as the Holland Tunnel to him. The first and last idle thought that floated in his confused mind was, *What in the hell is an Islamic terrorist doing with an old antique rifle when they were all supposed to be supplied with new smuggled in AK-74's?*

The individual at the other end of the rifle appeared short and thin, maybe somewhere in his upper eighties in age, it looked like. The old man had a fierce, angry look in his dark eyes, a weathered face that had the look of soft, tanned leather. The white beard covering his face had a sprinkling of gray. Clay could see at one time the man had been dark haired. Small clumps of white hair carelessly stuck out of a very unusual hat, setting purposefully on his head. Clay noticed it looked somehow familiar, but couldn't place it for a moment. Then it came to him in a flash. *Holy shit!* he thought. He saw the hat was faded and weathered now, but still worn proudly. It had once been a unique khaki color he realized, as recognition dawned on him. Above the short brim was a faded red star and attached to the back of it a flap of frayed cloth to protect the wearer's neck from the sun. Clay couldn't believe he was looking at a man wearing a garrison cap belonging to a member of the Imperial Japanese Army of World War Two. Further confirmation came when Clay gazed at the faded and patched military type blouse on the man. He wore a pair of course straw-colored pantaloons and well used tire-track sandals. Clay could see there appeared to be a great deal of pride and fighting spirit still in the old soldier.

Realization flashed over Clay like the rapid unreeling of a motion picture. He had recalled touring a World War Two military museum the small town of Mabalacat in the the Northern Philippines, near the former Clark U.S. Air Force base. There had been a small display of military weapons, including the one the old soldier held with such practiced confidence. Clay recognized it as an Arisaka assault rifle. And the man looking down at him, a former Japanese soldier, one of the one's who'd fled to the jungle after U.S. forces had invaded and retaken the Philippine Islands.

The old soldier looked every bit as military, after all these years, as he must have been in his younger years. Clay could see the man was still very proud and a fighting spirit still dwelled in the man, even after all these years. Very fit looking, an unusual anger appeared to be burning in those dark eyes that Clay couldn't begin to comprehend.

"Tate! Tate!" the man shouted angrily, gesturing upward with his rifle. Clay had no idea what the man yelled at him, as he began to struggle to his feet. Stryker was going berserk, barking wildly, straining at the chain and trying to get loose, with full intent of tearing into their tormenter. Clay looked backward over his shoulder and noticed the chain had begun to become undone. The old Japanese soldier seemed to have lost all tolerance, raising his rifle and pointing it toward Stryker. Clay knew he only had moments to defuse the situation or the dog would die.

Chapter 23

Geezus! This old guy still thinks the war is going on! Now what in the hell am I gonna do? Gabe, where the hell are you? John Wayne! Where are you when I need you?

The angry man screamed a torrent of Japanese at him while brandishing a vintage bolt-action rifle threateningly. Clay, totally befuddled by the strange confrontation wondered where he had come from. How had he so quietly snuck up on him and what does he want? The questions flew through his mind in rapid-fire succession.

As if in answer to the man's words, a female voice said from behind the him in broken, but understandable English, "He say, 'Get up! 'Stand up!' to you two times! He lose patience with you! Do now, or he shoot you and your dog! You make him very angry!"

Not taking any chances or wasting another minute, Clay scrambled to his hands and knees and clumsily managed to get upright. Stryker wildly barked and tried to break loose. Fearing for the dog, Clay said in a harsh, commanding voice, "Stryker, quiet! Sit!" He said it twice more before the dog seemed to understand and finally stopped the tirade. Still on the alert, he stood in place staring hard at the stranger with the rifle.

The old soldier eyed Clay's pack and two rifles on the ground. Pointing his lethal, bayonet-tipped weapon at Clay's chest, he yelled twice, "Te o agero!"

Clay looked back at him totally puzzled, having no idea what the man yelled at him. In a few seconds, a Philippine woman stepped out from where she had been hidden behind the man. She appeared small and aged like the soldier, but he guessed her to be ten to fifteen years younger. Even at this stage of her life, he found her to be still very attractive. Sprinkles of gray peeked through her lustrous black hair. Her clothes were simple, lose fitting peasant garments. Her face told volumes of the apparent hard life she must have endured. Clay had a questioning look on his face and seeing this, she said, "He say, 'put your hands up!'"

In response, Clay slowly raised his hands up to shoulder level, stalling for time while his mind raced, looking for a way out of this strange situation. Breaking the silence, in between the exchanges of the two of them, Clay said, "Why? I'm no threat to him or you!"

She relayed this information to the man rapidly, and the burning, angry look flared anew in the man's eyes. Pointing with his rifle at the weapons on the ground, he spat out the angry words, "Omae wa watashi no hitojichida!" then accusingly said something additional to the woman.

"What did he say?"

"He say, 'You are my prisoner.'"

"What? Prisoner? Why?" Clay retorted angrily, now more puzzled at why this old soldier was accusing him, in so many words.

She replied, "Because he say you are a soldier and his enemy!"

"I am *not* his enemy! In fact, I can help him!"

She relayed this to her man and after a short, cynical laugh, he said something further to her. "He say you are the enemy because you have the weapons of the enemy!"

"No, that is not right! I took them *from* my enemy!"

Another quick conversation followed between the two, then the man gave a cynical laugh and raised his rifle to his shoulder as if he were going to fire. Clay pushed his hands forward in a gesture of supplication and said, "No, please, wait, wait, I am not your enemy! Please believe me!"

The woman looked at Clay for a moment and said, "You are American?"

"Yes."

"Then he say you are his prisoner of war!"

"The war has been over for many years!"

"He say you lie! And why do you carry the weapons of our enemy?"

"Let me try to explain," Clay said, unconsciously beginning to lower his arms. His mind a whirl, wondering how could he possibly explain to this old warrior and his woman where he had come from?

Seeing this move, the old man yelled at Clay, brandished his rifle like a pointing stick and motioning upward.

"He say, 'Put your hands up'. He means business! He is a very angry man!"

Clay raised his hands back up and tried to reason with them. "Please explain to him that the war between Japan and the United States has been over for more than sixty years now. We are at peace with Japan."

"He say you lie!"

"No! It is true! We are close allies with Japan and help to defend her from would be aggressors like North Korea!"

"Korea belong to Japan," the man said as a forgone conclusion.

"No, that has been over for many years. After World War Two, Korea split into free South Korea and Communist North Korea, the aggressor. I would not make up a wild story like that!"

A brief look of doubt appeared on the man's face, as he quickly said something to Clay. The woman translated, "He still don't believe you! What proof do you have?"

Clay replied, "I have proof and can show him, but not now - later." Continuing, he said, "So what are we going to do? We can't stand here all day!"

Stryker chose this moment to disobey his orders and erupted in another burst of angry barking at the old soldier. He strained hard at his chain, doing his utmost to break free. The soldier took a step to the side, giving him a clear view of the dog, which stood behind Clay. Raising his rifle, the man took careful aim at Stryker,

In a pure panic, Clay yelled at the top of his lungs, "No! No! No! Don't shoot him!" He leaped back, directly in front of Stryker, unmindful that he might get shot in an attempt to block the aim of the rifle.

In the sudden confrontation, the man yelled something, but the woman seemed paralyzed in fear and said nothing. Clay dropped to his knees and took Stryker in his arms. He turned his back to the soldier and used his body to shield the dog. "Go ahead and shoot me, you God Damn coward! Shooting a defenseless dog! You are nothing but the lowest of the low! Crawl back under the rock where you came from!"

His angry burst seemed to have jolted the woman out of her silence and she quickly translated to her man. The soldier seemed surprised by the impudence of this individual who was clearly his prisoner and he lowered his rifle. Still keeping it at waist height and leveled at Clay, he replied to his wife and she translated now that the situation appeared to be somewhat defused. "He say, he do not understand you Americans and your animals. You would die for that animal?"

Clay looked him steadily in the eye and said, "You wouldn't understand! Maybe someday, if we survive I'll explain it to you!"

Another rapid exchange followed between the two. Looking at Clay, she said, "No, explain! He wants to know now!"

Addressing both of them Clay replied, "This is my friend! This is my partner! We take care of each other and he would gladly give his life to protect me...and I would do the same for him! That's something you are incapable of understanding."

Both the man and woman seemed stunned by his response. Looking down for a moment, the soldier grunted and spoke to Clay in his language and then turned to her to translate. "You are wrong! Maybe we do understand. You don't know everything!" She translated, then stopped, unable to suppress some tears that coursed freely down her cheeks.

Clay could now see and begin to understand that somewhere in their past life, this couple had suffered a personal loss. He had no idea what it was and felt sure they wouldn't tell him, a mere stranger and apparent enemy to them.

In his exhaustion he knew he had slept much too long and any survivors of the terrorists would be coming up the trail soon. There had to be some way to convince this old soldier that he meant no harm to the two of them and they all needed to leave at once.

Choosing a direct approach, omitting an explanation of the doorway, he explained how he had returned with fresh water and had run into the terrorist patrol attacking his friends. The soldier listened and grunted his acknowledgment a few times as Clay explained all the previous events that had led him to this spot.

Pointing at the rifles Clay said, "I took these weapons from my enemy, your enemy too ! We cannot stay here. They are coming after my friends ahead of us and myself. If they catch us, they will kill us all and that includes you two!"

"How can we be sure you are telling the truth?" the woman asked.

"These guerillas are al-Qaeda terrorists that are after me. I have tried to slow them down, but they may have gathered reinforcements by now. They are sure to be on their way and we must leave now!"

A rapid exchange in Tagalog between the two followed and Clay heard the man mention al-Qaeda and Abu Sayef in the exchange. The old soldier grunted again, nodding his head up and down a number of times, apparently in understanding, Clay hoped. Both looked at Clay straight in the eyes, searching for any hint of dishonesty, he figured.

"My man says he still don't believe you, but you are right, we must go! We know al-Qaeda, they are bad people!"

"Okay, but how are we going to do this!" Clay asked.

"He say you unload the small rifle and carry it. The long one with the scope, you will carry on your shoulder."

"Okay, fair enough," he said, cautiously kneeling down, under the watchful eye of the man. He picked up his AK-101, released the magazine and set it on the ground. With the rifle pointed away from the couple, he ejected the one round in the chamber and put it in his blouse pocket. Picking up the magazine, he reinserted it in the rifle, but did not load a round in the chamber. He knew if he had to, he could charge the weapon in seconds and be ready to fire. Showing the rifle to the man, he said, "Okay? Can we go now?"

The soldier looked at Clay and with a half smile on his face, said, "Okay," It surprised Clay that the man had said it in English.

Setting his AK-101 down, Clay shouldered the pack and slung the Draganov onto his right shoulder. Picking up his AK in his left hand purposely to show that he wasn't going to try anything, he slowly stood upright. Stepping over to Stryker, he undid the chain and looped a double wrap around his fist. Moving past the couple with the dog, in the direction of the trail, Stryker started a low growl aimed at them. Clay immediately reacted and commanded in a stern voice, "No! No! No Stryker! Let them be!" The animal looked up at Clay, a questioning look on his face, as if to say, *Are you sure this is what you want to do, boss?*

Clay smiled down at him, in an attempt to reassure the dog, saying, "It's okay Stryker, they're friends." The woman followed through by rapidly translating every word to her man. He gave a brief smile and nodded his head in understanding. Clay pushed his way through the thick brush of the tiny game trail toward the main pathway. The couple followed a safe distance behind him.

Reaching the primary track Clay, did not immediately step out of concealment. Being very cautious, he carefully parted the foliage to observe in every direction of the pathway. Stryker, at the same time, sniffed the air for any sign of the enemy. Satisfied that no one had detected them and waited for their appearance, he stepped out on to the corridor and briskly moved up it with the dog leading. The old couple picked up the pace and followed.

With Stryker straining eagerly at his leash, leading the way, the group advanced at a vigorous pace up the main track. They had gone three or four miles when the dog slowed to sniff and investigate the ground. If Clay had to guess he figured the dog might have picked up fresh some scent from mere hours ago. Clay was concerned as to what or whose scent the dog had picked up.

Excited that they might be getting close to his friends, Clay insisted on picking up the pace and moving at close to a trot. Soon, he came across that which he missed, on reaching the branch of the trail the previous evening. Heavy drag marks gouging the soft earth of the trail were evident - this was a heartening indicator to him. Thinking about it, Clay figured that his team had deliberately picked up and carried the travois litters, in an effort to confuse the enemy as to the direction the group had taken. They had not realized that it had also steered him up the wrong branch and almost gotten him killed. Fortunately, it turned out in his favor.

An hour later, winded by the strenuous pace he'd set, Clay came upon a long, heavily overgrown bend in the pathway when someone up ahead cut loose with a burst of automatic rifle fire in his direction. They all dove for the nearest cover. Screaming at the top of his lungs, Clay yelled, "Hey! Stop firing! Friendlies!"

A shaky voice replied, "Halt where you are and be recognized!"

Royally pissed off, Clay shouted back angrily, "Hey! You dumb ass! You're not standing guard post outside some stateside barracks! This is the fucking jungle! Now cool it!"

For a few seconds silence followed, then the voice said, "Stand up and show yourself!"

Clay yelled back, "You better not shoot at me again or I'll kick your miserable butt all the way back to California!" He then stood up with his hands in the air as a precaution and stepped into the middle of the trail.

"I don't believe it!" the voice said, "It's Clay! We all thought you were dead! We had heard a lot of shots and explosions in the distance and thought they'd gotten you."

"Well they didn't, but you almost did, O'Reilly!" Clay had recognized the youngest member of his team. "What'd they do, give you *Tail End Charlie,* rear guard duty again?"

"Afraid so. I'm really sorry about taking a shot at you. We are very spooked. We've been hearing a lot of movement around us and aren't taking any chances."

"Okay, pal, you're off the hook. I'm alive and well and I've brought some new friends with me."

Clay watched in amusement as the guard registered a surprised look on his face on seeing the Japanese soldier and his woman. "Where in the heck…" Before he had a chance to finish, one of the other team members made an appearance.

Clay noted the surprised look on his face also, as he said, "Never a dull moment around you, huh Clay?"

Replying in a calm voice and wondering how they all would take it when he explained the presence of the couple, Clay said, "I guess you could say that, Babcock…and oh, by the way, in case you're wondering about the uniform, this gentleman is a member of the Imperial Japanese Army! Also, I'd like to inform you that we are all his prisoners of war!" Clay noted the immediate amazed reaction on their faces. "He is of the belief that Japan is still at war with the United States!"

"Prisoner of war?" O'Reilly said. "You can't be serious!"

"Never more serious in my life!" Clay said. "And I think it might be a good idea to join up with the others before he gets antsy and decides to shoot one of you two. He kind of likes me!"

That was enough for the other two. Both turned without another comment and led the group up the trail toward the team's location. On reaching the temporary encampment, Clay could see a perimeter had been set up, facing down the trail, as if they had been expecting a fight. They all stood up and got out from behind temporary firing positions and either slung or lowered their rifles.

All were happy to see that Clay had survived. Rick couldn't contain his curiosity, saying, "What about the terrorists? We all thought they had gotten you!"

"No, I've been very lucky and able to keep one step ahead of them."

Nodding toward Stryker, Rick said in his typical, wisecracking, Philadelphia way, "So what's with the hair bag? Where'd you pick *him* up?"

Clay grinned and said, "Don't talk about my new partner that way! His name is Stryker and he might get hurt feelings." He laughed. Stryker seemed to realize he was the center of attention and wagged his tail a few times, then relaxed and sat down, comfortable next to his new master. Clay went on to briefly explain how he had taken the wrong branch of the trail and how he had discovered the dog. "He's a trained K-9 patrol dog and he's damn good at sniffing out the bad guys. I found out!"

Rick asked, "So what's the story on those two?" indicating the man and woman.

"That's a long story, but here's the short version," Clay replied and then went on to describe his meeting up with them. "And oh, by the way, I forgot to mention. I am officially his prisoner of war!" Seeing their confused expressions, he continued, "And so are all of you!"

"You are joking, right?" Rick said, half in jest, but with a serious look in his eyes. "Tell me this is one of your lame jokes!"

"No joke! I have never been more serious in my life!"

As the two spoke, Clay glanced over at the couple and noted the woman had been rapidly translating every word of the conversation to her man. Everyone had their eyes on him as he stepped forward and faced the group. He spoke rapidly in Japanese, holding his rifle at port arms, diagonally across his chest and ready for instant use. Clay recalled the words the man had spoken to him from his early encounter.

The woman spoke slowly and clearly to the group. "He says you are all his prisoners!"

Disbelief showed on the faces of every member of the team. They remained silent for a few moments in total shock at the strange proclamation. The young team member, O'Reilly uttered the first words. Clay recalled the man was a somewhat brash individual, from the Bronx, who had a habit of popping off without thinking. Taking an aggressive stance and moving a few feet toward the old soldier, O'Reilly sneered, "He's got to be kidding, right?" When no one answered, he went on, "That old antique he's carrying can't hurt anything and probably won't even shoot! Hell they most likely don't even make shells for it anymore!"

The woman didn't even have to translate because the old man picked up the message clearly from O'Reilly's voice and body language. The rifle came up in a flash, the butt locking into the man's shoulder tightly. An audible click and the safety was released. The instant flash of anger appeared on the man's face as the rifle came swiftly up and

pointed at O'Reilly's head. O'Reilly's eyes became as big as saucers as
he realized his fatal mistake in judgment.

Clay leaped forward in a desperate effort to step between the two.
"No! No! Don't do that!" he yelled. Too late! The flat crack and instant
echo of the rifle firing reverberated around the small clearing, stinging
their ears. Everyone reacted immediately and dropped to the ground
for *any* kind of cover.

Chapter 24

No one blinked or moved a muscle. All eyes locked on the old warrior and O'Reilly. Speechless, Clay watched as O'Reilly, totally dumbfounded, slowly sagged to his knees staring straight ahead in complete shock.

Out of the corner of his eye Clay watched in fascination as the old soldier flipped up the bolt of the rifle with the palm of his hand and slapped it back in a blur of motion, ejecting the spent shell casing. With the same automatic, fluid motion, he pushed the bolt forward, stripped off a new round, and chambered it. The bolt handle slapped down, and he was ready to fire again. His wife picked up the spent shell casing and dropped it into a small pouch hanging from her shoulder.

That ought to take the brash edge off O'Reilly for a while! He'll remember the moment for the rest of his life! Clay thought.

O'Reilly, completely chastised, looked beseechingly at the old warrior, a pitiful look on his face. "Please don't shoot me!" he pleaded. "I'm sorry, I apologize!"

The woman translated the words and a brief smile cracked the corner of the man's mouth. Clay realized that the man had slightly raised the muzzle of the rifle a moment before he fired. The minute amount of elevation at his end had been magnified as the bullet flew toward O'Reilly and passed harmlessly over his head. Clay doubted if anyone had detected the move and his respect for the old warrior went up several notches. The man could have easily killed O'Reilly and still held them all at bay. Clearly, he was not a cold-hearted killer as the façade he projected. It was a warning and had claimed everyone's undivided attention.

"Any more dumb statements, O'Reilly?" Clay tensely asked, his ears still ringing from the shot. "You didn't think he was serious?" Nodding toward the soldier.

"Well, I…"

Clay cut him off. "Couldn't you tell by the look on his face that the man wasn't joking?"

"But…"

"No buts about it, pal! Very bad move! I'd been trying to build a little bit of trust in the man regarding our intentions and you just blew it for all of us!"

"Sorry…"

"Yeah, well we all may be sorry now!"

The team stood up and watched the man to see what he would do next. He had them cold. They all had their rifles ready but it was a standoff. Everyone realized he'd get one or more of them before they got him so no one made an aggressive move.

Swinging his rifle in a slow arc and back around the group, the old soldier spit out a brief torrent in Japanese.

"What did he say?" Clay asked, the first to have the courage to utter a word.

"He say, 'I wonder if anyone else wants to challenge me'?"

Looking at the two of them, Clay said, "This is very important. I repeat, please try to explain to him that we mean no harm to both of you. Bear with me for a few moments while I try to figure out how to show him."

She spoke again without translating, "Hurry, because time is running out for my husband and me!"

Clay realized the woman was absolutely correct. Time was running out – for all of them! They couldn't afford to stay here another moment, they must get moving. A terrorist scouting party surely had to be on the way to investigate the gunshot.

Clay had everyone lower their rifles, then back off. Speaking to the woman he said, "You are correct, we must leave immediately. But we have a problem that must be solved first. We have to somehow reach a truce with your husband or we won't be going anywhere! He needs to give us a chance to prove what we have been trying to explain to him. The war is long over and we are not your enemy! The enemy is out there!" He indicated, pointing down the trail and around them.

The pair held a hurried conference as Madeleine translated to her husband. "My husband and I have talked it over." Nodding to Clay, she continued, "If you give us your solemn oath of honor that you nor any of your friends will betray us, then we agreed to what you have asked."

"Yes, I agree. We all agree," he said as they all nodded their heads.

"Good! Now let us get moving!" she answered.

Clay and Rick quickly checked the map, estimating their position and got the column moving up the trail at a brisk clip. Clay guessed they had a little over five miles to what looked like a dirt road on the map that appeared to pass close to a deserted World War Two Japanese airfield. Clay and Rick had discussed it and figured it would be a good landing zone for a rescue. As a precaution Rick had a rearguard of two men lag behind them by a hundred yards so any pursuing terrorists would not catch them by surprise.

Walking along with the couple Clay kept racking his brain on how to prove to the old soldier what he had been saying. He kept thinking about it, and then inspiration hit him a few minutes later.

"Hey, Galloway?" he said to one of the soldiers up ahead. "You still have that stuff you were told not to carry with you on patrol?"

"I don't know what you're talking about, Clay?

"Oh, come on, you know what I mean! The pictures!"

He reluctantly replied, "Yeah, I have them in my pack."

"Good! Come back here and show these people."

When Galloway came over to the couple, Clay said to them, "I'd like to introduce you to Specialist Galloway. He has something he'd like to show you."

Galloway pulled his pack off and rummaged around in it until he came up with a small, brown leather-bound folder and handed it to Clay. Taking it, he gave it to Madeleine, saying, "I would like you and your husband to take a good look at these pictures. They are of my friend here, his Japanese wife and their children."

Both Madeleine and the old soldier paged through the photographs, commenting to each other. Turning to Clay, she said, "My husband Kenji wants to know where they were taken?"

"They were taken in present day Tokyo,." Clay said. "At a famous American amusement park called Disneyland and around the city."

The husband showed visible shock. "He say, 'This can't be'!"

"Please believe me, it is! I wanted to show them to you to prove the war is over and we are at peace with Japan!" Clay said.

There was a quick exchange between the two, and then she said, "He say, 'I find it hard to believe this is really Tokyo'!"

"But it is! Now are you willing to believe us?"

They discussed it again and she said, "He say, 'Yes'!"

"Good, then let's keep moving."

Seeing a sharp bend in the trail up ahead, Rick slowed the column down while he sent two men ahead to check it out. It was clear to Clay he did this to ensure there were no unwelcome surprises beyond the bend. With the pace slowing a little it gave Clay an opportunity to ask some more questions. "I hope you don't mind, but how did you and your husband meet?"

"I found him starving in the jungle. When the Americans returned, he was very frightened because their leaders had told them all that the Americans would execute them. That is why he fled into the jungle. I took him back to my hut and nursed him back to health."

"That's very commendable. But why are you running now?"

Before she could answer, the word filtered back the all clear and they moved off again. Clay took his turn helping to carry the travois litters and then rejoined the woman and her husband.

Madeleine said, "We were married and happy for a long time. We moved to a small village in the mountains and had two children, a boy and a girl. They were grown up and ready to begin their own lives when the terrorists came. They demanded that the village support them. The village chief refused and they killed him. Everyone fought back, but were no match for the guerillas. Both our children died in the fight. My husband killed many but the village was practically wiped out. Some terrorists got away but we knew they would come back, so we had to escape to the jungle. That is why my poor husband is so angry. The terrorists ruined our lives and killed our children, can you now understand how he feels?"

"I am truly sorry. It must be difficult – your loss!"

"More than you can know."

"What will you do?"

"We hid all our possessions in a cave and hope to return for them some day soon. Then maybe we can live in peace. So how did you and your men happen to be here?"

Clay briefly explained how their helicopter had been shot down and the fight with the terrorists. They were curious why he had lagged behind his team and he explained his role. "Now, our plan is to get to a good, open extraction point so the rescue aircraft can safely come and get us. We should have enough battery life left on our emergency radio to contact passing aircraft."

The old warrior spoke briefly and his wife said, "He says that is dangerous! He was a radio operator in the Army and is worried that the terrorists will home in on your signal and pinpoint where you are!"

"Very true. Our only hope is the rescue aircraft can get to us before the terrorists."

She translated and then replied, "My husband said that is taking a very dangerous chance. He has seen those big hovering birds - they are very slow. He would like to know what is you destination?"

Clay knew the man was making reference to the helicopters he had seen passing in the air. He asked Rick to pull out the map, stepped to the side of the moving column and lay the map on the ground. Clay, Rick and the couple grouped around it. Pointing to an area of the map, Clay explained, "Located here is the remains of an old Japanese fighter strip, from the war that was carved out of the jungle. It is in the open with no encroaching mountains to cut off radio signals, so communications should be fairly good for contacting aircraft passing in the vicinity.

Clay listened while Rick determined where they were at this point and how far they had to go. Rick said, "As far as I can determine, we are located about here," he said indicating a spot on the map. "The trail we are traveling crosses what appears to be a dirt road that heads south from the area near the air strip. When we reach that road, we should be able to take it toward the airfield pretty easily and maybe there before dark."

The old warrior looked closely at the map, pointing at two different spots, in close proximity, to the airstrip. Touching the map in each spot with a calloused finger he shook his head and said a few words to his wife.

"He has traveled around much of this area in the past. My husband said to go this way would be very dangerous. What he is pointing at are two large encampments of terrorists just a few miles from the airfield, what you would call training camps. If you must go to the field, the best way would be to travel at night and hide in daylight. You would still be taking a very big risk!"

"Well, what do you think? Is it worth taking the risk? I don't see any other alternative, do any of you?" Clay asked the group.

Rick and the group all agreed this was the best chance they had of rescue. Before the discussion went any further, after a quick, muted conversation between the pair, Madeleine said, "There is one other possibility."

The man bent over the map and pointed to a spot, which appeared to be about a half a mile from where their trail bisected the dirt road leading toward the airstrip. The man said a few words to his wife and she turned to the group, "He say it is too dangerous to go to the air strip and strongly recommends against it. At the spot he is indicating your group can make their way safely to the sea. Once on the coast you should be able to hire or find a boat big enough for all of you."

Everyone peered closely at the map where his finger pointed. Clay said, "I don't see any kind of a road or trail there."

Madeleine replied, "He said there is none! By going cross-country he feels this is the best and shortest route to the coast and safety."

On hearing this, Clay and Rick held a quick strategy session to determine what was best for all of them. Clay watched closely as Rick bent over and measured the distances involved in the two alternate routes.

After discussing it a little further, Clay said, "He's measured between the two and it is approximately twice as far to the coast as it is to the airfield. With luck, we should be able to get to the airstrip faster and have a better opportunity of contacting our aircraft. We've chosen to stick to the original plan and head toward the field."

On hearing this, the old warrior replied through Madeleine, "He thinks you are making a grave mistake. But that is your choice. Since we now feel it is no longer safe for us to remain in the area, we will go with you - if it would be possible for you to take us with you on your aircraft, and we can begin again in a safer area."

"We understand your concerns but this appears to be the simplest solution so we will take the chance. Yes, we would be happy to help you and will take you with us. Now we must get moving. We have no way of knowing but the group to our rear may be getting closer."

Finishing up, Clay, Rick and the couple rejoined the moving column. Clay stationed himself with the couple near the head of the group with Rick. Clay, aware that the danger of being detected by the terrorists had increased, approved when Rick sent out two scouts ahead of the main body.

A half mile from the juncture of the trail and the road to the airfield, they were crossing a shallow dip in the ground about fifteen feet wide when the old warrior held up his hand, motioning them to stop. Pointing at the washed out area crossing the pathway, he spoke. "He say he has seen where this dry stream bed goes. It winds in a gradual gradient course, draining into the sea. During the monsoon, heavy rains build up and the rushing waters have created this gully. This is the other route he spoke of earlier," Madeleine said.

Clay inspected the arroyo with a practiced eye. It had a sandy, level bottom with a sprinkling of small, sparse bushes growing in the center. He recognized they would not hinder their progress should they have to use this route. It looked very inviting, but he knew they had decided it would be a last resort, due to the extra distance, which he didn't feel they'd need.

Clay had a funny feeling about their situation. He passed it off as a sixth sense or maybe a hunch, it didn't matter, he just had an uneasy feeling. Stepping over to where Rick moved with the column, he said, "Rick, I'm having an uneasy feeling about the route to the airfield. I think we need to cover our bases."

Rick listened, then said, "And how do you plan to do that?"

"Okay, we know a guerilla scouting party is somewhere down the trail. Could be a mile, could be four or five miles. We have no way of telling. The main body will be behind them by a couple of hundred yards or more.

"What do you have in mind?"

"Okay, here's what I'm thinking. The chances are good we havev some time – time we can use to our benefit. What I'm recommending is we set up a defensive position here at the arroyo, while our scouting party checks out the dirt road."

"I don't understand? Why are you saying that?"

"Okay, here's the way I see it. From the map it looks like that dirt road is fairly developed. I'm just getting a bad feeling with that terrorist training camp nearby. They may have regular patrols along it – and if we walk into one, we could be in a lot of trouble."

"True, if that happens."

"It's a simple thing. I just want to keep our backdoor open in case we have to make a hasty exit. The scouts check out the road, and if they give us the all okay we head up the road. How about it?"

"Okay, we'll try it your way."

Rick took charge of setting up defensive positions, while Clay continued on toward the road crossing. The scouting party, which was two hundred yards ahead of him was no longer in sight. Clay was not worried, guessing they had reached the other road and were now reconnoitering up it. He could feel anticipation and excitement growing within the group. They were close to their destination and eminent rescue, but they still had a few obstacles to get by, he realized. Clay figured they'd go as far as they safely could undetected, in daylight, then lay over in concealment till nightfall, continuing on to the field. This time they would make sure the rescuers brought enough air to ground support so they could safely affect the rescue.

Now, some distance ahead of the main body, Clay could see the dirt road ahead. He immediately noted it would allow the movement of vehicles. It was a lot wider than their trail and should allow them to get to the airstrip a lot faster, he concluded. His mind was preoccupied with these thoughts, when he suddenly heard a heavy machinegun. Moments later he heard the crackle of rapid automatic rifle fire in answer. The rattle of rifle fire continued for a few seconds, then abruptly ceased. The heavy hammering of the machinegun continued unabated.

Rick ran toward the sound of the firing. Clay pulled the Draganuv off his shoulder and handed it to Rick when he got up to him. "Stay here and watch out for the others! Let me check it out!" Clay said, without thinking.

With his AK in one hand and Striker's leash in the other, Clay ran toward the road. He didn't have far to travel. Up ahead, the two scouts came tearing around the juncture of road and trail, running hard.

One of them breathlessly explained to Clay, "One of those damn pickup's, a Technical, mounting a heavy machinegun, spotted us and opened up. We have no idea where it came from. One moment the road was clear, the next, there it was! The Technical is about four hundred yards up the road and advancing toward us at a good clip."

Clay realized his inner fears had been realized. Quickly he said, "That thing was probably sitting, hidden, off on the side of the road waiting under cover. That could mean they've been tipped off! They might be in radio communication with some other group. Rick, I recommend you get everyone ready to use the alternate route, while I check out the road!"

"Hey! You can't do this all by yourself! We're outgunned!" Rick said.

"Can't I? You'll see!" Clay replied. He ran back to where the two travois were lined up in the procession. At the one containing the extra equipment, he grabbed the RPG launch tube and the pack containing the rocket grenades. Slinging the pack over his shoulder, along with his rifle, he ran forward with the launcher in one hand, Stryker's leash in the other.

Approaching crossroads a few yards ahead of him, he dodged into a copse of head - high shrubs, concealing him from the dirt road. Working his way forward twenty-five yards parallel with the track, he spotted a shallow ditch by the side of the dirt lane. Dropping onto his hands and knees, he and Stryker scooted forward and slid into it. Laying the launcher down on the dirt, he carefully peered, just above the lip of the ditch, to determine if the terrorist's vehicle had seen him. Satisfied, he got himself ready for the attack, feeling confident in his plan.

Watching the vehicle, he noted the Technical was still at least three hundred yards away and not close enough for the slam-dunk type of attack he needed. Not being totally familiar with the launcher, he knew he had to have the vehicle very close to him so that he would have a guaranteed hit. Opening the pack, he pulled out one of the three grenades and loaded the round in the launch tube.

Cautiously he raised his head again and peeked ahead at the vehicle. He noticed it had slowed in its approach. He wondered why. Either they have a radio and are calling in reinforcements or they believe the two of our guys they jumped, can't get away! he thought. He then noticed in alarm that two flankers had joined the Technical team, one walking on each side of the pickup, on the shoulder. Both carried fully automatic AK-74's. It would complicate the matter, he thought.

With his eyes peering out from under his camouflage hat, just above the lip, he stealthily watched every move of the group as they came closer. When he felt it was within his kill range, he picked up the weapon and shouldered it. Not being familiar with the RPG's sighting process, he took a chance and went ahead anyway. Standing up, fully exposed to the terrorists, he aimed the weapon. He put the sight picture on the cab of the truck. The approaching group apparently still had not noticed him. He had wrapped the leash around his leg once, so both his hands would be free. As he depressed the trigger, he felt Stryker's chain jerk slightly. He couldn't take his eyes off the enemy, but guessed the dog had caught scent of the enemy and reacted. He felt the grenade launch at the truck.

He noticed that the driver and gunner reacted as they spotted the telltale rocket exhaust headed toward them. Moving instantly, the driver tried his best to turn and evade the oncoming round. The gunner ducked behind the cab. A moment later the rocket reached the vehicle. Clay watched in wide-eyed amazement as the round passed miraculously between the top of the cab and then just under the long barrel of the machinegun, exploding harmlessly in the distance.

Now the tables were turned, Clay realized. He watched in horror as the driver quickly recovered, wheeling the agile, small vehicle in his direction. Clay could see the driver screaming and watched the gunner pop back up and take control of his weapon. As the truck barreled toward him, bouncing up and down crazily on the rough track, the gunner sprayed the area wildly with his gun, hoping to get lucky. Clay also noted in alarm the two flankers had disappeared.

Dropping back down, out of sight, he grabbed another grenade from the pack and shoved it into he launcher. He loosely wrapped Stryker's chain once around his ankle and stood up, the weapon on his shoulder. The truck advanced rapidly toward him. He coolly took his time with bullets flying all around him and sighted again on the enemy. They think they have me now! I only have a second or two at best! Taking steady aim just above the bumper of the truck, he jerked the trigger firmly, feeling the rocket fly out of the tube. Seconds after firing he was shocked to hear the sudden and continuous rattle of automatic rifle fire erupt to his rear where his team waited.

Technical Gun Truck attacking Dixon

Chapter 25

Clay ignored the machine gun bullets slapping wildly into the low, dirt berm. He coolly watched the telltale path of the RPG headed for the target. The approaching threat to the team had to be taken out at all costs. Moments later it slammed into the grill of the Toyota gun truck, just above the bumper. The vehicle exploded in a huge ball of fire and stopped dead in its tracks as if it had been whacked by a huge sledgehammer. Seconds later the fuel tank went up, adding to the conflagration.

Relieved that he'd been lucky and neutralized the Technical, Clay relaxed a little for a few moments. He'd made Stryker stay below the dirt shoulder to protect him from the machine gun. He noticed the dog suddenly tense up. Clay guessed that Stryker might be picking up the scent of the approaching flankers he'd spotted earlier, next to the mobile gun truck. He didn't want to deal with them nor did he have the time because it sounded like the team was under attack.

He shouldered his AK101 with the RPG in one hand, Stryker's chain in the other and headed toward the team cross-country to save time instead of taking the road. He moved at a fast trot, extremely worried that somehow the main body of the al-Qaeda terrorists had managed to catch up with the team.

When he reached the area where he thought the team might be, he stopped and listened. The gunfire was steady, but intermittent, almost as if the guerillas were holding the team in place with a delaying action. He figured they were waiting for the arrival of the main force.

Forcing his way through the heavy underbrush, Clay blindly pushed ahead as fast as he could, ignoring the noise he created. He burst through another heavy growth of brush and Clay found himself face to face with one of the terrorists, forty yards away. Apparently the man had heard his approach and turned to face the sound. Clay could readily see the guerilla had him dead to rights. He knew he could not get the rifle off his shoulder and aimed in time. Figuring he had nothing to lose, he chose to give it a try.

Watching as the man quickly brought up his AK-74, Clay saw the man's eyes glance off to the right for a moment and suddenly get as big as saucers. Instead of finishing off Clay, the man turned and ran in fear. Surprised and totally at a loss at this strange behavior, Clay suddenly saw a flash of brown fur pass him in a blur, accompanied by a bone-chilling growl.

Clay recalled he had originally set down the empty launcher, not wanting to be encumbered by it as he fought his way through the underbrush. He slipped the chain from his hand, but had not tried to pick it up as he figured Stryker would follow him. Apparently Stryker had his own plans and had doubled to the end of the growth. Finding a small opening he worked his way through. Gaining on the fleeing terrorist, Stryker leaped, became airborne and landed on the man's back, knocking him to the ground.

Not wasting a second with his unexpected reprieve, Clay ran over to the man, knocked his rifle out of reach and then scanned the area for the other guerillas. The man lay frozen to the ground with Stryker's bared fangs close to his face.

Trying to get a better fix on where the others were, Clay guessed there were about four or five more in the party. He knew he had figured correctly about their delaying tactics. Had the main force arrived, he knew they would have been able to overwhelm the team. In an exposed position and about to duck down, Clay heard increased firing coming from the team, possibly choosing this moment to initiate a counterattack. Now on the enemy's flank, Clay joined in firing several long bursts in the direction of the enemy's fire. Apparently they had had enough and chose to break off the attack shortly thereafter.

Clay kept his prisoner under close guard until Rick and the other team members hurried over to him. Surrounding the prisoner, they watched Clay ease Stryker away from the frightened man. The group respectfully parted for the old Japanese soldier and his wife as they made their way over to Clay. Speaking to the soldier and his wife, Clay said, "Can you see if you can get some information from this prisoner for me?"

The old man intuitively seemed to know what Clay wanted because he spoke rapidly to his wife before she could translate. "My husband wants to know what information you need?"

"Tell the prisoner I need to know the size of his main body approaching us."

After the translation, the old soldier got an evil smile on his face and snapped into place the razor sharp bayonet on his rifle. In a flash, he stepped on the man's chest with one foot to hold him down, put the bayonet at the terrorist's throat and angrily said something to the man in Japanese.

Speaking to the prisoner in Tagalog, Madeline said, "My husband says you look a lot like the one who killed our son and he wants to gut you with his bayonet!" A frightened look appeared on the man's face; he lost control and wet himself. She continued, "If you tell us the truth, we may let you live!"

Looking up at the old soldier with eyes bulging in terror, the man babbled something quickly to Madeline. She replied in Tagalog, "We need to know the size of your main force that is approaching?"

He replied quickly and she said, "He claims he doesn't know!"

With the evil smile getting bigger, the old soldier pressed the blade against the man's throat a little harder and drew a small amount of blood. The prisoner gurgled pitifully, and looked over at Clay with pleading eyes.

Clay gave him a look that said, there's nothing I can do about it, shrugged his shoulders and started to turn away.

The man quickly babbled something and stared at the old soldier with abject horror on his dirt encrusted face.

"He says there are about thirty men in the group," Madeline reported.

"Okay," Clay said, "Let him up. We'll take him with us. Tie his hands behind his back."

The look on the old soldier's face reflected disappointment, "My husband wants to kill this little roach!" Madeline told him.

Clay replied to both and Madeline translated at the same time. "A promise is a promise. I did say I'd let him live."

Pulling his bayonet away from the frightened man and stepping off of him, the old soldier said something to Clay with a mischievous smile. "He said the prisoner didn't really look like the one who killed my son, but it worked for us! He needed to be motivated!" Madeline translated.

Clay smiled and winked at both of them saying, "That it did!"

Rick wanted to know about Clay's encounter with the truck. Clay explained quickly, then nodded at the old soldier and said, "I think his idea of using the arroyo to evacuate to the coast is the best. It would be too dangerous to try for the old airfield. When the al-Qaeda terrorists discover they've lost the truck, they'll send more. We better get going before this group shows up," he warned, pointing down the trail.

Minutes later the group moved down the gulch toward the sea. Clay insisted on hanging back as rearguard with another man. When they were near the coast, Rick called a halt. He sent two scouts up the coastline to see if they could find some kind of vessel, boat, or truck. The team moved quickly into temporary, defensive positions.

Over an hour later, from where he lay concealed, Clay watched the steady advance of the enemy. Sending his teammate back to warn the others, Clay prepared himself to initiate a stalling action with the captured AK-47 and the spare ammunition. Like a lizard crawling up a garden wall, Clay stealthily worked his way up the ditch. On top, he snaked his way to a deeply eroded section that cut into the gully wall. Wiggling into the cut, he had enough room for him and Stryker while totally concealed. He pulled out all of his magazines and lay them on the ground close by for easy access. Checking the AK-47 again, he prepared to spring his surprise.

The approaching guerillas appeared overconfident and were grouped closely together, he noted in satisfaction. Maybe this will shake their trees a little, he thought. Clay let them get within three hundred yards, then rose up from hiding and fired off a long, carefully aimed burst at the closest group of men. Watching, he knew he'd hit several of them as the rest scattered for cover like a covey of quail taking flight. The enemy lay down a heavy return fire as they slowly tried to advance, dodging and zigzagging from bush to bush in the sparsely covered arroyo. Clay continued to lay down a continuous rapid fire, delaying their advance to gain time for the team.

Down to his last magazine, Clay fired several more long bursts of fire to keep their heads down. The rifle empty, he dropped it, grabbed Stryker's chain and jumped down into the gulch, running crouched over toward his team with the dog loping ahead of him. He figured the enemy, still off balance, wouldn't realize their tormentor had left, for a few critical minutes. He quickly retrieved his rifle and launcher from where he'd stashed it and rushed back to the team.

Just beyond the perimeter, he stopped and scrutinized the team's positions. Set up in a U position with the spread, open ends facing the advancing guerillas, Clay could see they were hoping to suck the enemy into and past-the open ends-then close the door behind them. Clay chose a spot near the top of the left leg with Stryker by his side.

They didn't have long to wait as the enemy came down the gully fast and furious. Clay figured they were being goaded and driven by the vengeful guerilla chief. They seemed determined to overwhelm the defense, no matter what the cost.

The fight was hard, fast and merciless with Clay's team having the upper hand from their better defensive positions. It almost appeared as if they were throwing themselves away as if they didn't care. They were making it too easy! He mused. As the fight started to peter off to sporadic firing, someone to the enemy's rear started firing an RPG-7, using anti-personnel grenades. The gunner appeared to be inexperienced because the grenades were landing harmlessly behind their perimeter.

Something has to be done because sooner or later that clown is going to get lucky and get the range, Clay thought. Crawling from his position, Clay wormed his way back on top of the gulch, moving quietly toward the sound. He kept a good distance from the edge of the arroyo, creeping from bush to bush undetected. A little over three hundred yards from his lines, he heard the blast of the RPG firing and knew he had it pinpointed. Coming to an open area, he knew he couldn't cross it without being spotted, yet he knew the RPG gunner had to be close by. Releasing the safety on his AK-101, he took a risk and stood up for a better view. He immediately spotted the gunner and another man about a hundred and fifty yards away.

One terrorist, obviously the loader, was in the process of pulling another grenade from a canvas satchel, when the gunner saw Clay. Clay knew the gunner had an empty launcher and was not a threat, but the loader was another matter. In a blur of speed, the man dropped the grenade and dove to the ground. A few moments later he came up, with his AK-74 and blazed away wildly in Clay's direction.

The sonovabitch just might get lucky if I don't do something quick! Clay aimed and fired off a short burst, forcing the man to duck. Putting his sight picture on the gunner, Clay fired another burst, dropping him like a stone. The loader popped up again, but Clay was ready for him this time. He carefully aimed and fired, putting the man down permanently.

Rushing forward, Clay picked up his prize and found to his disappointment, he had ruined the launcher. Disgusted, he inspected several holes where his shots had hit the launcher. He dropped it, and grabbed the satchel of grenades without checking them, satisfied that at least he'd stopped the gunner. Knowing he'd be discovered at any moment, Clay threw caution to the wind and took off running back toward his lines with Stryker practically pulling him along.

He'd gone about fifty yards when he heard angry shouts behind him and bullets started stitching the ground around him. Zigzagging and dodging behind any available bush, Clay kept running hard until suddenly he felt a burning sensation in his right leg, a moment later the close-by sound of a shot. He fell to the ground feeling like someone had slammed him in the leg with an iron bar. His rifle dropped to the ground and slid out of his reach. Not realizing he'd released Stryker's chain, the dog kept running ahead of him, unaware of what had happened. The dog stopped fifty yards further, saw Clay on the ground and started to come back.

Pulling himself around, facing where the shots apparently came from, Clay reached for his rifle. Two more shots were fired, ripping up the ground between Clay and his rifle. He recognized the warning and froze in place. A hundred yards away, a man in a well-worn, faded camouflage uniform and headband boldly stepped out of concealment behind a large clump of high bushes. Clay recognized immediately the weather-beaten face and the cold, dark eyes of the guerilla chief. Apparently, Clay realized that the man had carefully worked his way in close to the team's positions. A chill raced up Clay's spine as he thought, now he's finally going to settle accounts with me. He helplessly watched as the wily old guerilla raised his rifle, taking his time, carefully taking aim at him. Clay took one last look at the crisp, blue sky, then into the cold, dark and vengeful eyes, once more thinking, It'll be all over in a moment! I hope Stryker gets away.

Chapter 26

Clay waited for that final, fatal moment, but to his utter amazement nothing happened. He felt positive the old guerilla had pulled the trigger on his rifle, yet it didn't fire. An angry look crossed the man's dark, leathery face as he rapidly checked his weapon, pulling back the bolt to check the chamber of the weapon. Letting the bolt slide home, in a blur of long-practiced motion, one finger pressed the release button, ejecting the empty magazine, while the other hand whipped out a full one from his canvas vest. Tapping the bottom of the magazine twice against his thigh, to seat the ammunition, the man smoothly hinged it into his assault rifle and locked it in place.

During those same moments, Clay, surprised at the fleeting, unexpected reprieve, reacted as only a desperate man could. With the pain from his wound stabbing at him, he lunged for his rifle just out of reach - his only option. An odd thought flashed through his mind about the guerrilla chief, Most experienced fighters usually put two or three tracer rounds into the magazine as an indicator to let the shooter it is almost empty. He didn't and I wonder why? Unless…he had someone else load it for him. Bad move.

Clay groped forward and grabbed the stock of his rifle, pulling it to him while at the same time; he stole a furtive glance up at the guerilla chief. With a deft, practiced motion, the man drew back the charging handle and released it, stripping off a fresh round and chambering it. The weapon, ready to fire again, the guerilla brought the rifle up to bear on Clay.

Accepting his fate, Clay watched as the final seconds ticked off. A mere second later, Clay blinked once, not believing his eyes as the old guerilla chief stiffened, followed by the thunderous loud crack of a rifle from behind him. Totally amazed, Clay spotted the tiny, dark hole that appeared above the bridge of the guerilla's nose. The man stood there for a second or two like a statue, and then the AK slowly slid from his grasp and clattered to the ground. The man collapsed in a heap as if he were a rag doll.

Rolling over, Clay found himself totally floored, having no idea of where the shot had come from. Less than one hundred yards away, stood the old Japanese soldier, with practiced ease, in the process of reloading. He slapped back the bolt, ejected the spent cartridge and chambered another before Clay could blink his eyes. The old man had a satisfied smile on his face and gave a short bow to Clay. Clay automatically nodded his head in respectful reply.

Painfully, Clay began to wedge himself up to a kneeling position using his rifle as a brace. Before he could manage to get upright, he noticed the old soldier bring up his rifle and take aim again. Swiveling his head, Clay was jolted to see that another terrorist had materialized from hiding, determined to finish the job his leader had begun. Clay guessed in those fast-moving seconds that the man had been stealthily snaking forward, getting into position to finish him off. Twenty-five yards away, closing the distance fast, Clay had no idea where the man had come from. With his rifle and bayonet thrust out in front of him, firing wildly from the hip, Clay knew the terrorist would be on top of him in seconds. With leg throbbing, Clay clumsily prepared to fend off his attacker.

Another thunderous, flat crack of a rifle split the air and the guerilla stopped in mid-stride, as if he'd been slapped in the face by a wooden two-by-four. His rifle flew into the air, he went over backward while his feet kept moving forward for a second, the last signal from his brain — then he was down, permanently.

Turning around, Clay saw the old soldier reload quickly, then reach down and retrieve his spent cartridges, putting them in his pocket. I wonder why they both do that? he pondered, recalling seeing Madeline had done the same thing. I'll have to ask them first chance I get.

Clay struggled to his knees using his AK as a crutch when the old soldier ran up to him, looped his arm under Clay's at the shoulder, "Ike! Ike!" he grunted, "Let's go! Let's go!"

Clay had no idea what the man was saying, but he got the point and needed no further encouragement. They had to get out of there immediately as Clay knew they were closer to the guerrilla's lines than their own. If the guerrillas saw their plight and got up the courage to charge them, they wouldn't stand a chance.

With his arm over the old man's shoulders, Clay limped as fast as he could toward their lines, ignoring the bullets landing dangerously close around them. This is the guy who should be getting the Silver Star for bravery, Clay thought as they hobbled and stumbled toward the safety of their lines.

Nearing the team's perimeter, Clay noticed the enemies' gunfire had become greatly reduced and sporadic. The team members, in an effort to cover for the two, now advanced in a counterattack, pouring out a withering fire. When Clay and the old soldier met up with his advance teammates, they both stopped and looked back toward the terrorists' positions. The firing had become widely scattered and greatly reduced. Apparently the killing of their fearsome leader had taken the will and fight out of them. In true guerilla fashion, they appeared to be melting back toward the jungle, knowing they'd lost the upper hand. A few minutes later the firing from that direction had ceased completely and there was no further sign of the terrorists.

Clay and the old soldier continued on until they had reached safety and then Clay had to sit down to rest his leg. The man gently helped

Clay get down on the ground as Madeline hurried over to them. Pulling a small pack off her back she reached in and pulled out a tin container and opened it.

"What's that?" Clay asked.

"This will help relieve the pain," she replied, starting to roll up his pant leg.

The medic came up to them at that moment and slipped his medical kit from his shoulder bag. With scissors in hand, he moved to cut open Clay's pant leg.

"Hey! What the hell do you think you are doing?"

"I've got to cut open your pant so I can treat your wound!"

"No! Absolutely not! This is my only pair of pants. I'll pull them down."

The medic and Madeline inspected it. "It's a flesh wound. No damage to bone or muscle that I can see," the medic said. "Let me clean the area around the wound first."

"Okay, then let her apply the salve."

"What kind of salve is it?" The medic asked Madeline.

"It is a very old herbal remedy from my people ages ago, for treating wounds. It takes the pain away."

Looking at the medic who had doubt written across his face, Clay said, "Let her go ahead anyway. It can't hurt and maybe it will help."

After Madeline applied the salve, the medic applied his medications as a precaution, bound up the wound, and gave Clay an antibiotic shot to stave off infection. Clay felt the salve Madeline had applied worked as the pain began to rapidly dissipate.

Turning to Clay, Rick said, "Why don't you and your two new friends come over here. I'd like your input and thoughts on the best approach to leave the area, in the least amount of time. When Clay, Madeline and her husband had joined the group, Rick unfolded the map so everyone could clearly see it. "Here's approximately where we are right now," he said, pointing to a spot near the coastline. "Up the coast about two miles, in this area, it looks like there's some kind of inlet or cove bending around in a hook so it's hidden from the coastline. Now we can't be totally sure this to be true because the map is a reprint from and old one and often inaccurate. It has to be checked out physically."

Clay looked closely at the map, "True, you never know, it could just be tidal flats now or blocked by a sand bar. I noticed the dirt road from the airfield just seems to disappear on the map not far beyond were it crossed our original trail, but it seems to be aimed directly toward the inlet."

As they continued to discuss the images on the map, Madeline gave her husband a running commentary. As he replied, she quickly translated. "What my husband said is that the road runs all the way to the inlet. He's seen it, but it is not shown and they carefully camouflage it from prying eyes in the air. This is how they get weapons and supplies up to the camps near the airfield."

"Then we need to check it out right away. I'll go," Clay volunteered.

Rick looked at Clay and smiled saying, "No you won't! Not a chance. You're wounded and I really think you should stay with the team for now."

Clay thought about it for a few seconds, and then reluctantly acquiesced. "Okay, I think I've had enough excitement to last me the rest of my life anyway."

Rick laughed. "Yeah, sure. The way you've been running around here like a combination of Rambo and John Wayne - that's not going to be very long. Rick continued. "These two guys can move fast, you can't for now. You never know, maybe we just might get lucky and find something we can use like a hidden truck or a small boat that will hold everyone."

"One can only hope." Clay said.

"Okay you two, you better get going," Rick said to the two volunteers. "Get up there as rapidly as you can move and then get right back down here! We need to know which direction we're going to move, up there or down the coast on foot. It's going to take a little while to get together to move. We have to patch up a few minor wounds and get the travois litters set up again. By the time they return, we should be at the coast."

Three hours later, Clay settled down tiredly onto a fallen palm tree, in the shade of another and watched the rest of the team move onto the beach area. Even though they all felt there was very little threat, the team set up a light defensive perimeter. Now all they had to do was wait for the return of the scouting party.

They didn't have long to wait, the two men came trotting back and everyone eagerly gathered around to hear their report. As Clay listened, they explained that on finding the inlet, it opened up into a manually improved cove well hidden from the ocean. One of the men explained further, saying, "We found what looks like a very large schooner. It's tied up in the cove and extremely well hidden with net camouflage interspaced with tree branches."

Curious, Clay asked, "What kind? Can you describe it?"

"Well, what it looks like to me is a very large regional trading vessel that brings mail and supplies to all these small islands around the archipelago," one of the men said.

Clay was disappointed as he had hopes for something fully under power. "That might be difficult because I don't think anybody here know how to sail," he said.

"That's the whole point," the other scout replied, "we don't have to worry about that. It has power along with the sails. We checked it out below deck after we overpowered the guards. The boat is at least eighty feet long and has two big Volvo engines."

"What about the guards?" Clay asked.

"There were two. We eliminated the one by the gangplank quietly, but when we went aboard, the other one spotted us and ran inside the bridge. He appeared to be calling for help when we broke in and stopped him in mid-sentence."

"Radio! That's great news! At least we can now radio our base and get help out here to us," Rick said.

Embarrassed and with downcast eyes, one of the scouts replied, "Sorry boss, we couldn't help it. The only way to stop him was to shoot him and some of the shots damaged the radio!"

"Is it workable?" Rick said.

"I don't know. We didn't check it out before we left. It might be repairable."

Regional Trading Vessel, *Southern Trader*

"Well, that settles it," Rick said. "Maybe, for us, that boat might be what used to be called the Disneyland "E" ride ticket. The best ride in the house! We need to get up there like yesterday!"

"One more thing," the other scout said, "the inlet ended a short distance beyond the cove. We noticed tire tracks leading down to the beach and on closer inspection we found a well camouflaged dirt road leading away from the cove."

"That confirms it, the road on the map goes all the way through and that's where the terrorists will be coming from if we don't get up there and on that boat immediately," Clay said. "You've got to figure they're going to come looking for that Technical I took out, when it doesn't report back - then they'll come looking for us fast with more trucks and heavy machine guns that'll turn this boat into kindling wood if we don't get out of here!"

Arriving at the cove, Clay and Rick walked around the ship, inspecting it. At the stern, Clay noticed some paint peeling off the name of the ship that the terrorists had haphazardly covered over. Curious, when he boarded the boat, he went to the stern and bending over the back, used his knife to scrape away the paint. It came away easily and reading upside down, he read the name, Southern Trader, Surabaja. "Looks like somebody paid a dear price! This has the look of a regional trading vessel that plied the coastal waters delivering mail and supplies. The captain and crew were most likely overwhelmed by pirates and were murdered." he said.

"Pirates! You've got to be shitting me!" Rick said.

"No! A fact of life in this day and age and a growing problem in these waters," Clay replied. "Well armed, they either loot the ship and sink it or take it for other uses - like this one, probably used for running arms and explosives. Brutal!"

Everyone hurried about his assigned tasks with renewed urgency. They edged away from the mooring place and departed in the late afternoon under power. Just before they started the engines and cast off, Clay could swear his ears picked up the sounds of vehicles headed in their direction. Worried, he urged the team to hurry up and get under way. Needing no further invitation, minutes later, with engines growling smoothly, they cleared the inlet and into the open ocean under power. They lost sight of land when the sun dipped into the ocean; suddenly, almost instantaneously the inky blackness of night enveloped them. The steady, powerful thrum of the big Volvo engines comforted them for the first time that day.

Rick and some of the others took turns steering, while Clay went over the map with a compass and gave the helmsman steering coordinates. A few hours later, he conferred with Rick, saying, "According to my calculations, I believe we're probably still in Philippine waters and not international. There is a good chance we may run into a Philippine Navy patrol boat and they can help us steer an exact course to our base and maybe even escort us. We should be near our home base sometime late tomorrow afternoon."

A huge moon rose and lit up the sea as if it were daylight. The sky was cloudless and crystal clear, the stars twinkling in the inky black heavens like millions of tiny diamonds. Coming up to Clay, Rick commented on the awesome scene above them. "Looks like we'll have a nice, peaceful moonlight cruise back to the base."

"Yeah, sure, we can only hope so. I'm still a little worried about what that terrorist may have gotten off to his pals on the radio just before he was stopped," Clay replied.

"Hey, it's a big ocean and we're just a tiny fly speck on it and hard to find. I think we'll be okay and it will be an uneventful crossing," Rick said.

A few hours later, one of the men who had been steering the vessel and had been relieved, came up to where Clay rested with his head against his pack. Stryker lay comfortably next to him. In a concerned voice he said, "Clay, I'm really sorry to bother you, but I need to talk to you."

Clay had been trying to sleep, but with the effects of the medicine apparently wearing off, found his leg starting to throb again and been only dozing off. He came instantly to full alertness. Stryker picked up on it and lifted his head from Clay's other thigh where he had been resting it, twitching his ears in expectation. "What is it?" he asked.

"I may be seeing things, I don't know. The ocean plays tricks on the eyes at night. Could have been the reflection of a fish jumping or something, but all I know is, I could swear for the briefest moment I spotted a tiny flash of light. There's something to our rear following us! I swear it!"

Uneasy about the unusual sighting, Clay roused Rick and they all went back to the stern of the ship. They strained their eyes for several minutes, but could neither see nor hear anything. A small knot of concern began to grow in Clay's stomach as he stood watching the ocean to their rear. Can't anything ever go easy? He wondered. "You two go ahead and try to get some shuteye. I just can't sleep and I'm wide awake! Would one of you do me a favor and wake Madeline? Ask her if she wouldn't mind applying some more of that pain relieving salve she has; my leg is starting to bother me again. I'm going to stick out here with Stryker and keep our eyes open and see if anything develops."

Not long afterward, Madeline came forward and applied another treatment of her natural pain remedy. The pain began to dissipate and he finally began to feel drowsy, the day's events catching up with him. Minutes later, his eyes dropped closed.

Chapter 27

"Clay! Wake up! Wake up! We've got company!" one of his other teammates kept repeating, anxiously shaking Clay's shoulder. Coming out of a deep, dreamless sleep brought on by the tension and exhaustion of the previous day, Clay cracked his eyes open. After Madeline had applied her salve again, the pain from his wound had abated and he finally dropped off.

Stepping over to the stern of the ship where Rick and several others stood, Clay looked at the ocean. The sea at this time of the morning was calm with shallow troughs and a light mist hung just above the surface; the heat of the coming day had not yet blanketed them. Their boat had a slight roll as they progressed through the sea, but they were still able to focus on objects in the distance. Visible through the mist, Clay identified two craft, side-by-side, following, he estimated, about eight hundred yards or more out.

"Looks like I wasn't seeing things after all!" his teammate, who had reported seeing the flash of light the previous night, commented.

"You're absolutely right. On a dark ocean, in the middle of the night, even someone lighting a match can be seen for great distances. So you weren't going round the bend on us, pal," Clay replied.

"Yeah, but the big question is, who are they?" Rick asked.

"Okay, being logical, since we are still probably in Philippine waters, the chances of them being Philippine Navy patrol boats are pretty good," Clay said.

"Okay, but why didn't they close on us last night and try to identify themselves?"

"Maybe they did, but remember, the transmitter was shot up and destroyed when our guys had to overpower the radio operator. If they are a Navy patrol, they may have tried to contact us and failed, deciding to get a better look at us in daylight. Remember, they're probably not taking any chances either because they might think we're drug smugglers, gunrunners or whatever," Clay reasoned.

"Okay, but we're moving away from the mainland, in the opposite direction that drug smugglers with a shipment, would normally go," Rick said.

"Look, I don't have a clue. Common sense tells me that maybe they're thinking they might have spooked us had they had approached us in the night," Clay said.

"You've got a point there," Rick replied.

"There's only one way to find out," Clay said, getting up and moving over to where his rifles and gear were stored. He shouldered the Dragunov SVD and moved back to the stern. He placed a towel over the sturdy stern railing to cushion the long sniper rifle, popped off the protective rubber covers off the scope and gently set the rifle down on the hardwood rail. His eye to the scope, he picked up the vessels in the distance and worked the adjusting knobs to bring the images into clear focus. While the mist still obscured the boats, he was able to get a slightly better picture, even if distant, of the two patrol boats.

"What do you see, Clay?" Rick asked.

"Years ago, in boot camp, my drill instructor once told us to 'Believe none of what you hear and half of what you see and you'll get along okay in this world'," Clay said, "From what I can determine at this distance, they appear to be Philippine Coastal Patrol boats but I can't be one-hundred percent positive. I can't quite tell because the early morning mist, the vibration of the ship's engines and the rolling of the boat in the sea are combining to obscure my image of the boats. According to the graduations on my scope sight, I figure they're about nine hundred yards out, so I can't be totally sure. For that matter, I don't have a clue what their patrol boats look like. In any case, I can tell that from the bow waves they're increasing speed and closing on us. The men I can see are dressed in white and look like sailors, but I'm not going to assume anything until they get a little closer."

Clay and Rick discussed the situation and made a decision not to stop and wait for the boats to catch up with them. Clay felt that it was better to be cautious since the boats hadn't tried to signal them.

A half hour later, Clay noticed the boats had closed to within five hundred or more yards and were not running side by side as they had been; they had now split up as if to bracket their boat. Clay found this troubling and picked up the Dragunov again to get a closer look. Peering through the scope, he gasped, "Jesus Christ!" Gone were the Donald Duck uniforms; this was a joking military inter-service reference to the sailor uniform worn by the Disney cartoon character. The white sailor uniforms had been used to get close to the pirates quarry. Gone were the white uniforms and into their place the filthy looking group of cutthroats had changed into a motley collection of well used camouflage and civilian clothing. Most had red sweatbands wrapped around their foreheads. Clearly the fake window dressing of the uniforms had worked like a charm! he thought disgustedly. Now he realized they were in real trouble. The boats approaching were Malaysian pirates intent on getting their boat back. That had to be the only answer! I wonder how many poor, unfortunate people these bastards have fooled with this phony little trick? Plenty, I bet! His anger welled up like bitter bile in his throat. Not this time around you bastards!

With his eye still glued to the scope, Clay observed something else that gave him an involuntary chill. At the stern of each vessel an RPG-7 gunner stood, with the back end of the grenade launcher hanging over the back of each boat. Moments later what Clay observed next removed all question and doubt from his mind. A blood red flag was quickly hoisted up the mast of one of the ersatz patrol boats.

A cold chill raced up Clay's spine by what he saw. It was a depiction of a pirate flag with a difference. Below the gaping skull was an unusual set of "crossbones". The left side moving from left to right was a black bone. Crossing over that bone from right to left was a picture of an AK-47. The intent to terrorize was clearly evident. The inscription on the bottom of the flag in Latin clearly indicted to him they were in for the fight of the lives ; a fight to the death. In Latin if spelled out the words : Mortem Contemnere Qui Hoc Signum. Clay dug deep into his early schooling when he was required to take a course of study in Latin and had to translate Caesars Gallic Wars from Latin into English. The inscription meant Death To all Who Defy This Flag. They were approaching very fast and Clay knew they had no choice; they couldn't outrun them, he knew they had a fight on their hands to the bitter end.

"Incoming! Take cover!" Clay yelled. Everybody ducked down behind anything they could find. Retrieving the Dragunov, Clay focused on the gunner on the patrol boat to the right. Seconds later, the man fired his RPG at them. Clay quickly lined up his shot and fired, but the roll of their ship in the ocean swells threw off his aim slightly. The shot glanced off the boat's deckhouse and missed the man by a scant inch. The pirate immediately ducked down.

Clay took aim at the other gunner, who remained standing to watch the path of his grenade. Clay put the crosshairs of the scope in the center of the man's chest and squeezed the trigger. He watched as the man flinched slightly, grabbed his shoulder by his neck and leaped out of sight. Disgustedly Clay knew from experience that at a distance of five hundred yards, even the minutest deviation or movement, under these difficult conditions, transmitted to inches off the target, at the receiving end of the bullet.

The first RPG grenade landed to the left side of the ship about seventy-five yards out, hitting the ocean and exploded harmlessly. Everyone watched in horror as the second grenade followed, coming from the right, lined up dead center on the ship, but a little too high. It flew through the upper rigging, glanced lightly upward off of one of the furled sails, passed on through, exploding without damage a hundred yards beyond the ship.

Pirate's flag with their motto at the bottom of the flag

It was too close for comfort as far as Clay was concerned. "We were lucky with those two shots, but it won't take long before they get the range on us! We've got to do something to throw off their aim!" he yelled.

Rick yelled to the man in charge of the controls, "Increase our speed! Take it all the way to the stops - maybe we can outrun them!"

"That might help, but I have a strong feeling this barge can't outrun those patrol boats!" Clay replied.

"Think of something!"

One of the other troopers offered, "How about if we start zigzagging?

"Yeah, that should at least throw off their aim with the RPG's," one of the other men suggested.

"Good thinking," Clay said, "I should have thought of that."

"But that'll slow us down and they'll be on top of us in no time," Rick replied.

"I don't mean extreme zigzags," the man said, "Just stagger our course enough to keep them guessing."

"That way they won't know which way we're turning next," someone else added.

"Good thinking. I'm willing to take a crack at anything at this point," Rick replied, giving the order.

The helmsman immediately initiated a slight course change and continued to do so in random directions every few minutes. But it wasn't enough as far as Clay was concerned. It seemed to have the desired effect because the pirates stopped firing RPG's, but Clay noticed they were steadily gaining on the Southern Trader. I've probably got them a little gun shy after shooting at them and they are probably wondering what I'm using at this distance, he thought. Time to teach them another lesson so they'll keep their heads down.

Clay scooted down behind the Dragunov and picked it up, focusing on the nearest boat approaching from the right. He lined up the crosshairs and picked a man standing foolishly on top of the deckhouse with a pair of binoculars to his eyes. He was furiously working the focusing knobs when his view came to rest on Clay. In that moment Clay could almost visualize the man yelling a warning as he squeezed the trigger. The rifle bucked and a moment later the binoculars flew into the air and the pirate flipped backward into the boat.

Clay continued to squeeze off shots at randomly spaced targets watching with satisfaction as each pirate slumped out of sight. Because of the sound of their own weapons, the pirates didn't get it for a few vital minutes. Under the conditions, it was not the easiest of shots, but Clay managed to get a few more before the pirates wised up to what was happening and took cover. Quick learners, next they started a process of more than one popping up and firing, making it more difficult for Clay to focus and fire on multiple targets. About the time he would line up and fire, they popped out of sight and another two or three would appear and fire. He was beginning to waste precious ammunition and more often than not cutting thin air, until he ran out of ammo.

From the ammo pouch that were with the rifle, Clay reloaded another full magazine, moving his attention over to the boat on the left, the occupants having no idea of his tactics yet. He began the process all over again. From training, he knew the rifle had excellent first-round hit probability at the range, and he was successful until the pirates probably realized their ranks were being steadily decimated, and changed their stratagem.

"Why don't we take a shot at them with our RPG?" Rick offered.

Clay vetoed the idea, replying, "We only have a few rockets and I don't want to take a chance of wasting any. I'd like them to get closer."

"How much closer?" Rick said, in a concerned voice.

Clay smiled and replied, "I'll let you know! Trust me this one time, okay?"

Over a half hour later, the patrol boats had straddled the motor-sailor and began heavily peppering it with a constant rain of gunfire. Clay immediately knew they clearly meant to keep the team's heads down while they closed on their ship with intentions of boarding them. Fortunately, the sturdy teak construction of the Southern Trader afforded them ample protection and there were no causalities.

While the return fire from the team kept the pirates at a distance, Clay knew they couldn't keep this up indefinitely. Fully aware that they were getting low on ammunition, Clay realized that if the pirates managed to overwhelm them with their firepower and get in close to board them, it would be all over for all of the team. He racked his brain continuously for some kind of solid solution as the pirates edged in closer.

An hour later, the team's ammunition dwindling, the pirates smelled blood, sensing this by the reduced fire from the Southern Trader. Like a pack of hyenas closing in on a crippled victim, the two boats began to converge on the motor-sailing ship.

Now realizing the situation had gone critical, Clay gave the order, "We're running low on ammo, pick your targets before you fire." With the last magazine in the Dragunov Clay knew he was low ammunition. He concentrated on making each shot count.

Suddenly the gunfire from both boats intensified and Clay quickly found out what the attackers had in mind. The heavy fire accomplished its purpose and kept their heads down. From cover, Clay watched their next move in horror.

An RPG gunner popped out of hiding on each boat in a coordinated attack and took aim. Clay realized that the old saw, shooting fish in a barrel didn't come close to reality. It would be more like dropping a grenade in a barrel, he thought, the bastards couldn't miss.

Clay yelled the warning, "RPG gunner on each boat. Get them!" Before the words were barely out of his mouth, he heard the telltale flat crack of the Arisaka firing and saw the gunner slump over the gunwale of the boat, dropping the RPG overboard.

"Nice shot!" he yelled, as he glanced in the direction of the rifle report and saw the old soldier spread out in a solid prone position on top of the deckhouse. A brief smile crossed Clay's face as he watched the man reload like a well-oiled machine and pick another target.

Rick looked over at Clay and said, "Now?" No further words were necessary. Clay shouted back, "Now! Before they bring out another RPG."

Rick yelled to the nearest man, Rutherford, telling him to get their captured RPG-7 loaded, saying, "Take out that bastard!" Another man nearby pulled a rocket out of the pouch, loaded it and Rutherford took aim. The ocean had gotten choppier, the swells deepening. The gunner waited a few seconds until he figured he had the deckhouse on the patrol boat lined up and then fired. The ocean swell at that precise moment dipped the other boat down and the rocket glanced off the top of the target, continuing off into the distant sea where it exploded harmlessly.

"Jesus Christ!" Rick yelled in exasperation. Rutherford flushed in embarrassment and they rapidly reloaded and he took aim. More cautious this time, he depressed the trigger and fired. A blast followed as they all watched the telltale path of the rocket. It hit squarely in the deckhouse this time, exploding into a ball of flame and shrapnel. Clay guessed it was an anti-personnel rocket as it took out most of the crew. The boat slowed, and then stopped dead in the water, no longer a threat. Morbid curiosity caused the whole team to watch as burning pirates threw themselves into the sea.

Everyone had momentarily forgotten the RPG gunner on the other boat, but it appeared he hadn't forgotten them. About the same moment, Rutherford pulled the trigger on his rocket, the pirate fired his RPG at the Southern Trader. Moments later, it struck their ship a little above the water line toward the stern. They all felt the explosion below deck as it rocked the ship and smoke immediately began to pour out of open ports.

Rick yelled the alarm. "Find fire extinguishers!" Clay dove down the steps to the lower deck, grabbing a large fire extinguisher strapped to the wall and raced toward the door to the engine room; several other team members followed finding extinguishers as they ran. Clay placed the palm of his hand against the door testing for heat, then the doorknob. Both cool to the touch, Clay turned the door handle, while all stepped back in case the extra oxygen might cause the fire to flare out of the doorway. Carefully pulling open the door, he leaped out of the way, but only smoke came out. They dropped to their hands and knees and crawled into the engine room under the billowing smoke.

Spotting the origin of the fire, they concentrated their extinguishers on it, dousing it quickly. Clay felt extremely lucky that it had not reached the fuel tanks. Vents had been installed around the room for cooling and they jerked them open to clear the room.

Coughing, with eyes watering, Clay looked at the engines. The devastation from the rocket looked serious and after a rapid inspection of the damage, Clay figured the engines were probably beyond repair. He could feel the ship had slowed to a stop, now dead in the water, a sitting duck for the attackers. As Clay looked around the room, he couldn't quite figure why the destruction had not been more extensive from the rocket. "If I had to make a guess I'd say that when the rocket hit the side of our ship, instead of exploding, it penetrated at an angle, then exploded. The whole room should have been destroyed but wasn't. That could mean many things such as the rocket was old or faulty from exposure to the sea air, it could be anything! In any case it could have been worse than it was," he said to the men with him.

Seeing there was nothing more they could do, they all raced back up topside to see what was going on as the sound of increased gunfire reached their ears.

As they kept low and crawled out on the main deck, Clay could see Rutherford and his loader were examining the rear of the rocket with distressed looks on their faces. When Clay spotted the problem he immediately blamed himself. His bullets from when he had attacked the terrorists on shore had apparently hit or ricocheted into the area between the Sustainer Motor and the Booster.

The gunner and his partner peered at the deep indentations in both elements of the RPG. "What I'm really afraid of Clay, is that one of the rounds might have damaged the Stabilizer Fins and the RPG might not deploy properly," Rutherford said.

"Look, it's not your fault. It couldn't be helped! Just give it your best shot! Be careful it's a PIBD round and could explode if there's any damage," Clay said to them, concerned that the impact-detonating feature could explode prematurely. Accepting Clay's advice and cautiously loading the rocket into the tube, the two men scooted over to the heavy teak gunwale.

Poking the launcher over the top, the gunner aimed and fired. The rocket exited the launcher, performing normally, heading directly for the approaching boat, but in mid-flight it started rotating erratically and deviating from the course, nosing down into the ocean and exploding just short of the pirate vessel. With a look of hopelessness on his face, the man loading it showed Clay that they were out of ammunition.

A few moments later, Rick, having observed the flight of the rocket, crawled over to them. "Well, I've got a little more good news for you," he said. "I checked around and we're on our last magazines of ammo."

"Shit! You've got to be kidding me! You mean we've used up everything?"

"Just about. Sorry, but we are tapped out."

Raising his head at eye level above the heavy wooden railing, Clay saw something that caused a chill of apprehension in his stomach. With the news from Rick and now this, there is no way we can stop the pirates from boarding them now, he thought. The faux patrol boat was now rapidly headed for them and he knew they had full intentions of climbing aboard the Southern Trader. If that happens, it will be a slaughter, he reflected with a combination of burning anger and despair. Well Goddamn it! They're not going to get any of us without a fight!

With Rick's nodded approval, Clay yelled, "Everybody! Listen up! Never thought I'd ever have to say these words, but, fix bayonets and get ready to repel boarders!"

Chapter 28

As he fired at the approaching pirate vessel, Clay saw two warning tracer rounds leave his rifle. With his magazine just about empty he tried to make his last few rounds count, then set the weapon on the deck. With no more of the special ammunition the sniper rifle required, he avoided the furious return fire, ducking below the protective teakwood railing for protection. He pulled his Beretta out and pressed the magazine release, sliding it out, checked it quickly to make sure he had a full load, then pushed it back into his pistol and thumbed off the safety.

He guessed the others felt as he did and steeled himself for what would be the do-or-die final, bloody assault on the Southern Trader. Clay vowed not to go down without a fight, hoping his teammates felt the same way. There would be no prisoners with these animals; they would murder everything in their bloody path.

His thoughts were interrupted by one of the other troopers who had been below deck making sure the fire was totally out and had not spread. "Rick – Clay - ya gotta come below. Right now!" he called to them. "I found a small gift from Mister Remington!"

Both crawled on hands and knees and followed the trooper below deck. He led them down the narrow passageway, stopping in front of what turned out to be the former Captain's cabin. Curiosity got the better of both of them as they followed him inside. On the floor were three large, unfinished shipping crates made of pine. The raw pine lid's had been pried off and lay loosely over the crates, concealing the contents. As he lifted the top off the first one, the man said, "As I said, we have received a gift from Mister Remington!"

Inside the crate, securely fastened to the mount was a set of six Remington pump shotguns, side by side in a row. Shocked beyond belief, Clay watched as the trooper lifted the lid off the other crate where another set of riot guns was exposed.

"And now," the man said, lifting the lid off the third crate, "The best part. A full case of double-ought buckshot shells!"

"Hold shit! Possibly this is our salvation." was all Clay could manage, choked up with emotional relief. The trooper took one of the cardboard boxes out of the case, opened it and dumped it on the bunk. He picked up one of the shells as if he didn't believe his eyes, and showed it to both men. "I accidentally stumbled on this stuff when I came in here and saw the crates under the bunk. Why they were hidden in here, I haven't a clue!"

"And we don't care either," Rick added, pulling one of the shotguns out of its Velcro securing strap and pumping back the slide. Turning it over, Rick grabbed a handful of shells off the bunk and started loading the weapon. Clay and the other man followed suit.

After a quick parley with Rick, Clay handed his to the trooper with a box of shells. "Here's what you need to do. Take these two up on deck and distribute them."

"Okay. Anything else?"

"Cycle the team down here two at a time. We'll pass out loaded weapons and ammo so that everyone is armed. Here, you take this third one." He handed the loaded riot gun to the trooper. "One more thing," Clay said, "Make sure you tell the men to find a good hiding spot away from the railing and no action until we give the word. It needs to be a complete surprise to work."

"Okay, I'll pass it along to everyone," he said and left the area.

A short time later, everyone armed and under cover, the wounded, hidden below deck with pistols for defense, just in case, Clay and Rick stealthily watched from concealment, back on deck, as the patrol boat approached.

The team listened while Clay spoke. as Rick nodded his approval. "I think it best to let the first group get on board, then we'll spring the trap! This is our only chance, so we've got to play it close to the vest!"

Turning to the old soldier and his wife, Clay said, "I'd like you both to take cover someplace safe. I don't want to take a chance of either one of you getting hurt." Pointing to the small, upper-deck day cabin a little beyond the midpoint of the ship, Clay said, "Why don't you both go in there and close the door till it's over."

The old soldier argued with Madeline for a few moments but finally gave in. Clay knew the man was concerned about the safety of his wife.

Turning to one of the other men, Clay said, "I want you to take Stryker down below with the wounded. Tie him up so he can't come back up here and accidentally get hurt." Then talking to Stryker and handing the leash to the trooper, Clay said, "I want you to go with this man!" Stryker whined mournfully, as if imparting thoughts that he didn't want to lose another partner.

As they all tensely waited for the pirate craft, Clay felt the bumping of the patrol boat as it came to a stop against the Southern Trader. Moments later several grappling hooks flew through the air and hooked onto the ship's railing. Less than a minute later, the first of the pirates came over the top and dropped to the deck, followed by another group and then a third group. The men stood there in a kind of surprise and shock that they had gotten this far unopposed. Watching from cover, Clay figured that this had to be what they were thinking. An older, better dressed pirate, apparently the leader, gave an order to one of the men, who broke off from the group and headed for the day cabin at a trot. Oh shit! This is not exactly going as I hoped it would, Clay thought.

Clay watched anxiously as the pirate rushed up to the closed door. He held his AK- 74 at waist level, straight ahead, finger on the trigger and he threw open the door. It swung wildly outward and banged with a clatter against the front of the cabin. He pointed his AK into the opening as he stepped through the hatch. Clay made a wild guess and thought, I bet he's expecting to find a crowd of cowering civilians! A moment later Clay recognized the familiar loud reverberation of the old

Southern Trader under sail, fleeing the pirate's attack

soldier's Arisaka. A second later a pirate toppled backward out of the hatch and dropped dead to the deck.

Shit! The surprise is blown! Clay thought, standing up and taking aim at the nearest pirate, as he yelled, "Now!" The rest of the team opened fire simultaneously from concealment or standing up. The first pirate took a load of buckshot at close quarters, in the chest and went down permanently as Clay immediately picked another target. The sound of the riot guns firing drowned out the few shots that the pirates managed to get off. The acrid smell of cordite filled the humid air as the fight intensified. Caught totally by surprise, the pirates went down like butter melting in a hot frying pan. It was all over in the space of a few minutes.

Several of the team members rushed over to the gunwales and caught the remaining pirates trying to escape back into their boat, and finished them off. The remaining men aboard the boat took cover and continued to fire. Clay turned around, scanning the bodies littering the deck and spotted what he had hoped to find a few seconds later. He stepped over to a dead pirate and pulled a hand grenade off the man's bloody garment. One of the other men guessed what Clay had in mind and did the same. Both crawled over to the gunwale, keeping out of sight, pulled the pins on their grenades and held the spoon tight, until Clay nodded. They popped up and dropped the grenades into the patrol boat, ducking back under cover. Before any of the enemy could react and try to throw the grenades back up to the ship, they went off with a deafening explosion. Clay thought that should have finished them off, but as he took another look over the railing he noticed a few had survived, including the pilot of the boat. The pilot kept under cover as best he could and desperately worked to steer the boat away from the Southern Trader while the few remaining pirates alive fired sporadically in an attempt to keep the team under cover. Clay knew they had taken the fight out of them. Clay let them go, as he thought, Maybe next time they'll think twice before attacking a ship.

Clay scanned the carnage on deck for any pirates who might be playing possum, when he noticed Rick propped up against one of the canvas covered hatch covers. He rushed over to him and saw that his pal was badly wounded in two places. Clay yelled for help and a few seconds later a medic rushed over and began to give aid. Rick, one of the few injured, had taken hits in the right upper shoulder and a wound in the thigh. Ignoring his own wounds, Clay picked Rick up and carried him to a shaded area up forward.

Clay automatically took command. "Okay, check to be sure they're all dead, collect their weapons and get the bodies over the side." The men set about the grisly task. Next, Clay sent two men below that he recalled had mechanical experience in hopes that they could get the engines going or to cannibalize enough from one to get the other working. Two hours later, they reported back that it was hopeless, due to vital components being damaged beyond repair. The news left Clay frustrated. He had to get power for the ship.

While Clay wasn't his usual energetic self, the medication from Madeline allowed him to move about with a minimum of soreness at this time. He was fully aware that when it wore off, he would pay the price in discomfort. With Stryker back at his side, he visited Rick who had been made comfortable on a bed of several sleeping bags.

"So? How are you feeling, buddy?" Clay asked as Stryker licked Rick's outstretched hand, his tail wagging.

"I'm ready to get back to work," Rick replied.

"Hah! Now - that's a joke! You ain't goin' nowhere with those wounds, pal. You're going to need proper treatment and soon."

"Speak for yourself!" Rick said, pointing to Clay's thigh.

"The only thing I'm concerned about right now is getting this tub going! The engines are not repairable and we're stuck," Clay replied.

"No you're not," Rick pointed his finger upward. "You've got plenty of power. Wind power."

"No one on board knows anything about sailing," Clay said.

"But I do," Rick replied. "I have a little experience with small craft and this is no different, just bigger!"

"Okay, what's our first step?" Clay asked.

"When I looked up into the rigging I noticed some of the lines were fouled. You need to get a couple of men up there to get them straightened out. Then I'll show everyone how to deploy the sails," Rick explained.

"I'll get right on it," Clay promised.

Walking over to trooper O'Reilly and another man nearby, Clay said, "Okay guys, I need your help." Pointing up into the rigging, he continued, "The lines are tightly tangled and have to be freed. I need you two to climb up there and get them loose."

"Whoa!" O'Reilly said, frowning, "I can't go up there!"

"What do you mean you can't go up there?" Clay said, anger forming in his gut. "Are we going to have another problem with you?" He remembered the recent shooting incident.

"No, boss, you won't. I'm just afraid of heights and freak out!"

"No you won't, I'm going to go up there with you!" Nodding at the other man, Clay said, "I'm going up instead of you."

"But your leg?" O'Reilly seemed to be looking for any way to wiggle out of the chore.

"Screw my leg! Let's go! I'll be right below you."

Hesitantly, O'Reilly started up the rope ladder attached to the gunwale. Clay followed closely behind, ignoring the twinge of pain he felt radiating from his leg.

Three-quarters of the way up to the mast, Clay moved next to O'Reilly and pointed out what they needed to do. O'Reilly hung on so tightly his knuckles were turning white. He started to look down when Clay yelled at him, "Don't look down! Look at me. Now, let's get this job done."

O'Reilly slowly edged over to where Clay had started one-handed to loosen the tightly tangled lines while he hung onto the ladder with the other. It was wound so tight it looked like the Gordian Knot to him.

"Help me get this loose," he called.

O'Reilly edged closer, wrapped his arm through one of the ladder holes and tightly grabbed on to a vertical section. With his other hand, be began to work on the tangled portion with Clay. They had been working on the rope for several minutes when Clay, not so much heard, but physically felt the parting of air passing, very close, over them in the rigging. A moment later, a loud, shrill sound, similar to the sound of a fighter jet passing overhead, rattled their ears.

"What in the hell was that?" O'Reilly asked.

"I have no idea! Let's get this done and get outta here!"

Seconds later, in the direction of the sound, the ocean exploded in fire, smoke and a huge cascade of water.

"That looks like…" Clay never finished his sentence as another rush of hot air passed close above their heads. A moment later, the same harsh sound assaulted their ears followed by an explosion closer to the ship.

"Somebody's shooting at us!" Clay proclaimed in shock.

"I've had enough! I'm outta here!" O'Reilly screamed, starting to descend.

"No! Wait! Get back up here! The rope has to…!" Clay yelled as he reached to grab O'Reilly's shirt to stop him.

A split second later, a sharp dagger of excruciating pain from his wound, shot up Clay's leg, through his side and up his arm. It was so bad, he lost his grip on the rope, and then lost his balance, falling backward. As he swung out into open space, he unconsciously made a desperate grab for the thick outer strand of the rope ladder with his other hand, managing to clamp his fingers tightly around the rope. Swinging out into space, he glanced down at the deck below and felt a dizzying sensation. Turning back to O'Reilly he gasped, "O'Reilly! Help!"

Chapter 29

The strain on his hand felt as though someone had taken a pair of red-hot vise grips, squeezing down hard on his fist. The burning sensation made him want to cry out and he didn't know how much longer it would be until he lost his grip. Swinging slowly back and forth, he dared a glance downward at the hard, teak deck below. The small knot of troopers gathered below him stared up helplessly. The sight made him dizzy and he involuntarily closed his eyes tightly, not knowing how much longer he could hold on. Even now he felt his fingers losing their grip.

It seemed only a moment later, a strong, confident voice spoke to him from above. He knew that voice, but it couldn't be. Perched several rungs up the ladder sat Gabe, a smile on his ruddy face, holding onto the rope confidently with one hand.

"Where'd you come from?" Clay gasped in surprise.

"I've been with you all the way, keeping an eye on you."

"This can't be. I'm hallucinating," Clay said.

"No, you're not. I'm here. Listen to me carefully, Clay. You can make it. Trust me. Just believe in yourself."

Clay looked up again, but Gabe had disappeared. Gabe's words penetrated his inner core and determination took over. He forced his mind to focus on survival, to hang on a little longer. A few moments later he found himself totally shocked to hear another familiar voice close to him.

"Try and swing your body over toward my arm."

Clay couldn't believe his ears. "O'Reilly! You came back!" he croaked out of his dry mouth.

"Yeah, and I'll probably regret it the rest of my life," O'Reilly said with a smile. He dangled in space over the rope ladder from the waist up, his legs securely intertwined in the open spaces of the ladder.

The strain on his hand forgotten, Clay forced himself to start a pendulum movement with his other arm outstretched toward O'Reilly's arm. He made three tries, just barely missing each time. Beginning to lose the feeling in his arm attached to the rope, he thought desperately - I've got to do it right this time or there might not be another. Forcefully, making his body swing outward as much as he could to gain enough momentum as if he were on a child's swing, Clay swung forward. His mind totally focused and determined, he saw the outstretched hand.

Connecting, O'Reilly slapped his hand around Clay's wrist and held on with a claw-like, iron grip. Clay's fingers wrapped around O'Reilly's wrist and hung on as if his life depended on it...it did. Pulling Clay toward him, every muscle in his body screaming, O'Reilly arched his body backward to bring Clay closer to the lead rope. "I have you! When I pull you close to the rope, let loose and grab it," O'Reilly said.

Swinging toward the edge of the rope, Clay felt his arm brush against its rough surface. Knowing this to be his only chance, Clay released the man's wrist and made a desperate grab for the rope. Disregarding the pain that burned like fire through his body, Clay's fingers wrapped like an eagle's talons around the rope and clamped shut.

"Nice going, boss! Now for your next trick..." O'Reilly said.

"Give me a moment, okay?" Clay closed his eyes and let the strain of the last few moments wash out of his body.

"Okay, Clay, but we've got to get your leg over the rope next."

Looking downward, Clay saw one of the other troopers scampering up the rope ladder to help. The other man positioned himself slightly below O'Reilly on the ladder. "Swing your body up toward the ladder and we'll both try to grab your leg and pull you over," O'Reilly instructed.

Straining every burning muscle in his body, Clay started a swinging, pendulum motion. As his leg swung up toward the rope, he thought he had missed, but a moment later, four strong arms wrapped around his leg and bodily manhandled his body onto the ladder. Clay gratefully scrambled the rest of the way and lay flat against the rope, exhausted. Drained of all emotion and energy, Clay lay next to O'Reilly for a few minutes.

"O'Reilly, I owe you big time."

With his sweat soaked head lying against the rope, he smiled at Clay, "I really am afraid of heights, boss. Never again, okay?"

"Okay, deal," Clay said, as the two of them set about untangling the fouled lines. Thinking about the shots that came through the rigging, he added, "I'm really worried where they came from. We've got to get the sails unfurled and deployed to pick up the wind as soon as possible."

On the horizon, heading directly at them, Clay saw what appeared to be a fishing trawler similar to the huge tuna boats he'd seen docked in San Diego years ago. He could see some kind of deck gun or small artillery piece positioned on the bow. The gun fired again and a moment later, the shell landed with a deafening explosion of fire and smoke in the water fifty yards in front of the bow, showering the ship with a huge misty spray of ocean.

A moment later the sound of another shell came at them and landed a hundred yards from the stern of the Southern Trader.

"I think they're trying to send us a message," Clay said. "We better get down to the deck and see if we can get the sails up. We've got to somehow put some distance between us and them."

Everyone put in an all out effort to get the sails deployed. Peering through the scope of his Dragonuv, Clay focused on the approaching ship. He could see they had taken a small howitzer and mounted it on the bow.

Setting his rifle down, he picked up one of the captured AK-47's, released the magazine and stripped off a round. Inserting it manually into the chamber of the Dragonuv he slid home the bolt. He was taking a wild chance that this would work. Clay fully realized that the Dragunov used the older 7.62-54R cartridges instead of the standard 7.62 AK-47 round. He did it in desperation, to keep the attacker's heads down long enough to gain time for the team to get the sails operating.

Focusing, to get a crystal clear picture, one individual stood, clearly the leader. Clay set the crosshairs on his chest and began to steadily squeeze the trigger. A moment later before he fired, a huge column of water, smoke and fire erupted in front of the ship. Seconds later, another geyser of water erupted next to the first. The ship abruptly reversed course.

Now a ship approached them. Focusing the image, Clay recognized the unmistakable lines of a US Navy Fast Frigate heading their way at flank speed. He'd never seen a more welcome sight. Moments later, the Navy ship's automatic deck gun fired again. Clay could see the other ship had completed its turn, as the shell hit near the fantail, bursting into fire and smoke. They'd had enough, turned tail and were running. A wild cheer went up from everyone including Clay.

A short time later, the frigate hove - to near the Southern Trader and a zodiac craft carrying sailors came over with a radio to check on the condition of the crew. Clay concluded that more than one listening ear had tuned in on the pirates' radio transmission before the team had stormed the Southern Trader. In the meantime, the captain had positioned the frigate fifty yards from their ship. Receiving instructions over the handheld radio from the Senior Chief Petty Officer, a pilot line fired from the stern of the frigate landed in the bow area of their boat. Everyone pitched in, pulling the heavy towing hawser line aboard the Southern Trader. The sailors efficiently secured the towline and a short time later, they were underway headed home.

Arriving near the large pier jutting out into the water at the main base, the frigate slowed to a stop. A sturdy workboat appeared and moved alongside the Southern Trader which had drifted to a stop and gently nudged it up to the pier.

As soon as the gangplank was in place, several people dressed in white, which Clay figured were medics, came aboard and immediately began to assist the wounded down to the pier. Some of the others with stretchers carried the more serious wounded down to the pier, putting them in an ambulances.

With Stryker leading the way, Clay painfully hobbled down the gangplank. Noticing a tall, dark haired nurse in a crisp white uniform giving orders, Clay made his way over to her. "Miss, we have some very badly wounded people on board. One is the copilot and the other my friend, Rick. They are in need of urgent care."

Her smile showed sincere concern. "Take it easy, soldier. We received a radio message from the Navy ship and we're on top of the situation. I've got medics on board right now. We know the serious condition of your friend and the copilot. Transportation has been arranged to take them to the airfield, then to a hospital in Manila."

"Why not here?"

"They are very seriously wounded and our small medical unit is not equipped to give them the proper care."

Clay looked closely at the woman, thinking, *She is absolutely beautiful. I am beginning to believe that a person can fall in love at first sight.*

Coughing, he asked, "Do I call you Captain?"

"You can call me Carolyn. I'm not in the Army. We're all volunteers from several church groups back in the States. Since there is a shortage of medical personnel over here, the government donated and equipped this medical facility to help everyone in the area, civilian and military."

"Okay, I understand, but I've got to get the rest of the men up to the base so they can get a decent meal and clean up," Clay said, starting to move away.

"Where do you think you're going?"

"With my men."

"No, you're not. You're wounded in several places and in no condition to go anywhere. You're going with me up to the hospital for proper treatment before those wounds get infected."

Feeling his stubborn streak rise to the point of exploding, Clay said, "No I'm not. I've got the responsibility of taking care of my team now that Rick is gone."

"You ever heard the word *gangrene?* If that leg wound isn't treated properly soon - you could lose it. You're coming with me to the hospital," Carolyn said with iron determination in her voice that the argument was over.

"I'll stop by later, I'll be fine," he assured her, starting to step away. Suddenly he felt weak all over and everything started to spin. Clay staggered, trying to get his balance as he fell toward Carolyn. He felt her grab him under the arms to hold him up, yelling, "Bring a gurney, quick!" Then he blacked out.

Regaining consciousness, Clay found himself on the gurney in a huge tent. He guessed this had to be the small base hospital. Focusing, Clay found himself staring up into the most beautiful blue eyes he had ever seen. He could see the authentic concern in them. "Are you okay, soldier?" Carolyn asked.

"Call me Clay."

"Sure, Clay. Are you okay now?"

"Never felt better. I've gotta get up to my men."

"Yeah, sure. Your men are fine and are receiving care. You're going nowhere. You're going to be here for a while. And by the way – I'm Carolyn Carter."

"What? No I can't do that. What about my partner?"

"Your partner?"

"Yeah, his name is Stryker. Where is he?"

"Oh, you mean the dog?"

"He's not just a dog - he's my partner."

"Okay, okay, he's fine and right over there napping. He hasn't left your side since we brought you in here. Wouldn't even eat. Seems he's taken a great liking to me and I was able to get him to eat."

"Thanks, I appreciate it. He's special."

"After you passed out, the doc injected you with a light sedative. You were pretty banged up and exhausted. You slept for over twelve hours."

Clay checked his bandages and then ran his hand over his face. "Who cleaned me up?"

"I did and I shaved that barbed-wire bristle off your face. You almost look human," she replied with a smile.

"Okay, that's nice and I thank you. Now - when can I get outta here?"

"So, what's your rush? So, maybe you don't like my company?" Another mischievous smile played across her attractive face.

"On the contrary, I could look at you forever and a day and still not get tired of the view." Surprised at what he had confessed, he felt his face flush in embarrassment.

Blushing herself at the compliment, but deeply pleased, Carolyn said, "Oh, wow! That's a really old line."

"It's not a line. I meant it."

"Look, you *are* pretty banged up. Most of your wounds are superficial scratches and will heal quickly. The leg is a different matter. Thankfully, the bullet didn't hit the bone, but it is serious. You're not going anywhere for a while."

"A while? How long is that?"

"Until it heals properly. If you start running around playing *Rambo* it'll open the wound again. You're stuck with me for a while."

"I wasn't playing at *Rambo*. I did what I had to do to save the team."

"Not the way I hear it - from some of your men. The way they tell it, you came across like a one-man army. You know, you were damn lucky. If that bullet had shattered your leg, you might have been walking with a limp for the rest of you life."

"I had a guardian angel."

"And what was his name, Gabe?"

"How'd you know that?"

"You were delirious and raving in your sleep, calling for Gabe. Who is he?"

"A good friend, a friend who helped and guided me."

"*Where* is he? I didn't hear of anyone by that name in your group."

"Oh, he's around all right." *When you least expect him, he's there,* Clay thought, recalling the surprise when he showed up on the ship's rope ladder.

"Oh, I see," she said doubtfully, wondering if he had been hallucinating. "Look, some of your men have been talking to me about you. They tell me you have a habit of taking unnecessary risks."

"If you're given the chance to set things right, you do it and don't think about it," he said with conviction.

Not understanding the mysterious statement at all, she looked at Clay appraisingly for a moment and felt a growing affection for this brash character. She hadn't felt this way about anybody since she had lost her husband, and then devoted all her time to her work. Wanting to get through to him, she said, "Look, there's more to life than running around playing *Rambo.* Sooner or later you're going to draw a bad card and your luck will run out. That's it, finis, game over!"

"I've accomplished what I set out to do, that's what's important. So what else is there?"

"A lot more to life, if you just give it a chance. What do you or did you enjoy in the past?"

His memory very vague, he seemed to recall he never had time and was always working. "I love a good book, most kinds of music, but especially Dean Martin and Frank Sinatra. I also love slow and close dancing," He looked at her closely to see her reaction. He liked what he saw in her sparkling blue eyes.

"Really?" she said, "That's very coincidental because Dean's one of my favorites too and I have a couple of his C D's. Well, I've got to go, other patients to check on, but we can talk some more this afternoon."

Clay leaned back against his pillow thinking about Carolyn as Stryker moved over to the bed and rested his chin on Clay's good leg. "What do you think of her, buddy?" he said to Stryker, not expecting a reply. Stryker idly wagged his tail from side to side and looked up at Clay as if he understood every word.

Clay's emotions were in turmoil about Carolyn. On one side he found himself strongly attracted to her. But, on the other, the vague, painful memories of his past marriage failure hung in his mind.

Days passed quickly and as his wounds healed, Clay looked forward to Carolyn's visits every day He never tired of seeing her. Their conversations about books, music, movies and the simple, enjoyable things of life stimulated him and drew him closer to her. He loved it when she leaned close to him to check his bandages because he could smell the clean, fresh scent of her perfume, like wildflowers in a field.

In a few weeks she was nagging him to get out of bed. Her mischievous grin told him she had something up her sleeve. "I think it's time for you to stop being a *lazy slug*, get out of that bed and do something," she said jokingly, "Time for you to take a walk." Clay found himself pleased to hear this as he'd been getting out of bed and taking a few hesitant steps when she wasn't around to catch him.

Taking her hand, they walked around the camp, set in a cleared area that appeared to be the remains of some kind of plantation. He felt like a teenager in love, holding her hand, savoring every moment. In return she squeezed his hand in reassurance of her feelings.

Clay no longer wanted to return stateside, even though his time in country had expired. He had obtained an automatic extension of two months while he recuperated. The two of them began taking long walks near the ocean in the evenings, continuing their long discussions and savoring the time they had together.

He couldn't deny it, he was deeply in love with Carolyn. One evening, on the beach of a small, isolated cove near the camp, watching the surf crashing on the beach, Clay made his decision. He put his past troubled marriage behind him forever and turned to face Carolyn. Taking her gently in his arms, he looked deeply into her eyes and seeing no resistance, kissed her passionately in a long and lingering embrace. She returned his kiss hungrily. Afterward he said, "Look, I don't know how this happened, but it just did."

"I know. I feel the same way and I wanted it to happen. I haven't felt this way about anyone since I lost my husband."

"What happened to him?"

"Plane crash on his way home from a business trip. I went into a deep depression, threw myself into my work, then suddenly I found myself here. My memory is very hazy, almost a total blank. *I'm* over it now."

Noting the similarities to his own previous life, he said, "Strange, my memory is the same, but I do know I haven't had these kind of feelings for as long as I can remember."

A few more weeks went by and Clay calculated through his mental calendar that his extension time had passed. No one had caught it and he figured it was either a paperwork foul-up or they were too busy with other, more important matters. He chose to keep quiet because now he didn't want to leave Carolyn. He had a small, inner fear dogging him that if he did leave, he might never see her again.

He had learned from several knowledgeable people at the base that Mindanao had become a major training ground for al-Qaeda terrorists. Based on his recent experiences, he knew this to be true. The rumors of growing terrorist strength bothered him greatly and he feared for Carolyn's safety in the exposed base hospital and lightly guarded base camp.

Their evening walks became a regular event, except when she had the duty. As they became more comfortable with each other, their time together became more intimate and sensual. He loved hearing her soft moans when he kissed her on the neck and behind the ear. Carolyn kissed him back hungrily, which in turn caused a rekindling of old fires he thought he had lost. He loved exploring her exquisite body as they held each other. He just couldn't get enough of her.

One late afternoon she stopped by to see him just as he was getting ready to take a shower. She told him she would meet him at their spot at the cove later that evening.

As he came down the dirt path leading to their secluded meeting place, he heard the unmistakable velvety voice of Dean Martin, belting out *You're Nobody 'Til Somebody Loves You* on what had to be a portable stereo. Stepping around the small bend that opened out onto the cove's half-moon shaped beach, he saw with surprise that Carolyn had laid out everything for a picnic. A soft, canvas cooler held two chilled bottles of wine, and she had set out cheese and crackers on plastic dishes. Two candles in holders were on top of the closed picnic hamper which added to the intimacy.

He stood watching her for a moment, marveling at her exquisite beauty. She wore on a light tan colored, sheer, loose fitting cover up dress, and underneath a revealing two-piece bathing suit. As he knelt down on the blanket, Carolyn looked at him with a big smile. Grinning, Clay asked, "What's going on? You went to a lot of trouble with this set up. What's the occasion?"

"I'm celebrating us…and the moment! Life is too short to not savor and enjoy it every chance we get."

"I'll sure agree to that," he replied. He moved over to where she knelt, took her in his arms, and gave her a long, passionate kiss. Her mouth trembled on his when she returned it, then after a few moments she stood up and said, "Let's take a stroll along the beach."

Hand in hand they walked along the beach among the scattered seaweed and shells. He had anticipated the possibility that they might go into the surf, so he had worn a borrowed bathing suit under his shorts. He watched her as she dropped the sheer, silky dress exposing her sensuous body now clad only the tiny two piece suit which she had borrowed from another nurse. He shed his clothes down to the borrowed suit. Before it had fit him perfectly. Now it seemed too tight.

She ran ahead, squealing at the cold shock of the water. She laughed like a giggling teen-ager and he found himself laughing as well. He caught up with her and together they felt the weight of the pounding surf as the cold wave carried them away, but even the tremendous pull of the wave could not separate them.

They again met a wave head-on, but it seemed not as cold to them. "It's feeling warmer," Carolyn shouted above the raging water.

"I don't even feel the cold anymore," he answered her. *I'm hot as hell,* he thought, his whole body trembling.

He pulled her from the water and she didn't resist him. As they threw themselves into the sand, he said, "This is like something out of an old movie."

"No, it isn't," she said, smiling up at him. "This is not a film – it is us and very real – we are very much alive." She stood up, reached for her towel and began to dry herself off. He did the same and in minutes, they found themselves drying each other. She stood perfectly still as his hands explored her body. She did not even breathe as he touched every soft, rounded, firm part of her and she gasped, her whole body trembling as he finished his search.

"Let's sample the wine," she said softly and he could feel her warm breath upon his face. He could have proceeded without the wine at this point, but at this time, he also did not want to break the spell. "It will be my courage," she told him, touching his trembling chest.

He could have died right then and there....

After – he could remember opening the bottle, pouring it, gulping it at first – for *his* courage – and then suddenly she was removing his suit – God, he hoped she hadn't torn it because he would have to return it in the morning.

After – he could remember the moonlight shining on her breasts, the passion in her embrace, the urgency he had felt to climax, but in the back of his mind – he wanted to please her too.

After – he had felt a tremendous, complete feeling as they ended it together.

They lay on the blanket, side by side, each enjoying the afterglow of their lovemaking. They held hands, each lost in their own thoughts. Clay's mind focused on the future and how much he wanted to spend it with Carolyn. Leaning on his elbow, Clay said, "I love you with all my heart. It has been a very long time for me and I almost forgot how our kind of love felt."

Looking at him with adoring eyes, she said, "I know, I'm experiencing the same feelings."

It had grown dark when reluctantly they packed up and departed, neither one wanted to break the magic spell that surrounded them.

They met for lunch the next day and while Clay was bursting with the urge to propose marriage to her, he wanted the moment to be special. They agreed to meet the following evening, at a small, romantic restaurant just outside of town, near the base. It would be a time they would remember always, he hoped.

Clay knew that sooner or later his paperwork would catch up to him. There were several things of importance that needed to be taken care of, but he felt he wouldn't have the time. He had hoped to help Toshiro, the old soldier and his wife, Madeline retrieve their belongings from the cave and help them set up a home, enlisting the assistance of his buddies. Clay knew it might take some time figuring out how to get Stryker cleared to be shipped to the States without a hassle. He guessed he'd maybe have a week, if he lucked out, maybe two, before they finished his paperwork at the base. Then he knew he'd be shipped out to Manila, and then ultimately the States.

He wanted to find a minister or a priest, and with Carolyn's agreement, he hoped, get married before he departed. But there was a nagging, hazy thought in the back of his mind, from his other reality, that he couldn't do so. There was some kind of a recollection that he thought a divorce was in the works. It was all very confusing at this point and he put it off until he could think about it later. He planned that as soon as he had his Army discharge, he'd quickly return and finish up everything left hanging. Stryker would be safe with Carolyn until then.

The following morning, after breakfast, Clay found a form on his hospital bunk explaining he'd been released from the hospital that day. He figured he'd be sent to the transient barracks to await processing and transfer. He guessed it would take at least a week, before he could get everything completed, giving him the time he needed.

Clay had just finished packing his duffle bag when a courier in a *Humvee* showed up with orders to take him to headquarters. Totally puzzled, he was shown into the office of the commanding officer and told to take a seat. "Clay, you are to be commended for the part you played in the safe return of the team. Something has come up that is extremely urgent. We have a plane ready to depart and one spot left. You've got to be on that plane."

"But sir, I have a few personal things that I have to take care of this evening. Why can't I go tomorrow?"

"Sorry, but you must go - now. It will be the last plane out. The prisoner you brought back with you has divulged a wealth of valuable intelligence information. We have confirmation of an imminent attack by the al-Qaeda guerillas. Everything will be shut down and nothing will be going in or out till this is over."

"Then let me stay to help fight them," he replied.

"Sorry, orders are orders. They've come from the very top. When you reach the States the Army needs to impart all of your knowledge and recent experience to a special group coming over here soon. You must go now."

He tried to call Carolyn from the small, base airport but was informed she was assisting in the operating room and wouldn't be available for a while. Totally upset at not being able to contact her on reaching Manila, Clay tried desperately several times to phone the hospital, but was informed by the base operator that only military communications were being allowed to be connected. With fear for Carolyn's safety hanging heavy on his mind, Clay boarded the transport.

That evening, Carolyn waited at the restaurant for two hours. Not knowing why Clay had not shown up, but fearing the worst, she broke down in heart-rending sobs. She felt heartbroken and abandoned. Thinking Clay had changed his mind and no longer desired to be with her, she left the restaurant. It had grown dark as she looked for a cab in vain. None were around anywhere and the night was filled with gunfire and explosions. Fearing the worst, she began to run back to the hospital.

Chapter 30

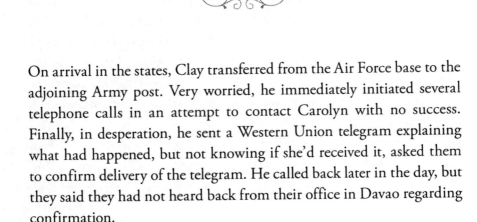

On arrival in the states, Clay transferred from the Air Force base to the adjoining Army post. Very worried, he immediately initiated several telephone calls in an attempt to contact Carolyn with no success. Finally, in desperation, he sent a Western Union telegram explaining what had happened, but not knowing if she'd received it, asked them to confirm delivery of the telegram. He called back later in the day, but they said they had not heard back from their office in Davao regarding confirmation.

He spent the better part of a week relating his experiences regarding the terrorists to a counter-insurgency training cadre, soon to be sent to Mindanao. With this responsibility completed, he processed out of the Army by the weekend.

With his discharge papers, a government airline ticket to the city of his enlistment on the east coast and his back pay in hand, Clay put his return plan in motion. He knew he'd now need a passport; he applied for an accelerated one and expected it in a few days. He purchased everything he'd need, clothes, shoes, suitcase and a one-time use cell phone at a discount chain. At an Internet café in the strip mall, near the base, he surfed the internet, finding the names of prospective employers. From his room, in a small motel, in the same area, he began to set up appointments for job interviews.

After several phone contacts with logistics and security firms, he set up two face-to-face interviews with prospective overseas employers. The final interviews took place at offices close to the military base. He had heard from others at the camp that these companies actively recruited former military personnel because of their training, experience and discipline. Both made offers and Clay accepted the job from the one operating closer to the base near Carolyn.

The next contingents of new employees were not slated to transfer to Mindanao for over a month. Clay couldn't wait that long; he felt he had to go as soon as possible. Since the company wanted him because of his recent experience, he reached a compromise. He agreed to pay his own way and meet up with them and begin his employment as soon as they arrived.

On arriving in Davao, he managed to connect with a courier heading to the base. He couldn't help but notice the evidence of a terrorist attack. Fearing the worst, he raced up the dirt road leading to the hospital tents.

Nearing the largest tent he heard the velvety sounds of one of their favorite singers, Dean Martin, belting out *Return To Me* on a portable stereo. Instantly his heart jumped a beat, it could only be Carolyn, she was okay. A moment later, a big furry body knocked him to the ground, joyfully licking his face. He looked up and saw a pair of concerned, deep blue eyes staring down at him. A smile with concern and a bit of anger creased her beautiful features.

Crawling out from under Stryker and standing up, he grabbed her by the shoulders and pulled her to him, hugging her fiercely. "The commanding officer insisted I take the last seat on the last plane out. I tried to explain to him, but he would have none of it. On reaching Manila I tried several times to reach you, but they told me only military communication was allowed due to security."

"I know, I found out later. I waited for two hours and didn't know what to think. A passing *Humvee* picked me up and returned me here during the terrorist attack. They were beaten back, but the rumor is they plan on returning in force."

He kissed her passionately, and said, "But you're safe, that's the main thing. I love you like I've loved no one else. I don't know what I'd do if I lost you, I couldn't bear it. I want us to spend the rest of our lives together."

With a mischievous smile, Carolyn said, "Is that a proposal?"

He had not forgotten, and reaching in his pocket he pulled out a small box. The ring fit her perfectly. "Will you?" he asked.

"Yes, with all my heart," she said, tears of joy streaming down her cheeks. Stryker stood next to them, his tail wagging furiously, sensing their happiness.

Over coffee during the next hour he explained what had happened to him, while she filled in the details of the terrorist attack

Over several months Clay enjoyed working for the security firm. Grateful for his role in rescuing the team, Clay had received approval from the commanding officer for a reconnaissance flight to make a short diversion to the cave where the old soldier and Madeline had hidden their possessions. Clay had accompanied both of them on the flight. On landing back at the base the old soldier had bowed and thanked everyone profusely. Bowing back, Clay had one nagging question about the couple still in his mind. "Mr. Watanabe, my curiosity had gotten the better of me. Why do you and Madeline always save the empty shell casings after you've fired your rifle?"

With Madeline translating, he replied, "Ammunition has been close to impossible to obtain. With the help of some friends I was able to obtain reloading equipment and supplies so I could reload my own ammunition. That's why I always save the empty shells."

Carolyn had been instrumental in contacting the Japanese government about the plight of Toshiro Watanabe. Officially still on the rolls and with promotions over the years he received a substantial amount of back pay dating back to 1943. With the funds Clay and Carolyn helped them find a nice home, in a safe village, so they could enjoy their retirement.

Clay continued operating with and protecting supply columns from guerillas and terrorists; the Army couldn't be everywhere. But there were serious drawbacks and the work could be grueling and tension filled, always followed with the threat of what lay around the next bend. Taking a page from the previous war in Iraq, the terrorists relied heavily on I.E.D.'s. The improvised explosive devices were a constant threat that could rip through a column at any moment.

To release his tension, he made the trip down to the base on the weekends to spend the time with Carolyn and Stryker. When Sunday night arrived and he had to return, Clay found it harder and harder. They had long discussions about leaving this danger filled business. Clay realized he no longer received the rush from the action as he had in the past. Two weeks before the end of the month over dinner, Clay agreed to give his notice with the condition she and Stryker accompany him back to the States. She agreed and with a firm departure date, the fear for his safety left her. During the final week, the company insisted he be part of a particularly dangerous supply run to a remote outpost in the middle of a hostile region. He had a bad feeling about the trip.

Everything went well. The supplies were delivered and they headed back. They passed a narrow choke point in the road, the site of a previous ambush. They were almost out of the narrow gorge when a huge blast occurred up ahead. A black, oily cloud of smoke immediately curled up into the sky. The heavy rattle of automatic weapons fire could be heard working its way in their direction. Clay figured they had to fight their way through to open ground, their only option and began steering his vehicle out of the stalled column. A moment later, a bright flash of heat filled light blinded him and for a second it felt as if a sledgehammer had slammed into the side of his body, then blessed blackness enveloped his consciousness, dropping him into a dark void.

His mind sent him a signal; there were voices in the distance coming closer. Standing over him now, they were talking about him as if they were discussing a piece of meat. Those were medical terms, his mind informed him. *Where am I?* he thought, struggling to move. Voices louder now. "He's coming around, call the doctor!"

Again he tried to move, but it felt like someone had tied him down with duct tape. His eyes felt as though they were glued shut. Feelings of frustration overwhelmed him as he grunted, "Shit."

"He's coming out of the coma. Check his vitals."

Clay felt a soft, moist sponge dabbing around his face and eyes. Cracking them open slightly, the images standing around the bed at first indistinct and blurred, then slowly began to clear. Opening his eyes wider, he focused on them; all were dressed in white.

"Hello, Clay. How are you feeling?" A man's voice said from his right side. Looking up, he saw a serious, gray haired, older visage with a stethoscope around his neck. "Raise up his bed a little," the doctor said. Clay heard the sound of a small motor as the bed elevated. Now able to see everyone, he croaked with a dry mouth, "Where am I?"

One said, "In a government hospital outside of the city."

"Am I back in the States?"

"No, you're still in the Philippines, up north on Luzon."

"What happened?"

"An I.E.D. exploded right by your vehicle. From military reports, it may have been remotely detonated - they think."

Doing an automatic check, Clay could see that both his legs and arms were attached, much to his relief, but when he tried to move nothing happened.

"You were very lucky. They told us the device went off near your vehicle; apparently you had pulled out of the column and were at an angle and not right next to the device, so you were somewhat shielded from the explosion. Had it gone off next to your *Humvee* there would have been nothing left."

"What about the others?"

"All dead, your vehicle totally destroyed. You are the only survivor."

Hesitatingly the doctor continued, "Your burns and shrapnel wounds will heal. But you are permanently paralyzed from the waist down. You will be feeling pain, but we hope to keep it under control."

Clay felt himself going into shock. *Paralyzed?* The doctor seemed in a hurry to leave after giving Clay the news. "I've got rounds to make. I'll check back with you later today."

That afternoon, a Philippine aide appeared. "My name is Rudolfo. I will be administering your pain relieving shots."

Several days later, a dull, throbbing pain began to grow in Clay's lower back. He rang for Rudolfo and the man came and gave him a pain relieving shot. It immediately dulled the discomfort. Clay tried, several times, to call Carolyn, but for some reason could not get through. Whenever he asked anybody, they were vague and avoided his questions. He now feared the worst.

The shots continued morning and night over the next few weeks. As time passed they seemed to have less effect on the ache as his body acclimated to the medication. He began to need more and more. Desperate, Clay begged the man for additional shots, but Rudolfo refused, citing hospital orders. Then one evening, he appeared by Clay's bedside as Clay lay there wracked in pain. Slipping a small plastic bag under the bed covers, he said, "Take two of these whenever the pain hits you." He then handed two of the dark brown capsules to Clay with a glass of water. Clay hungrily gulped them down and shortly thereafter the pain left and he felt euphoria.

Over the next several weeks a brisk business relationship developed between the two men. When he told Clay he couldn't steal any more from the pharmacy, Clay told him he had money if he could make a connection outside the hospital.

One afternoon, almost out of capsules, Rudolfo appeared, but he had no plastic bag with drugs only a letter from one of Clay's buddies at the base. The news floored Clay. The large terrorist attack had materialized and the two-story building where the hospital had been relocated had suffered major damage. Carolyn was missing and feared dead.

The next piece of news sent Clay into a tailspin, now thoroughly hooked on the drugs. Rudolfo told him he couldn't get him the drugs anymore as he had been fired from the hospital for illegal drug dealings. Devastated by the news about Carolyn, now this, Clay felt he had nowhere to turn. The man reluctantly gave Clay a name and a phone number. He said the source might be questionable.

Clay hated himself for what he felt he had become. He began to regret having made the choice to relive a part of his past. The prophetic words of Gabe pealed like a loud bell in his mind. Despising himself, he still had to feed his growing habit or he'd go crazy with the pain. Calling the number, the man at the other end seemed cautious. Clay identified his connection and the man gave him an address.

Desperation winning over caution, Clay managed to get dressed and knowing they would not let him leave, sneaked down an unused freight elevator that afternoon. Flagging down a cab, he arrived at the address, a seedy, rundown section of town adjacent to the huge shantytown. The address appeared to be a door up a dim, foul smelling, filth-ridden alley. Darkness quickly approached as he wheeled himself up the to a door, bearing the address he'd been given, partway up the passage. A single, bare light bulb illuminated the dirt encrusted door. Banging loudly several times, he waited, but the door remained unanswered. Clay began to sense an uneasy feeling. *This is a mistake; get the hell out of here, now!*

Hearing a sound to his far right, he wheeled around toward the entrance of the alley. *What's this?* he thought. Seeing the images at the head of the alley, an involuntary chill raced up his spine. A group of four shadowy figures slowly, with studied arrogance began to move toward him. His heart skipped a beat with the cold realization he had nowhere to run, even if he could.

The group approached and stopped in shadows as the apparent leader spit out gruffly in broken English, "Is this him?" Stepping between the men, Rudolfo appeared in the dim light near Clay and said sneeringly, "Yeah, that's him. That's the crip. He's loaded with bucks."

The leader stepped forward next to Rudolfo. Clay saw the face of a merciless killer, lined, weather-beaten, dirty with cold, dark, dead eyes like a shark.

"Can I have my money now?" Rudolfo squealed. Reaching into the pocket of his jacket, the leader pulled out a small wad of cash and handed it to Rudolfo who immediately counted it. "I thought you said you were going to give me more?" Looking up from Clay to the aide like a bird of prey, the cold, dark eyes burned right through the informant. Knowing better than to push it, Rudolfo said, "Okay, okay, this is enough." He immediately skittered away, up the alley, like a frightened crab.

Clay couldn't resist, shouting angrily, "Got your thirty pieces of silver, Rudolfo?"

"Yeah, crip, and now you're gonna get relief from your pain… permanently," he shouted, running from the alley.

The three hoods advanced threateningly, until they stood in a semicircle at arms length in front of Clay. Even at this distance, Clay could smell their fetid body odor, like decaying flesh. Slipping his dirt encrusted hand inside his leather jacket, the boss thug pulled out a clear plastic bag of black capsules and waved it in front of Clay just out of his reach. "This what you looking for crip?" in broken English.

The desperate need for the drug overwhelmed Clay as he nodded anxiously.

"Then show me the money," the man sneered.

Digging deep into his jacket pocket, Clay pulled out the thick wad of bills.

The hood stepped closer with the plastic bag thrust forward. His other hand was outstretched, palm up, for the money. Clay reached for the capsules while offering the money. Just out of Clay's line of sight, one of the other hoods reached over and snatched the money before Clay could react. The boss immediately snatched the drugs back and reached inside his jacket.

"No, you can't do that! I need that stuff," Clay blurted.

Laughing hideously, the thug replied, "Can't we?" The rest of the gang all laughed at the leader's joke. Whipping out a lethal looking butterfly knife, the man flipped the handle open, rolled his hand and snapped the two halves of the black handles together, faster than a switchblade. Clay stared at the wicked looking blade, fear welling in his stomach like a big rock.

In a flash of movement, the leader stepped around Clay, grabbed his hair and placed the blade on the side of Clay's pulsing throat. In a rehearsed move, the other two grabbed Clay's hands and clamped them down on the wheelchair handles.

"Don't! Please! I've got more money. I promise I'll give it to you," Clay pleaded.

"Sure you will. Rudolfo said you wanted to die anyway. Said he heard you babbling in your sleep about suicide."

"No, that's not true. I've changed my mind, I want to live."

"Too late for that now. Don't worry. I'll make it quick unless you give me more trouble, then I'll make it slow," he sneered The thug applied pressure with the blade and Clay could feel the sting of it breaking his skin, feeling the rivulet of blood roll down his neck. Closing his eyes, Clay waited for the inevitable.

"I wouldn't do that if I were you!" A booming voice echoed from the head of the alley. Surprised, Clay snapped his eyes open as all three hoods turned their heads around at the sound of the voice. They watched wordlessly as the husky, shadowy form with a large dog on a leash advanced toward them.

The leader reacted swiftly, placing the blade on Clay's jugular, snarling threateningly, "Don't come any closer or I'll slice his throat right now."

"You better not or I'll guarantee you'll have a very slow and painful death." The voice came across firm and mean.

A little shaken by this bold intrusion, the boss yelled furiously with spittle flying from his mouth, "He's mine. Now get the fuck outta here before I kill you too."

"I don't think so," the stranger said, slipping closer. Stepping into the weak light of the overhead bulb, a man dressed in a tweed walking hat with a low brim just above hard, piercing eyes appeared. He wore a tan shooting jacket and rough canvas pants.

"Gabe! You're here," Clay croaked at the sight of his mentor, his heart fluttering with hope. Noticing Gabe had inched closer to one of the thugs, Clay watched as a moment later, Stryker leaped at the hood to the right in a blur of movement while Gabe quickly took out the other one, leaving his body an inert pile in the dirt. Stryker hit the first one in the chest with flashing teeth, going for his throat. Skittering away from the dog on hands and knees, he stood and fled from the alley screaming in terror.

The leader, his attention momentarily drawn by the scream, felt his knife hand roughly ripped away from Clay's throat and twisted back. The thug fruitlessly tried to counter the attack, but in a few swift, brutal moves, Gabe finished it. The thug fell against the far wall and slid to the ground, the knife buried to the hilt in his chest. He had a glazed look on his vicious face as his last breath left him like a deflating balloon.

Stepping in front of Clay, Gabe looked down at him with a mixture of relief and sadness. Cutting the tape loose on his hands with a knife from one of the others he said, "Think you'll make it okay?"

"You came back!"

"I told you I'd always be there when you needed me."

Seconds later, a ball of fur crowded out Gabe as Stryker jumped up, paws on Clay's lap and began furiously licking his face.

Picking up the baggie of drugs, Gabe said, "Do you honestly want to spend the rest of your life with the claws from this garbage dug in your back?"

Without a moment's hesitation Clay said empathically, "No. It's just the pain…"

"I can help," Gabe said, dropping the bag to the ground and grinding it under his heel into the dirt and filth of the alley. Reaching down, he picked up the wad of cash the thug had dropped and slipped it into his pocket.

Gabe looked Clay straight in the eye and said, "I want you to think back, real hard." After a few moments, he went on. "You accomplished what you set out to do. You saved your buddies from a gruesome death. I can tell you now that had you not intervened; it would have ended as in your nightmares. Except for one small thing. It changed you as a person along the way. You found out the hard way you are not immortal. You also learned that you are a good person with a life ahead of you."

Clay stared at his lifeless legs with regret and said, "Yes, I guess I did…and now I have to live with it…somehow."

"Do you honestly want to spend the rest of your life like this?"

"You know the answer to that. But I'm stuck."

Silently Gabe took the handles of the chair, turning it around and began to wheel him deeper into the dim alley.

"Where are you taking me?"

"You'll see. Be silent." As he slowly wheeled Clay, Gabe took the moments to reflect back on his *own* recent experiences and his other duties, while he'd been away from Clay. He recalled being back at the base, sensing an urgent, panicked call for his help. He appeared amid a scene of complete chaos. The terrorists, keeping their threat, had launched a second, larger strike on the base. Rushing to the two-story building where the tent hospital had been relocated after Clay left, he could see a fire engine crew desperately trying to extinguish an out of control blaze that engulfed the whole building. Wondering if his attempt was hopeless, he told Stryker to stay, then raced into the building anyway, amid shouts to stop. Reaching the stairs, he raced up them, knowing the building might collapse at any moment.

On the second floor ward, running past empty beds, he found her. He recalled the lump in his throat he felt seeing Carolyn lying there, unmoving, face down on the floor. Kneeling, he felt a weak pulse, picked her up, held her upright and spoke into her ear.

"Carolyn, listen to me. Help me. We must get out of here...now!" After saying this several times with no response, he yelled in her ear, "Carolyn, is this the way you want your life to end?"

Amid the crackling noise of the fire, he heard her painfully whisper, "No."

"Then help me. Walk. We must leave now before the floor collapses."

Holding her arm over his shoulder, he walked both of them haltingly to the far entrance to the ward. Hearing an ominous rumble behind him, Gabe looked over his shoulder. The floor began collapsing in fire and smoke like an undulating snake moving at express train speed toward them. Gabe only had time to say, "Hold on to me tight," as he stepped under the arch of the doorway just as the collapsing floor reached them. A moment later the heat, smoke and fire were gone, replaced by a kaleidoscope of bluish-green, swirling lights spinning around them. Gabe smiled now at the memory. It had been too close, but he had managed to save her. After seeing her safely back to her reality, he returned, to finish his business.

Coming back to the present, nearing the end of the alley, he pushed Clay up a gentle ramp ending at an old, rusting corrugated tin warehouse.

Clay remained silent as they reached a padlocked door. Turning his head to Gabe he said, "It's locked."

"It is? I don't think so."

Turning back, a black, impenetrable opening stood before him where a moment ago the door had been. Looking closer through the opening, Clay saw a black, opaque sky filled with the tiny dots of a billion stars. *What is this?* he thought, then said, "Wait."

"No time. We must go now. Time is up," Gabe replied, pushing Clay through the opening with Stryker by his side. The moment they entered the opening, everything closed around them and the bluish-green kaleidoscope of lights and mist swirled around them with a fresh smell of a newly mowed lawn. He felt Gabe pushing him through a long, tunnel-like tube. Clay's mind spun as he again heard voices and snippets of conversations, but this time from the recent past.

A few minutes later, they were again in semidarkness. Clay turned, and found the tunnel had disappeared. Gabe stood in front of him and said, "Take my hand. Stand up."

Feeling a bit unsure, but obeying, he took the outstretched hand and found he had the use of his legs back and could stand. Looking around him in the dim light, he could smell the damp forest, the earth and recognized where they were.

"Come," Gabe said firmly, "We must get back."

Needing no further encouragement, Clay moved along the dimly lit trail, recalling the first time he had been here. Happening to glance down at himself, he found his hospital garb had been replaced with the same rumpled suit he had worn on that fateful night. Turning, he noticed Gabe wore the same white suit once again.

Crossing the stream, Gabe led him up to his wrecked Mustang. As if reading his mind, Gabe said, "Don't worry, you'll be able to get it rebuilt, good as new. Trust me!"

Clay smiled at the words he had heard Gabe utter so many times.

Gabe steered him to the open car door. Suddenly Clay felt tired, totally exhausted. "Why don't you sit down for a moment while I get some water. Close your eyes and rest," Gabe said, putting his hand on Clay's forehead. Clay's eyes dropped closed.

It seemed like only a moment later when he felt a hand shaking his shoulder. "Gabe, you're back already?" he muttered.

A voice replied, "Gabe?" Who's Gabe?"

Opening his eyes to a strange face, Clay looked at the man and his clothes. On his white uniform, above the pocket, he saw the name of an ambulance company embroidered on his shirt.

"My name is Roger. Who's Gabe?"

"A close friend. How'd you get here?"

"Very weird happening. We had delivered a patient to the hospital for elective surgery. We were off duty and didn't want to take any more calls. I don't know why, but we were drawn to take this old road back down. As we came around a tight bend, a big German Shepard barking furiously appeared in our headlights in the middle of the road. When we stopped, he kept running down the hill and coming back till we followed him. That's how we found you."

"Yeah, lucky for you - we found you. A couple of hours more and you would have died of exposure. The dog saved your life," the other paramedic said.

Clay looked beyond the two men and seeing Stryker waiting patiently, called him over. Stryker put his paws on the edge of the car seat and began to happily lick Clay's face.

"Here, this must have fallen out of your pocket. I found it on the floor by your feet," Roger said, handing Clay the large wad of cash he'd had that night in the alley. It hadn't been a dream.

THE END

Epilogue

Leaning against the porch railing of the hillside home, Clay watched the sun slowly dip below the foothills to the west. He reflected back how everything seemed to fall into place. Returning to his house he had found papers from a law firm representing his wife, filing for divorce. After the divorce was final and the house sold he'd left the state with his share of the proceeds. Starting a small security-consulting firm, based on the needs he'd experienced, it had become an instant success. With his new partner, Carolyn, they'd already secured two overseas contracts. He didn't want to ever let her out of his sight again, she was too precious to him. After his marriage to Carolyn they'd come here to Prescott, Arizona and purchased a house in the mountains outside of town.

His mind drifting back he recalled that afternoon in the grocery store. Coming around the corner of an aisle he'd accidentally run his cart into a display of canned goods trying to avoid another cart just coming around the next aisle. Kneeling down he began rebuilding the pyramid of cans. Mildly surprised he noticed the other person had stooped down to help. Turning to give his thanks he received the shock of his life. A pair a sparkling blue eyes and a crooked smile looked back at him in equal surprise as Carolyn looked as shocked as he felt.

"Carolyn, I thought…," those were the only words he could manage as emotion choked him.

"I thought I'd lost you forever too." she replied, tearfully.

Leaning over he hugged her and said, "I'll never, ever, lose you again."

Looking up the aisle toward the back of the store he saw a familiar figure, dressed in starched white shirt, grocers apron and wire rimmed glasses, standing at the back of the store, smiling at them. "Gabe!" he said, amazed to see him.

Glancing up at Gabe, Carolyn expressed surprise at the name, "No, his name is *Raffa*."

"Raffa?" He replied.

"Yes, Raffa, short for Raphael. He brought me through my own *Doorway*, just as he did for you."

"We owe him a lot. He helped both of us to find each other."

Both watched as their mentor gave them big smile, and a parting salute. Turning, he opened the warehouse door. Both saw nothing but a dark void with twinkling stars. Looking over his shoulder once more Gabe winked at them, then disappeared through the opening.

Coming back to reality, he looked down the gentle slope, watching the newly restored, vintage maroon colored Mustang wend its way up the winding driveway. The driver's door opened and Carolyn stepped out and looked up at him. Clay looked down at her with a loving smile that said everything. His life complete, he knew he had accomplished what needed to be set right in his life, at long last.

Carolyn leaned the front seat forward and Stryker leaped out with his new partner, a female German Shepard and both raced up the stairs toward him.

Clay looked at the red sunset and thought, *I wonder if we'll ever see Gabe again?*